Blue-Eyed Son

a novel

Melissa Tomlinson Romo

RED SHIP BOOKS

www.melissatomlinsonromo.com

Acknowledgements

This book is for my parents, Rusty and Liz Tomlinson. Thank you for teaching me not to wait for my ships to come in.

It is also for my husband, Agustin Romo. Thank you for the time to start writing, encouragement to keep writing, homemade lentils delivered to me at the keyboard, and Heimat. This book is in the world because you nourished its author in all the ways.

Thanks to Susan Fitter Harris for being the first to know, the first to read, and for that life-changing breakfast. Thanks to Elly Lonon for knowing my characters (and me) better than I did and keeping me honest.

Thanks to many people who read these pages and whose knowledge, insight, and wisdom are woven into every line of this book: Rob and Cyndy Shearer, Charlotte Otter, Brigitte Lund, Anke Blasco, Teara Kuhn, Chantel Martinez, Karen Bernal, Sarah Maschoff, Anna Blake, Bobbie Ford, David Kazzie, Suzanne Haynes, Max Widmer, Harrison Kinney, Tim Dalton, Linda Klein and Liz Tomlinson. Special gratitude goes to Matt Phillips for his copy editor's eye (if not for you, hyphen infamy). I explored early ideas about this novel with the talented writers of the Montclair Write Group, The Creatives and the Hoboken Writers Group, without whom I would have spent many years writing in the wrong direction.

Thanks to Agnieszka Cisło, Agnieszka Woronowicz, and Andrzej Golec for help with the Polish and to Bernd and Judith Daser for help with the German. Thanks to Paulina Kubiak for helping me understand the workings of a Polish farm and for bringing to life for me all the sights and sounds, right down to the barking dogs. The six of you helped me know where you come from better than any book could tell me. Any mischaracterizations of either Poland or Germany are despite your strenuous efforts to help me get it right.

Thanks to all my colleagues at Grey Warsaw for making me feel like I belonged and for giving me so many heartfelt reasons to write this book.

Thanks to skilled author and illustrator Joanna Young for your artistic guidance on the cover ingredients and for putting your heart and soul into helping me just because I asked.

Thanks to Mary Kay Downes, who helped me publish my first book and never stops reminding me that people do indeed read the copy.

Thanks to the entire Romo clan for their warm exuberance, and to Warren and Amy for your boundless excitement, support, and the occasional piece of grammar wisdom. Thanks to Graham for making me more real than I would have been otherwise and hopefully a better writer because of it.

Thanks, lastly, to my sons Julian and Ian for reminding me what's important and for sharing me with this little brother.

July 1994, Chicago

ONE

In Which His Daughter Attempts a Wedding

Agnes's mother handed her a package to open. It was a box inside a box inside a box. Inside the last one, her mother's pearls—graduated until they were no bigger than the periods at the ends of sentences. Each one round like a planet, the imperfect white of baby teeth. Her mother swept Agnes's loose blond curls aside, looped the necklace around her neck, and secured the clasp. They looked at each other, at the young bride in the mirror with her neck so adorned. Agnes was happy to have the necklace, of course. She had counted on it.

The story of Agnes and her fiancé Krys was a happy one, mainly because they were oblivious to so much while simultaneously dating and growing up. Agnes had decided oblivion could make anything good for a long time, and she embraced the notion without considering the hazards.

They had met in the seventh grade. Agnes could remember how he looked on that black Huffy bike—the cool kid with shaggy hair and a brown leather jacket with the elbows worn almost white. She used to watch for him on the way to school and back, around the schoolyard, along the path under the Kennedy Expressway. He might have watched for her back then, she couldn't be sure. She never asked. She assumed he was like all boys at that age, who think girls are still kind of gross.

When they were fifteen, he took Agnes sledding in a lake-effect snowstorm. The heavy snow delivered by moisture of the vast Lake Michigan was of the driving kind that enveloped everything in its path. So many layers of white ice accumulated over the course of the winter that it was possible to forget what was once below. Every October, firemen circled the neighborhood, taping tall wooden sticks, painted red on the top, to every fire hydrant so they could be found after the snow had concealed the hydrant for the duration of winter. In so many ways for Agnes, finding hidden things was a way of life.

Only one hill stood near where Agnes and Krys lived in Chicago, in Sikorski Park. Krys led her there, their boots punching through several feet of snow, as both of them squinted through the wind. When they reached the hill, it was clogged with kids descending at ferocious speeds and haphazard angles. He walked with her across the bottom and up around the side. When they reached the crest of the hill, he put her in the sled and kneeled behind it. She looked at him, urgently, with eyes that implored him to ride down with her. His grin implied he wouldn't. Agnes gripped the side of the sled and just then Krys pulled back on her hood, slipping it off her head. He rocked the sled forward and back, the snow beneath getting slick. The sled jerked forward and left the grip of his hands. She sped away with one big push. Halfway down the hill, she heard him yell, "I love you, Agnes!"

She stopped breathing, stopped blinking, as if trying to be sure she heard him right. *Love?* Air froze her lungs and snowflakes melted in her wide open eyes. Nobody had ever said that to her before. She wasn't gross to him. She wasn't gross at all. He loved her.

At the bottom of the hill, Agnes's sled hit a rock and it flipped over, sending her shoulder-first into a drift. Krys ran down the hill. When he reached her, she pulled the bottom of his jacket and he came to his knees. They kissed in front of the whole crowded hill of kids. Some teased and gave into outbreaks of laughter. It was a good kiss. The kind she still thought about years later.

After the kiss, he taught her how to say "I love you" in Polish: *Kocham cię.* That's how they always said it to each other after that day. *Kocham cię.* It was the only thing she knew how to say in Polish and in that way it became their little secret. Their little Polish secret.

***

Agnes's mother decided to wear a peach dress on her daughter's wedding day. It wasn't a good choice with her auburn hair, but Agnes was too polite to usually tell people what she thought, especially her own mother. *It fits you well* was all Agnes could manage. Her mother took it as a compliment and Agnes let her.

"Do you want to put on your dress, honey?" her mother asked.

The makeup artist's brush hit Agnes across the cheeks, and she felt them getting redder. Maybe too red. She didn't know for sure because she couldn't turn to check the mirror.

"After the makeup," Agnes said, garbled, her mouth puckered.

The makeup artist patted an oversized puffball across Agnes's nose and told her to shut her eyes. When Agnes couldn't see anymore, she absorbed the noises: her mother's crinoline mesh scraping under her skirt, the sparrows squawking from the elm outside, the creaking girth of the six-columned mansion, the tinkling of acorns dropping into the eaves, the string trio in the manicured garden downstairs playing Bach and Strauss.

Agnes had told them not to play any Beethoven. Except maybe the *Moonlight Sonata*, to which her father interjected that the *Moonlight Sonata* was too brooding for a wedding. *Really Agnes. Tsk, tsk, tsk.* Agnes adored her father, but sometimes he could be, in her way of thinking, very European. By this Agnes really meant he could be a snob. She never told him this and didn't dwell on such thoughts. Anything bad about him she tried to forget as quickly as possible, whitewash over it, start fresh. She made sure he was always a perfect thing in her mind. Isn't this what daughters do?

***

Agnes's father, Bernd Mueller, was a German and an architect, two things that went beautifully together. He worked in downtown Chicago, but kept a studio on the first floor of their townhouse where he sometimes came if he needed to work uninterrupted. Growing up, disruptions included Agnes, but if she snuck in quietly with a pad of paper and a pencil he would let her sit under the drafting table. This is how she became so good at drawing. First figures of hands and feet, fingers bending, toes from the front view. Then forms of people running, standing, jumping. Two forms together embracing. Faces were harder. The eyes she drew always looked angry. When she was younger, she worried it was a sign of some misunderstood rage deep inside herself. No, her father reassured. It's just hard to draw eyes. Eyes are like pools of water or ribbons of smoke, always moving, always changing. They aren't like buildings or bridges. They defy drawing.

Her father had been born in Munich, orphaned during World War II when his parents died in a car crash. Agnes could never get him to talk about them so she knew nothing at all about her birth relatives in Germany. A couple in Berlin named Mueller adopted and raised him, but there seemed to have been some falling out he never explained. The father died before she was born. The mother almost never made contact as long as Agnes had been alive. Her father was nearly without family except for his wife and daughter. She felt lonely for him.

He came to the United States in 1963, four years before Agnes's birth, and four months before Kennedy's assassination. He had seen Kennedy speak in Berlin, and he told Agnes once that Kennedy's murder disoriented him, more than he could have imagined. Kennedy had been his reason for immigrating to the United States and without Kennedy in charge, her father had told her he felt like a man without a country, even an adopted one.

From his arrival, he studied architecture at the Illinois Institute of Technology's School of Architecture. Mies van der Rohe had come to the school in the 1930s—Germany's really bad years, her father called them—bringing his Bauhaus School style of architecture into the curriculum. He was a much admired figure in Agnes's household. Truthfully, Agnes heard a lot more about Mies growing up than about the grandparents in Berlin. Her father's architecture school was a magnet for German students, but it happened to be in Chicago, which happened to be the largest Polish city in the world after Warsaw. It never occurred to Agnes that there was any irony in this at all.

***

"You look so, oh God ..." Her mom choked at the last word and covered her mouth.

They stood next to each other in front of the full-length mirror. She in peach and Agnes in white, the two of them like a summer dessert. Her mother adjusted the pearl necklace for what felt like the sixtieth time. She straightened the pearl tiara around the crown of Agnes's head and the bobby pins swerved, pulling her hair out of place. Agnes told her it was okay, but it was useless to say that anymore. Her mother had always been a detail person, and the tiara and pearls only several of a thousand details she was trying to stay on top of. Agnes watched her fussing and reflected how it was a shame she was Lydia Mueller's only daughter. Lydia Mueller was great at putting a wedding together.

When not planning her daughter's wedding, Lydia worked as a public relations executive in the third largest public relations firm in the US. People always said she was masterful at catching the tiny details many miss while they focus on the big picture. Her philosophy centered on details mattering more than anything. Even if the big picture looked perfect, the wrong details were like a leak in a boat. Details made it into the public subconscious and could make a company go under years after thinking a corporate gaffe had been fixed.

Ford was her biggest client. During the past month, she had been almost too busy for a wedding, thanks to O. J. Simpson using

7

a Ford Bronco to evade police after he allegedly murdered his wife and another man. The phone rang constantly during the final weeks leading up to Agnes's wedding: the calls were either about cake, flowers, dress fittings, or O. J. Simpson.

"Are you thirsty?" her mother asked.

Agnes was, but the makeup artist had already applied lipstick. She pointed to her lips.

"It can be reapplied," her mom said.

"It's fine." Agnes sat on the stool by the dressing table with one eye looking out the window. "Have you seen Papa?"

Her mother's eyes rolled. "He told me he had an errand."

Secret errands usually thrilled her mother, but not this time. Her father was famous for them. One Saturday afternoon before Christmas he had left on just such a secret errand and came home with a brand-new Mercedes Coupe for his wife with a bow on top, just like in the commercials. Agnes glanced out the window, at the tree-lined driveway, remembering the car. Her father's secret errands always turned out to be something good.

"Is Krys here yet?" she asked.

"Oh, yes." Her mother was holding her middle three fingers to her mouth, like a little muzzle, and Agnes could tell she was desperate for a cigarette. She had kicked the habit five years earlier, but at moments seemed on the verge of lighting up again. Agnes always felt a little bit guilty if the moment had something to do with her. "Three of your bridesmaids are on the stairs keeping him from sneaking up here."

Agnes looked to the door and heard the voices of Paulina, Lauren, and Cate, their high-pitched chatter mingling with a deeper voice. She strained to hear. The sound of Krys trying to be persuasive made her smile. He was good at that, she thought, even adorable. She turned back to the mirror and fussed with a blond curl that didn't want to stay pinned to the back of her head. She knew she had cut her hair too close to the wedding date; the side layers were too short and looked chopped and heavy next to her face. The longer hair in back had no shape at all—it just lay straight behind her shoulders. She had decided to wear only the pearl tiara instead of a veil—Krys's request, to show off her blond hair—but now it seemed like a mistake. She considered, in an irrational jolt of panic, if a wig were possible.

***

For Agnes, the most attractive thing about Krys Sobota was his pride, even if it edged toward being abrasive. He told her it was a Polish thing, and she didn't try to challenge it or change him. They had their first date—if it could even be called that—in the eighth grade, at the Kingpin Bowling Alley in Avondale. This was the year before the *Kocham cię* snowstorm. He was terrible at bowling. Nearly every one of his balls went into the gutter. She knew he was humiliated. He grew more frustrated, embarrassed, and played worse on every turn. After seven frames, Agnes told him she had a stomachache and asked if he could walk her home. He was so relieved that he took her hand when they were halfway home and held it the rest of the time. It was the first time she felt important to another person, feeling her hand deep inside of his. She wasn't sure if she loved him, or if she just loved the feeling of being important, but she loved something that day. She loved it very much.

A few months before they graduated from high school, when they had said *Kocham cię* to each other for years already, Krys took her on a tourist boat on the Chicago River. Despite the late March wind, they sat in the back on a bench on the upper deck. Agnes dropped her head against the railing and let her hair fall, flying, his fingers gathering it. His lips came to her ear and kissed it. She didn't turn her head. Agnes Mueller closed her eyes and prayed she would love him exactly like this through college and that she wouldn't forget how she felt at just that moment. Nobody had ever been so important to her. Or was it really this: she had never been so important to someone else? As if he could hear her prayer, he told her neither of them would forget. *Kochanie,* darling. She turned into his arms and let them wrap around her, the boat rocking them, the motor swirling the river's surface, still green from the Irish holiday.

***

Agnes realized she had gotten dressed in her wedding gown too early. Already she had had to go to the bathroom, been thirsty, hungry, and even wanted to lie down. She put off all of it because she was already made up and dressed. The wedding was supposed to start in thirty minutes.

"Papa's here?" she asked her mother again.

Her mother shook her head, the fingers still in their muzzle formation. "Not yet."

"It's only a half hour." Agnes looked searchingly at her mother. She wanted to hear something reassuring, something an in-control details person would say. Her mother remained silent with her fingers across her lips and said nothing. "Do you know where he went for this errand? What it was for?"

Her mother shook her head again and dropped her hand, starting to leave. "It was too risky to run out this morning. I told him. I'm going to send someone to look for him."

As her mother left, Paulina poked her head through the open door. "Krys is driving us crazy out here."

Agnes waved at her with both hands. "Shut it!"

Paulina slid through the crack in the door before closing it, muffling the hammer-like pounding of Lydia Mueller's high heels descending the hardwood stairs. Paulina sat on the pink cushion of a wicker rocking chair. The sky-blue bridesmaid's gown, the stiff taffeta, fought to fit between the armrests. The blue gown and the pink chair reminded Agnes of a hospital nursery. It was horrid. Agnes couldn't believe she had made her friends wear such a dress. It was probably the least flattering garment she had ever seen on any of them.

"Is your mom okay?" Paulina asked.

"My father's not here. Did you send him for wine or something?"

Paulina shook her head. "He'll be here. Try not to stress."

A hard knock shook the door, and Agnes hoped it was her father. Then from the other side she heard the unmistakable sarcasm of her groom's voice, "Agnesssska?"

"Krys, go!" Her eyes darted from the door to Paulina. "He can't see me!"

But it didn't matter what she said, it usually never did. He was irrepressible. The door swung open and Krys stood in the room. He shrugged his shoulders and grinned. "You need some better bouncers, *Kochanie.*"

Paulina stood and started pulling him by one elbow, but his body didn't budge.

Agnes felt addled. Her father was missing. She had to pee. All she could do was give in to him, her usual pattern. "It's okay. Can you give us a second?"

Paulina threw up her hands and left. Krys sidled toward Agnes, sheepish. "I know the whole bad luck thing, but I couldn't wait another second to see you."

She cocked her head and couldn't help but smile. It was impossible to be angry at him. "We're getting married. You're going to see me for the rest of your life."

He slid his arms around, closing her in. Since that day on the hill when they were only fifteen, he had grown to over six feet tall with broad shoulders. He was full of a brusque passion, alluring but distant, that he seemed to draw from his family of mostly men, his dad and four older brothers, the long arguments Agnes had witnessed at the dinner table over things like Solidarity and Martial Law. *When would Poland be free of the Soviets? Never?* Before coming to the States, Krys's father had been a factory foreman in Gdańsk and an avid hater of the Soviet regime. He once spent three nights in a cell in the basement of the central police station for questioning— yet he was never questioned, never told what they wanted to question him over, and was eventually released without explanation. The same morning he brought the family out of Poland under the floorboards of a freight truck that passed through Czechoslovakia, then Austria. Eventually they found their way to Chicago. A year later, Krys was born. The only American in a house full of Poles, looking for a way to get back, to fight back, or both. Krys kept Agnes at arms' length from that fight, calling it useless politics. Agnes agreed. It was only noise behind their American childhood, their falling in love. Poland was so far away, and seemed so unimportant from where they lived, deep inside the borders of the land of the free.

After college, Krys had become an architect, something that Agnes thought would please her father. But her father hadn't remarked on it, or even helped Krys get a first position after college. Agnes didn't want to admit it to herself, but she felt that Krys was going to be a more successful architect than her father. Maybe because he took more risks. Maybe he cared less about consequences or what people would think. It was still early in his career, but already Krys was designing things that experts looked at and called impossible. He designed the renovation for a college library in Cincinnati that everyone said couldn't be built—too expensive, it defied engineering—and yet it *was* built. Was this why her father distanced himself from Krys, because of professional envy?

Still holding her close in the upstairs room, Krys drew a green-velvet box from inside his tuxedo pocket. The velvet had worn off on the corners, the gold rim of the lid tarnished to bronze.

"I forgot to give these to you before." He stepped back and opened the box. "I was hoping you would wear them at our wedding."

Two sterling silver earrings, swirls of silver like a chignon of metal, sat mounted on a green-velvet cushion. A small honey-colored amber stone rested in the center of each. Even though the box was shabby, the silver earrings had been polished to a brilliant shine. They took Agnes's breath away.

"My grandmother wore them at her wedding. Her mother before. I guess her mother before that. They're old."

For a moment, Agnes considered that they didn't match the

pearl necklace her mother had just given her, but she was going to wear them anyway. She secured the first amber, then the other and checked them in the mirror. She saw him standing behind her; he looked so pleased.

"How are they?" she asked.

They looked at each other in the full-length mirror, just like she had done a few minutes earlier with her mother. But the feeling was different, of course. Before she was drawn into her past, her childhood; here she was now, looking at her future. Krys's arm circled her waist and he kissed the crown of her head through the veil. She thought she could have left with him, right then, without a wedding. She had everything she wanted. She didn't know it was the last time she would feel that way for a long time.

***

Things happened quickly after her mother rushed back upstairs. She burst through the closed door and caught Krys and Agnes in the preliminary grip of lovemaking, on the edge of the bed, him trying to be careful with his future wife's face and dress. *How is that for details?* Agnes thought. None of them said a word. Her mother just shooed Krys out.

Her mother explained that she had sent a colleague of her father's to look for him. Agnes straightened up and went to the window.

"Did he say anything to you this morning? Was he upset about anything?"

"Nothing at all. We were just rushing around. He went early to get his suit at the tailor. That was it."

After hours of resisting, her mother finally pulled out a pack of Parliaments and lit up. Smoke billowed around her. Agnes opened the window a bit further.

Paulina entered the room. Behind her, Agnes could hear that the house was noisy and full of guests. Later, the details of what was happening downstairs at that moment would be filled in by witnesses. Two of Agnes's college friends had started arguing in the rear garden, an old battle, about how one of them hadn't supported the other in a falling-out over another friend's drug problem. In the kitchen, her mother's nervous sister Margot was on her third helping of shrimp cocktail, eating from a tray that hadn't even been passed yet. Several cases of wine arrived in the back of her friend Peter's Ford Explorer, not very good vintages. And Krys, having just parted with his great-grandmother's heirloom earrings, was stopped inside the front door by an arriving guest, nearly late, out of breath. He was the British husband of an old work colleague of Lydia Mueller who probably didn't know a soul at the wedding. He was carrying an envelope with Agnes's name on it.

"Beg your pardon. Do you know where the bride is? I suppose this is meant for her. Agnes?" He held the envelope out to Krys. "A chap at the front gate asked me to pass it on."

Krys took it and looked at it, glancing back at the guest. "What chap?"

The guest shrugged. "Sorry. He didn't share his name. He didn't look as if he were coming in, so perhaps he wasn't invited?" He nodded at the envelope. "Would you be good enough to pass that on?"

Krys's mouth parted in a wry smile. "I will," he said.

***

But he wouldn't. Then the organ started to play. In the upstairs room, Agnes's mother snuffed out her cigarette. "Let's go. We're having this wedding. With or without your father."

Agnes blanched. "No," she said, her back stiffening. "Are you kidding? I can't get married without Papa."

"It's too late, Agnes. It was his choice not to be here."

"How can you be so sure it was a choice? Aren't you even worried about him?"

"I can't be worried about him now. I'm worried about *you*. What do I tell everyone downstairs? We're supposed to be having your wedding!"

Ah, yes. *What will she tell people? How will it look?* Agnes tried to be patient. "People will have to understand. Tell them there's been an accident or something." Agnes felt it was too ominous to think about accidents at that exact moment and tried to push the thought out of her mind. "Nothing serious," she added. "Just something that means we have to delay."

Then Agnes turned to look out the window, just in time to see her broad-shouldered, irrepressible Krys stomping down the driveway. He was striding away from the house, arms swinging, clearly angry about something. She watched him, dumbstruck, and couldn't react fast enough to run down after him. To her amazement, when he got to the front gate, he turned out of it and disappeared. She stared at the far-off shadow of gravel where the last step of his shoe had been, willing him to reappear, trying to process what had happened. Seconds passed. There was only gravel, a gate, the bend of elms, a plink of acorns, the organ still playing. She was alone. Her father was missing and her groom was not coming back.

***

A few minutes earlier, while Agnes was trying to back out of a wedding that didn't involve her father, Krys made it three steps up the landing with the letter in his hand before he stopped. *What chap?* He held the sealed envelope between his fingers and looked more closely. *Would he be able to read any of it through the paper?* He backed down the stairs. There was a powder room underneath, a tiny art deco space with a smoky gray wall. He entered, locked the door, and sat down on the stool in the corner—upholstered in black and white satin with a pattern of the Chrysler Building. *What chap?* He flipped the envelope over. The paper was too thick to see through. Looking at it again, he noticed it was sealed with drafting tape. *Drafting tape?* He tried to think if any of the guys in his office had had their eye on Agnes.

He held the envelope up to the light, but he couldn't make out any of the writing. The light was too dim. He tried the seal and pulled at the corner of the tape to see how much it would open without showing any damage. The sound of ceremonial chords on the organ drifted from the garden. He checked his watch: it was time. Voices quieted and he sensed people receding from the foyer to be seated for the ceremony. Krys's heart pumped under his pleated white dress shirt as he studied the envelope. With a short breath, he pulled at the seal and it opened with a tear. He glanced at the door and then back at the torn paper. Now she would know it had been opened. Now he couldn't give her the letter, whatever it was. So he read it:

> *Dear Schatzie,*
>
> *I tried to come. I didn't leave on an errand like I told your mother. I was away trying to convince myself not to worry about your marriage. But I do worry. That war isn't so long ago. There are things you don't know about our family, about my birth father. Once Krys knows he's married to the granddaughter of Herr Kommandant Klaus Schneider, that he's your blood relative, I don't see how it couldn't affect you both. I should have told you about him a long time ago. That's my fault. Then maybe you could have talked to Krys. But if one day he knows, he will resent you and won't be able to accept it. Or even if he does, his family won't. I know you think I don't really know him, but I know how he is.*
>
> *I'm afraid for you. I think a marriage between the two of you could never go well, that's all. It just can't go well. I should have said something about this a long time ago. That's my fault, I know.*
>
> *I'm sorry... Es tut mir leid meine liebe Tochter*
> *Papa*

TWO

The Brief Tales of the Childless Mothers

Klaus Schneider lived with his wife Liesl in a small apartment on Salvatorstrasse, a few blocks from the Odeonsplatz, in the center of Munich. They had lived there since getting married in the spring of 1934. He was a watchmaker, a family trade that went back three generations. Klaus often thought how lucky he was to have won a girl like Liesl as his bride. A sparkling blond beauty, with a heart-shaped face and round in the hips, she was much more striking than any of the women in his family. How could he have married so well?

They were a happy couple, as happy as a couple could be during a time of great economic difficulty for Germany. Nevertheless, Liesl tended the apartment and cooked for Klaus as any wife would, and he provided for her. All was as it should be. Then war came, and the demand for a luxury good like a watch, which had already been greatly reduced, withered to almost nothing. Klaus decided he would have to put his manual dexterity and mechanical training to other uses, so he joined the armaments wing of the German Army with a job building and tuning the detonators of bombs. His work was demanding and technical, just the kind he liked. He felt joy being alone, working with his hands, fixing the switches and wires of explosives as expertly as he had assembled fine timepieces. He never thought about the destruction these bombs would bring. To him, a bomb was just another machine he wanted to make function flawlessly. The truth was, Klaus Schneider was a smart man, but not a wise one.

Liesl and Klaus had tried to have a child for many years. There was no reason for it not to work. The doctor told them it was just one of God's mysteries. Klaus accepted that they would be childless, wishing Liesl could also. He satisfied his parental instincts by volunteering to lead a troop of the Hitler Youth, young men who were the future of the Reich. The mission gratified him. But Liesl kept yearning for a child of their own, slipping into bed next to him most nights with a hopeful glow in her face. But that glow was soon replaced by a pallor of disappointment when weeks passed with no sign of a pregnancy.

After joining the army, Klaus worked in one of the Klupp factories outside of Munich that had begun specializing in the production of artillery. Every day he traveled close to an hour in the back of a truck with two dozen other enlisted men with similar technical skills. They worked until nine o'clock at night when another shift came on and the truck would take the day workers back to town. There was talk of lodging all technicians like him at the factory, and Klaus hoped that wouldn't happen as he knew there wouldn't be room to bring spouses and family along. If Klaus had to live separated from Liesl, it would be one more thing standing between them and having a child. He wouldn't be able to bear Liesl's despair if that happened.

In the Klupp factory, Klaus had his own worktable in the southwest corner of the first floor. It sat by one large window and all day long the sunlight poured through, something he enjoyed so much it surprised him. One morning in the spring of 1941, as Klaus was setting up his equipment, an SS officer by the name of Ernst Bormann came to see him on the factory floor. He told Klaus they needed his skills for a special project. Klaus liked the sound of it.

"We need a bomb. Very small. But it can't look like a bomb." Bormann reached inside his coat and slapped what looked like a small, dead animal on Klaus's work table. Klaus jumped back.

"What is that?"

Bormann chuckled and smiled out of the left corner of his mouth. "It's a rat bomb." Klaus stared. Something like a pencil protruded from its anus, which Bormann pointed at with fascination. "This is the fuse. And here," he ran his finger over the carcass "the entire body is filled with plastic explosive, covered with the rat skin. We intercepted these from the British. They have given us an idea."

"Do you want more rat bombs?"

Bormann wrinkled his nose. "Certainly not. But we do want bombs in disguise, just masked as something else. Something small, something innocent."

The words *small* and *innocent* set Klaus thinking. He thought of the boys in his youth group. He had seen a few of them playing with small model airships, like the Hindenburg that had exploded a few years earlier in New Jersey. The boys liked pretending to fly them through the air, diving to evade enemy planes, or exploding and tumbling to the ground. Maybe the association with a terrible explosion gave him the idea.

"How about a toy airship?"

Bormann's eyebrows arched. "Can you make them small? And about twenty of them?"

Klaus adjusted his glasses and stared back at the dead rat with the fuse sticking out of it.

"I can try."

"Very good."

Klaus touched the back of the rat where the fuse was. "Is it meant to be detonated like this?"

Bormann circled Klaus's worktable, examining it, but Klaus felt that more than his table was under inspection. "No. That's the difficult part, and why we are coming to you. Each bomb needs to have a remote detonator. We have to be able to control when it goes off, when the time is right."

Klaus thought about the remote detonator. The technology was expensive and not that reliable. In a small bomb, he had never heard of such a thing. "Why so small?" Klaus asked.

Bormann pursed his lips, almost a pucker. "Because that's how we want them."

He buttoned his coat. "I'll leave the rat with you. As a prototype. I'll be back in ten days to collect your mini-toy airships."

Klaus watched Bormann walk to the far end of the factory floor and leave through a pair of swinging wooden doors. Klaus was already mentally sketching schematics, furiously, because he was trying to put out of his mind why the German Army would want to disguise a small toy as a bomb. *Just do what they ask,* he told himself. *Keep your head down and yourself out of trouble.*

It would be close to impossible to design such a small bomb, and then build twenty of them, in just ten days. He got to work right away. He started by taking a conventional bomb, about the size of a large melon, and disassembling it completely. He laid all its components across the worktable, brushing aside wrenches, pliers, stray wire, and bits of rubber insulation. He examined each part to determine how to best replicate it, only smaller. Methodically, he copied each wire and switch as a smaller version of itself. He gave a list of materials he would need for the airship casing to the foreman and four days later—such speed was unheard of and Klaus realized Bormann must have said something to the foreman—he had what he needed to finish building the mini-toy airship bombs.

As he had promised, Bormann returned ten days later to collect the toy airships. The work had been so complex, Klaus hadn't slept more than a few hours during that time. When Bormann entered the factory floor, Klaus presented all twenty toy airships lined up across his work table, and behind each one lay a remote detonator he had designed himself.

Bormann was pleased and smiled at Klaus, not hiding his

admiration. "Very impressive, Herr Schneider. We will have to give you a promotion." Bormann waved to a junior officer. "Box these and put them in the back of the truck in the next caravan to Wrocław. Make sure they're out of sight."

The junior officer smiled at the display of mini-toy airships. "Bravo, Schneider."

Bormann cackled and added, "Now we will have to call you something a little nicer. How about Kommandant Schneider, Kommandant of the mini-toy airship fleet." He smiled, his mouth full of big teeth. "Ja?"

Both officers laughed, and Klaus realized they were patronizing him. As the junior officer carried the box out, Klaus considered the destination, a city in Poland. That didn't surprise him, but he still wanted to know more. Why a toy for boys?

"If you don't mind," he paused, "can I ask what is the mission in Wrocław that these airships are for?"

He hoped Bormann would consider the zealous dedication he had shown to the task and decide to answer his question. Bormann circled the toe of his boot on the factory floor, scraping over grit.

"This floor is dirty, Schneider. Make sure it's cleared today," he said, turning to leave. "As for these bombs, they're taking care of a little pest in Poland."

"Pest?"

"Indeed. Little boy pests." Bormann slapped his leather gloves into the palm of one hand. "These boys are running their own little underground war, running messages and weapons." With his free hand held high, he made a wiggling motion with his fingers to imitate the mischievous children. "We have been a little careless to ignore them. No more."

Bormann said nothing else, just gaped at Klaus as the implication became obvious. He looked almost gleeful as his mouth silently made the shape of one word: *Boom*.

"They will be effective, I hope, Herr *Kommandant* Schneider?"

Klaus looked out his one large window and watched as the crate of mini-toy airship bombs was put into the back of an Opel

Blitz truck. A hand came from behind a canvas flap and slammed the gate shut. Klaus turned back to Bormann and struggled with his facial expression. His mouth had gone dry and his heart beat against his tongue. He realized what he had done and couldn't believe his naivety. Bombs for armies were just a part of war. Bombs for children weren't.

"Yes," Klaus whispered, "they will work."

Klaus thought of Liesl. Perhaps because of her longing for a child for many years, he felt the need to appeal the children's lives. "But Herr Bormann? Are these not just children? What harm can they bring to Germany?"

Bormann walked closer and glared with disapproval. Once they stood nearly nose to nose, Klaus smelled Dijon mustard on Bormann's breath, so strong it stung his eyes. "Am I to understand that you are not supportive of the mission, Herr Schneider?"

Klaus had never been outspoken, but it seemed that this might be his last chance to do some good, if it were even possible anymore. "I just don't see how killing little boys is going to help the Führer in Poland?"

Bormann stared, studying him, disgusted. Klaus could read in his face that Bormann was deciding something very important, right then.

"I can see I have answered too many of your questions, Schneider. You will be sorry you asked them." Bormann backed away, then he looked at Klaus's table and saw several sheets of paper that held the technical drawings Klaus had made for the mini-toy airship bombs and their remote detonators. He grabbed them and quickly rolled them up. "I'll keep these," he said.

Herr Bormann took one more step back and raised his hand in a shadow over Klaus's face. "Heil Hitler!"

Even though Klaus had made the gesture many times with his youth group, he hesitated, as if he had never done it before and wasn't sure how to position his hand. When he finally returned the salute, he looked more carefully at Bormann and noticed that the small rosette over the brim of his SS officer's hat wasn't a rosette at all. It was a skull and crossbones. He wondered how he had failed to notice this earlier. He wondered how he had failed to notice many things.

***

Germany's war had turned Liesl into a light sleeper, so she had no trouble hearing the gentle knock at the apartment door on Salvatorstrasse a few days later. She left Klaus stretched out and snoring in bed and went to answer. When she opened the door, two SS officers in long, gray coats stood in the hall.

"We'd like to talk with you, Frau Schneider," said the first officer, removing his hat.

She gestured to the back bedroom. "Let me get my husband."

"No need. This is about you." The second officer had somehow slipped into the apartment and taken one of the ladder-back chairs from the kitchen. He placed it between them and extended his hand in a gentlemanly way. "Please, do sit down."

Liesl sat and looked up at them with clear blue eyes.

"Frau Schneider, is it true your family is from Austria?" the first officer asked.

Liesl reached up to smooth the morning knots out of her hair and after a pause, she nodded.

"We have reason to believe your uncle there, Josef Richter, is … plotting against the Führer," he said, pacing soundlessly in front of her. "Why would we have reason to believe that, Frau Schneider?"

Liesl was stunned. She hadn't seen her father's brother since she was a young girl. Uncle Josef had drifted away from the family shortly after he finished school, but she never imagined his life could turn so sinister.

"I just don't know," she answered. "I don't have contact with Uncle Josef."

"Do you want to help the Reich?" the first officer asked, leaning over her. "Do you think you are in a position to do that?"

"I hope so, yes." She looked at both of them, her loyalty

sincere. "What do you want me to do?"

"That's good, Frau Schneider. You are eager, and we have a lot to tell you. Why don't we go somewhere we can discuss this more discretely, shall we?"

One of the officers helped her out of the chair and gestured for her to get her coat, a blue cashmere pea coat with onyx and pearl buttons. Klaus had given it to her the previous Christmas after a particularly disappointing run of doctors' appointments. It was more than they could afford, and the extravagance of the gift only reminded her of her failure to bear him a child. She hadn't wanted to keep it, but he had been so proud when he offered it to her.

"Right now? I should tell my husband—"

The first officer held his palm up. "Don't worry," he said. "We'll make sure he receives word."

The second officer replaced the ladder-back chair to its precise spot in the kitchen without so much as a tap on the floor, while the other one held open the door. She approached it, apprehensive. She walked out of the threshold Klaus had carried her through seven years earlier as a new bride. The door clicked shut as the group departed and Klaus slept on.

***

Klaus always awoke from the same dream: Bormann driving off with his mini-toy airship bombs, Polish children in a basement or a hidden room, then … his eyes would fly open. He turned to find comfort with Liesl but found only the impression of her head on the pillow, her sheets brushed aside. He went into the kitchen expecting to find her, as it was normal for her to cook his breakfast and wake him with the aroma of eggs and sausage. But the kitchen was dark with no familiar smells. When he heard a knock at the door, he figured Liesl must have gone to the store to get something for breakfast. He hurried to help.

He opened the door to an empty hallway, and to his surprise, Liesl wasn't there. Nobody was. He looked down and saw a small, square package wrapped in newspaper at his feet. It was wrapped in the previous day's edition of the *Vöelkischer Beobachter*. He recognized the story on the front page that he had read the morning before, about a celebration for Adolf Hitler's birthday. The day before was April 20, 1941 and the Führer was fifty-two years old. He picked up the parcel and brought it inside, momentarily distracted from his search for Liesl. As he unfolded the paper and opened the box, he was overjoyed to see an ebony-cased mantel clock that looked exactly like one that had once belonged to his father, something he coveted as a boy, but could never touch. It was exquisite. He didn't stop to question where it had come from and why it was placed, gift-like, on his doorstep that morning. He turned it over in his hands, running his thumb down the smooth side of the dark walnut case, tracing the tips of his fingers across the glass enclosure, admiring the elegant roman numerals that rounded the mother of pearl face, counting out the time.

Just about the moment Klaus thought of how much he longed for his days in the clockworks, he felt a tickle in his fingertips. A millisecond later, the tickle was followed by a deafening thunder as the elegant clock blew to pieces in his hands.

***

Three hundred and sixty-three miles to the north and a year later, Gertrude Mueller kept herself busy like she did every morning after her husband, Albert, went off to work. She put on the gramophone, usually a concerto or a waltz by Strauss, and cleaned their two-bedroom apartment in the center of Berlin. It took her the whole morning and she did it every day. With the world feeling like it was crumbling around them, the war closing in, the regularity of cleaning calmed her down. At twelve-thirty, she changed into a dress and a pair of small-heeled Italian shoes and met several of her women friends for lunch in one of their apartments. Occasionally, Gertrude hosted.

Despite the war, Albert and Gertrude Mueller lived as comfortable a life as a couple could in those days. Albert was a lawyer for the German government and Gertrude, aside from keeping the house, adored cooking and was skilled at needlepoint. She kept especially busy during the year creating needlepoint crafts of every kind that would be sold in dozens of Christmas markets across Germany. The previous year, she took three girls as apprentices to keep production high. Her homemade crafts amounted to a humble and meager industry, but it was still one she was proud of.

Even though born in America, Gertrude had spent her whole adult life in Germany and was German to the depths of her soul. She agreed with her husband that Germany had been horribly wronged by the Treaty of Versailles that concluded World War I. No, not wronged. Humiliated. Albert and Gertrude agreed on almost everything: the music over dinner, walks in the evening, the most significant literature of the day, and the importance of Germany surviving this war better than they had the last one.

But there was one detail about Gertrude that didn't fit the prevailing vision of a German wife during those years, and that was that she did not desire children. She was able to have them, as far as they knew, but she just didn't want them. Gertrude felt that becoming a mother was nothing more than a cliché. She knew that cooking and homemaking were equally clichés, but those things made her feel accomplished and joyful. Somehow she never felt motherhood would give her the same pleasure. Child rearing was a burden that a married woman was expected to bear, and Gertrude never did anything that was expected if she could get away with it. It was something Albert loved about her from the day they first met as teenagers.

As far as having children, he respected her feelings even if he didn't share them. He wanted children, and the older he got the more urgently he felt the need for at least one. Albert tried to convince Gertrude many times with many different arguments. Even Hitler tried to convince her: Germany's birthrate had fallen dramatically during the previous decade and was literally shrinking in population as the elderly died off. Germany needed its mothers.

Gertrude was now in her early forties, perhaps too late for her to bear children, but Albert wanted to think that there was still a short window of time left. He knew that their childlessness was something they would regret, not only for themselves, but for their whole nation. Reproduction seemed like a veritable duty, and not doing his duty was never part of Albert's character.

But at the same time, Albert's allegiance to Germany was being tested. He knew from his government work what Hitler had planned for Europe and it scared him. The whole continent seemed to have just stumbled backwards into another world war because of a few acts of Germany's that had met with little resistance. The Sudetenland first, Czechoslovakia, even the invasion of Poland. They were there for the taking and Hitler took them, and what did the rest of the world do? Not very much. The UK and France declared war but kept their troops a safe distance away from the occupied nations in the east. They didn't try control Hitler, they only wagged their fingers at him. When the Japanese attacked the American's navy in Pearl Harbor on December 7, 1941, America finally entered the war. Albert remembered from his youth that when America entered World War I, it was over within the year. He hoped the same would happen now, but Hitler's operation to dominate Europe seemed to only quicken after the Americans became part of the fight.

At the beginning, Albert quietly directed the more junior lawyers in his office to find any legal or economic technicality that would slow things down. One such case arose when Holland owed Germany taxes on its imports. In the winter of 1940, they had been able to persuade Hitler that it was in Germany's best interest to collect taxes before launching an invasion. There was less chance of a country's cash reserves being hidden. Partly because of these arguments, the German Army didn't move to occupy Holland until May. Albert tried to convince himself that the few months' delay saved lives, it gave people time to get out, and that he had done a good thing. But he knew he was rationalizing his own complicity. More and more he felt he was taking part in something he wished he could totally abandon. Couldn't they leave Germany? Could they go back to Gertrude's family in America? Whenever such ideas crossed his mind they struck him as cowardly, and Albert couldn't bring himself to even talk about it with his wife.

So they stayed put in Berlin and Albert made sure his office continued to cast doubt on the prudence or timing of every military action. In the early days of war, this worked. Hitler wanted to appear as if playing by some kind of rulebook, and Albert had been quietly determined to use this tactic against him. But with every new brief and injunction, it was getting harder for Albert to conceal his motives. Every day when he arrived at work he feared that one of Hitler's officers would point a finger at him and label him a saboteur.

Albert remained close with a friend from his school days named Frank, but lately their relationship had grown complicated. That was because Frank didn't have any hesitation about Hitler's actions or the war in general. For Frank, the Second World War was meant to be Germany's recovery from the first one. Since their youth, the two men had lived nearly parallel lives. They served as stewards on the *SS Vaterland*, before she was seized by the Americans during World War I and left to rust for years in the port of Hoboken, New Jersey. When there was almost no war left to fight, she was put into service as an American troop transport and renamed the *USS Leviathan*. It broke Albert's heart that Germany never got her back.

After the war, Albert and Frank joined the German Navy, such as it was, and rose to become officers. After that came law school in Bonn. Albert and Gertrude, who had been married since the navy days, tried to pair Frank with any girl they thought might suit him, but none seemed to. So Frank remained Albert's bachelor buddy, sticking close to his old friend and eating Gertrude's cooking several times a week as he had nobody of his own to make him a decent dinner. Gertrude's needlepoints even filled Frank's apartment.

Now in Berlin, Albert and Frank met each other every Thursday morning for coffee at Frau Bader's café on the way to the government office where they both worked. One Thursday in the fall of 1942, Frank started chatting about a topic that, at first, seemed to Albert to be only idle conversation.

"Have you noticed, Bert, that there are a lot of," he paused, looking for the word, "*loose* children around lately?" Frank cut the tip of a cigar then circled his hand in the air to indicate the haphazard cavorting of unattended young people.

Sitting across at the small café table, Albert studied the heavy growth of Frank's eyebrows, the sag of his half-open lids, how his age showed. *Loose children,* Albert thought. *What a term.* Frank closed his lips around the end of his cigar and lit it. He drew a breath and the end of the cigar glowed bright orange as the fine tobacco caught fire.

"You and Gertrude don't plan to have any kids?" he asked.

Frank offered Albert a cigar, peering at him with the same look he always gave Albert when he was daring him to do something. He had to know by now that Albert didn't enjoy cigars, but Albert took it and was soon puffing away on the distasteful thing to Frank's satisfaction.

"We talk about it," Albert said.

"Sure," Frank smiled. "So it just hasn't happened yet?"

Albert felt the question was a little too personal, even from an old friend.

"Something like that."

Frank leaned forward over the table and tapped his cigar ash into a porcelain Limoges dish.

"Did you ever think to adopt?"

It didn't surprise Albert that adoption would come to Frank's mind. His friend had transferred to a new job the previous year, several departments away from Albert, working on something connected with family services in Germany. Albert wished for such an assignment because he could live with himself if he knew he were helping families stay together, not preparing invasions that tore them apart.

Albert didn't reply and they smoked their cigars for a few moments in silence, watching the morning traffic out the window and people hurrying in and out of the café before work. Albert considered the question of adopting a war orphan, one that had never entered his mind. The truth was, he hadn't paid much attention in the streets and hadn't really noticed a sudden rise in the population of children begging or appearing alone. There hadn't seemed to be any more than usual, but maybe Albert was turning a blind eye to a growing problem. He hated to admit it, but it wouldn't be the first time. Frank's words—*loose children*—sank deeper into Albert's mind. It began to make sense that there was indeed something he and Gertrude could do to help. They were in the middle of a war and whole cities had been bombed. There had to be hundreds, if not thousands, of children who needed families. Couldn't they do this, for Germany? For a single child?

Albert began to feel that it was their duty to take in a child, and to sit by and do nothing while children needed homes was not only careless but cruel. And while he didn't want this to be part of his reasoning, it also crossed his mind that adopting an orphan could reinforce his loyalty to the Reich at a time when his job—he didn't want to think about what else—might be in jeopardy. Adopting a German orphan would prove his commitment even while he worked against Hitler's purpose. As for his wife, unless she had a heart of stone, she couldn't refuse to take in an orphan so he discounted the need to even discuss it with her. Regardless of their politics or lifestyle preferences, this was a humane thing to do.

By the time they finished their cigars, Albert arranged for Frank to put their name on a list to receive a child. Months passed. Albert waited, and his wife knew absolutely nothing.

***

One day close to Christmas 1942, an administrator from a Lebensborn home on the East side of Berlin called their flat and only Gertrude was home to answer. The female voice on the line informed Gertrude that they had a boy ready for them.

"I'm afraid I don't know what you mean?" Gertrude said.

"You are Frau Gertrude Mueller, ja?"

"I am."

"And you've asked for a child?"

What was this? Gertrude thought. *A child?* This must be a mistake.

"I'm afraid I'm not sure what you mean."

"Do you want me to remove your name?" The woman on the other end made no effort to hide her disapproval. Gertrude winced, still unsure what any of this was about.

"No, that's fine."

"Then can you come tomorrow? We have a boy, age almost one year, if you don't mind. You can see him and if he doesn't suit you there are several others."

Gertrude fumbled for a piece of paper, took down the address of the Lebensborn home and hung up. She immediately called Albert at work, but he was in a meeting. She left several messages that day but he never called her back.

When he arrived home that evening, she was sitting at the kitchen table waiting. She didn't want to assume he had deceived her, but that's what it felt like.

"Albert, why would a Lebensborn home call us about adopting an orphan boy?" she asked.

Albert was still in the middle of taking off his coat and fleetingly thought *A son!* He set down his bag and answered without looking at her, buying time to prepare his argument.

"Isn't it obvious, Gert? There are children in Germany who have lost their parents now, many children. It's our duty to help them," he replied, his back still to her. "Isn't it?"

"Our duty? To whom?"

He turned and sat down at the table with her.

"We owe Germany."

"Owe Germany?" she huffed.

Albert saw the exasperation in her face. The war was wearing on her, or maybe he was. He didn't want to think that though.

"Do I owe Germany for the food shortages? For the blackouts? For the air raids?" She looked up at the ceiling as if their building were roofless and the sky filled with bombers. "Is that what I owe Germany for?"

He put his hand across hers on the table.

"I know you're upset. But we can't act that way. We need to act as if we owe Germany everything."

Gertrude pulled her hands away and put a palm on each side of her face, shaking her head from side to side. "How could you get into this arrangement without talking to me? I can't raise a child. I did not hide that from you," she said.

"I'm sorry, darling, but we must do this." Albert's tone had changed. "I'm not going to beg you. We need to show some commitment. We don't have a choice now. You know what my office has been doing. We need to show that we're part of the fight." He paused and touched her on the arm. "Do you understand what I'm saying to you? This is something they're asking us to do, to take this boy, and we're going to do it."

Albert watched her, still with her face in her hands, and felt a sudden bitterness toward her. He saw her as selfish and childlike. He couldn't understand how his wife could grant neither Germany nor her husband what they wanted. War or not, he longed for a child. How could she not understand this? How could she stand in the way of that?

"When is the appointment with the home?" he asked.

"Tomorrow," she said.

"Okay, then."

He stood up and left her sitting at the kitchen table by herself. In the living room, he poured himself a glass of the best brandy they had, the Asbach Uralt, and fell into his leather armchair by the front window. The night had long since descended, but Albert didn't bother to turn on a light. A few moments later, he heard his wife's footsteps in the hall and then the bedroom door shut almost soundlessly. He sat motionless in the dark room. The brandy, usually smooth, only burned the inside of his mouth.

***

The next morning they sat in a tram crossing Berlin to visit a baby boy who was meant to be theirs. Gertrude rode next to her husband, watching the street life flit past as they traveled toward the Lebensborn home. She couldn't look at him and kept her face pointed toward the window. Her life felt suddenly snatched from her own hands, her future not hers anymore. Albert had put her on a new path, against her will, from which there was no turning back. He had no right to make such a huge decision without even talking to her. The worst part was that she didn't even deserve to know about this plan. How could he treat her so presumptuously? She resented him and was angry for letting her marriage become one where she was so unequal. She imagined every possible escape route from her current situation, including leaving him and the child, but she couldn't bring herself to consider it. She was stubborn, but not cruel.

The tram stopped to pick up more people. A young couple boarded, smiling at each other as they held on and the tram started moving ahead. The young woman nuzzled the chin of the man and then laid her head on his shoulder. *What a fool!* Gertrude thought as she watched. Love is for fools. Marriage is nothing more than a woman's prison. That young girl has no idea what lies ahead.

Albert reached for his wife's hand, momentarily touching it. She jerked it away and tucked it under her elbow, out of his reach.

***

When they arrived at the Lebensborn home, the cacophony of children playing on stairs, in corners, and up and down hallways vibrated through the building. Children filled every bed and chair—too many to count, of all ages. Gertrude was shocked. She had no idea the war had created so many orphans.

A nurse led them up a flight of concrete stairs to a large room on the second floor, crowded rail to rail with small cribs holding babies younger than a year old. On the right side of the room, all the way at the end, Gertrude couldn't help but notice a baby boy reaching up to the top of his crib railing, trying to pull himself up. Each time he pulled and dropped down again, his wisps of fine blond hair fluffed into the air. A nurse led them toward him. As they reached the crib, Gertrude saw his head pop up again as he finally managed to pull his body to a stand.

"What happened to his family?" Albert asked.

The nurse flapped open a thin file. "He came to us only one month ago, just with the birth certificate and a report from the authorities in Munich that his parents died in an automobile crash."

"So not war casualties?" he said.

The nurse shook her head. "It seems not." All three of the adults looked at the bouncing boy in the crib, wobbling in his standing position. "But regardless, he has no parents now and no other family to take him in."

Gertrude moved closer to the crib rail and kneeled to come to eye level with the boy.

"What's his name?" she asked.

The nurse looked again into the file. "Bernd," she said. "Son of Liesl and Klaus Schneider of Munich." She closed the file.

Gertrude felt sorry for the parents as she looked at their child, now alone in the world. He stopped jumping and looked straight into her face with his wide, round eyes. His eyes shined blue and clear like an April sky. He gurgled and grinned, wobbling, but proud of himself for standing up so long. He stretched his arms over the railing, directly toward Gertrude and spoke the only word he knew: *"Mamo!"*

To Gertrude's astonishment, she couldn't remember the hopelessness she had been feeling the night before or that morning on the tram. She couldn't remember feeling trapped or wanting to run away. All she wanted to do was return this baby's smile and grasp the tiny hands he was holding out to her, so she did.

THREE

Secrets between Fathers and Daughters

Agnes didn't want to leave the upstairs room where she had put on her wedding gown, where her mother had placed her pearls on her neck, where Krys had given her the amber earrings, where everything had been prepared. She wanted to stay in that room because in that room she was still getting married. Her mother had been at the window with her when Krys rounded the gate and disappeared. They remained silent for what felt like hours, though it may have only been a minute. She had wanted Agnes to get married without her father and Agnes wondered what she would do now that there wasn't even a groom. The day had slipped out of her mother's control. Losing control usually sent her mother over the edge. Her mother's hand came to rest on her shoulder, and Agnes waited for a tension-fueled lecture, but she didn't get one.

"I'm sorry, Agnes," she said. "I'm so sorry, darling."

They both kept staring at the end of the drive. A knock sounded at the door and a moment later Agnes's three bridesmaids entered the room. Again, her mother stayed calm.

"Girls can you please let our guests know that we are very sorry, but we will have to postpone the wedding."

Lauren, Cate, and Paulina all gaped at Agnes apologetically.

Agnes hated that look. She shook her head and turned back to the window. In her state of shock, it hadn't even occurred to her to cry or be angry—two things she felt sure would come later. Her bridesmaids started to leave.

"Wait," Agnes said. "Can Paulina take me home?"

Agnes knew her mother would want to whisk her away from the humiliation of being left at the altar by both her groom and her father. But she wanted to be with Paulina now. She needed to clear her head, something she could do with her best friend but almost never with her mother.

"I can take her," Paulina said.

"Sure," Agnes's mother answered, a bit wounded. "Do you want help getting out of your dress?"

Agnes stood up and pulled the skirts of her dress up above her ankles.

"I just want to go, Mom. I'll change at home."

Paulina held the door open and Agnes walked through. She looked down the landing into the foyer of the house which was filled with guests milling about, unaware. She turned back to Paulina.

"How do we get out of here?"

Paulina took her hand. "There's a back stairway to the kitchen at the end of the hallway."

They moved toward the back stairs. Every few seconds, Agnes recalled the vision of Krys walking away, through the gate, and it made her throat ache. She wasn't far from crying now. "What happened to make him leave like that?"

Paulina started down the stairs ahead of her and didn't answer. She was good at keeping Agnes's head above a problem by simply ignoring it or telling a light-hearted joke. Paulina had always been far more practical than Agnes, more in command of her emotions. They reached the last step and entered the kitchen at a point between the industrial stainless steel dishwasher and a butcher block counter loaded with professional standing mixers. The Lincoln Hill Mansion was famous for its exquisite on-site catering.

A young woman dressed in a server's uniform was leaning over the wedding cake, swiping her finger along the plate just at the edge of the fondant. When she saw the bride come barreling into the kitchen, she snapped her finger back.

"Oh!" she said.

They all stared at the cake. Paulina looked at Agnes and then back at the cake.

"Yes, do it," Agnes said.

Paulina walked over to the counter and took a large carving knife from a magnetic mount on the wall. She turned and stood over the cake, looking back again at Agnes.

"Are you sure?" Paulina asked.

"It's my cake. I paid for it."

In one swift motion, Paulina hacked straight through the middle, from the top tier down, splitting it open, chocolate crumbs flying, fondant curling back, raspberry coulis dribbling out of the incision. The woman in the server's uniform gasped. Agnes snatched a flat box from another counter and started assembling it. She handed it to Paulina. Wordlessly, the two women put chunks of the chocolate cake into the cardboard box while the server watched, gaping.

As Agnes boxed the cake, she recalled how she and Krys had tasted more than twenty different cake and filling combinations before deciding on the chocolate with raspberry coulis. They figured it would please almost everyone. Paulina and the server watched Agnes closing the lid of a cardboard box, both of them with those same apologetic looks that her bridesmaids gave her upstairs.

"It's okay," Agnes said, wanting them to stop looking at her that way. "Thank you."

Agnes looked from one side of the kitchen to the other and touched her gown. She'd had a change of heart about wearing her dress now that she'd seen so many people still in the house.

"Is there a place down here I can change? I don't think I actually want to drive away like this after all."

The server pointed to a side door. "Under the stairs. There's a powder room."

"Pauli, do you have anything I can put on?" Agnes asked.

Paulina opened her bag and pulled out a pair of jeans and a T-shirt. Agnes swirled around the counter that held the cake and pushed the swinging kitchen door with her palm. She could tell that Cate and Lauren had started breaking the news because the foyer of the house had become a chaos of guests not knowing if they were meant to wait or leave, take their presents or leave them, say good-bye to the wedding party or leave without a word. She could hear all the debates swirling. The powder room door was immediately to the left, just beyond the kitchen entrance. She stepped toward it and slipped inside before anyone could see her.

She pulled the wedding dress up and kept pulling and pulling until her head was free of all the layers of the skirt. She dropped the whole dress on top of a stool with a pattern of the Chrysler Building in New York City—she recalled the building was one of Krys's favorites. She pulled on Paulina's jeans and T-shirt and looked at herself in the mirror. Despite everything, her face looked rather good. Her blue eyes appeared even bluer in the halogen light of the powder room, emphasized by the tones of cream and smoke that the makeup artist had applied to her lids, the same tones that covered the walls of the powder room. It was possible her eyes had never looked so good. Unfortunately, Agnes saw a watery film gathering in them and knew tears were imminent.

She exhaled sharply and turned to gather up the gown before she spent another second alone in the powder room and had a complete breakdown. As she grabbed the last fold of white satin into her arms, she saw a torn corner of paper on the floor next to a used curl of drafting tape. She picked them both up. The paper looked like the top flap of an envelope. She turned it over to see if anything was written on it but there was nothing. She tossed the paper and tape in a wastepaper basket next to the toilet and pulled the door open. As she came out she ran into one of her guests, nearly knocking him over with the billowing cushion of a white dress that protruded in front of her.

"I'm so sorry!" she gasped.

The man she had collided with took a few steps back and recovered. "No worries, it's quite all right," he said with a thick British accent. He looked at the dress she was holding and his eyebrows arched. "I don't suppose you're the bride?"

For the first time Agnes felt the full humiliation of what had happened. She wanted to get away from him, from everyone, and into Paulina's car as fast as possible. "Yes. Would you excuse me?"

He slid out of her way. Agnes had nearly reached the kitchen door before he said something that made her stop in her tracks.

"I do hope all of this wasn't due to that letter I was handed."

Agnes turned and walked slowly back to him.

"Did you say someone handed you a letter?" She recalled the torn envelope flap and tape she had just thrown in the powder room trash.

"Indeed. Didn't you receive it?"

Agnes looked at the powder room door and back at him. She couldn't stand seeing his apologetic face get even more so.

"Oh, right. *That* letter. Yes of course, that was just something from the caterer."

The guest smiled and Agnes wished him a nice day. She wanted to apologize about the wedding but just couldn't manage it.

When she entered the kitchen, Paulina was putting more pieces of cake into cardboard boxes. More food remained lined up on the counters, waiting to be served—little finger sandwiches on silver trays, shrimp cocktails, skewers of chicken satay, mini meatballs. What would they do with it all?

"Can you have all this sent out to shelters or food kitchens today?" Agnes asked the server. The woman assured her she would.

Agnes pulled Paulina out the back door, and they got into Paulina's Honda Civic. Once the car doors were shut, Agnes told her about the guest in the foyer.

"Where's the letter?" Paulina said.

"I have no idea, and I have no idea who it was from. All I know is that it was a letter for me."

Paulina started the engine and pulled around the front of a three-car carriage house and toward the driveway that led to the main road.

"I have a hunch about what happened," Agnes said.

"What?"

"I found a piece of what looked like a torn envelope in the powder room, with some used up tape. Someone got that letter and opened it in the powder room."

"You think Krys?"

"It could explain why he's not here."

"But what on earth could be in the letter that would make him leave without a word?"

"I'm not sure. It's not like I live a sordid, secret life."

"An old boyfriend?"

"I never dated anyone who would care enough to disrupt my wedding, not after this long. Krys and I have been together forever."

Paulina's Honda fell into a line of cars leaving the property by the front gate, the same gate she had seen Krys walk out of. There were three kids in the back of the van in front of them, facing the rear window, pulling at their clothes. One of them pulled off a nice-looking navy blazer and tossed it to his feet.

The kids started making faces and drawing things on the window with their fingers. Agnes wished the windows of Paulina's car were tinted. She didn't want anyone to see how her eyes had started to water and how the tears now fell, fast and heavy.

***

Paulina drove Agnes back to her parents' house on Crenshaw Street, on the Northwest side of Chicago. Thick trees ran along both sides of the old street, trees that covered the road with a canopy of leaves in the summer. Brick row houses lined Agnes's side of the street and 1920s bungalows lined the other. Paulina had grown up in one of the bungalows at the end, not far from Sikorski Park, and her parents still lived there.

By the time Paulina pulled up in front of the Mueller's three-story brick row house, Agnes's sobbing had reduced to mere sniffling. She stepped out of the car, Paulina right behind, and they both approached the front door. Agnes stopped short when she saw a piece of paper taped there. She tore it off.

"The letter?" Paulina said.

Agnes unfolded the paper—it wasn't even in an envelope—and quickly realized she couldn't read much. It was all in Polish. She looked at the bottom and saw Krys's name scribbled there. She handed it to Paulina.

"You will need to tell me what this says."

"Here, out loud?"

"Sure." Agnes closed her eyes, resigned. It was a hot day, with a glorious sun. It would have been a good day for a wedding.

"Why would Krys write you a letter in Polish? He knows you won't understand it."

Agnes kept her eyes closed. "I think this is his way of being spiteful."

Paulina read it out loud, hesitating as she translated each line:

Agnes,

First off, whatever your father thinks about me, he has no right to mess up our wedding day. I've always been good to you, haven't I? I'm a good guy, yes? He seems to not care about any of that and just wants to ruin us any way he can. I don't get it.

Secondly, your family has been keeping something from me and it isn't cool. I don't know what to think. Ask your dad, that's all I want to say. Ask your dad why he wasn't at our wedding, and then figure out if you want to tell me about the reason why. What are you guys hiding? Whatever it is, if I should know, don't try to hide it from me. I deserve to make up my own mind about whether or not I care about some Kommandant grandfather of yours.

I don't know what to do now. I might take the honeymoon trip *with my brother so maybe we'll talk when I'm back. I need to cool off.*

Krys.

When Paulina stopped reading the letter, Agnes sighed and opened her eyes. Thoughts and memories rattled her. *Her grandfather? That was the reason for all this?*

She put her hand on the doorknob and pushed the door open. In the front hall, she called up the stairs.

"Papa, are you here?"

There was no sound in the house. She continued to listen, looking down the hall and back up the stairs, then back at Paulina.

"Agnes," Paulina said gently, "I think he's not here." She held out the letter. "Is this the letter the guest was supposed to give you?"

Agnes took it. "I don't think so. But it sounds like Krys knows why my father wasn't at the wedding, and if he knows, then there must have been another letter that Krys read." Agnes pointed at the middle of the paper. "This thing about the Kommandant ... that's my father's father. Krys doesn't know about that." Agnes went into her father's home studio, off the side of the front hall. "At least, he didn't know about it before today."

She slumped into one of the two Barcelona chairs positioned across from her father's drafting table and dropped her head into her hands, the letter flopping between her fingers. "He's angry. I guess he expected I would talk to him about it."

Paulina sat down in the other chair and there was a pause like the kind when a person walks a tightrope, every movement a calculation. "What did your father's father *do* ... exactly?"

The afternoon light slanted sharply into the front windows of the studio. There had been a nice breeze that morning, and they had left the air conditioning off. But the room had collected sunlight all day and now felt as humid and stifling as a greenhouse. For a moment, Agnes thought about the letter before this letter, the one Krys must have seen. It must have been a letter from her father to her. She was angry with Krys for being so cagey, even if he was angry. But she felt relieved to know there was a reason her father hadn't come to the wedding, even if that reason were going to complicate things between her and Krys. If there were a reason then it meant that her father hadn't had an accident. He wasn't at her wedding because he had a reason not to be there, and somehow Agnes was surprised how much that small fact calmed her. He wasn't hurt somewhere, or worse. He was just hiding. This didn't surprise her because in one way or another, he seemed to always be hiding, always emotionally out of reach. She knew he adored her but often, even when he stood right next to her, he seemed miles away.

Paulina waited for an explanation but Agnes didn't know where she could possibly start. And how would Paulina feel once she knew? Agnes had to hope that they were good enough friends and that the history was far enough in the past that it wouldn't matter between them. She peered across at Paulina in the other chair.

"I guess you could say that my father and I have a secret," Agnes said. "And the only other person who knows about it is your Aunt Eva."

***

October 16, 1978, was a Monday. At 6:18 in the evening, local time, the senior Cardinal Deacon Pericle Felici stepped onto the balcony of St Peter's Basilica and spoke to a crowd of thousands. They had gathered there since the previous Friday to know who would succeed Pope John Paul I, who had suddenly died after only thirty-three days in office. Three days and eight ballots later, a curl of white smoke had appeared above the rooftops of the Vatican.

On that Monday evening on the balcony of St. Peter's, following the appearance of the white smoke, Felici neared the microphone and delivered this pronouncement in Latin:

I announce to you a great joy:
HABEMUS PAPAM!
The Most Eminent and Most Reverend Lord,

Lord Karol Cardinal of the Holy Roman Church Wojtyła
Who took himself to the name John Paul

The crowd in St Peter's Square stilled and there were shouts of *Who? Who was this Wojtyła?* Was this name Japanese, or African? Then a news reporter toward the center of the crowd, who was carrying in his hand an exhaustive list of all the candidates, was heard yelling at the top of his voice, *"Polacco! Polacco!" It's the Pollack!*

Karol Wojtyła was the first Polish Pope in the history of the Catholic Church and the first non-Italian Pope in more than four hundred years. The last conclave of the twentieth-century had delivered them all a Pole, a Cardinal from Krakow.

Agnes was eleven years old when the Polish John Paul II became the leader of the world's seven hundred million Catholics. But in her Methodist household, the news of the first Polish Pope was barely discussed. In the house of her best friend down the street, however, it was all anyone wanted to talk about. This was a sign, Paulina Malbek's family insisted. Now Poland had its own guardian angel, which it desperately needed.

The families of Paulina's parents, Brygida and Witold, had left Warsaw during World War II, when the two were still children. After a few years in New York City, both their families ended up in what was becoming a very Polish Chicago. Brygida and Witold married and quickly had two sons, Daniel and Aleksander. Paulina was born ten years after Aleksander. Mrs. Malbek always insisted that Paulina was a surprise, not an accident, and that there was a difference.

While growing up, Agnes had been invited many times for Friday dinners at the Malbek's, which were long and boisterous, filled with the aromas of dill and vinegar, sausage drippings, and the tartness of of some pickled vegetable. Brygida's sister, Eva, who was unmarried, was usually there. Eva taught mathematics at a Chicago high school, and she often talked about Warsaw, about going back one day and teaching there. Eva had been eight years old when the family left Warsaw, in the middle of Nazi occupation.

Over dinners at the Malbek's, Eva always spoke longingly of Poland and of how it used to be. Witold was quick to bring her back to reality: it had become a downtrodden, Soviet-controlled nation and it was nothing to go back to. Agnes wondered why Eva made such a fuss about Warsaw when so many people were trying to get away from it, or stay away. Something there kept a hold of Eva, like the gauzy grip of a ghost.

One of those ghosts was a brother of her's and Brygida's named Rafał. In the Malbek house, he was mentioned the way a long lost friend would be mentioned, in phrases that started with "do you remember how he used to …" and so on. Agnes didn't know what happened to Rafał. He wasn't with them in Chicago, and Agnes was fairly certain he wasn't with them anywhere. Rafał seemed to have died many years ago; his end was never referred to but it was always there, like the edge of a reef in an ocean that drops into a chasm so deep and dark that even fish can't swim into it. They talked about memories of him being alive, not the memory of how they lost him. The subject of Polish ghosts—if not Rafał, then others—was one that Eva often brought up at dinner.

"Did any of you happen to hear about that Polish woman in Archer Heights?" she said one night at a Malbek dinner.

"No, what about her?" Witold asked, his mouth half full.

"She just found her long-lost brother, living in Hamburg. He's been there since the war, but he swears he doesn't remember her."

There was an intrigued silence around the table.

"How did they find him?" Brygida asked.

"The Red Cross," Eva said. At the mention of the Red Cross, Agnes looked up.

"The woman has three brothers, all missing and presumed dead, but she has been looking for them since the end of the war. On this one, she says she has proof."

Eva raised her hand to touch the back of her neck.

"She said this brother had a birthmark here, like a wine stain."

"So does the Hamburg guy have the birthmark?" Paulina asked.

"The article didn't say. It just said she's flying over to Hamburg to meet him."

"It seems a bit desperate, if he doesn't want to meet her," Witold said. "By now, I think she should just leave him alone."

Everyone stayed quiet. Witold peered across the table at his wife. Agnes observed them trading a look that they wished Eva would be quiet.

"But if he's alive," Eva said, "I don't see how she possibly could."

Like always, everyone at the table knew who she was really talking about.

***

Not long after, Agnes sat at the Malbek's kitchen table after school, struggling over an algebra assignment. Eva came into the kitchen and started making the girls a snack to eat. She stood at the sink and started peeling oranges, then cutting sections and arranging them on a plate. When Paulina went upstairs for a moment, Agnes left her homework and went to talk to Eva.

"You always feed us oranges," Agnes remarked, watching her peel in her expert way.

"Did you know that the children in Poland now, most of the time, can't have oranges? There's only one ship that comes from South America to Gdańsk every year, loaded with oranges. Only one. The radio stations announce its position and everyone follows its progress across the sea. When the ship docks in Poland, it's front page news."

"Sorry," Agnes said, "but Poland doesn't sound very nice. Why would you want to go back there?" She realized the question sounded rude, but Eva never seemed to take things personally. Agnes liked how that made it easier to talk to her.

"That's who I am." Eva paused and stopped peeling. "I'm Polish. I want to be in a place I belong, and I belong there."

It was the perfect moment to ask about Rafal, and Agnes longed to know more about him, but she couldn't bring herself to say his name, or to inquire about his end. She recalled the conversation a few weeks earlier about the Hamburg man and the Red Cross.

"How do people use the Red Cross to find other people?" she asked.

Eva finished peeling the orange and she lifted the plate to carry it to the table. "Why do you want to know?"

"I just wondered. Just, if I ever needed to find someone or something."

Eva raised an eyebrow, her angular East European features accentuated by the piercing look she gave Agnes. "Anyone in particular you want to find?"

Agnes shrugged. "No," she said. "It was just a question."

Eva ate a segment of orange and tilted the plate toward Agnes. "I supposed you have to just call the Red Cross and ask them for help."

Agnes hunched her shoulders and nodded. "That makes sense."

Eva looked down at Agnes's homework with that way a teacher has of assessing a person's entire future by the look of one sheet of exercises. Doomed, or destined for greatness.

"Are we talking about the Red Cross because you don't want to finish your homework?"

Agnes expelled a long sigh, slid the worksheet across the table, and popped another piece of orange into her mouth.

***

Although she wasn't ready to tell Eva about it, Agnes had her own kind of elusive family spirit, a person who haunted Agnes in strange ways. Her grandfather—her father's birth father—was the same kind of ghost in their family. Only nobody had any memories of him because he died when her father was only a baby. Agnes knew his name was Klaus, and that he was from Munich, but she knew almost nothing else and wished she did. She wished she knew about his wife Liesl, her grandmother. She had asked her father about them and always got the same answer: *I didn't know them.*

But that wasn't entirely true. The year before, around the time the papal conclave was voting to select Karol Wojtyła as the next Pope, Agnes wasn't able to sleep and she overheard her parents talking in their room. A few times she heard the name Klaus, which made her roll up in bed and listen as hard as she could. It was something about a family tree her mother had been working on, a long piece of paper that was permanently unrolled and in progress on her desk in the bedroom.

"Why are they on here? Take them off," her father said.

"… Off?"

"There's a reason. I don't want to go into it. Just take them off. You write 'Albert and Gertrude Mueller' for my parents if you have to put something on a damned family tree."

"It's not a *damned family tree*. This is for Agnes."

Silence followed, then the muffled sound of her mother's decorative bed pillows being tossed on the floor. It was a fussy detail that irritated her father.

"And the Schneiders?"

Agnes craned until she was nearly off the side of her bed. She didn't want to put a foot on the carpet as the floorboards in the old house creaked hideously.

"Bernd?" her mother pressed him. "What about the Schneiders?"

She heard a finger snap loudly against paper. The angry finger had to be her father's, and the paper must have been the parchment of the family tree.

"This man," another snap on the paper, "was a Nazi, Lydie! I don't want to see his goddamned name! Not on anything!"

Agnes winced at the word Nazi, a word she had heard at Malbek dinners, in newspapers, on the TV news. It was a term she knew, and she knew it wasn't good. Another long silence followed, broken only by the sound of bedsheets rustling.

"Okay," her mother paused. "But many men his age in Germany were, weren't they?"

"He was worse than most, Lydie. Far worse."

Their voices grew quieter. Agnes took a quick gulp of air and slowed her breathing to hear.

"If you ask me," her father said, "it was a good thing for a lot of people that his car crashed when it did. If only it had been sooner."

***

On Eva's encouragement, Agnes pulled the phone book out of the pantry and flipped it open on the kitchen counter. Neither of her parents was home from work yet. After some fiddling through *The Yellow Pages*—advertisements for tax preparation and rodent extermination—she found a listing for the American Red Cross among the government numbers in the white section. She dialed and waited through what seemed like twenty rings, far too many for an organization that was supposed to help people in emergencies. Just as she was about to hang up, someone finally answered.

"American Red Cross."

"Hello? Is this the Red Cross?"

"How can I direct your call?"

"I wanted to find out about someone from World War Two. Someone who was in the military."

"You probably don't want the Red Cross. Maybe try Veterans Affairs."

"He wasn't in the American military. He was in the German military."

"Then you probably want their Veterans Affairs. Whatever that is."

"But what if ..." Agnes twisted the cord of the phone and looked searchingly around the kitchen. "What if the person committed a crime during the war? Would the Red Cross know about it?"

"It depends on what that person did."

"I don't know what they did. That's what I'm trying to find out."

"Sweetie?" the woman's voice turned patronizing. "How old are you?"

"I'm seventeen," she lied.

"Then what do you care about World War Two?"

Agnes shook off the question. "If I have his name, would the Red Cross maybe have some record of him?"

"As the war happened in Europe, record keeping would have been under the jurisdiction of the International Committee of the Red Cross. But you need to submit a written request."

"Where do I call them?"

"You said this person was in the German military?"

"Yeah."

"Then you can try West Berlin. I'll transfer for you."

Agnes quickly thought through how she would explain a call to West Berlin on the phone bill. Maybe she could convince her parents she had called Gertrude to say hello. It was more than a stretch, but it was all she had. "Okay, sure."

"Good luck, sweetie."

Agnes started to say thank you, but there was an abrupt click on the line, then two high-pitched beeps. Then the phone made a long beep like it was ringing somewhere far away, a foreign ring. A female voice answered.

"*Rotes Kreuz, Berlin, Bechtel, Guten Tag.*"

The woman spoke quickly and Agnes could barely interpret the German, even though her father had spoken to her in German off and on since she was born.

"Is this the Red Cross in Berlin?"

The woman switched to an accented English. "How may I help you?"

"Do you have records about people in the military from World War Two?"

"What do you need, specifically?"

"I wanted to find out about a person in the military who might have committed a crime during the war. Like, what kind of crime it was."

"Are you American?"

"Yes, but this person in the military was German."

While Agnes waited for the woman to say something, her mind started whipping through scenarios of what could happen because of her phone call. What if Klaus had done something really awful and it were traced back to her, and then her father? Would her father be in trouble? Maybe she was making a huge mistake.

"Requests for information should come in writing. With identification. Yours and the service member's. Your identification should show that you are over eighteen years old. It should also show that you have some right to the information, if you do. Like a family relation."

Agnes didn't hesitate, especially because she knew she was meant to. "Do I request it to you?"

"A humanitarian request, yes. We can run a report from our Tracing Service. But that's all you can get. Unfortunately, there are no military records remaining. All personnel rosters of the German military were burned in the air raid of Berlin in 1945." The woman paused. "Another place you can look up this person is his city of birth or residence."

"I think he lived in Munich."

"Then I give you the number for the Rathaus in Munich. Also they will ask for a written request for information with proof of identification of all persons. And I don't know their policy on releasing information to a non-German." Agnes scribbled down the number as the woman read it out. "You want that I send you a request package for the Tracing Service here also?"

"Yes, please."

Agnes gave the woman her address in Chicago. As she finished, the front door swept open and Agnes could tell by the sound of the steps that it was her father. She thanked the woman with a whisper and hung up, slapping shut the phone book and sliding it back into the pantry. She quickly folded the paper with the number of the Munich Rathaus and shoved it deep into her pocket. She heard her father walk into the studio and unpack his bag. She stood by the phone a few more seconds, thinking about how she would come up with some kind of identification that showed she was over eighteen, or find someone who was old enough—and willing enough—to do it for her.

***

Two weeks later Agnes received a thick white envelope from the International Committee of the Red Cross, which she fortunately intercepted and took up to her room before either of her parents returned home from work. She sat on the bed and opened the envelope. Inside were several brochures about the work done by the Red Cross around the world, a stapled packet of instructions, and three forms in triplicate with carbon sheets between each page. Agnes heaved a sigh. It was a lot to fill out, and the forms were all in German.

The next afternoon, Agnes walked down Crenshaw Street and knocked at the Malbek's door. Paulina answered and Agnes asked her if Eva was home.

"I need some help with math," Agnes explained.

Paulina called behind her toward the kitchen and in a moment, Eva appeared at the door. Agnes asked her if they could find a place to study, somewhere else, because she had a really tough assignment. Eva took her purse off a table in the front hallway and pulled the door shut.

"The library's a bit far for a walk. How about the Chopin Diner? It's after the lunch rush so it should be quiet. I'll buy you a milkshake, how's that?"

Agnes agreed. They walked up Crenshaw toward Milwaukee Avenue and turned right. Five blocks up on Milwaukee they arrived at the establishment owned by Wojtek Kubelski and his wife Magda, both from the Polish city of Torun. The giant star on the diner's map of Poland placed Torun north of Warsaw, toward the Baltic Sea. A small plaque next to it of a man holding a globe and a sextant mentioned that Torun was the birthplace of Nicholas Copernicus. Patrons at the Chopin ordered off what Mr. Kubelski called "The Polish Hero's Menu," which included the Marie Curie Curried Chicken Sandwich, the Copernicus Clam Chowder, and the latest addition, a Pope John Paul Fish Fillet. Agnes's favorite was the Pulaski Pulled Pork Sandwich, named after the Polish military general who saved George Washington's life in the Revolutionary War.

Agnes and Eva walked in and Mr. Kubelski lit up when he saw them. He spotted Agnes first. "*Blondynka!*" he cried.

His nickname for her meant *little blondie.* Mr. Kubelski treated Agnes like the granddaughter he never had; he was the grandfather she always imagined having. He slipped her powdered *pączki* donuts whenever Magda had made a new batch, sliding them off the hot cookie sheet, wrapping them up, shooing her out the door before Magda could see that he was giving them away. He was stout and jolly, like Santa, with a stiff gray mustache that stuck out over his mouth like the bristles of a broom. When he smiled, Agnes could never quite see the smile, only the upturn of his mustache and the squint of his light eyes, which sometimes would give her an energetic wink.

They took a seat at the counter and grabbed two menus from the amber-studded metal holders that kept them standing upright on every table. Magda Kubelski, always fiercely energetic, burst out of the kitchen. She was counting something on a notepad and didn't look up. "*Czesc*, ladies," she said. Agnes started to open her mouth, but Mrs. Kubelski threw up her hand. "Let me guess. You're here for your milkshake?" Agnes nodded. "Chocolate?"

"Yeah."

"That's good. And I put the *pierniczki* on the side." Agnes loved the soft gingerbread cookies that had been Torun's specialty for centuries. Mrs. Kubelski gave a quick nod and a wink, both so quick somebody might have missed each gesture if not watching carefully.

"Can I have the same, Mrs. Kubelski?" Eva called after her.

"*Tak, tak,*" she called in a singsong voice as she walked back to the kitchen.

Eva tapped Agnes on the back of her hand. "Okay, so tell me about your assignment."

"I need you to request something from the Red Cross for me," Agnes said.

"Excuse me?"

Agnes opened her book bag and instead of pulling out an algebra textbook, she produced her father's birth certificate and passport, the thick white envelope from the International Committee of the Red Cross, and the paper on which she had written the phone number for the Rathaus in Munich.

Eva gaped. "Agnes what is all this?"

"I called the Red Cross, like you suggested. I asked them how to find out about people from World War Two." Agnes explained what the woman in Berlin had told her to do next. "I don't know how to do all this, I'm just a kid. We have to send a request in writing with some proof of relationship," Agnes slid the documents toward Eva, "and they said they could look up my grandfather. If there is any record of him."

"So that's who you were talking about before? What are you trying to find out?"

"I think he did something bad during the war."

Magda appeared from the kitchen with a pair of milkshakes, setting them down in front of them on the counter. As promised, each milkshake was accompanied by three soft *pierniczki* cookies.

"Don't you think this is something you should talk to your parents about?" Eva said.

"I just can't. I think it's something my father is very upset about." Agnes took her shake and brought the straw to her mouth. "And I don't think my mom knows much."

Eva picked up her father's birth certificate. "So what do you want me to do?"

"I need help with the forms. They're all in German."

"Sweetie, I don't know any German. Not much anyway."

"But I thought, you're smart, you're good in math and things. You would know how to fill these out."

"Thanks, but knowing math isn't the same thing as knowing German."

"Sure, of course. I know."

They both looked at the three forms in triplicate with the carbon paper. Eva picked one up. "Did you bring your English-German dictionary?"

Agnes pulled it out from the bottom of her bag. Eva read the first line of the application and flipped through the dictionary for a moment. She took a pen from her purse. "Okay, who is making the request? You?" she asked.

Agnes presented her father's birth certificate. "Bernd Heinrich Mueller, born Bernd Schneider."

Eva held the pen in the air. "Oh, Agnes. Are you sure?"

"It has to be someone over eighteen with a family relation. I mean ... who else is there?"

Eva hesitated and then started writing her father's name on the top of the forms. They went through two rounds of milkshakes completing the entire set of forms, including the names of Klaus and Liesl Schneider, her father's birth information, and their location in Munich. They got to the bottom of the form. "Where do you want the information sent?" Eva asked.

After getting lucky to intercept this envelope at home before her parents, Agnes realized it was too risky for anything else to be mailed home.

"Could you put your address?"

Eva wrinkled her mouth, doubtful. She looked up and down the form.

"I guess we need to change this, your father's address. It needs to be mine."

Eva crossed out what they had written and put the address of her apartment house nearby.

"I hope they still accept it, with that address changed."

The diner was starting to fill up with customers coming in for an early dinner. Magda kept crossing in front of them to get things from behind the counter, then crossing behind them to bring things to people sitting in booths. Eva gathered up the forms they had filled out, and the documents Agnes had brought.

"I'll need to photocopy all of these at work tomorrow to put them with the request. I'll mail the request and bring these by your house tomorrow, is that okay?"

Agnes thanked her and they finished their milkshakes. She couldn't imagine that the absence of those three documents, buried deep in the bottom of her mother's desk in the kitchen, would be noticed in just one day.

Agnes glanced at Eva as they got ready to leave and noticed a worried look on her face.

"Agnes, are you really sure you want to know what your grandfather did? That war is long over now. It might just upset you, and it doesn't sound like something your father wants you to know."

Agnes took a bite into her last *pierniczki*. "He won't know that I know," she said. "And yes, I do want to know. How can I not?"

Agnes knew she was talking to the one person in the world who completely understood that question and probably asked it to herself every day of her life.

***

Two months later, Eva received a report from the Tracing Service of the International Committee of the Red Cross. She met Agnes back at the Chopin Diner, this time in a booth in the back corner of the restaurant. Agnes opened the thin envelope that contained only two pieces of paper. The first was a page printed on a dot matrix printer, faded, with information that appeared to come from a database. The second was a blank information request form from an organization called the World Committee for Crimes against Children (WCAC). Eva held the printed page and they both read it together. Agnes found Klaus's name and next to it, the printout read, "National Socialist No. 4872, WCAC Case No 312, Deceased 1941, cause: unknown." Underneath his was the name Liesl Schneider, "National Socialist No. 669, Missing Person Case

No. 1211, Deceased 1949, cause: cancer of cervix."

Eva picked up the blank form from the World Committee for Crimes against Children, which they realized wasn't entirely blank. At the top a name and case number were already pre-typed in the form: Klaus Schneider, Case No. 312. At the bottom of the form was an address in Copenhagen for mailing.

"Is there anything more?" Agnes said, picking up the empty envelope.

"This is it, just some case numbers."

"Why this thing about crimes against children?"

Eva laid all the forms down on the table. "I think you have to ask this WCAC for more information."

"Should I?"

"At this point I don't see how you couldn't."

Agnes sat back. "Something doesn't make sense about their dates of death. My father was born around Christmas in 1941, and I know they died sometime the next year in a car accident. So why does it say that Klaus died in 1941 and Liesl died in 1949?"

"It's possible your grandfather died before your father was born?"

"But what about Liesl? If this is right, she was alive until my father was seven years old."

"You said he was adopted?"

"Yes, by the Muellers, at the end of 1942. But why was he in an orphanage if his mother were still alive?"

"I don't—"

Agnes rose to his defense. "Did she not want him?"

Agnes felt a pang of heartbreak for her father and wondered if this was really why he never wanted to talk about either of his birth parents. His mother didn't want him.

"You don't know the circumstances, Agnes, so don't make any assumptions just yet. I didn't live in Warsaw through to the end of the war, but I can tell you that Europe was in a complete chaos during those years. Maybe his mother just couldn't manage after her husband died."

Agnes saw Magda walking toward them holding a pair of milkshakes.

"You ladies snuck in without me even seeing," she set the milkshakes down, "so I thought I would save you trouble to order."

"Sorry, Magda," Eva said.

"It's fine. You hide out as long as you want." Magda winked and walked back to the front of the diner, where the booths were full of customers and the sound of Polish being spoken. Agnes heard Mr. Kubelski, out of sight in the kitchen, his bellowing laugh.

Agnes lifted the WCAC form with Klaus's name at the top. "Can we send this one back?"

"You're sure?"

"Like you said. How can I not?"

"Okay then. I'll let you know when I have the report back." Eva put the papers back in the envelope. "And don't jump to conclusions about your father and his mother, sweetie, please."

"No, no," Agnes promised. "I won't do that."

***

It was nearly summertime when Eva received a long report from the World Committee for Crimes against Children. Because it was so large, she asked Agnes to come to the Malbek's house rather than meet at the diner or in Agnes's house, and be interrupted wading through so much information. Agnes came after school while Paulina was at a piano lesson and Mr. & Mrs. Malbeck were both at work. Eva sat with her at the Malbek's kitchen table and let Agnes open the envelope.

Inside was a photocopy of a three-page report, typed on what seemed like an old typewriter, with letters misaligned and some characters faded. Behind it were nearly twenty photocopied pages of press clippings from the late 1940s about a trial in Nuremberg, Germany. Behind those were four more photocopied pages with the names and details of what were called claimants in the case involving her grandfather, Klaus Schneider. Agnes picked up the three-page typed report and started reading aloud from the beginning.

> *Trial of Scientists, Wunderwaffe, Nuremberg Military Tribunal*
> *Palace of Justice*
> *Nuremberg, Germany*
> *6 April 1948—23 June 1948*
> *Indictment: Schneider, Klaus Wilhelm, SS, Chief Artillery*
> *Kommandant, German Army High Command*
> *Delivered posthumously: 4 June 1948*
> *Sentenced posthumously: Execution by hanging*
> *SCHNEIDER, KLAUS WILHELM, SS, MÜNCHEN:*
> *Found guilty of inventing seventeen variations of high-impact concealed*
> *explosives charged with remote detonation used by the Germany military*
> *from 1942 to 1943 in one hundred and sixty campaigns targeting Polish*
> *Allied Underground forces in Wrocław, Szczecin, Poznań, Lublin,*
> *Lodz, Gdańsk, Krakow, and Warsaw, with a number of victims*
> *estimated to be 6,400, principally male youth of the Polish Underground*
> *. . .*

Agnes stopped reading and noticed that Eva's face had turned pale. Eva stood up from the kitchen table, as if in a trance. She took a glass from the cabinet and turned on the tap. Agnes watched the back of her, stoic, drinking from the glass and looking straight out the kitchen window. What had it been? Rafał? He was young—a *male youth* like the report said—and had disappeared during the war. Could he have been part of the Polish Underground?

"Are you okay, Eva?"

"It was just like that, actually." Eva's voice was strangely hollow. "Things happened to people. You saw it with your own eyes, or knew about it. And you had to act like you didn't see, or you didn't know. Because if you did anything, or said anything … it would happen to you."

Eva said nothing more and didn't turn around. She just stood there. All Agnes could do was look at the back of her head, her cropped brown hair, the slight hunch of her back, as she took another drink of water. Agnes thought the silence in the kitchen would make her crazy. She was beginning to feel horrible for ever having involved Eva.

Eva turned to face her with cheeks clear of any trace of tears and her color returned. "Do you think you found what you were looking for?"

Agnes shifted in her chair, wanting to reassure her about Rafał but she couldn't dare mention his name. "Don't jump to any conclusions, Eva. Like you told me in the diner. You were right."

"Of course not," she said. "It's hard to know anything about that war now, isn't it?"

Eva put the empty glass in the sink and came to sit with her again at the table. "I think you might be done looking. You probably don't need my help anymore?"

"Thank you," Agnes whispered. "I'm sorry I got you involved."

"No." Eva touched her hand. "Sometimes we just have to do things, for ourselves. It's nothing to be sorry about."

Agnes kept her hand underneath Eva's, which was soft and warm. "Why haven't you asked the Red Cross for help?"

Eva must have known what Agnes meant. She smiled gently and rested both her hands in her lap.

"I'm not as brave as you think I am."

Agnes couldn't imagine Eva not being brave, let alone herself being braver. Their eyes met for a moment, held there, and then Agnes looked down at the table without saying more. She took some of the photocopied pages and turned them over. There were at least three dozen news articles documenting the Scientists Trial. "What do I do with all this?"

One article contained headshots of all the men named in the trial. Underneath one was the caption Schneider, Klaus W. Agnes held it up and studied the photocopied black and white image.

"Is that your grandfather?" Eva asked.

Agnes studied the picture. He had a full face, jowly and clean shaven. His mouth and brow were strong, making him look

intelligent and determined. He was bald in the front, and the rest of his light hair combed over across the top. He wore a military uniform with striped ribbons across the shoulders, but unlike the other men, he didn't have any medals pinned to his chest. Agnes looked for some resemblance to her father but had trouble identifying anything that reminded her of Bernd Mueller. In fact, he looked like a complete stranger. Eva gently pressed Agnes on the arm and lowered the photocopy.

"My advice is to just keep this to yourself. It sounds like your father already knows. He probably lived through the fallout of these trials in Germany, so it might be very personal."

"But it wasn't his fault. It was his father who made these explosives, not him. Why does he have to feel ashamed about it?"

"I've never really gotten to know your father, but he seems like a noble person. I imagine he feels some connection to this because it was his father, and he probably feels some connection for you. Maybe he's wanted to make it up to the families of those kids and there hasn't been a way. There will never be a way. It will always be unfinished business. Do you see what I mean?"

"I guess so," Agnes said.

"Don't let him ever know you know about this. It could only make the shame worse for him."

Agnes agreed, but she didn't know if she could agree forever.

FOUR

Fairy Tales and Frog Princes

On the afternoon of what should have been her first hours as a new bride, Agnes rose from the Barcelona chair and shut the French doors leading from the foyer into her father's studio. The heat of the room seemed to rise instantly, the sun sinking lower, now like a horizontal disc of light cutting through her eyes. She turned to her father's desk, next to his drafting table, and started looking across the surface. On the left side sat notes on graph paper from current and past commissions for architectural work. Three books rested on the right side: *Merriam-Webster's English Dictionary*, *The Bourne Supremacy* by Robert Ludlum, and *Lost Baltimore: A Portfolio of Vanished Buildings* by Carleton Jones. At the front of his desk was an acrylic pencil cup with a small American flag perched in it. His checkbook was there, next to the phone and a list of reminders. Agnes picked up the list and saw the third reminder that said "*Check on Mamo's test results.*"

Paulina came to the desk and stood next to her. "You found something?"

"What do you think this means?" Agnes showed her.

"Mamo is Gertrude?"

Agnes nodded. "What is she having tests for?"

"It must be something that isn't just routine if your dad feels like he has to check on them."

Paulina put a hand on one of the drawers. "May I?"

"Of course." Agnes opened a drawer on the other side and they both started looking for clues about where he might have gone. The second drawer down was where her father usually kept cards and letters that he felt obligated to keep, but needed to have out of the way as he didn't like clutter. The top few cards were from Agnes, to celebrate his birthday that past Christmas and Father's Day in June. She opened the one for Father's Day and saw what she had written: *Happy Papa's Day my dear, dear Papa—can't wait for you to walk me down the aisle. You will be the most handsome man there! Don't tell Krys! I love you, Schatzie xxxxoooo*

She put the card face down on the desktop and kept sorting through more cards and letters. A small lavender envelope had slipped and gotten stuck on the side panel of the drawer. She picked it out and flipped it to the front. It was from G. Mueller in Berlin. Gertrude.

She showed Paulina. "Do I read it?"

"I don't know why we're looking through his drawers if we don't intend to look at what we find in them."

"True." Agnes opened the flap and read. After a minute, she sat back in the chair, her hand on her forehead. After a few moments, she had to stop reading as it was news that she wasn't prepared for.

"What does it say?" Paulina asked.

"Oh poor Gertrude. She says she has Stage 4 breast cancer."

"Jesus. When?"

"This is from March."

"She would be having really aggressive treatment ... or just palliative care if it's that bad. But if they're doing tests, I would assume they are trying to eradicate it." Listening to her technical explanation, Agnes recalled that Paulina's grandmother had died from breast cancer while they were in high school.

"Why didn't he tell us? Or me?" And just as Agnes asked the question, she realized it would have surprised her for him to share the news. Again, the retreating, the emotional distance. He had planned to weather this storm on his own.

"Would he have gone to Berlin to be with her when he dropped your wedding?"

Agnes looked again at the note, and Gertrude's beautiful penmanship. She wasn't sure she had ever seen Gertrude's handwriting. "It seems kind of extreme doesn't it? And he would have had to buy a ticket last minute, unless he had been planning for a while not to come to our wedding, but I can't believe that."

Paulina opened another drawer. "Where does he keep his passport?"

Of course. Agnes stood up and went to a bookcase behind the Barcelona chairs, to a false book that kept important family documents. It was a box, painted to look like Tolstoy's *War and Peace*. She opened it and pulled out three American passports, one for each of them.

"He didn't go then?" Paulina said.

Agnes rummaged further through the box and then put it down on the coffee table. "No, he did go. His German passport isn't here. If he went to Germany, he would have used that to travel."

"So maybe he did go to Gertrude's. Do you know how to reach her?"

Agnes returned to the desk and slid open the center drawer, a shallow one that held pencils and small pads of graph paper. Next to a pad of graph paper she found a thin, brown leather Filofax where he kept his contacts. She flipped through. Gertrude Mueller's contact was in pencil, at the end of the "M" section, after dozens of engineers, drafters, and college friends from IIT. She held the book open and dialed Berlin.

After a moment, a dazed voice answered: "Hello?"

Agnes glanced at the clock; it would be after midnight in Germany. She must have woken Gertrude up.

"Oh … I'm so sorry about the late hour," Agnes said in a rusty German. "This is Agnes. Bernd's Agnes."

Gertrude coughed and her voice came clearer. "Oh, dear.

Hello. How are you?"

It seemed like a question Agnes should be asking her. But she thought maybe she wasn't supposed to know about the cancer, so she carried on as if life were normal for Gertrude, not possibly approaching its very last days.

"Okay. Well, not entirely okay, to be honest," Agnes said, hearing how badly it all sounded. "My wedding was today. But my father has," she paused, "disappeared. I'm wondering if he made plans to come see you in Berlin?"

There was a long silence, which Agnes expected meant that yes, he was on his way there. Relief washed over her.

"I'm so sorry, dear. How terrible. Come to think of it, he did say he might check in on me. But I don't know if he meant now. It's a long way to come, isn't it?"

"Yes," Agnes said. She was thinking, with a little bitterness, that it was such a long way that Gertrude had never been to visit them in America. "So you haven't heard from him?"

"No, I don't recall that I have." She stopped. "I just don't recall. I'm sorry."

Agnes still felt the need to inquire about Gertrude's health. But how? Something vague.

"Are you feeling all right?" she asked.

"Oh me? Just the same. Same as always," Gertrude said, speaking in such a cheerful way in the middle of the Berlin night that Agnes knew it must not be true.

"Do you think it would be okay if I came to visit you sometime?"

Gertrude coughed again, this one more rambling and it went on for a long moment.

"Well, dear. If you'd like to, of course. I'm not very entertaining now at my age."

Agnes forced a short laugh. "That's okay. I don't need to be entertained. I've actually never been to Berlin. I can wander around." Agnes heard how false her voice sounded, as if coming to Berlin were nothing more than a touristic lark.

"That's fine," Gertrude said. "When were you thinking of coming?"

"Is this week okay?"

"This week?"

"Are you home on Tuesday? I can probably arrive on Tuesday."

Agnes had no idea what she had planned. She had her passport, she was a grown woman, she could fly if she wanted to and had two weeks of a honeymoon vacation from work. If there were any reason to go to Berlin other than the huge hunch her father was on his way there, then maybe it was because this could be her last chance to meet the woman who raised her father. The woman he called Mamo. Regardless of his emotional distance to everyone else, there was something between her father and Mamo that didn't exist between him and anyone else, not even Agnes.

"I can't wait to meet you," Agnes said, and she did mean it.

"It will be nice for me too, dear," Gertrude said.

They hung up. Paulina had been standing at her side and gave Agnes an incredulous look. "You're flying to Germany?"

"I just have this feeling he's there. Or on his way. When do you have to be back in Warsaw?"

Paulina had left their neighborhood in Chicago the year before, following her Aunt Eva back to Poland after the Berlin Wall fell, when Lech Wałęsa was elected President, when the country had opened up. She took a job working for an American ad agency, slipping into the culture like she had been born and raised there. After all, she was a dual citizen and grew up in a house where Polish was the main language. Poland was probably more home for her than she realized. Agnes wished Germany had been that way for her, but she didn't even have a German passport even though she had a right to one.

"I'm supposed to be back next Monday. We have a photo shoot for a new client."

"Can you come with me to Germany, before you go back?"

Without Paulina even responding, Agnes knew the answer was

yes. There was one person who would never say no to her and that was Paulina.

∗∗

Agnes's mother came home after dark in a cloud of Parliament smoke, her eyes bloodshot, the front of her peach dress stained with the round, white rings of salty tears. It looked like she had cried much more than Agnes. What was it that made older women so much more prone to sobbing? Aunt Margot shuttled things back home from the Lincoln Hill Mansion all evening until well after dark. Late that night, Agnes and her mother sat at the kitchen table in a kind of dazed silence that seemed impossible to talk through.

"Have you heard from Krys?" her mother asked.

Agnes shook her head that she hadn't. Krys's angry Polish note was now concealed in the top drawer of her dresser next to years of mementos of their being together. His letter made her feel too ashamed of … something. She didn't know if it was her infamous grandfather or unforgiving groom.

"You will, darling. You will. I'm so sorry."

Her mother lit another cigarette and her robe hung open a little. Agnes wondered if she had been drinking. Getting drunk was something Agnes had never tried as a way to calm herself down. She wondered how it worked, if it worked. She wondered if she would feel calmer being drunk, or just more nervous and disoriented. That was another thing about aging that Agnes didn't look forward to: the plethora of coping mechanisms.

"Has Papa called you?" Agnes asked.

Her mother blew a jet of white smoke from her nose. "No."

"Do you think something could have happened to him?" Despite Krys's note, Agnes still had a lingering fear of her father having met with disaster.

Her mother pointed with two fingers, the ones clutching the cigarette, at the front door. "No. The police would have shown up by now."

It only took her mother a few minutes to get through the cigarette and light another. After observing her mother's furious efforts to cope for a few minutes, Agnes felt like sharing at least a little of what she knew.

"I think I might know where Papa is." Her mother raised an eyebrow. "I called Gertrude when I got home."

Her mother sat straight up in her chair. "Mueller? His mother?"

"She's his only living family. I just thought, if he were really having some problem, maybe he would reach out."

"Has he?"

"He did call." Agnes didn't say anything about Gertrude's cancer. "He said he might come, to check on her."

Her mother rolled her eyes. "That's good. At least he's not neglecting his mother." Her sarcasm, while sometimes funny, was in this case decidedly unattractive.

"Paulina has to go back to Warsaw next week. So, on the way, she's going to come with me to Berlin." Agnes said it all quickly, a plan already made, even though she was still trying to book herself a plane ticket. She didn't want her mother to try and talk her out of it, or suggest she come along.

"What about Krys? Are you going to at least talk to him?"

"I'm not sure why Krys left the wedding," Agnes lied. "But whatever the reason, don't you think he's the one who needs to be calling me?"

Her mother snuffed out her cigarette and tapped the loaded ashtray. "And if he calls here?"

"Tell him I'll be back in a week."

Agnes stood up and went to her mother, kissing the top of her head. Her mother squeezed her on the shoulder. "I'm sorry, Agnes. I was trying too hard today. I wanted everything to be perfect for you."

Agnes kissed her again, longer. "I'm not a client, Mom. I'm your daughter. You don't have to make me perfect."

When Agnes pulled away, her mother held her arm a moment longer. "Don't you understand by now? It's not you I want to make perfect. You already are. I just want everything else to be as perfect as you are."

***

Two days later, Monday evening, Paulina and Agnes were on a Lufthansa flight from Chicago to Berlin. It would arrive at 8:30 in the morning, flying over the Atlantic Ocean, through the black night. Krys still hadn't called, and Agnes was a little relieved, even though she missed his arms in a terrible way. Especially his arms. And his little Polishisms, she called them, *Kocham cię* among them. Would she ever hear him say that to her again? Describing her eyes once, he had taught her how to say the Polish word for blue, which was *niebieski*. It sounded like *knee bees ski*, he told her. After that, whenever she saw anything blue she had an absurd image of a drone of bees, their knees covered with tiny knee pads, skiing down a hill. Thinking of it on the plane made her giggle.

After takeoff, their flight climbed into the clouds and the sky ahead darkened rapidly as they flew away from the setting sun. They ate a mediocre dinner of sauerkraut and pork. Agnes spent a few minutes trying to watch a movie that neither she nor Paulina had ever heard of on a screen fifteen rows ahead that hung from the ceiling. Eventually they both drifted off to sleep. Agnes dreamed about Germany, about her father. An old dream she had often since she learned about Klaus Schneider and his infamous crime.

The scene rose up in her mind of a man, so handsome, strong, and intelligent, but harboring the will to kill thousands of people in cold blood. He was standing next to a fence, tossing a baby into the air over and over again. Agnes was always afraid for the baby. But then the baby giggled, and she felt relieved. Then the man brought the baby to his chest and patted him on the back. He nuzzled the baby and Agnes saw the man's uniform, the ribbons on his shoulders but no medals on his chest. *Was this Klaus and her father?* She saw the man's lips moving, like a silent movie. *Here is my son* Agnes read on his lips. *Here is my boy. My boy. And my boy is just*

69

like me.

The moment of the father's declaration jerked her awake and there was a surge of panic as Agnes reached the last part of the dream, about her father being just like his own father, just as evil. It could never be, she tried to tell herself. In the seat next to her, Paulina lifted off the patches covering her eyes.

"Are you okay?"

Agnes ran her hand across her forehead. "I was dreaming."

"Flying does that."

Agnes laid her head back. "I guess."

She closed her eyes and opened them again, looking out a window. A moonless sky filled the space above the North Atlantic Ocean. The darkness of water and air had no beginning and no end, the clouds were invisible. A sense of being in between nothing, hung in a void of all substance and meaning, sent a vague chill of panic through her. Or was it the dream? Fatigue gripped her. She closed her eyes again and dreamed about a train trip with her father when she was in the fourth grade, a journey from Chicago to Washington, D.C. to visit the monuments. Her mother had decided to meet them in D.C. after an event there for one of her clients, so the train trip was a rare time alone and one she always remembered.

Agnes had been sitting next to him, watching the farms of Indiana and Ohio unfurl from the window. Then they passed through the hills of the Allegheny Mountains, and finally the green horse pastures of Maryland.

"What made you decide to come to America?" she asked, as they pulled out of Baltimore's Union Station. Agnes was curious because he always referred to America as *your country*, meaning hers and her mother's, but not his. It almost gave her the impression that he didn't like being here. But when she watched him gaze out the window of the train, with his head back on the seat and his eyes relaxed, it seemed that she might have gotten the wrong impression.

"Do you know who John Kennedy was?" he said.

"He was President?"

"Yes. And he came to Berlin when he was President. I went to hear him speak. I guess you could say I ended up here because of him. Because of something he said in Berlin."

"What did he say?"

"Lots of things. My girlfriend Ursula and I went to the Rudolph Wilde Platz to hear him speak and were so moved by him. It was a time when we wanted to be inspired by someone like him, moved to do something. Ursula wanted to be a veterinarian, but she had a job as a waitress. I guess I must have been around twenty-one or twenty-two. I was still living with Albert and Gertrude, trying to figure out what I wanted to do. I fiddled with design, making little drawings, things like that. But I was trying to find my purpose in life, do you know what I mean?"

Agnes didn't really know, but it sounded exciting to be grown up and have a purpose in life. "What did Kennedy say that made you want to come to America?"

She leaned into him and looked through the window as the train picked up speed past the Inner Harbor.

"He spoke about freedom and prosperity. His view of the world, how things could be, sounded to us like a fairy tale. Simply impossible. But it still moved us very much. Then he said, about West Berlin, 'You live in a defended island of freedom.' There it was, the truth. West Berlin was an island. Even though it was free and democratic, we were still separated from the rest of the world by the territory of East Germany all around us, which was controlled by the Soviets. The Berlin Wall cut right through the city, near Albert and Gertrude's apartment. I saw it every day. To a Berliner, the city felt like an island, like Kennedy said. We were isolated from the whole world. I didn't really want to be isolated, not like that. So a month later I left."

"And what happened with Ursula?"

"She was going to come with me, but her mother was sick and she couldn't leave. So that was it," her father said. He pursed his lips, faintly melancholy.

"Did you love her?"

"Well, maybe." He tweaked Agnes on the nose. "Then I got caught up with a couple of pretty American girls and never looked back."

Agnes giggled. "Are you glad you came to America?"

"I wouldn't have lived my life any differently."

"But don't you miss Germany?"

"I don't think about it much." He looked out the window at a horse pasture with a red barn at the far end. "I just hope the Berliners can tear down that wall someday. It would be a good thing for Germany." Her hand was flat on the seat and he brought his hand down over it. "I hope it happens in your lifetime. It would be nice for you to know Germany the way it was, without a wall. One country, not two."

He squeezed her hand and she looked with him, into the very far distance, until the little red barn disappeared from view.

***

Their flight landed thirty minutes early and Paulina and Agnes emerged into Berlin's Tegel Airport, groggy from too little sleep during the nine hour flight. They walked down the jet ramp, collected their baggage, passed through passport control and customs, and found the taxi rank outside the arrivals hall. They climbed into the back of a white Mercedes taxi, one in a long line of Mercedes taxis. Agnes gave the driver Gertrude's address, a turn-of-the-century apartment building in the Charlottenburg section of the city.

As they entered the city, Agnes looked for traces of the old Berlin Wall. It had been torn down five years earlier, like her father had wished. She hoped he would be glad to see the city without it.

Agnes gnawed on the corner of her thumbnail during the entire ride and Paulina kept silent. Soon the taxi pulled up in front of a six-story apartment building, each floor lined with tall French doors and gleaming black shutters, Juliet balconies, and a stone façade adorned with carved ornamentations. They let themselves in through a glass door with brass spindles across the panes and found the elevator. The elevator car was small with a lustrous, red carpet like the ones in old movie theaters. Once the elevator got to the fourth floor, they found Gertrude's door on the left, halfway down a long hallway wallpapered and lit with white ceramic sconces. It probably hadn't changed at all since Gertrude moved in decades ago. Agnes wondered how sick Gertrude would look, and if she were in any pain. She still didn't know how to talk about the cancer. She smoothed her hair as Paulina came up beside her.

"I forgot to tell you. She doesn't speak English," Agnes quickly said.

"Don't worry about me."

"And she's very old. Mid-nineties I think."

"Wow. She must be a tough lady."

Agnes agreed that she must be. She pressed a tiny white button by the doorknob and heard an insistent buzz inside, beyond the door. "Ja?" a frail voice called almost immediately.

"Frau Mueller?" Agnes called. She had never been able to bring herself to call Gertrude her grandmother. *"Es ist Agnes."*

The lock jostled loose and the doorknob turned. Gertrude Mueller stood in the open doorway wearing a baby-blue knit dress, pearl earrings, and necklace to match. Her thick white hair was swept up and pinned behind her head, and her face was made up with a cheerful pink rouge and lipstick. Agnes felt drab standing in front of her, especially after her night spent on an airplane.

"My dear, please come in," she said in her musical German.

Agnes introduced Paulina and they followed Gertrude to a sunny sitting room, made large by the obvious vacancies left by missing objects. It looked as if Gertrude were in the process of slowly moving out. Several vibrantly colored rectangles were visible against the faded green wallpaper, spots where paintings must have hung for many years, protecting the paper from the sunlight. A map of Germany from the early twentieth century, before World War I, hung over the mantel. Before both the wars, Germany had been a much larger country. An antique desk was positioned between two French doors, the summer sun flooding in, lighting up the dust. Above the desk hung a small clock with a fox on the minute hand and a rooster on the hour, the fox giving chase to something it would never catch. Agnes couldn't place why, but she found the symbolism unsettling, like a moonless sky.

Gertrude sat on a flower-patterned settee, with Agnes and Paulina in opposite chairs. A tray of coffee and water with small china teacups rested on the table between them.

"I'm sorry your wedding was disrupted," Gertrude said as she poured coffee.

Agnes took a coffee cup from her. "Thanks." She had sent Gertrude an invite for the wedding, but then she hadn't known about Gertrude's cancer, and even a healthy woman in her nineties would have difficulty traveling. "Have you heard anything from my father?"

"Not yet. I suppose then it's just *you* checking on me, isn't it?" Gertrude raised her cup as if making a playful toast and looked at Agnes over the rim. "You know I would have liked to be at your wedding. I just don't travel very well now. Not since Albert died."

"Sure," Agnes said. "I understand."

Agnes put her cup down and stole a glance at Paulina. She knew Paulina wasn't following much of the conversation, but probably knew that Agnes still wasn't broaching the real subject at hand. In the taxi from the airport Paulina had encouraged her to ask Gertrude about her father and Klaus Schneider. Maybe between the two women, they could help her father resolve his issues over Klaus's crimes. Agnes had no idea how to start that conversation. She picked up her cup and took another sip. Her hand trembled a bit and some coffee spilled over the edges.

"Gertrude," she started. "I think Klaus Schneider had something to do with my father not being able to go through with my wedding."

Gertrude's eyes widened.

"My. That's a name I haven't heard in so many years."

"Yes, I know about him."

"Your father finally told you?"

"Not exactly, but I know about him now."

Gertrude appeared remorseful. "The trial of those men was unfortunately very public, and I had already explained to Bernd who his real parents were by that time. I wished I hadn't."

"It seems he feels some kind of blame, or even that maybe I should," Agnes said.

"Oh, no. You really shouldn't."

"I don't." But it wasn't entirely true. It was Agnes's legacy, wasn't it? Just as if her grandfather had discovered a vaccine, designed an electric car, or published a book. It was his life's work, meant to be remembered by his descendants. "But there is always something I wondered about. Maybe I could ask you?"

"Of course."

"I talked a long time ago to the Red Cross in Germany. They told me that Liesl died in 1949, and Klaus in 1941. I thought my father's parents died in a car accident together in 1942?"

The room was stone quiet. Paulina reached for more coffee and traded a look with Agnes.

"That's odd, isn't it?" Gertrude eventually said.

"And they said Liesl, before she died, was listed with German authorities as a missing person. Did you know she was missing?"

Gertrude looked blankly at both of them. "It's the first time I hear that."

"Maybe I could talk to someone at the orphanage in Berlin. Maybe they know?"

"I'm afraid you can't. The orphanage closed after the war. As for the Schneiders, I wish I could help you more, but I never did know them."

Gertrude was spinning a thin charm bracelet around on her wrist. When she saw Agnes watching, she stopped and gave a confiding look. "It's possible the Red Cross is wrong, dear. It was a confusing time, during that war."

"Yes, it's possible," Agnes said, but didn't really believe they could be wrong.

Gertrude went to the antique desk, under the fox and rooster clock. Inside a bottom drawer, she lifted out a thin manila envelope. It almost looked empty. She returned to Agnes and pulled two pieces of paper out and handed them to Agnes: one long form, official-looking and old; the other a small scrap of lavender notepaper. At the bottom of the long form, an eagle gripped a lightning bolt in each claw, each bolt looking like half of a swastika. Agnes knew it was the early emblem of the National Socialist government. The name at the top, typed in all caps: Schneider, Bernd Heinrich. It was her father's birth certificate, the original. The one her mother had at home must have been a copy.

"This birth certificate is what the orphanage gave me when we took Bernd in. I don't know why I need to keep these documents anymore," Gertrude said, handing the papers and envelope to Agnes. "Somebody in your family should have them."

Your family? Agnes read what was written on the lavender paper. As she did, it occurred to her that Gertrude was divesting, divesting the way a person does at the end of their lives. It made her feel indescribable sorrow, all in one blow, that this woman's death wouldn't have much impact on Agnes's life even though it should have a huge one.

Agnes took a breath and focused on the lavender paper: the name *Petra*, underlined twice. Next to it *b. 1920*. Another name: *Georg*, also underlined twice. Next to it *b. 1922*.

"Who are Georg and Petra?"

"Georg is Klaus's brother. Petra is Liesl's sister. I found their names a long while back, but we never made contact. But I thought maybe your father would want to know them. They are his uncle and aunt."

"Do you know where they are?"

"I believe Petra lives near Munich. I don't know where exactly." She paused. "Ah! I have an old phone number for Georg." Gertrude went back to the desk, opening another drawer, another envelope, sliding out a small piece of white paper with a phone number written in pencil. "This number must be over thirty years old. It might not help, but you can have it. Georg lives in Düsseldorf. Perhaps he might be someone you can talk to about what the Red Cross told you."

Agnes looked again at the dates on the lavender paper and calculated that Petra and Georg were in their seventies now. Aside from being likely out of date, the phone number for Georg was barely legible. Agnes put it all back in the large envelope. She waited that afternoon as long as she could at Gertrude's apartment for her father to call, going through three pots of coffee with Paulina. Finally the jet lag gripped her. She was too tired to stay awake and felt herself overstaying her welcome.

"Paulina and I will be at the Bach Schlosshotel." She handed Gertrude the number. Any other grandmother would have insisted Agnes stay with her, but Agnes didn't have any expectations of that. Gertrude wasn't really any other grandmother. She wasn't really a grandmother. After the past few hours, Agnes felt as much a stranger there as if she had come off the street to sell her a vacuum. It felt like nothing connected them, not even her father. They kissed each other on the cheeks politely and said not much more than just good-bye.

***

Paulina hailed a taxi and another white Mercedes appeared at the curb.

"Mercedes are everywhere," Agnes remarked.

"They're made here," Paulina reminded her.

Paulina gave the driver the address of the Bach Schlosshotel, which she had booked for clients previously and so knew it would suit them. They passed through the Tiergarten, coming out to a section of town that was less leafy than Charlottenburg. Agnes peered through the windshield. Ahead of them, one of the largest reconstruction projects in Europe was underway in the Potsdamer Platz, and the Reichstag was being refurbished and prepared to support Norman Foster's luminous glass dome.

Winding through some quieter side streets, they arrived at the boutique Bach Schlosshotel. The taxi pulled through the front gate, its black iron rails wrought together and hung between two pale stone columns on either side of them. Magnolia trees lined the driveway that circled up to the building, their hard, glossy leaves knocking the windows of the car as they drove through. True to its name, the Bach Schlosshotel looked like a castle, complete with a tiny moat and two fortified towers on either side. It was a little absurd in Agnes's opinion.

The lobby of the hotel resembled a shadowy, medieval chamber, a welcome shelter from the high afternoon sun outside. A massive iron chandelier loomed directly above the center of the lobby. Draft sketches by Kandinsky hung behind the front desk, framed in black, each lit with a tiny halogen light that arched over them on a wire. During the drive, Agnes had explained her conversation with Gertrude.

"When we get to the hotel, I'll check us in, and then I have to make a work call." Paulina held up a Nokia cell phone, her work line. The agency did work for Nokia so everyone had their latest model cell phone, which had just that year started to sweep through Europe as a must-have electronic for everyone from businessmen to blue-haired grannies. "You go straight upstairs and call this Georg person. It's the best lead you've had yet."

"You think the number is even good anymore? Is he even still alive?"

"Seventy-two isn't that old."

"What do I say to him?"

"How about 'Hi, Uncle Georg'?"

"That sounds odd."

"At least you'll get his attention."

***

Agnes left Paulina in a secluded corner of the lobby to make her work call and went up to the fifth floor of the hotel where theirs was the last room on the left. She entered and noticed the room's heavy curtains were drawn almost to a close. Matching winter-scene paintings hung over each twin bed, displaying snow-covered Alpine castles and frozen lakes. Agnes put her purse down by the side of the bed and sat next to the phone. Lingering mildew in the room made her feel congested. She reached into her purse for the envelope and dug out the paper with the phone number for Georg Schneider in Düsseldorf.

Agnes studied the number. She started to dial, though she hardly expected a thirty-year-old phone number to still be the right one. But after one ring, a man's voice answered, sounding deep like a drum.

"Schneider, guten Tag," he said.

When she heard him speak, she recalled what Klaus, his brother, had been accused of doing, and she found herself expecting Georg's voice to sound menacing in some way, the way she would have expected Klaus's voice to sound. It didn't seem fair of her, but that's where her mind went. But he didn't sound menacing at all.

He waited a long moment for her to speak as she fumbled longer than she meant to. In the best German she could manage, she told him who she was and who he was, her great-uncle. She could hear furniture shuffling on the other end of the line, like a chair being scraped back and Georg taking a seat. The silence on the phone lasted longer than she would have expected. To steady her nerves, she started counting little repeating figures of frog princes that were embroidered on the bedspread.

"I'm afraid you'll have to explain," he replied.

"When Klaus and Liesl died, they had a son. Bernd. He's my father."

"Who told you they were the parents of this Bernd?"

This Bernd? "His orphanage told us. Klaus and Liesl's names are on his birth certificate."

As Agnes explained, she started to wonder: *where was Georg when his nephew became an orphan?*

"Well, I'm sorry to disappoint you, Fräulein. But the father of that boy couldn't be my brother. Klaus and Liesl never had a child."

She turned on the edge of the bed, not sure she had heard correctly.

"What do you mean? They didn't have a child that was put up for adoption?"

"They would never have given up a child. They wanted a child very badly."

Agnes took the birth certificate Gertrude had given her out of her purse. "I'm holding his birth certificate in my hand. It says he was born in Munich, at the Krankenhouse Schwabing, December 26, 1941. Mutter: Liesl Richter Schneider, Vater: Klaus Schneider."

"If that's the date he was born, it would be impossible to have Klaus and Liesl as his parents. The explosion killed them both in the spring, earlier that year."

Agnes sat up rod straight. "Explosion?"

"Yes. In their apartment. A gas leak. I remember the day, twenty-first of April, 1941. Everyone thought it was someone making an attempt on the Führer's life, on the day after his birthday, but it wasn't him who perished. It was my brother and Liesl. It was a terrible day." Sweat beaded on her forehead. Georg didn't know about Liesl dying years later, and being missing before then. How could he not know? Or was the Red Cross mistaken like Gertrude had suggested? Now a third story. An explosion? It didn't seem possible there could be so many stories about one couple's death.

"One of the reasons I wanted to call you was because the Red Cross told me Liesl died in 1949. Of cervical cancer. But the orphanage said she and Klaus died in a car accident in 1942. I never knew which was right."

Georg Schneider emitted an abrupt sigh. "It sounds like you have altogether the wrong couple, Fräulein. It doesn't sound like my brother and Liesl are the parents you are looking for. Maybe your father was the child of another Liesl and Klaus Schneider of Munich?"

"For some reason they are listed on his birth certificate, with their full names. And I have your name, and Petra Richter who is supposed to be Liesl's sister?"

Georg didn't answer immediately.

"Yes, Petra is," he said. "How did you get our names?"

"The woman who adopted my father had them."

"Then I think you need to ask her. I don't think any of the information you have is correct. I'm sorry I can't help you."

"No, that's okay. You've been … very helpful. Thank you for speaking with me."

"Of course," he said. "Good luck—"

Agnes gripped the receiver of the phone. *What about Klaus and the trial?*

"Wait. Could I ask you something else?"

"Yes?"

"Was Klaus in the military?"

He cut her off. "I don't know anything about what he did for the military. My brother had a lot of his own problems. But he was a good man, a simple man." Georg paused. "Please, can you just remember that?"

"Of course. I'm so sorry to bother you."

"Good-bye then, Fräulein."

Georg Schneider hung up with a loud click. Agnes reached to the nightstand, laid the receiver in its base, and brought her hands to the side of her face, pressing her temples with her fingers. One hundred and thirteen frog princes had been embroidered into the bedspread. She stared at their squatting bodies, their happy green faces, topped with yellow-pointed crowns.

***

By Thursday morning, when there had been no sign of her father in Berlin, Agnes had convinced Paulina that they needed to go to Munich before she returned to Chicago.

"What was Georg talking about? An explosion? And before my father was even born?"

"So what do you hope to find in Munich? Bomb residue?"

Paulina asked, packing her bag.

"Come on. My father was born there, for one thing. We can see if there are any records of Klaus and Liesl in the Rathaus, something about their address, a record of the explosion or their deaths. And surely the hospital in Munich where he was born will know about him?"

"You would hope so."

"This isn't just about what happened on my wedding day. Klaus Schneider is from Munich. He's haunted me my whole life. Maybe, for no other reason, I just want to walk the streets where he walked because it will somehow connect me to him. Somehow help me understand something about him and be able to stop wondering about him."

"After everything you've learned, you want to be connected to him?"

"I want to understand him. And then I want to forget him. Don't you have to connect with someone to understand them?"

"You know he's not there to meet you for a coffee," Paulina chided.

"Yes, I realize that. I'm talking about a metaphysical connection. Being with him in the same space, even if I can't be with him in the same time."

Paulina shut her small, wheeled Samsonite. "I can go with you for a few more days, and then I have to go back to Warsaw and earn a living. Is that okay?"

"That's fine. Where else can I go after that anyway?"

Paulina left the room to go to the front desk to book their flight to Munich. Agnes sat on the frog prince bedspread and called Gertrude, one more time.

"I talked to Georg Schneider after I left your apartment," she started. She relayed all of what Georg had told her, none of which seemed to come as a surprise to Gertrude.

"It's like I told you, my dear. That war was a confusing time."

"But Georg Schneider isn't a bureaucracy that has confused its records. He's Klaus's brother. Why would he know nothing about my father?"

"I just don't know. It's very strange."

"Is it possible the orphanage got my father's documents mixed up with another child's?"

"Of course. Those things are always possible."

Agnes stared at the painting of a castle over the bed. "Before I go back to Chicago, I'm going to stop in Munich. I guess I just want to see where he was born, know a little more about it."

Gertrude made a noise. Agnes couldn't tell if it were a sigh or a muffled groan. "Then if you'll be there, perhaps you should talk to Petra. She's in a town called Kowald, west of Munich. She runs a dairy farm."

Agnes closed her eyes. How was it that Gertrude suddenly knew more about Petra, things she hadn't told Agnes the day before? But regardless, Agnes reminded herself that Gertrude was elderly and very ill and Agnes just had to be patient.

"You know how brothers are," Gertrude said. "They don't keep in touch. It is odd, but still Klaus could have had a son without letting his brother know. Liesl may have been closer to her sister than Klaus was to his brother. Maybe there was a rift between them?"

Yes, Agnes thought. A rift. She thought of how emotional Georg became when Agnes asked about Klaus's time in the military and a rift didn't seem likely. They seemed very close.

"If my father calls …" she said. Then stopped. "I'll call you. I don't know yet how you can reach me there."

"Have a safe trip, Agnes."

***

Paulina sat next to Agnes on Lufthansa flight 73 that left Berlin's Tegel Airport at one o'clock Thursday afternoon. They would land at the airport in Munich one hour and ten minutes later.

Agnes stared out at the wing, hypnotized—the wing on the tarmac, the wing taking off, the wing in the clouds. The same wing. So many thoughts and theories were churning in her head that she was grateful to have nothing to do but sit and stare. Early in the flight, a summer rain shower hit them and the plane fought against the turbulence. She counted the beads of rain that slipped across her oval window in a jet stream of air.

Agnes had tried to keep Krys out of her mind, but now it had been too many days, too much confusion, too much turbulence, and she missed him fiercely. She felt that catch of pain in her chest, that fear and loneliness she felt whenever she and Krys were quarreling, when he wasn't at the end of the telephone line or waiting for her after a hard day. When he was nowhere. She squeezed her eyes shut and tried to snuff out thoughts of where she would have been now if things had gone according to plan: on a beach in Cancun, as Mrs. Sobota.

In the middle of the flight, a young woman in a blue and gold pantsuit came down the aisle and offered them tea or coffee. They both took coffees. Agnes drank quickly. Paulina lingered over hers, flipping through a copy of *Mode Spiegel* that a passenger on a previous flight must have left in the seat pocket.

"Can you even read that?" Agnes asked.

"It's fashion. What's to read?"

Agnes flipped the inflight magazine to the city map of Munich. She dropped her finger on a square in the middle of town. "There. We go first to the Rathaus. Every resident of a German city will be registered at the Rathaus."

"Do you really think we'll find records about the Schneiders from the 1930s and '40s?"

The coffee had helped Agnes's mood. She turned her head up, haughty, affecting a fake German accent. "Ov corze, fräulein. Didn't you know? Ze Germans keep recordz on *everyzing*."

***

A short time later, the plane descended for landing. Agnes hated landings, but especially this one. The engine of the Airbus 320 kept slowing, dipping, then revving. The fuselage pitched and the wings wagged in wide circles. She hated flying in the summer when the air was hot and angry, convections building unstable clouds, creating the worst turbulence for planes. Agnes looked out the window and saw green pastures bordered by ribbons of road and dotted with the orange rooftops of houses. She wished she were on the ground.

The plane hesitated slightly as it neared the runway, the eerie sensation of the engines nearly turned off and the fuselage floating only a few feet above the ground. Finally the wheels tapped the tarmac. The plane lurched up in a hop, shimmied to either side, and came back down again. The pilot thrust the engines into reverse and the turbines roared. Agnes pitched forward and put her hand on the back of the seat in front of her. She clenched her eyes shut and touched the inside of her diamond solitaire with her pinky—the first time she realized she was still wearing it and maybe shouldn't be—and thought how it calmed her down to hold Krys's arm during landings like that one.

A half hour later, through the terminal, they dropped their bags into the trunk of a black BMW 325i that they rented from Sixt. Agnes tapped the rear closed with a perfectly engineered *click*. She settled behind the steering wheel. The inside of the car smelled like leather heaven, if there were such a place.

She drove them toward the center of Munich. Brightly colored flower boxes perched on the rail of every balcony and sill of every window. Munich seemed opulent, even elegant—from the inside of the car, to the whitewashed façades of buildings and perfectly tended flowers and lawns. Images of her father came to mind, his blazers and their suede elbow patches, his designer watches, the tasteful elegance of his building designs. It made a little bit of sense that he was from Bavaria, maybe not raised there, but definitely Bavarian at heart.

When they pulled up in a block near Munich's City Hall, the Neues Rathaus, Agnes wedged the BMW into a tiny parallel parking spot. As they got out, she pulled a piece of notebook paper out of her purse and unfolded it. She had looked up some of the more technical terminology. The *Anmeldeformular*, for one, was the form any resident of Munich had to complete and file with the City Hall. She would ask about the Anmeldeformular for Klaus and Liesl.

They walked across the Marienplatz toward the Rathaus. The hollow clang of organ pipes sounded outside as the Glockenspiel on the front of the building began its display of jousting knights above the square. Agnes looked up, squinting into the sun. The entire square was filling with people, shoulder to shoulder, holding cameras to their faces and framing the clock in their lenses. She and Paulina pushed through the gathering crowd of tourists and arrived at the entrance to the Rathaus.

"*Guten Tag,*" she said to the uniformed attendant. He was young, so she took a chance that he could speak English. "We're looking for some records on some people who used to live in Munich, in the 1930s. We want to look up their An ... mel ... de ... formular." Agnes stumbled over the terminology, but the young man seemed to know what she meant.

"For that you need office on floor three, to *Kreisverwaltungsreferat,* and you will pay fee there," he said. He had such a heavy accent she could barely understand his English, but was grateful that he could speak it.

"Okay, *Dankeschön,*" she said.

He had already turned back to a magazine with dirt bikes on the cover. "It's welcome," he mumbled.

They walked through the center hall on the ground floor of the Rathaus and took the elevator to the third floor. The elevator opened opposite a glass door labeled with black letters and a crest with a black eagle: "*Landeshauptstadt München Kreisverwaltungsreferat.*" They walked through the door and into the long room beyond. The high ceiling gave it the aura of an enormous library stretching the whole length of the Rathaus. Bright white sunlight streamed through the windows along the south side of the room, facing the Marienplatz. Agnes could hear the Glockenspiel still chiming; its song was even louder and more out of tune when heard from inside the building. They walked toward a woman standing behind a counter in the center of the room. The woman was young, like the attendant downstairs, but her businesslike demeanor made her seem older.

"We're looking for the residency records of two people who lived in Munich in the 1930s—a Liesl and Klaus Schneider. And their families," Agnes announced.

To Agnes's surprise, the woman didn't hesitate when she heard the request. She turned almost robotically to a neatly labeled cabinet to her right and pulled out a form from one of the cubbies. The woman pushed a long sheet of paper across the counter and asked her to fill it out and sign at the bottom. As if she could tell what Agnes were thinking, she mentioned that the Rathaus held records as far back as the Middle Ages, should Agnes need them.

Not even two minutes later, Agnes had completed as much of the form as she could. It asked for birthdates, places of birth, family relations, occupations, addresses, and telephone contacts. Agnes had almost none of that for Klaus and Liesl. She put their names, with Munich as their residence, Bernd Heinrich Schneider as their child, then lastly the names of their siblings. That was all she knew. She returned the form to the woman and sat with Paulina on a long oak bench in front of the counter and waited.

"What if they can't find them?" Paulina wondered out loud. "You didn't give her much to go on. Just a bunch of names."

Agnes watched the woman tapping at a computer on her desk, then saw her get up and walk into a back room. "Don't worry. If anybody can find a needle in a haystack with nothing to go on, it's a German."

The Glockenspiel was quiet. Agnes looked through the windows up to a sky full of clouds so white looking at them almost hurt. The building seemed to creak in the hot wind, the windows rattled and tapped in the small places around the perimeter where the old glass had come loose. A man in green corduroys and a black cap stood on a scaffold repairing spots in the wall where the white paint had started to flake. He lost his balance momentarily and Agnes straightened, nearly standing to help him, but he recovered. He removed his cap and wiped his brow with the inside of his sleeve and said something sharply to himself in German. Agnes looked forward and saw the young woman returning with a large, black leather-bound volume in her arms. The sight of a faded swastika imprinted on the cover in gold leaf startled Agnes, but then she remembered that the volume was merely a government document and the National Socialists were the government in power when it was made.

"Here you go. They are in this volume here, which is the Official Tax Record. I marked the page for you. There are a lot of Schneiders, but there's a record with Liesl and Klaus listed together. I assume that's the one you want. Unfortunately, we can't photocopy these big books. But you can write down whatever information you need." The woman slid the volume across the counter and pointed to a table in the waiting area with a wooden box containing paper and small pencils.

Agnes took the book to the counter and peeled open the top cover to the marked page. The paper stank of mold and Paulina held a hand in front of her mouth. As the book settled open, a plume of dust emerged from the pages and curled into the rays of sun above the table. On the marked page, five columns had been drawn with ink and a straight edge. Whoever made them must not have had a long enough ruler because she noticed that the bottom third of each vertical line was started anew and drawn to the bottom of the paper, slightly misaligned. The entries in the first column appeared to contain names, and the one just to its right contained addresses. Agnes ran her finger down the column of names until she found the two she was looking for.

"Schneider, Liesl, Klaus. This is them." She touched their names and looked to the next column. "This must have been their address—Salvatorstrasse 31."

"This is so weird isn't it?" Paulina beamed wonderment. "They were real. They really lived."

"I know. This feels like the first piece of information that makes sense to me," Agnes replied.

"What else does it say?"

"Look." Agnes pointed at a bunch of numbers next to their entry that clearly signified amounts of money. It was hard to read the column headings, which were in German and written in an old Gothic script with ink that was either smudged or faded, or both. "The woman said this was the Official Tax Record. So these must be their tax payments."

They flipped through several pages and followed the tax payments of Klaus and his wife Liesl. On 10 June 1937 there was a payment of 25 Reichsmark. Every year displayed three or four payments, the last one on 15 November 1940.

"When did their car accident supposedly happen?" Paulina asked.

"1942." Agnes looked down the page and turned to face Paulina. "But if they stopped paying taxes in 1940, it supports what the Red Cross told me. That Klaus died in 1941 and Liesl disappeared."

"Or that there was an explosion that killed them both in 1941," Paulina said.

"Right."

"Do any of these entries list occupation?"

Agnes pointed to the column just to the right of their address. "Here. It says Klaus was an *Uhrmacher.*"

"What's that?"

"Clockmaker."

"That sounds harmless enough, doesn't it?"

"But I thought he was in the military?"

Agnes recalled the letter from the World Commission for Crimes against Children. In the Scientists Trial at Nuremburg, Klaus was named as the Chief Scientist for the German Army High Command. It seemed incongruous with being a clockmaker. How could he have gone from being a clockmaker to having such an important military post?

Something else on the page caught her eye, something that looked like it could be important because not all the entries had them. With the volume laid open across her forearms, she walked back to the counter. "Excuse me?" Agnes heaved the book onto the counter. "Can you tell me what these double crosses mean next to Klaus and Liesl Schneider's names? Here?" Agnes pointed to two small crosses marked in a different pen at the far right end of their entry.

"Ja. The double cross means no descendants."

Agnes stared at her, realizing this corroborated what Georg said.

"Perhaps I am not using the correct English word?" the woman said. "I mean, they had no children."

Agnes wanted to label it as a mistake. The lines in the table were crooked. Maybe these crosses applied to the people in the lines above or below Klaus and Liesl.

"But they did have a child," Agnes pressed.

"Not according to this."

"Are you sure?"

The features of the woman's face drew together, and she gave Agnes a stern glance. "Our records are quite in order."

Agnes pointed to the columns of money. "And you said these are tax payments?"

"Indeed."

"Did people stop paying taxes after 1940? If they were in the military maybe?"

The woman pulled a pencil from behind her ear and tapped the point of it twice on the counter, her irritation as palpable as the chimes of the Glockenspiel which would soon sound again through the building and across the square.

"During the war," she said, "every German paid."

FIVE

Lost in Bavaria

On Friday morning, Paulina drove them out of the city center and north toward the Krankenhaus Schwabing, which had been listed on her father's birth certificate as his birthplace.

"You know this is the end of the road, don't you?" Paulina said.

"What do you mean?"

"If this hospital doesn't have a record of your father, then storks brought him and he has no parents."

"Please don't joke."

"I just want you to be prepared."

"I don't think I can possibly be prepared for that." Agnes sunk into the leather upholstery of the passenger seat. "This has to all be some kind of mix-up with his paperwork."

"Germans don't seem like the type to mix up their paperwork."

"Have you been thinking about where your dad is now? Any hunches?"

Agnes sighed. "I'm trying not to be worried. I think my mother was right about the police. We would have known right away if something had happened to him. For now, we just don't know where he is."

They reached the gate of the Krankenhaus Schwabing, and

Paulina pulled the BMW up in front of a red and white drop barrier. The barrier rose and Paulina drove through, finding a parking spot in front of what looked like the main building. The Krankenhaus reminded Agnes of an American college campus with its smooth, green lawns, and clusters of long, three-story, dorm-like buildings. Orange tiles and dormer windows roofed each whitewashed building. Here and there a window was open a crack and the wind pulled corners of lace curtains through the openings. Agnes pointed to a larger building with three arches that displayed a sign for the hospital across its cornice.

"Let's try there first."

When they entered the building, a nurse with a jowly chin was sitting just inside the door. Her smile jutted like a two-sided arrow into her cheeks. "We're looking for the hospital administration?" Agnes asked. The nurse pointed with a chubby finger toward a dim hallway of marble tile and gray walls that lead off the lobby. From there, they were directed to the maternity wing in a separate building at the rear of the complex which they were told would hold birth records. They walked from the main building alongside a shallow canal lined with what looked like cherry trees. She was glad to think of her father being born in such a beautiful place, although it was possible it looked different in the middle of a war.

At the end of the canal, they found the maternity wing. Just inside the front door, they came upon another office. Framed pictures of newborn babies lined the walls. A nurse stood at a high table by the window, going through paperwork. Her straight brown hair was neatly held away from her face by a white cap.

"Excuse me?" Agnes said in her halting German. The nurse looked up. "Is this where we can find birth records? We're looking for the records of a baby born here on December 26, 1941. We think his parents were listed inaccurately on his birth certificate."

The nurse's face was clear and healthy, plump in some places and lined in others. It gave her the impossible aspect of someone who was both wise and youthful. She smiled, her teeth white and straight. Then she answered, in perfect English, "You are? What makes you think the birth certificate is incorrect?" Agnes heard her accent and realized the nurse wasn't German.

"Are you American?"

"Yes, I'm from Boston. My name is Leslie Anderson." She approached them. "So why do you think his birth certificate is wrong?"

Agnes started her explanation as Nurse Anderson invited them into an inner office. Agnes and Paulina took their seats in two white wicker chairs positioned in front of her desk. That was something Agnes noticed about hospitals in Europe, especially in Germany: they were rarefied places offering retreat and comfort, not the test-running and drug-dosing factories Agnes was used to in the States. She imagined her father would enjoy designing a German hospital, if he ever got the chance one day. Agnes looked across the desk and glanced at the silver plaque which identified Leslie Anderson as Head Nurse. Agnes was thankful that, maybe, they had found the right person. It felt like a gift.

"What year did you say he was born?"

Agnes pulled her father's birth certificate out of her purse. "This says 1941."

Head Nurse Leslie Anderson looked the certificate over and her face wrinkled. "That's strange. I'm not sure why this hospital would be listed as his birthplace. Krankenhaus Schwabing didn't have a maternity ward until *after* the war, when the Allies came in and used it as a military hospital. By then, they had started treating soldiers here, mostly Americans still in the European theater, and their families. My understanding was that they felt this hospital wasn't suited for maternity, but so many babies were being born to soldiers that they had to set up the ward. But before then—you said 1941?—I don't think any babies were born here."

Agnes felt a tiny, imaginary crevice start to open in the earth underneath her feet, a tectonic shift rumbling deep within her that threatened a seismic quake to come. "Would you mind checking your records anyway?"

"Of course. Just give me a minute."

While they waited for her to come back, Agnes started counting the pens and pencils in the mug that sat at the top edge of the desk. Paulina sat with her, likely knowing better than to crack another joke. Nurse Anderson was gone for what felt like a long time, and Agnes hoped that meant she had found something.

"What if he wasn't born here?" Agnes said.

"He was born somewhere," Paulina replied.

The door opened and Nurse Anderson sat down behind her desk holding open a manila file folder. "I looked into both paper and digital archives, under his name and both the parents' names for the first five years of the maternity ward's operation. There's no record of his birth, or of either of his parents being patients. And as I assumed, the first birth we had here was the twelfth of April, 1946. It was a boy, born to Major William Warren and his wife Annie. From Lakeland, Florida. I'm sure that was the first one." Agnes dropped her shoulders. "I wish I could help you clarify things with your father's birth certificate, but I just can't. I'm fairly certain he wasn't born here, not in 1941 or any time after that. I'm so sorry."

They stood up and thanked Nurse Anderson. When Agnes shook her hand, she felt a small pulse of sympathy pass between their eyes and fingers, something she felt like she so rarely encountered in the world anymore.

"You might want to talk to the Red Cross," Nurse Anderson offered.

"I did already."

"Well you might want to go back to them again. Ask them about Displaced Persons from World War Two." Nurse Leslie stopped, but a look from Agnes implored her to continue. "I'm just suggesting that if your father's birth certificate is suspect, perhaps he was separated from his family during the war."

Agnes considered all the scenarios in which a baby could be separated from his family during a world war. Perhaps he was rescued during an air raid. Perhaps they were refugees and being separated from his family was safer than being with them. Agnes walked with Paulina back to the car, numb, scrounging through her mind for possible explanations of finding no record of her father's parents and no record of his birthplace. Her wedding day had only been six days earlier but it seemed like sixty years. She had lost track of time and place. Where her father was, she still didn't know. Where her father had come from, she didn't know either. The second one was a question she didn't even know she would end up asking.

Back in the car, she pulled her father's birth certificate out of her purse. She looked at the photocopy of the old document, how carefully it was typed. The typewriter that had been used had a broken *r*; that letter was always slightly higher than all the others. She tried to imagine who had typed it, when and where they had been sitting. In a small office, maybe in a large building. Had it been a man or a woman? Had they known they were typing up a sheet of lies? The mistakes didn't seem like accidents anymore. "Is everything on this piece of paper made up?" Agnes heard herself utter.

Paulina looked at the paper with her. "Maybe your father was just found somewhere and nobody knew where he came from so they had to make something up?"

"But then why not just say that? Just put 'unknown' in the spaces for mother and father? Why fabricate the whole story with the Schneiders and them dying in a car accident? Somebody made all of that up, don't you see? All of it. Somebody wanted to make sure that people thought the Schneiders were his birth family. But why them? Why my father?"

"No idea. But if the Schneiders were not his real birth parents, then who was?" Paulina added. "And where was he born if not here?"

Agnes looked beyond Paulina into the thick forest surrounding the hospital compound. She had the sensation of being the victim of a crime, in that moment in the car, in front of that hospital. Something was being ripped away, like a bag off her shoulders, like valuables out of a locker, like something stolen out of her room or off her desk. Something was gone, faster than she could even see it go. She had been mugged once, in downtown Chicago, when she was home from college and out for dinner with a few girlfriends. She watched the man run up the street with the ripped handle of her purse in his grip. The purse swung as it got smaller, and she struggled to remember what was in it, figuring that once it was out of view she wouldn't be able to recall the contents anymore. Her wallet, yes. Inside that, a few bills, a few quarters for parking, a fortune from a Chinese restaurant. It said: *Life is your own invention.* As if life could be invented. She liked the idea then, but now it seemed perverse. Everything in the stolen purse was replaceable. Her father had reminded her of that to make her feel better. Nothing was really lost, not for good. But then he had hugged her with such a force, as if the threat of losing *her* for good was never far from his mind.

Now she felt that feeling about him, that he could be lost to her forever. He could be lost to all of them. Maybe he already was.

***

After leaving the hospital, they returned to the hotel in the center of Munich, where Agnes had a similar, awkward conversation with a woman named Petra Richter, the sister of Liesl Schneider, as the one she had with Klaus's brother Georg. This time, she didn't insist on being Liesl's granddaughter, but she did say there was a possibility. It was a shame to hear Petra react with such a hopeful sound in her voice, because Agnes had all but given up on the possibility that she had anything to do, genetically, with the couple from Munich and their siblings. Now Agnes just wanted to know where to turn next, and Petra was the only stone left unturned. They agreed to meet at Petra's dairy farm outside the little crossroads village of Kowald the next morning.

Kowald was forty miles to the west of Munich, down a short stretch on the Autobahn, then along three separate country roads. It was Saturday morning and quiet, a week after her wedding day, a week into what should have been her life as Mrs. Sobota.

Agnes was grateful for the drive, as being behind the wheel helped her think. Paulina had fallen asleep only a few miles outside of Munich, which reminded Agnes of how tired they both were. To keep alert she turned down the air until it was uncomfortably cold. She had to stop once as a farmer led a line of cows across the street, the biggest one heading up the line and each one of them progressively smaller until the last three looked barely larger than newborn calves. It was late for baby animals, Agnes thought. Paulina stirred in the seat next to her. "Where are we?"

"Near Kowald."

"How much longer?"

"Only ten minutes, I guess. We'll be early. I think I'm driving too fast but I sort of figured that Germans don't care about that."

"Germans with a herd of cows might."

Paulina sat up straighter in the seat and pulled her hair back into a ponytail. The road made a hairpin curve then rose quickly to the right, past a rushing brook and a line of cypress trees that separated the bank from the shoulder, but only barely. Their car leaned toward the brook in places, and Agnes could see the curved backs of mossy rocks in the water, silverfish glinting in between them, the sun coloring the surface with long white brushstrokes. The road crested at the top of a small hill and, as they headed down the opposite slope, a lone house came into view at the far end of a field. It was brown with a steeply pitched roof, still a mile or so away, but she knew it had to be the home of Petra Richter as there were no others anywhere nearby.

Agnes held the steering wheel tightly as she maneuvered around several more curves and over a small bluff to where the road straightened. Petra's house, with its dark brown timbers and white gingerbread eaves, was now clearly visible. Three separate herds of cows meandered in the large pasture behind the house, their bodies motionless in the July haze, some of them lying down. Two stainless steel silos were visible behind another brown structure, which was larger and less decorative. Agnes guessed it was a barn. Maybe it had a hayloft, a place a child could play. As she slowed the car, she experienced a flash of wishful thinking: a vision of a boy growing up in this brown house tucked between the green slopes of pastures and forests, near a brook full of fish, the majesty of the Alps in the distance. How different her father would have been if he had grown up here, raised by someone who was his true family. But if the Rathaus, the Krankenhaus, and Georg Schneider were to be believed, Klaus Schneider died childless. Either Liesl Schneider gave birth to her father after she was widowed, or not at all.

As they drove up the gravel turnaround, a heavyset woman came out of the house and stood on the broad deck that stretched from one side of the house to the other. A blue flowered handkerchief tied her gray hair back, and she placed her hands on her hips waiting for the girls to get out of the car. Agnes stopped the car and she and Paulina met Petra on the deck.

"So you're the impossible granddaughter?" Petra said playfully in German.

"*Bitte?*" Agnes replied.

Petra switched to heavily accented but competent English, as if Agnes hadn't understood because of the language. "If you say you are my sister Liesl's granddaughter, then yes. You are impossible."

Petra stepped to the edge of the deck, her ice-blue eyes meeting Agnes's darker mid-ocean ones. Petra cocked her head and looked contemplative. "But it would have been nice if it weren't impossible."

"Could I talk to you about Liesl?"

"I was hoping someday somebody would," Petra said, leading Agnes and Paulina out of the high, hot sunshine and into the shade of a cathedral-ceilinged living room. It felt like a barn that had been turned into a house. The interior was especially dark, the windows too small for the space. Agnes's eyes were immediately drawn to the hearth, and the row of black and white photographs along the mantel. "Is Liesl in one of these?" she asked.

"In nearly every one!" Petra said, pulling the last picture on the end down and handing it to Agnes. Three adults stood close together, elbows and shoulders looped, the complicit posture of siblings, a kind of relationship Agnes had always longed for. Petra pointed. "Liesl's here, on the right."

It was the first picture of Liesl that Agnes had ever seen. Liesl was blond and tiny-waisted with an oval face and the outlines of womanly cheekbones just starting to show underneath the doughy flesh of childhood. Her golden hair was styled in large waves, like women did in the 1930s, pinned on the right side just above her ear so that the waves swooped gently around and cupped her earlobe. She wore a green tailored dress with a pleated front to the bodice and a thin lace collar at the neck. She was much more beautiful than Agnes had imagined. Their brother Stefan, who Petra said had made a career building ships in Hamburg, stood between the two girls like the steel beam of a skyscraper.

Petra motioned for Paulina and Agnes to sit down. Paulina had started to eat the sugar cookies fanned out on a wooden tray atop the coffee table. Petra sat heavily in the rattan chair opposite them. "What can I tell you about Liesl?"

"So many people have told me things. My mind is not entirely clear."

"That's fine, girl. I've run a dairy farm for close to fifty years in that condition. You can do anything until somebody stops you, no matter how muddled you are doing it. And the reality is most people won't bother to stop you, muddled or not, so you best get on with what you want to do in life."

"Maybe you can tell us how Liesl died?" Paulina interjected. "Was it an explosion or a car accident?"

Paulina's outburst must have been the result of now numerous meetings in which Agnes tip-toed around awkward questions before getting to the point. Agnes couldn't blame her for feeling the need to step in.

"Or was it a cancer?" Agnes added.

Petra pointed to Agnes. "Yes. That was the one," she said. "Klaus went with the explosion, yes, but Liesl wasn't with him that day."

"Why was my father always told they died together in a car accident?"

"Who told him that?"

"His orphanage."

"I have no idea why, but it's wrong. And it supports my theory that the explosion that killed Klaus was no gas leak. He was gotten rid of."

"Gotten rid of?" Paulina asked.

Petra took a cookie and raised an eyebrow at Paulina. "He must have done something. People were gotten rid of for lots of reasons back then. Your neighbor would be on the street one day, then the next day he would disappear, and it would be like he never existed. And nobody asked any questions. Everyone was just trying to stay out of harm's way."

"Do you know where Liesl was when the explosion happened?" Agnes asked.

"Not home. That's all I know. But a bit later, I started receiving letters. They came from a village called Spelzin, with a clinic of the same name, from late 1941 until the spring of 1946. But Spelzin isn't on any map, and I couldn't find anyone to tell me where it was. I even reported her missing. Then in late 1946, she called me and asked me to come get her at the Munich train station. She had been left on the platform in a wheelchair. I brought her here, but she wasn't well. She died three years later. She was only thirty-five years old."

"I'm so sorry," Agnes said.

Petra's mouth flattened. "It was a mercy, that's how I think of it. Liesl's life after Klaus was not good."

"What happened to her?"

"They experimented on her at this clinic in Spelzin, that's what she told me. Fertility experiments. I suppose they just thought they could make her produce children like a cow can produce tanks of milk."

"Klaus's brother told me she and Klaus couldn't have children," Agnes said.

"They couldn't." It didn't seem to Agnes that Petra had any children of her own. All the pictures in the house were only of her, Liesl, and Stefan. There was a warm-looking older couple in a few of them, their parents Agnes supposed. "Neither of us could, Liesl nor I." Petra clasped her hands together. "And do you know what you do with a cow that doesn't produce milk?"

Agnes shook her head. "I don't know anything about cows."

"You can either feed it better hay, yank harder on the teat, or kill it for hamburger." Petra slid the tray of cookies closer to them. "Liesl was exactly what they wanted to have more of: blond, blue-eyed, free of disease, not Jewish. And I'm sure they found it genetically impossible that such a superior body couldn't produce a child. By the time Liesl wrote me her second letter she had already been made to fornicate with 137 SS men."

Paulina choked on a cookie, and Petra moved a hand to give her a firm slap between the shoulder blades. Agnes instantly felt her mouth go dry, her skin prickle with goose bumps.

Agnes looked blankly at Petra. "She was forced to do this?"

"Liesl was a prisoner. The way she described it, Spelzin was a concentration camp pretending to be a hospital. She was watched almost constantly. She wrote letters in the lavatory, when she pretended she had to throw up. I guess no guard wanted to stand over a vomiting woman. The letters were all short and hard to read. And I don't know how she got them out. There must have been more that were intercepted and destroyed."

Agnes remembered the pretty, round-cheeked young girl in the photograph and the name that always was typed next to *Mutter* on her father's birth certificate. She never could have imagined this kind of hell for Liesl. And worse: she never could have imagined this kind of start for her father, if Liesl were indeed his mother, impregnated by some anonymous and racially correct soldier. Agnes felt nauseous. She started to sweat in the cool dark room. "What else did her letters say?"

"She asked me to come get her. In every one. But she couldn't give me any landmarks. Maybe there were none. I couldn't find this place called Spelzin. I tried everything I could think of. All the time, those Nazi doctors worked on her and tested things on her. Electric charges attached to anyplace they could think of—to her cervix, uterus, ovaries, labia, under the navel. She had sex while they shocked her nipples. They gave her toxic levels of vitamins because they thought it would increase her chances of conception. They dissected her fallopians and reinforced them with rubber tubing, like she was some kind of Frankenstein monster."

Agnes felt her stomach churn acidly. "You don't need to tell us all this," she whispered.

Petra seemed not to hear. "Her abdomen had been cut into so many times that she had five different infections at once by the time she wrote me the last letter."

"Those doctors were crazy," Paulina said in disbelief.

"People with white coats can get away with a lot," Petra said. "Like I told you. You can do whatever you want until somebody stops you, and nobody usually stops a doctor. I didn't know how to stop them. I didn't know where they were."

"But if Liesl couldn't have children, why did somebody put her name on Agnes's father's birth certificate?" Paulina asked. Agnes pulled it out and handed it to Petra. "Could there have been another Liesl Schneider, married to another Klaus, from Munich?"

"Did you check that at the Rathaus?"

"Yes," Agnes said. "There were lots of Schneiders, but only one listing of a couple with these first names, and with relatives matching your and your brother's names. It seems unlikely that the parents' names on his birth certificate refer to any other couple."

Petra stood and walked to a breakfront where a silver carafe stood in a cut glass bowl clogged with half-melted ice. Petra poured three glasses of milk, put them on a small wooden tray, and walked back to sit with Agnes and Paulina.

"I think the Nazis needed to fabricate your father's birth certificate, so they took the names of two people who they knew had already been gotten rid of," Petra said. "And perhaps it helped that Liesl and Klaus were considered genetically correct, by Nazi standards."

"Why would they need to do that?"

Petra handed them both a cold glass of milk. "Agnes, do you know about something called Lebensborn?"

"I don't."

"The word Lebensborn means *spring of life* in German. Sounds nice doesn't it?" Petra sipped from her glass. Her face seemed to lose its redness as her eyes grew as cold as the half-melted ice.

"What was it?"

"At the start, in the middle of the 1930s, Lebensborn was a plan to take care of mothers and children in Germany during a time when having a child was an economic hardship. Women were having many abortions and the birthrate was low. But it meant that Germany was aging and the population was shrinking. Our government—well, Hitler—wanted to reverse that trend, so they created hospitals and homes for pregnant women, even for unmarried girls. Women received money when they had a child. It became a financial salvation, then gradually, an honor. I was fifteen when the Lebensborn program started. I was looking forward to being a mother in a country like this one that prized mothers so."

"What does this have to do with Liesl, if she wasn't a mother?" Agnes asked.

"The Lebensborn became, closer to the war, more about breeding. Liesl's captivity was the worst of it. And at Nuremberg, those Nazi wretches swore that women and even girls were never forced to have sex during these years. It was a lie!" Petra stood and started pacing. "When I was seventeen, I was sent twice to a convention of Hitler Youth. I was excited and spent days packing as I knew there were two social events where the boys and girls youth camps would be brought together. At the first convention I went to, in May, I met a boy named Jonas. He was twenty years old." Petra moved slowly to the breakfront again and put her back to them. Her hands braced the edge. She lowered her voice so much that Agnes could barely hear when she said: "I had sex with Jonas."

A long silence settled in the room. Agnes and Paulina traded looks. Petra eventually walked back and sat in the rattan chair opposite them.

"I was so ashamed of myself. When I came home, I confessed to my mother. All she said was 'Are you late yet?' That was all. 'Are you late yet?' Three months went by and I was never late. Not once. When the next convention came in October, my mother encouraged me to go. But the way she said it, I knew I was being handed over for sex. 'Try again,' my mother had whispered to me." Petra peered at both of them, almost belligerently, like she was still fighting a battle she would never win. "My mother was asking me to try again for a baby."

"Did you go to the next convention?" Paulina asked.

"I did. I must have been brainwashed by then because I did try. I tried with four different boys during the week I was away from home. Like my mother said—'Try again.' So I did. I didn't want to fail her. But after I came home, I was never late." Petra paused. "Liesl and Klaus were already married and having trouble conceiving. That's when we suspected Liesl and I had the same problem. We couldn't bear children. In Nazi Germany, it felt to me like there was no bigger shame for a woman than infertility, and I carried that shame." Petra paused again, longer. "Someday … I *did* want to be a mother very much, just to be a mother. Not for Germany, you understand. For myself."

Agnes put her nearly full glass of milk on the coffee table. There was a question she dreaded asking, a question she feared the answer to so terribly that she thought she might leave without asking it. She bit her lip hard and forced herself to ask.

"When Liesl came to you, in 1946, are you sure she had never had a baby in those years she was at Spelzin? My father, perhaps?"

Petra's mouth flattened into a taut line like the seam of a punching bag. "Believe me. If a child had come out of Liesl's forsaken womb, we would have fought Hitler himself to get it back. There's no possible way."

Agnes moved her eyes around the room: the worn braided rug

at the door, the mantel of pictures, the ceiling high above, the tiny white windows hot with sun. She felt a dizzying vacuum. She squeezed her knees with both palms and realized she was holding on. Her relief at knowing her father wasn't the product of genetic experimentation was only equal to her panic that his origins were now completely unknown. No other stones remained unturned.

"Petra, I'm so sorry about everything that happened to you and Liesl. I wish something good could have come out of it for one of you, somehow."

Petra's tense lips relaxed. "You would have been something good."

"What do I do now? Where could my father have come from?"

Petra settled in her chair. "There was another aspect to the Lebensborn, though the Nazis also denied it at Nuremberg," she said.

"It sounds like the Nazis denied everything," Paulina huffed.

"They did. But there are children left who make this denial impossible. You see, Hitler wasn't satisfied with Germany's birthrate, even when the Lebensborn was in full swing. He wanted even more children for Germany. So Heinrich Himmler drafted a plan to steal them."

The feeling of the crevice opening came over Agnes, the tectonic shift finally failing and erupting like it had the force of nature behind it. "Steal them?" she stammered.

"They stole them right from their beds. Off the street. From their mother's arms. Any child who looked right." Agnes noticed that Petra was eyeing her face, her hair, the fair complexion Agnes was always careful to hide from the sun. "Does your father look like you?"

Petra seemed to be the kind of person who was full of theories, but here was one that Agnes sensed she didn't want to entertain. "I guess he does. Dirty blond hair."

"And blue eyes?" Petra asked.

"I don't see what's so unusual about that. Doesn't half of Germany have blond hair and blue eyes?"

"It's not by accident, Agnes. It's by design."

"My father looking that way doesn't prove he was a stolen baby."

"No, but it does make it a possibility." Agnes shifted nervously and Petra paused. "I'm sorry, I'm being coarse. But you don't know where he came from. You don't know where he was born or who his parents were. You have to consider that this part of the Lebensborn plan could explain why his birth certificate was faked. It follows the Nazi pattern. Children who were stolen were given fake names and fake birth certificates, entirely fake lineages. Their past identity erased."

"But stolen from where?" Agnes asked. Her heart raced. "Where do I start looking for evidence of a stolen fair-haired child?"

"There was one country in particular that was full of Nordic-type children and entirely under Hitler's submission. I would look there before anywhere else."

"Which one?" Paulina asked.

Petra picked up the empty tray of cookies, eyeing the crumbs, then set them down untouched.

"Poland."

Agnes's heart raced faster. She held her gaze on Petra so she wouldn't catch the eye of Paulina Malbek.

SIX

Finders and Their Keepers

Once he was in her home, inside her heart, little Bernd became
Gertrude's very own—his mother's child, a boy she held close
during the long days Albert was at work, who helped her with
every task in the house. He was pet, companion, love—a child
sweet and clever. He kissed her elbows while she folded laundry
and hugged her around her dainty waist. She taught his small
toddler hands how to knead bread. He liked to hide under the sink,
and they always laughed together when she pretended he was lost
and then found him hiding behind the sink's needlepoint-adorned
curtain. Bernd's prized possession was a white. stuffed rabbit that
Albert's friend Frank had given to Bernd when he was first
brought home from the orphanage. Later, Bernd named the rabbit
after him, Frank the rabbit.

Gertrude and Albert were both grateful when the war ended,
despite Germany's miserable defeat to the Allies. When the
bombing finally ended, the routine air raids a thing of the past,
they dared to hope that their son would grow up in peace. They
celebrated Bernd's fourth birthday on December 26, 1945, the war
all but extinguished, his life just beginning.

In Berlin at that time, the United Nations and the Red Cross were busily trying to resettle millions of what they coined Displaced Persons. Investigators were particularly interested in adoptions. One Saturday late in 1946, just before Bernd's fifth birthday, a pair of UN investigators knocked on their door. They introduced themselves to Gertrude as workers from the UN's Relief and Resettlement Agency.

Standing in the hallway outside the apartment, they removed their hats. Their cautious display of respect put Gertrude on edge. They spoke competent German, but Gertrude could tell by their looks and accents that they were Americans and something about their overly earnest faces was suspicious.

"May we come in? We'd like to talk to you about your boy," one of them said.

Gertrude allowed them in. Albert was home on a rare day off. He came from a back room of the apartment where Bernd was playing. They all stood around the kitchen table as if inspecting each other. Under different circumstances, thought Gertrude, they might all sit down for a cup of tea together, but Gertrude didn't feel like offering.

"Frau Mueller, Herr Mueller, we're sorry for the intrusion. May we ask you some questions about the boy?" the first worker asked.

"What is this about?" Albert asked.

"We're looking into adoptions during the war years." The investigator paused, careful with his words. "We have reason to believe that not all of them were legitimate."

"What do you mean?" Gertrude asked, stepping forward, gripping the back of the kitchen chair, sure she would fall over if she didn't. "We were called to his orphanage. He was there, without parents." Gertrude's voice rose nervously. "We didn't even *want* to take him!"

As soon as the words came out, Gertrude cupped a palm over her mouth and stopped herself, looking in the direction of where Bernd was playing. She turned back to face Albert and regret filled her eyes.

"Do you know anything about his parents or his family?" one

of the men asked.

"Yes. Our boy's birth parents were from Munich. They both died in a car accident," said Albert.

"Herr Mueller, do you know your boy's birth date?"

"Of course I do. It's the twenty-sixth of December, year 1941."

The men looked at each other. Gertrude sensed they knew something about Bernd that they weren't sharing.

"May we talk to him?" the second worker asked.

Bernd was making loud truck noises in the back room and Gertrude's eyes darted again to the back room.

"No, you may not," Albert interjected. "We already told you the boy's parents were from Munich and they died. I have his birth certificate. We have the papers from his orphanage. I'll show you if you don't believe me. His adoption is perfectly legitimate."

"Do you have the parents' death certificates?" the second worker asked. Albert shook his head.

"Sir, I understand your concern," the first worker started, holding both his palms in the air. "But you have to realize that there are many families in Europe now coming to us about missing children, mostly from outside of Germany, from the East and the countries Germany had occupied. I'm sure you can understand that for their sakes we have to investigate everything."

"Just ask his orphanage," Albert said. "We told you. He was there without parents, and we took him in. We don't get thanks for this? Only an interrogation?"

"We can't talk to the orphanage, unfortunately. The home was destroyed along with all their records."

"An air raid?" Gertrude's mind raced with memories of the children inside.

"No. We think it was destroyed intentionally by the Reich, just before the end of the war."

"But why would they destroy an orphanage?" Gertrude asked.

"They destroyed a lot of things to cover their tracks. It turns out that most of the cases we're investigating have that in common—the child came from a Lebensborn home that was later destroyed."

The suggestion of wrongdoing on their part, when they had acted so charitably, overwhelmed Gertrude. She left the kitchen and joined Bernd where he was playing.

Albert spoke. "Until I see proof of an issue or problem with our adoption, you are not welcome in my house. Do you understand me? I won't have you upsetting my wife or my boy. You can't walk into every home in Germany now looking for missing children."

"Sir, I understand. I know this is upsetting. But it's important that we eventually talk to the boy."

"No. You come back with proof or don't come back. I won't open my door to you again without it."

He showed the men out. They turned to say something else, but he had already swung the door closed in their faces. After they left, Albert Mueller stood with one hand on the knob and the other on his chest, trying to quiet his heart and slow down his breath. He heard Gertrude and Bernd laughing together in the back bedroom, Gertrude's laughter tinged with the brassy sound of fear. His heart beat on, awash with adrenaline. His heart beat like it was trying to save itself, like it was beginning to break.

***

The days that followed were some of Albert and Gertrude's worst. Gertrude alternated between pacing and cleaning. The apartment had never been so clean, or the living room rug so worn.

"What does all this mean? I don't understand how they're saying that Bernd's adoption isn't legitimate. This is some mistake," she said.

"None of it makes any sense," said Albert, bringing her to sit on the couch after they were sure Bernd was sound asleep and couldn't overhear them. Albert was holding a large envelope that contained all the documents the orphanage had handed over at Bernd's adoption. Gertrude thought about contacting someone in the Schneider family. She had started searching for Bernd's family, in case he wanted to know them in the future. She made notes with the names of relatives on a piece of her lavender stationery, people she had been able to locate through what was left of the civil registries. But she didn't want to acknowledge the suspicions that had been growing inside her ever since the very first call from the orphanage, ever since their visit when the walls crawled with children and it seemed impossible that they were all what the German authorities claimed they were. Some of the children were older and spoke foreign languages, a fleeting detail that Gertrude had tried to erase from her memory.

"We need to take him away," she whispered. "We need to leave here. They can't take him away from us. He doesn't know anything else but us. We're his family."

"We can't run with the boy like fugitives. Dear God! We are not criminals in this. They know that."

"Do they? We have a boy here, living in our house, who may have been adopted under false pretenses. Now that there are no records left, we're the only people left to blame!"

Albert patted her arm. "Nobody can blame us. How could they? We did what was right."

***

The following week, the two men from the United Nations called and asked to make an appointment to speak with Bernd. Albert felt like he couldn't refuse forever, so reluctantly he agreed. Gertrude decided she did not want to be home when they came. She left, telling Bernd she was visiting a friend. She kissed him on the forehead before going and asked him to be a good boy for his father.

When the UN workers arrived that afternoon, Bernd was wheeling through the apartment on a scooter. He had wanted to go to the park, impatient to move, but his father had kept him at home for their appointment. The men entered, removed their coats and Albert introduced them to Bernd.

They both sat on the couch in front of where Bernd was

playing on the floor with his rabbit. "Hello, boy," one of the men said in German.

Albert clapped his fingers to his palm gently to get Bernd's attention. "Son, these men want to talk to you. They want to ask you some questions. Can you please listen to them and do your best to answer?"

He stopped playing. "Okay, Papa."

"Thank you for talking to us, Bernd," said the first man. "We have a few questions, easy ones. Would that be okay?"

"Okay," he said, fidgeting. Albert put his hand on his son's shoulder.

"Bernd, who are your parents?"

Bernd giggled. "This is my Papa," he said, pointing to Albert.

"And your mother? Who is your mother?"

"Mamo is with her friend today," he said.

"That's good. Thank you, Bernd," said the man. "Bernd, tell me about the first toy you can remember playing with. Your favorite one."

Bernd clutched his rabbit by the ears and held it up. "Frank the rabbit!"

"That's good," the man said, recording the answer on a paper secured to a clipboard. He looked to the second man who was rummaging in his bag. He pulled out a child's toy, a small doll made out of hay and tied with green and blue ribbons. He handed it to Bernd.

"Bernd, do you remember this toy?"

The sight of the mysterious toy caught Albert in his chest and he held his breath. Bernd took the doll and turned it in his hands, looking at the way the hay was bundled with ribbons making a head, torso, and legs. He fingered the ribbons. "I don't really like this toy," Bernd said. "It's a doll. Boys don't play with dolls. Do you have any other toys?"

The two men laughed at his obvious indignation, and Bernd smiled, assuming that he had said the right thing.

"Bernd, we have one more question for you. Do you have any

sisters?"

Bernd seemed to find the question strange. Not quite sure what to say, he looked at his father.

"Answer the question, son," said Albert.

Bernd obeyed and shook his head. No, he didn't have any sisters.

***

When Gertrude returned that night, she was prepared for the absolute worst, to find her son gone. But when she opened the door, he ran to her and her heart leapt like never before.

"Mamo!" The word made her nearly collapse in front of him. She dropped to her knees as she always did and embraced him so intensely she expected him to complain of her squeezing too hard.

"*Liebling!* Did you have fun with Papa?" She wished her voice were steadier.

"Men came and they gave me a toy, but I didn't like it!" he said. Gertrude looked across the room at Albert, who shook his head.

"Did you talk to the men, my darling?"

"Yes! But the toy was boring. A doll. I don't play with dolls!"

"I suppose you don't," she kissed him on the forehead, grateful that it was still there to kiss.

After Bernd had gone to bed, Albert told her about the interview.

"They asked him a lot of questions about family, who his parents are, if he had any sisters. They showed him a toy and asked if he remembered it."

"Sisters? What did he say?"

Albert shrugged. "No, of course. He didn't remember anything."

Gertrude's nerves were frayed to almost nothing. "What did the men say after the interview? What's going to happen now? Are they going to take him away?"

"I don't know. They told me they would call to schedule an interview with us at their office."

Gertrude had started to hold her breath the week before and felt like it was still tucked inside, under her ribcage, waiting for a release that wouldn't come.

"What did the toy look like? *Did they say it was his toy?*" she whispered.

Albert barely lifted his eyes to look at her. "What does it matter, Gertrude? It was just a toy."

SEVEN

The Place that was Hammered Flat

When they left Petra's farm, Paulina took the wheel again. Agnes said she felt too weak in the arms to even hold the steering wheel. Paulina would take them first by the hotel to check out, then next to the airport, back to Berlin a day early before Agnes's flight back to Chicago and Paulina's flight to Warsaw. In the passenger seat, Agnes leaned toward the window and held the top of her face in her palm, her forehead tapping against the window as they drove.

"Is it possible Gertrude and Albert *stole* him?" she said hoarsely.

"You don't know that. Maybe he wasn't stolen. You just don't know, Agnes. Try not to assume the worst."

"Everybody keeps saying that to me." Agnes closed her eyes. "But things keep getting worse."

***

Once they landed in Berlin, Agnes told Paulina she needed to see Gertrude before she did anything else.

"Absolutely everything I've ever known about my father isn't right. His birth certificate isn't right. It's an official document and it isn't right. I have to ask Gertrude why."

"Do you want me to go with you?"

"No, I think I'd rather go this one alone."

Paulina hugged her.

"I'll be okay," Agnes said. "I'll meet you back at the hotel later."

Outside the airport, Agnes stepped into a white Mercedes and directed the driver to Gertrude's address in Charlottenburg.

Inside the building, Agnes left the elevator car and came up short in front of Gertrude's apartment door. *How do I even talk to her about this?* She pushed herself on and started rapping at the door. Heavy footsteps approached, too heavy to be Gertrude's. The door swung open, and Agnes saw her father standing in the yellow light of the vestibule.

"Papa?" she stuttered.

The sight of her father was simultaneously a relief and a horror. In the past week she had gone from being angry and confused to feeling such an array of emotions on his behalf that she was utterly drowning in them—heartbreak, fear, defensiveness, contrition. What did he know of his murky origins? Anything?

He stood with his hands out to his side, palms open, a surrender. For the first time in a long time, maybe ever, she really looked at him. His slightly wavy, dirty blond hair was tousled and not as well kempt as usual. She looked up at his eyes, gray blue, the penetrating eyes of someone who creates things and sees imagined things before they are real. His bow of a mouth, well-proportioned like everything else on his face, opened into a small smile. He reached his hand to touch her head, smoothing the side of her hair until his hand reached her shoulder where he gave her a gentle squeeze. They looked at each other for a long moment until he stepped back to let her in. As usual, he wouldn't make the first move. Agnes lunged at him and hugged him around the waist, squeezing like she could never let him go.

"Are you okay, Papa?"

"I'm a jerk, but besides that …"

She let go her embrace and looked up at him, shaking her head. "You're not. But why couldn't you talk to me?"

"It's your life, Schatzie." His shoulders drooped. "I didn't know how to stay out of the way and still be in your life at the same time."

"I know." She didn't, but she didn't want him to feel misunderstood while he also felt like a jerk.

They started walking back into the apartment. When they came into the living room, Agnes saw Gertrude sitting on the settee, her hands folded in her lap like before, and it reminded her why she had come.

"Gertrude said you went to Munich. What was in Munich?" her father asked.

"I went to talk to Petra Richter. She's Liesl's sister."

"Liesl, my mother?"

Agnes tried to read Gertrude's body language. Gertrude's hands were shaking. She showed no sign of wanting to say anything. Was Gertrude guilty of something? Did she know if the son she had adopted were stolen? Could she have committed the theft herself? Agnes felt a flood of questions banging through her head, each question spawning a dozen more, none of them easy ones to ask. Any question she asked now would possibly blow apart the relationship between the three of them and it terrified Agnes to imagine such a thing happening.

She turned to Gertrude, bracing herself, willing herself to just spit out the words that had to be said, no matter the consequences.

"Did you know that Liesl Schneider couldn't have children?" she blurted.

Her father stood next to her, dumbstruck. "What are you talking about? She obviously had me."

Agnes didn't take her eyes off of Gertrude. "No, she didn't, Papa. Liesl was infertile."

"Mamo, what in Saints is she talking about?"

Gertrude's reply was winded, breathy. "I just don't know."

Agnes didn't let up. She almost didn't know herself. Here she was, saying exactly what she wanted to say, without anyone having to prod her, the stakes incredibly high.

"You didn't *know*?" she continued. "Did you not know that Klaus died in a suspicious explosion, not a car accident? Did you not know that Liesl was a missing person during the war and after, and didn't actually die until 1949? What else did you not know?"

Gertrude's eyes bulged. "I swear to you both. I didn't know any of these things."

Something snapped inside Agnes. She pointed a trembling finger at her grandmother. "You are a liar!"

The Muellers used to have a problem with flies in their kitchen in the house on Crenshaw Street. It didn't matter what they did to prevent them—fly strips, sprays, candles, wrapping containers extra tight, keeping as much food as they could in the refrigerator, taping the edges of the screens. The flies still managed to get in and perch on everything. Agnes's mother had no problem swatting them whenever one caught her eye. The swat, the spray of gray and red guts, the splay of tiny-jointed black legs, then her mother would sweep up the mess with a paper towel and squirt the site with Clorox. But swatting at flies was never something her father could bring himself to do, just to raise his hand and leave the annoying insect dead with a quick downward thrust of the wrist. Maybe there was something about the quickness of it, the need to be brutal for just a split of a second, before the fly even had a chance to realize what was coming and get away. Her father wasn't a brutal man. In fact, he was the furthest thing from it. That's why, that day in Gertrude's living room, it seemed as if it took hours for her to figure out who had slapped her on the cheek so blisteringly fast, because it never could have been her father.

***

Agnes fled Gertrude's apartment and found a taxi at a rank down the street. She sat in the backseat, the brute contact of her father's hand on her left cheek still vibrating deep inside her face and head. She put a hand up and felt her cheek. It was still hot to the touch. She felt her eyes well and when she shut them, to hold off the crying, the tears dropped like torpedoes.

In her room at the Bach Schlosshotel, she huddled on the bed watching Paulina pack for her flight to Warsaw the next morning. Agnes was supposed to fly back to Chicago, but she wasn't making any effort to pack. She dreaded going home. She dreaded Paulina leaving.

"He'll get over it," Paulina said. "So will Gertrude. Try not to tear yourself up."

For once, Paulina did not try to joke or ignore her, and it made Agnes feel that things had truly turned for the worst.

"It's not only the slap," Agnes sniffed. Paulina got up and shoved some T-shirts and sandals into her duffel bag, pulling a pair of jeans out for the flight. "I can't see my father," Agnes choked. "Not now."

A terrible feeling came over her of wanting desperately to get away from a person she loved and actually being able to do it. Gertrude had probably forgotten about the Bach Schlosshotel, and so her father wouldn't know where she was staying. He couldn't even come after her if he wanted to. And she hoped that he wanted to, even if she didn't want to see him.

"You might not be ready for this suggestion," Paulina said, sitting on the edge of the bed and putting her hand on Agnes's bent knees. "You say you can't go home? Maybe it makes sense for you to come with me to Warsaw."

"What are you talking about?"

"Petra's right about Poland. There are so many stories like this, people missing, then found again. It's still a mess, even fifty years later."

"But I don't even speak the language. I don't even know where to look for information about him."

"Eva and I can help you. You've got another week before you have to be back at work. You'll stay with us. Let's see what we can find out. Maybe it's just a theory of Petra's and there's nothing to it. But you have the time. Maybe you have the time for a reason? Maybe you have me for a reason?"

"I think I've lost the will to keep looking."

"You haven't lost the will."

Agnes dropped her head between her knees and started sobbing. She felt Paulina's hand on the back of her neck. "I just want Krys," she cried, between heaving sobs.

Paulina pulled her close and hugged her, which somehow only made Agnes cry harder.

"I'm telling you, you haven't lost the will. And if you have, let's go get it back."

***

It was late afternoon the next day when Agnes and Paulina's LOT Polish Airlines flight glided to a touchdown on the tarmac of Warsaw's Okęcie Airport. As the plane descended, Agnes looked out the window at the striped farmland, land still plowed primarily by horses, not machines. The ground around Warsaw was so lacking in any kind of undulation it looked like it had been hammered flat. After they touched down, the plane taxied to the middle of the airfield and they took a bus to a small terminal with a beet-colored roof.

"Does your mom know you're coming here or is she going to be waiting for you at O'Hare?" Paulina asked.

"It's still early in Chicago. I'll call my mom from Eva's."

Once off the bus, they walked through sliding doors into the immigration hall. Paulina went toward a line for Polish citizens. There was a different line for citizens of the European Union, of which Poland was still not a part. Agnes took her place in the last line, the line for everyone else. Only one other person waited in that line. She listened to the sounds of the immigration hall. New arrivals were announced in a scratchy, high-pitched Polish over a static-filled loudspeaker. She heard no announcements in any other language, not even English or German.

Once they had collected their bags, Paulina led them outside, threading them through a swarm of hefty, shabby-suited men who leered at them and offered, *"Taxowka? Taxowka?"*

"Don't ever go with them. They're mafia," Paulina warned.

"There's a mafia here?"

"I just mean they're unofficial. And the price they charge will be unofficial, too."

Paulina led them to a taxi rank and after a few minutes in line, they got in the back of a white Renault.

"Ulica Polna," Paulina said, giving the driver Eva's address. The driver sped away from the airport, down a divided highway which was bordered by birch trees and weeds.

"Maybe you need to talk to Gertrude, and your dad?" Paulina suggested. "Sounds like it was a rough visit yesterday."

"I couldn't sleep last night. I wrote a letter to Gertrude in the middle of the night."

"That's good. I can send it express courier tomorrow morning from the agency. There's a courier that goes between our offices in Warsaw and Berlin twice a day."

Agnes wasn't sure about sending it. She had read it again, in the morning, before Paulina woke up. It felt like swinging punches at Gertrude, not apologizing. But maybe swinging punches was what she had to do now. She could recall every line she wrote, or thought about writing.

> *Dear Gertrude,*
> *I'm sorry for what I said.*

She wasn't sorry, not really, but she felt like she had to write it anyway.

> *My visit with Petra was disturbing. I was upset. She told me about Liesl and something called a Lebensborn. Did you know about this? Did my father come out of that? Petra has made me believe he might have been stolen. Is that possible?*
> *I talked to a woman at the hospital in Schwabing, the place where he was supposedly born. I went to the Rathaus in Munich. None of these places has any record of my father being born or of the Schneiders having had a child. It's as if he never existed before*

you adopted him. Where did he come from? I've been trying to come up with explanations. Wrong birth date? Wrong hospital? Wrong birth parents? I've thought of all those possibilities but it's just too much coincidence. How could so many mistakes be made about a single person? It doesn't seem very likely.

I found out about Klaus's bomb making when I was twelve years old. I saw the world differently after I found out I had a grandfather who had murdered children. The world was more sinister. Maybe I thought I was more sinister, my father too. It scared me, and keeping the knowledge to myself made me feel lonely. Maybe you felt that way too? Maybe there are things you are keeping to yourself for whatever reason?

Despite what Klaus had done, I still missed Liesl and wished I had known her. I even wished I had something of hers. I imagined she had something that a grandmother would have, like a handkerchief, maybe with a monogram, maybe the kind with lace on the edges. I felt like I never had a grandmother who could give me those kinds of things.

Agnes knew it was a dig but she didn't erase it. She kept writing.

I'm sorry that we don't really know each other. I wish we had seen each other more when I was growing up.

I'm going to Poland now, with my friend Paulina. I came here because of what Petra told me about the Lebensborn and stolen children. If you know anything about where my father came from, Gertrude, please, you have to tell me. You have to tell me before it's too late.

Agnes held her eyes shut tightly, fretting every line of the unsent letter, trying to bury the memory of her visit with Gertrude. In the back of the taxi, she listened to more scratching, high-pitched Polish that was coming through from the dispatcher. The radio burst with consonant-rich words that must have been times for pick-ups, addresses, taxi medallions, and phone numbers. The sounds swished together like the rapids of a river, meaning nothing to her. She opened her eyes and trained her gaze on the passing landscape, buildings coming closer together and higher into the sky as they left the suburban district of the airport and entered the city center. They passed a blue billboard that announced: *Warszawa. The Citibank city*. Beyond it, on the edge of a large roundabout, there was a billboard for L'Oreal. Claudia Schiffer flirtatiously nibbled the tip of her thumb. Her loose blond curls tumbled from the top of her forehead. *Jestem tego warta* was printed under Claudia's chin. *Because I'm worth it*, Agnes assumed. Of course she would be worth it, someone who looked like Claudia. Behind Claudia were larger commercial buildings and medium-sized skyscrapers with neon signs mounted on the top of them: Sanyo, Daewoo, Fujifilm, Elektrim.

They turned onto an avenue called Marszałkowska, three lanes of traffic on each side of a concrete median. The buildings on either edge of the avenue were a monotonous, blocky concrete with oversized windows and walls that seemed as if they must be at least two-feet thick. Agnes felt slightly intimidated, as if they had been built for giants and she were only small Agnes. The city looked uncannily like pictures she had seen of Soviet Moscow in one of her father's design books. Given the nearly half a century that the Soviets controlled Poland, it was probably meant to.

They turned off Marszałkowska and onto smaller streets. Wheeled carts dotted the intersections, loaded with flowers. Signs painted on the side of the carts all had the same word: *kwiaty*. A few minutes later, the taxi stopped in front of a nineteenth-century building with a graceful stone archway for an entrance, not unlike Gertrude Mueller's building in Berlin. It was also six stories tall with French doors from each apartment that opened onto narrow balconies encircled by decorative wrought iron railings. The apartment buildings on either side of Eva's looked like they had been built later, by the Soviets, constructed from painted cement and plaster with rows of small windows and no balconies. In fact, the buildings in all directions looked this way: unattractive, utilitarian boxes. Eva's building was the only one of its kind that Agnes could see from a different era. Later, Eva explained that hers was one of only fifteen percent of the buildings in the city that had survived the final bombing of Warsaw in August 1945, in which the city was reduced to almost nothing. For Eva the building was a special place, a place where she wanted to live for the rest of her life, because it symbolized Warsaw's survival.

The taxi driver pointed to his meter. It said *25 PLN*. Paulina paid him, and they stepped out to the curb just as Eva came through the archway wearing sandals and a blue skirt with a white knit top. Agnes hadn't seen her in over a year. The sight of Eva made her miss Crenshaw Street, her parents' house, and especially her father. She didn't want to think about how much it made her miss Krys.

"What a nice surprise to have you visit!" Eva opened her arms to embrace Agnes.

"Sure, but I won't put you out long."

"You stay as long as you want. I have the room."

She took Agnes by the hand and squeezed gently. Eva led them back through the archway, along a cobblestone driveway that must have once been used for horses and carriages. They stepped up onto a curb on the right side of the driveway, and passed through a pair of carved wooden doors with thin glass panes to a staircase that wound up through the building. As they ascended the stairs, the giggling of a pack of young children at play in the building's inner courtyard broke the silence. Agnes could hear a faucet dripping somewhere and caught the scent of standing water. The stairwell remained unlit, the worn steps blue from the early morning light that seeped in, somehow, despite the few windows. Their shoes scraped over the grit of dirt and dust as they reached Eva's apartment on the third floor, the lovely curve of the stairs encircling an open elevator shaft behind decorative iron caging. As they reached the landing, Agnes heard the sound of a woman's voice through an open hall window—that commanding sound of a mother with no time to waste—calling down to the children playing. *"Chodz!"* she yelled. *Come!*

Eva pushed open one side of a tall pair of oak doors and Paulina and Agnes followed her inside. A hallway led from the front door to the end of the apartment, with doors on the left and right opening into rooms. The first room on the left was a small, square living room. The next was a kitchen, then a door for the bathroom. The two doors on the right were bedrooms. Eva took Agnes to the last door on the right, which contained a twin bed with a trundle underneath and a small table. Eva had dressed the bed, table and window with white lace fabric. Agnes glanced at the closet and saw it was almost full with Paulina's things. She heard Paulina in the kitchen, the sound of glasses being brought out of a cupboard. Agnes turned back to Eva.

"I should call my mom. What time is it in Chicago?" she asked.

"Seven hours behind us," Eva replied. "There's a phone in the living room."

"I'll be quick."

"You talk as long as you need to, *Kochanie.*"

Kochanie. It was what Krys had called her. Agnes found the phone on the table next to the couch and dialed, like she did from Germany, the country code, the area code, then her familiar seven-digit number on Crenshaw. Her mother answered after only two rings. She let out a sigh of relief when she heard Agnes's voice.

"Did your father find you?" her mother asked. Her voice sounded distant and tinny, the quality of the line noticeably worse than it was in Germany or the US

"I saw him at Gertrude's place."

"Are you headed back?"

"Not right now."

"Oh, Agnes. You can't hide out in Germany forever."

Agnes heard a TV through the wall in the apartment next door. It was the same high-pitched scratching of Polish that she had heard from the taxi dispatcher and the airport loudspeaker.

"I'm not in Germany, Mom. I'm in Poland."

Her mother said nothing. Agnes thought she heard the flick of a lighter. Then came her mother's taut voice, her lips definitely around the thin barrel of a cigarette. "Why are you in Poland?"

"I visited Liesl's sister, Petra. Oh, Mom, it was terrible." She stopped. A painted crucifix on Eva's living room wall caught her eye. It was about ten-inches high, with dots of red blood painted on Christ's face just under the crown of thorns. In a macabre way, it reminded Agnes of all the fertility experiments that Liesl had suffered. "I found out that Klaus and Liesl Schneider weren't Papa's parents. But I don't know yet who his parents really are. And Gertrude won't say how she got him."

Her mother sharply exhaled a puff of smoke. "I don't like the sound of any of this," she said. "Come home now."

"I can't. Try not to worry. I'll be with Paulina and Eva. I just have to be here, for a little while, to look into something before I come back there." She paused. "Please, when you see Papa, tell him I'm sorry. Don't let him hate me."

"Why would he ever hate you?"

Agnes pursed her lips together as her eyes welled up. "He slapped my face, Mom."

A long silence followed without even the sound of her mother's lighter or smoke blowing. Just absolute quiet. "Oh, Agnes. Why would he do something like that?"

"Because … I called Gertrude a liar."

More silence, then: "I think you've both lost your minds."

"She claimed she didn't know anything about Papa's parents. I just don't believe it."

"Please be careful there. A few days. Then you come home."

"Don't tell Papa where I am. He'll come after me again. I'm twenty-seven years old. People have to stop coming after me."

Her mother cleared her throat, like she had something else to say. "This probably isn't the moment to tell you this, but I thought you'd want to know."

Agnes slid back on the couch. "What is it?"

"Something happened here the night after your father came

home. The Chopin Diner was robbed at gunpoint." Grief slipped inside Agnes like it came through a secret door. "The robber shot Mr. Kubelski after he opened the safe in the kitchen. He died before they could get him to the hospital."

Her mother kept talking, but to Agnes the voice became faint as if going into a tunnel. Grief lodged itself inside her uncomfortably, twisting her throat into a knot, making it hard for her to swallow or breathe. She saw Mr. Kubelski in her mind, the way someone sees a person they'll never see again, their figure more exceptional than it ever looked in life. She saw him on the sidewalk of Milwaukee Avenue outside the diner, helping Magda mix milkshakes, stocking *pierniczki*, greeting people at the door, calling her *Blondynka*. A quiver trembled across her lips.

"Is Mrs. Kubelski okay?"

"She wasn't there that night, thank God. But she must be in shock."

"Can I do something for her? Was there a funeral?"

"It was today. Anyway, your father was shaken. He wanted to go get you, especially after that happened. He knew it would upset you ... didn't he tell you?"

"No. I don't think he could."

They said good-bye, and Agnes leaned into a pillow with felt patches sewn onto the front. She was numb with sorrow, not even able to cry. The TV chirped through the wall, and the aroma of Eva's cooked cabbage seeped through the apartment. The only thoughts running through her head were of Mr. Kubelski. That Mr. Kubelski hadn't died. That Mr. Kubelski had been murdered. And she had spent enough time thinking about murder during her life to understand by now that a murder was a decision. It was a decision the murderer made to rob the whole world.

***

That night, Agnes dreamed of Wojtek Kubelski. She was sitting at his bar at the Chopin Diner and telling him about Warsaw and asking for advice about Krys, two conversations they would never have but she wished they could.

"I'll tell you something," his finger pointing to her nose. "Any man who would let you get away, is not smart man."

"I think he had reason to be a little angry."

"Still his fault."

"I'm in Warsaw now."

"Good thing. That's what we've all been waiting for, Blondynka, you see? The chance to go back to free Poland. Now," he said, spreading his hands, "there it is." He patted himself over the heart with both hands. "It's too bad I'm too old to pick up and start over in Warsaw. I would go in minute."

"You would?"

"Sure! *In a beat of the heart* is what they say, right?" Mr. Kubelski picked up a wad of receipts that had been poked onto an aluminum spear by the cash register. "Poland needs young people like you."

"What do you mean?"

"Ahh …" he threw his hands up, "it goes back for centuries, our problems. Everybody tries to end Poland, but they can't. Partitions, wars, Nazi occupation, then Communists ruining us, then that horrible Martial Law. It's a long and sad story. Poland deserves better story."

He reached out in the dream and touched her blond head. "It's good that you are in Warsaw, Blondynka. That makes an old Polish man happy."

She never saw him again, not in life or in dreams. That dream faded and ushered in a profound sleep on her first night in Poland, as if the departed Wojtek Kubelski were planting her there, pointing her soul in a new direction.

She would dream almost every night while in Warsaw, other dreams. She wasn't sure if it was the lingering, earthy smell of cooked cabbage or the drip of water in the courtyard or the coolness of the unlit stairwell. Something stilled her every day, a little more, so that during the night her imagination became more alive than ever. Agnes would have many dreams while she slept in

Eva's spare room, by the window over the courtyard, the courtyard that was filled with the sound of children playing and their mother calling them home.

EIGHT

A German Waits in Warsaw

When Agnes awoke Monday morning, she heard Eva moving hectically around the apartment. Paulina slept below, on the trundle bed, snoring. In the courtyard, the light was already high, a cheerful yellow.

Agnes went into the kitchen, which was painted pale blue, the paint peeling a little near the ceiling to show white plaster underneath. But the color was soothing, and even after only one day, Agnes liked being in that room. A narrow Formica counter with several white stools tucked underneath lined one side of the kitchen. Agnes sat and Eva put a plate of scrambled eggs down in front of her.

"I have to be at work all day today. Tomorrow I'm off," she said. "Anything you need, I can help you with. You tell me."

Agnes chewed and watched Eva move around the kitchen, pulling things out to defrost, checking the fridge. Eva had gotten a job as a translator for a British businessman whose identity she couldn't reveal. She said he was someone the entire world knew, and she had signed a contract that affirmed the confidential nature of the assignment. It was nothing sinister, Eva had assured. Her client was mainly interested in protecting his sizeable investments in Poland, and keeping his competition in the dark.

"I thought I would talk to somebody at the US Embassy. Is there one here?" Agnes asked.

"Of course. It's on Ujazdowskie Street. I'll write it on the map for you." Eva continued to whiz around the kitchen. "My client is trying to close a deal today. I have to go. Wake up Paulina. She's late." Eva left the kitchen still holding a half-full juice glass. She came back a minute later with a purse on her shoulder, set the empty glass by the sink, and kissed Agnes three times on the cheeks. "See if Paulina can get you a cell phone from the agency. I don't like not being able to call you." She scribbled her phone number on the back of an envelope. Then she pulled a city map out from under a stack of mail and circled a white, square icon on the west side of Ujazdowskie Street, across from a big park. "That's the embassy. And here's my cell number. I'll see you tonight."

Eva was gone and the apartment was quiet. Agnes glanced at the kitchen clock, one she had noticed before in an Ikea catalog on her mother's desk at home in Chicago. The large brushed chrome face sported a modern design with only the number four indicated in kelly green. The time now read a few minutes after eight. She left her breakfast and went to the spare room, where Paulina was lying face down and nearly sideways on the trundle bed, her wrists hanging limply on the wood floor. Agnes tapped the doorframe with her knuckles. "Madison Avenue is calling."

"There's no Madison Avenue in Warsaw," Paulina grumbled.

"Whatever it is, it's calling. Do you want coffee?"

"Please."

Agnes had heard all about Paulina's new employer, Weldon Bryce Stratham, in the days leading up to the wedding. While they tested hairstyles, manicures, and dress fittings, Paulina told her about the advertising boom in what was now a free, democratic Poland. Every Western company was setting up shop, whether they sold denim or diapers. Weldon was an advertising agency based in Chicago that had expanded into more than twenty countries in only the last five years, doing commercials for everything from airlines to cough syrup. Most of their best ads were often ascribed to the big agencies—Leo Burnett, McCann-Erickson, Young & Rubicam, or some other Madison Avenue titan. But many times they had been done by Weldon, with its cadre of art school creative directors and London-trained account planners. Weldon was the first Western ad agency to open in Warsaw, Bucharest, Prague, Budapest, and Moscow after the fall of Communism. They were reaping the benefits with the longest client list of any other agency in each market.

WBS Warsaw hired Paulina to be the account director for all the Polish advertising of a multinational client called Badgley's Limited, an enormous packaged goods firm based in the United Kingdom. Badgley's had such a fierce hold on nearly every segment of the European market—household cleaners, detergents, health and beauty products—that even American giant Procter & Gamble was having trouble breaking in.

By the time the coffee was brewed, Paulina trudged into the kitchen wearing cropped tan trousers and a white silk blouse with a funky necklace. Agnes told her she was going to the embassy.

"Eva wants you to get me a cell phone. Can you?"

"I'll find you one." Paulina closed her eyes and gulped the coffee. "I don't like not being able to call you."

"That's what Eva said."

"We feel responsible for you."

"It's okay here now … right?"

"Okay?"

"I mean not dangerous." Agnes looked dimly at Paulina. "Sorry. Is that a dumb question?"

"It's not 1945 if that's what you're concerned about. The Nazis are gone, the Soviets are gone, now you've got nobody to worry about but the capitalists."

Paulina placed her half-empty coffee cup next to the sink and went into the bathroom. Agnes dumped the coffee grounds in the trash and stopped to look out the window at the sidewalk below. A short man with a square gray cap was sweeping the section in front of Eva's building with energetic thrusts of a broom. Two elderly women passed, and he stopped sweeping, stepped to the side, and tipped his hat. He had a charm that reminded Agnes of Mr. Kubelski.

***

Agnes and Paulina left the apartment and took a city bus from Polna Street to Łazienki Park, where Agnes got off, six stops before Paulina would get off near the Opera House. Agnes walked north until she reached the edge of the park. The United States Embassy was across the street from the park, a Cold War-era steel and glass box of a building with closed-circuit cameras on every corner of the rooftop. A rifle-toting Marine stood at the guardhouse. Agnes showed her US passport and was let in through a high black gate. She climbed a few steps to the main doors and went inside. The hurricane-like air conditioning made her wish she had brought a sweater. She asked a lobby attendant if there were a department that could help a US citizen search for family in Poland. The lobby attendant was young, almost a teenager.

"You probably need to talk to the Poles about that," he glowered.

"Sure. I just don't know who that would be. Maybe somebody here can connect me to the right Polish agency?"

The kid looked at a directory on the podium next to him. Someone had arranged each page inside a plastic sheet protector and secured them inside a three-ring binder. Agnes watched him flip noisily through the pages. "Maybe there's some kind of citizen services thing? Or a legal aid?"

He looked startled. "It's for something illegal?"

This had to be somebody's kid, out for a summer internship. If this were the Ambassador's son, Agnes wondered how on earth he could embarrass himself by putting his dim-witted kid in the lobby.

"Could I take a look at that directory?"

She didn't wait for him to answer. She turned the binder so she could read it: Consular Section. Economic Section. Something about Agriculture. She scanned through several pages.

"Everything is by appointment." He took a black ledger out from a shelf inside the podium and opened it. "Do you want an appointment?"

She pretended she hadn't heard him. "What is this thing Office of the Historian?"

"I think that's in Washington, D.C. At the State Department."

A voice behind Agnes answered. "They're experts in past foreign policy, if that's what you need to know about."

Agnes turned around. A woman in a navy-blue suit stood just a few feet from them. She was small and semi-cheerful, but seemed like somebody who would pack a punch. She reminded Agnes of Mary Lou Retton, and Agnes placed her age as approaching forty.

"I don't think there's a department for what I'm looking for," Agnes said despondently. "I might be in the wrong place."

Mary Lou eyed the young attendant with a glint of annoyance. She motioned to Agnes. "Come to my office. Maybe I can point you in the right direction," she said. She brushed past the kid, and Agnes followed her down the hall to an elevator.

"Do you want me to put it in the appointment book?" the kid called, but neither of them looked back.

When they got to the elevator, Mary Lou punched the call button and whispered to Agnes. "Sorry about him. He annoys the crap out of me."

"Who is he?"

"Kid of an American businessman in town. Second summer he's here. We can't get rid of him, even though he's worthless." They stepped onto the elevator. "The Ambassador must owe some huge favors."

"He did have trouble helping me, I'll admit."

"You're not the first." She punched the button for the third floor and leaned closer to Agnes. "We call him Nepo. You know," she paused, a satisfied grin emerging as the elevator rose, "from the Latin *nepos*, root form of *nepotism*."

The elevator opened on the third floor, and they walked to big office at one corner of the building, with windows overlooking Ujazdowskie Street and the forested depths of Łazienki Park.

"My name's Bobbie Price," the woman said. She held out her hand and Agnes shook it.

Bobbie set her bag on top of an expensive-looking mahogany desk. Framed documents and photographs filled the walls. A flank of tall bookcases skirted the wall opposite the park windows, wrapping around to the door they had come through. Agnes studied one wall: MA in Government from Georgetown, PhD in Linguistics from Cambridge. The top of the desk displayed a picture of her standing next to President and Mrs. Clinton at the White House.

"I'm the Deputy International Affairs Officer," Bobbie said.

Agnes was sure she was in the wrong place. "Maybe I shouldn't take up your time."

Bobbie offered a glass of water from a carafe on the corner of the desk. "Don't worry. I just wanted to watch Nepo squirm while I circumvented his process downstairs. But let me help you anyway. It's the end of July and affairs are slow." Bobbie motioned for her to sit down. "What can I help you with?"

Agnes took a seat and studied the perfect application of Bobbie's makeup and the tidy updo of brown hair, held in place with a teal hairpin that clashed with the navy blue of her suit.

"Well ... it's about my father. He's German, now an American citizen," she stopped, glancing at an American flag propped up in a pewter pencil cup engraved with the crest of Georgetown University. "He was born during the Second World War, but I don't know where. That's what I'm in Poland to possibly find out."

Bobbie was sitting behind her desk, rolling her pen between her fingers and thumb, back and forth. She studied Agnes like she was trying to solve a crossword, a stare so intense it made Agnes look at the floor.

"This is a little more than needing help with a traffic ticket?" Bobbie finally said.

"Yeah."

"What makes you think he might have been born in Poland?"

Agnes told her what she had learned from Petra, about her father's false birth certificate and his supposed parents' deaths. Bobbie Price seemed to be studying her even harder. She put her pen down and tightened her lips to a near whistle, looking out through the bright row of windows.

"Do you know the names of any Polish relations he might have had here?"

"Nothing," Agnes said flatly. "Just his German name, Bernd Mueller. And the names of the people who adopted him."

Bobbie stood up in front of a tall, gray filing cabinet behind her. She pulled open the top drawer, then the second one. She looked through the second one for a minute, read something, then she closed the drawer, not removing any of the files. She sat back down behind her desk.

"There were records of people reported missing at the end of the war. They were called Displaced Persons. But I don't have anything about it here. They might be in the Polish State Archives, or still with the United Nations. Since the fall of Communism, Poland has been trying to get its archival house in order, but it isn't there yet."

Agnes remembered Leslie Anderson in Munich had mentioned Displaced Persons. "He probably wouldn't be in a list of Displaced Persons. He wasn't displaced at the end of the war. He was adopted by a Berlin couple in 1942. Gertrude and Albert Mueller."

"But according to his Polish family, he would have been missing. So from their standpoint, he would be a Displaced Person. You get me?"

Agnes looked again at the filing cabinet. "I guess that's true. Would he be in the Displaced Person records then?"

"He could be. But probably not as Bernd Mueller. Whoever would have reported him missing would have reported it under his Polish name."

"He was born December 26, 1941. Is there a way to look up

birth records from that date and somehow match them to a Displaced Person?"

"Civil records in Poland, including birth registrations, were almost all destroyed during the war, especially the ones in Warsaw. The Nazis removed a lot of other civil registries and took them to Germany. Marriage certificates, death records."

"Why would they care about all those records?"

"It was one way to erase Poland's statehood. One of many. Remove or destroy any record of a civil society." Bobbie picked up her pen again. "Do you even think his birthdate is correct, if so much else is incorrect?"

The question caught Agnes. She had never thought his birthdate was wrong. "It's the only date I know," she said.

Bobbie pulled out a blank sheet of paper and started writing at the top. She asked for Agnes's name and local contact. Agnes gave her Paulina's cell phone number. Underneath that Bobbie wrote: *Bernd Heinrich Mueller, D.O.B. Dec 26 '41 (?) Munich (?), US Cit. Chicago, False Birth Cert. (?) Klaus & Liesl Schneider parents (?) Berlin adopt. '42 Gertrude & Albert Mueller.*

Agnes couldn't help but notice that Bobbie had filled the paper with question marks. She stopped writing and looked across at Agnes, studying her again.

"What does your dad look like?"

Agnes knew what she was asking. It was the same assumption Petra had made.

"He's blond and blue-eyed."

Bobbie turned back to the paper and wrote *Aryan*, underlining it twice. Then she stood up and walked to a bookcase by the office door. She returned carrying a hard-backed volume entitled *The Ultimate Design of Nazi Eugenics*. A swastika decorated the front cover as well as the spine. She held the book out to Agnes.

"You might want to do some homework while I'm looking for the Displaced Persons records."

Agnes accepted the book and without thinking wrapped her palm over the swastika on the spine.

"You can get those records for me?"

"I have friends at the United Nations. I'll try them. And you're right, there's no department at the Embassy who will help. You'd have to hunt on your own, and it sounds like what you're looking for will be nearly impossible to find. Nepo will be upset all day about me seeing you without an appointment. The least I can do is make some calls."

"I don't know how to thank you."

"It'll just be a few calls," she put up a finger, "don't get your hopes up too high."

Bobbie nodded at the book in Agnes's hand. "That book talks about the Nazis' racial theories, the characteristics they considered *desirable*," she tapped the notes on her sheet of paper, "like being so-called Aryan." She turned more serious. "Hitler was mainly waging a war against race. Eliminating certain types of people—at Auschwitz, Treblinka, you know the places," she paused, "but at the same time he was increasing other types. The types he wanted. And he was as calculated and sinister as he could be about both."

Agnes turned the book over in her hand. "What am I looking for?"

"Breadcrumbs," Bobbie said without expression. "If you don't know *who* your father was, maybe you can find out *where* he was, before he was taken from home—if that is what happened to him—and after that. There was a finely honed process the Nazis called *Eindeutschung*," Bobbie made quotation marks with her fingers as she pronounced the last word in impeccable German. "It roughly means *alignment* or in this case *Germanization*. Place names in Poland were changed from Polish to German—Gdańsk to Danzig, Wrocław to Breslau. But they employed the same conversion with people's names. A child would have had to pass certain physiological tests to qualify as desirable. It wasn't just about blond hair and blue eyes. I don't know all the finer points. But that book will tell you. And it will tell you where they found desirable children, where they took them, and what they did with them."

"What happened if a child didn't pass the tests? Were they sent home?"

"No. Himmler was concerned that an Aryan-like Polish population, if left in Poland, could overwhelm the Germans someday. If they didn't qualify to be Germans, the children were usually sent to camps where most of them died."

Bobbie Price looked down at her notepaper and tapped the underlined word Aryan again with the tip of her pen. "It's funny about this word. It isn't even a racial term. It's from the Sanskrit, *arya*, meaning honorable or noble. It's a linguistic designation, nothing else. It refers to speakers of Indo-European languages that were native to Europe, Persia, and Northern India. It wasn't until the nineteenth century, when German writer Max Müller referred to the Aryan linguistic group as a race of people, that the term Aryan began to be more about race than language. When he used the word race, many linguists defend that he only meant tribe or grouping. He objected vehemently to the idea of a biological race of Aryan people. He said there was no such thing. But the racial anthropologists drowned him out. They managed to convince the world that Aryan was a subgroup of Caucasians, and a superior one, founded in ancient Germany. From everything I've read, there was absolutely no basis to it. Müller even pointed out in his writings that the earliest Aryan speakers were some of the blackest Hindus!"

"I never thought about the word," Agnes said.

"That's the problem. Nobody does now. After Max Müller, nobody defended the linguist point of view about that word. And then once Hitler latched onto it, the word was done for. It's not my favorite word, I'll tell you that. In my opinion, it was a linguistic atom bomb."

Agnes wedged the book tightly into her purse, concealing the black and red swastikas, as Bobbie pointed to it again.

"You should understand what they were thinking, what they were doing with their theories as it relates to race, then what they did with the kids that they took out of here." Bobbie paused and looked more pensively at Agnes. "Because if your father looks anything like you, he might have been one of them."

Agnes preferred to brush the comment aside. It felt, still, far-fetched that he would be kidnapped for his looks while still an infant.

"Is there anyone else in Warsaw, any government group or agency, I should contact while you're waiting for the list?"

"If you have someone to help you with the Polish ..."

"I do."

"Then you might try contacting some of the *Urząd Stanu Cywilnego*—these are the Civil Records Offices—in Poland's main cities. They're usually at the city halls. They may still have some records. It's worth a try."

"Okay, I will." Agnes stood up. Bobbie had started writing the letters of her father's name in a jumbled order on the bottom of her notepaper—B, D, R, E, N—and changing their order into different arrangements. "What are you writing?"

"When you look up the civil records, remember you're not looking for the name Bernd Mueller. Try looking for first names with one or more of these letters, especially the hard consonants—B or D. When the Nazis changed children's names, they tended to retain some phonetic resemblance to the original name. So the child would be less likely to question the new identity and it would subconsciously blend with the old one."

Agnes was dumbstruck by the level of calculation. "They thought a lot about this."

"They thought a lot about everything they did. Thank God they failed, because when the Nazis sat down to do something, they did a hell of a job."

"I just don't understand how they could get their hands on babies? Wouldn't a baby have been with its parents all the time?"

"They would have been, yes. So the Nazis didn't send in squads of soldiers. They used women. Pairs of them, they were called Brown Sisters. But they weren't sisters. They were women, in brown dresses, who went in pairs from village to village, looking for little blond children."

"It sounds like a story from the Brothers Grimm."

"Sure, but it wasn't a fairy tale. If the Brown Sisters saw a child who fit the profile, they would ask the child his family name. Then they checked the city hall for the family's background, especially religion. They couldn't be Jewish, of course. If they turned out to be Gentiles, you can be sure the child would be gone the next day. Right out of his bed."

"Wouldn't the parents have gone after their child? Or contacted the authorities."

"Remember who the authorities were during this time. Poland was occupied by the Germans. The authorities were the same people who took the children. They weren't going to help."

Agnes glanced at her own clothes, blue jeans and a cotton top. "Why did the women dress in brown?"

"Who knows? Hitler loved brown. The Hitler Youth dressed in brown, too. How would you dress your followers if you were paranoid about your own power?" Bobbie stopped. "Maybe brown is the color of submission?"

"It sounds too hard to believe."

"It was really happening. Thousands of Polish children every week. For two, maybe three years," Bobbie said. "It's just that so many other, worse things, were also happening. The Jewish ghettoes, the concentration camps, the mobile death squads. The theft of Aryan children from Poland has never managed to make its way into the headlines of history." Bobbie paused. "But Agnes, the reason I think you need to consider this is because historians are fairly certain that more than 200,000 children in Poland met with this fate during the war. These stolen children made up a significant part of the youth population of Poland at the time. And they vanished without a trace. Most of them were so thoroughly brainwashed that they have never known any other life, any other identity. So you coming looking for one of these children, it's a rare thing. It just doesn't happen. And it will happen less and less as we enter the next century. Their lives will be over."

Agnes didn't want to imagine that her father could have been one of these stolen children, but by now she was having a difficult time denying the possibility. She looked across the letters of her father's name that Bobbie had written and wondered how many Polish names contained some combination of those letters. There had to be dozens of possibilities, at least.

"I understand," she said. "When do you think you might have a list of Displaced Persons?"

Bobbie put her pen down. "It may take a while. Depends on how good my contacts are. I'll see if there's a way to gather a list of all Polish DPs who were under age five at the end of the war. Maybe you'll get lucky and the name Bernd Mueller will show up on the list."

Agnes didn't think it sounded all that lucky, and Bernd Mueller definitely wasn't a Polish name. "Is it possible my father could have been Jewish? I mean ... that he could have been in a concentration camp or a ghetto somewhere here?"

Bobbie's eyes turned brittle. "Agnes, Jewish children weren't missing at the end of the war," she said. "They were dead."

Again, Agnes was caught by her abrupt conveyance of the facts. Bobbie seemed to realize and gave Agnes a slight smile. "Sorry." She held up her hands, mea culpa. "What I mean is that the Nazis only took children who they could verify were Gentiles. That's what these Brown Sisters were up to. A blond, blue-eyed Jew would still have ended up in a concentration camp."

Agnes stood to leave, looking down at the newspapers that had been arranged in a stack on Bobbie's desk: *El País* and *Le Monde* poked out from the bottom, on top were the local papers, *Rzeczpospolita Polska* and the *Gazeta Wyborcza*. Sections of Russian and German newspaper had already been clipped and mounted on paper in a separate stack nearby for review.

"You can read all those?" Agnes asked.

"I get through the news from ten countries before breakfast. Then I start on Poland." She noticed Agnes's awe. "The secret to learning Polish is to make friends with the z. The z is everywhere, but it's not so scary," Bobbie smiled.

Agnes turned to go and paused as she reached the door of Bobbie's office. "Could you put one other name on your list, just a name to look out for in case you see it?"

"Okay ... what is it?"

"Rafał Rozbrat. He's a friend."

"Do you know anything about him?"

"He disappeared when he was about twelve years old, sometime during the war. His family told me he was a messenger, maybe with the Polish Underground."

She watched Bobbie Price write Rafał Rozbrat's name on the paper under her father's. After good-byes, Agnes stepped through the linoleum-tiled hallway of the building, riding the elevator back down to the lobby. Nepo saw her coming and held out a ballpoint pen.

"You need to sign out," he demanded.

Agnes returned a smug expression. "I never signed in."

She walked out, past the Marine guard, to the sidewalk along Ujazdowskie Street. The edge of Łazienki Park loomed, lined with a long bank of towering oak trees that shaded the sidewalk and part of the street. She crossed to walk under them, heading south, taking the long way home.

***

When Agnes reached Eva's building on Polna Street, she walked under the archway and started up the stairs. After only a few steps, a cascade of sudsy gray water came gushing down the stairs, running over her sandaled feet. The water was freezing, and her ankles cramped from the cold.

The pourer of the water came running, spewing words in Polish that Agnes guessed were *Sorry!* and *Excuse me!* and *I didn't see you!* He was a small, elderly man, mostly bald except for a ring of snow-white hair circling the back of his head from one ear to the other, like a woman would wear a mink around her neck. He had the face of a person who stayed busy all his life: carefree, yet tired. He clutched a square gray cap in his hand, and Agnes realized it was the same man who had been sweeping the sidewalk that morning. She held up her hand in a shy greeting and shook the water from her feet.

"It's okay," she said.

The old man brightened when he heard her voice. The skin around his eyes pinched as he smiled. "Amerykanska?"

Agnes nodded and managed a half smile. "Yes. Amerykanska."

He clapped his hands together, smiling broadly, and Agnes smiled back.

"Okay, bye," she said.

They exchanged waves and she continued upstairs. When she reached the landing of the second floor, she heard the man start to whistle. In the courtyard, the mother in the upstairs apartment was yelling down again, words Agnes couldn't understand, but that had become familiar anyway.

Inside Eva's apartment, Agnes dropped her wet sandals in the bathroom by the tub and dried her feet. After the conversation with Bobbie Price, she felt tense and nervous, full of edges. Bobbie had unloaded so much information that Agnes felt like it would take weeks for her to think through it all. She looked in the bathroom mirror, the wisps of her blond hair tied back from the heat, one small strand that curled near the side of her forehead, near the blue of her eyes. She closed her eyes and listened to the building. The mother had stopped yelling, and the TV in the neighboring apartment was quiet.

She went into the living room and perched on the edge of the sofa, switching on Eva's set. She clicked down past news shows, some foreign movies, until she spotted something recognizable. A yellow bird. Big Bird pointed with his padded yellow fingers to the number five that hovered on the screen. He repeated several times, in his cheery nasal tone, a word that sounded like *pinch*. *Pinch, pinch, pinch*. Agnes said it silently, moving her mouth: *pinch*. Five children danced around Big Bird, all of them chiming in: *pinch*. The color of the day had been *blue*. When Big Bird said it—*niebieski*—Agnes heard the familiar sound of the *knee bees ski* that Krys had taught her once. Her eyes welled up as she watched the yellow bird dance around on the screen and imagined bees on skis, flying down a snow-covered hill and someone yelling from behind them: *I love you.*

***

Agnes spent most of the afternoon on a white stool at Eva's kitchen counter trying to make headway through the book Bobbie Price had given her. It was unsavory stuff: in the early days, eugenics practice was considered merciful. If a child were born with deformities or mental retardation, parents could ask the government to put it to death and it would be done and everyone, including the dead child, was considered better for it. Closer to the war, parental permission was less of a requirement. Children would be kept in facilities "for their own good," and then would die there with little or no explanation to the family. She scanned the index. There was a chapter about eugenics theory in California, how it was the basis of Germany's approach. There was also a chapter about the euthanasia of the handicapped that was too repulsive to read. The Ikea clock was ticking loudly, drawing her attention away. She shut the book and went to look outside.

Down on the sidewalk, the gray-capped stair-washer was replacing the lids on top of the garbage cans on the street. The day had become hot, and she let down the horizontal blinds. Late afternoon sunlight came through the kitchen in slits of white and yellow. She walked to the spare room, kneeling on the bed, looking into the courtyard. Three boys were downstairs kicking a ball. It ricocheted off the walls of the building and after a few minutes, an angry man with a newspaper shook his fist out a second floor window. When the phone in the living room rang, Agnes was grateful for another distraction.

"How did it go at the embassy?" Paulina asked.

Agnes told her about Bobbie Price and the book. "I can't read more of this book right now. When are you done there?"

"An hour or so. Dinner at home tonight," Paulina said. "I'm bringing a friend from the agency."

"Do you need me to do anything?"

"Actually can you get flowers? There is Polish złoty in the kitchen drawer by the fridge."

Agnes remembered all the flower carts she saw on the roadside on their way from the airport, and the word *kwiaty.*

"Yes, I can do that."

***

An hour later, Agnes had successfully purchased a bunch of lilacs and left them in the kitchen in a vase of water. She went into the bathroom to take a shower. When she came into the hall, wearing nothing but a towel, a tall man wearing jeans and a checkered dress shirt was shaking out an umbrella in the entryway. As soon as he caught a glimpse of Agnes in a towel, he whipped around to put his back to her.

"Sorry about that," he called, a note of embarrassment in his voice. Agnes meant to slip into her bedroom, but found herself lingering, admiring the stretch of his dress shirt across his shoulders.

"No, it's me." She slipped into the spare room. "I'm gone now," she called. "You can turn around."

Agnes stayed in the bedroom longer than usual, trying on different outfits. Paulina had given her full rights to anything in the closet that would fit, but it turned out that Paulina was a little smaller than Agnes in all the places where it made a difference with clothes. Nothing seemed to zip or button well. She settled on a basic white T-shirt and jeans, emerging just as Eva was putting out the last plate. The man with the umbrella stood up from the table when he saw Agnes come in.

"Good to meet your jeans and T-shirt," he smiled. His eyes twinkled and he pursed his lips in a slightly mischievous way. "I'm Otto."

"Sorry again about that," Agnes said. They shook hands, her

fingers disappearing into his palms. While their hands were joined together, he leaned over and kissed her three times on the cheeks.

"Why do you kiss like a Pole and not a German?" Paulina ribbed him.

Otto sat back down and Agnes sat across. "I don't know what you mean."

"Three times on the cheek instead of two?"

"If you were me, wouldn't you take an extra kiss if you could get it?" Otto grinned like a schoolboy.

"Now I understand why you left Munich to come to Warsaw," Paulina sighed, putting a napkin in her lap as Eva started spooning out gravy-slathered hunks of beef onto everyone's plate. "The extra kiss!"

"You're from Munich?" Agnes asked. She started to say *so is my father*, but stopped herself.

"Yep. I came here to drive my father crazy. What kind of a person in law studies goes into advertising? And in Poland?"

"We have something in common then," Agnes said.

"Law?"

"No. The *driving dad crazy* part."

"I imagine nothing is good enough for a man's daughter, is it?"

Agnes started slicing her beef. "No, probably not."

"How did you do today, Agnes?" Eva asked.

Agnes put a bite into her mouth to buy some time to answer. "I found somebody at the embassy to help me."

"Oh?" Paulina said.

"Help you with what?" Otto asked.

Agnes wanted someone to change the subject. Her eyes darted from Eva to Paulina. "Just some … research I'm doing," she said.

Paulina took Agnes's cue. "Did I tell you? Badgley's killed the storyboards we presented today. All three of them. The creative director is giving me hell for being in the States for the last two weeks."

Agnes gave Paulina an apologetic look, as Paulina had been in the US for her disaster of an almost-wedding.

"No, Agnes, it's okay. He's just grabbing at straws. The ideas were terrible. I would have killed them myself if I had seen them before the presentation today."

"My advice?" Otto said. "Just take your client out for a nice dinner. Have your creative director change a few frames of the storyboard, and then present it again. He'll be calmed down and I bet he'll buy it."

"You don't know this client. He loves to kill things," Paulina said.

Otto looked unfazed. "I've had those before. The nice dinner works. Heavy on the cocktails. Let him complain to you about his kids' expensive private school in Switzerland and the Greek vacation his wife is nagging him for. Clients usually kill things because they need to beat their chests a little. They take it out on the creative work. You just need to give him another outlet."

As Otto ate, she noticed his meticulous manners, cutting carefully, bringing the food to his mouth with an upturned fork, not talking while he was chewing. These were her father's manners, but not Krys's. Otto drank two Żywiec beers during dinner. He told a few jokes toward the end of the meal, but said nothing about work, nothing about home. He seemed like someone who could enjoy himself.

"What do you do in Chicago, Agnes?" he asked.

"I make cereal commercials," she said.

"Like muesli, that kind of thing?"

"No, like Cuckoo for Cocoa Puffs. That kind of thing."

Otto smirked. "I'll never understand you Americans and your food."

"Well lots of people buy it."

"Personally … I wouldn't buy food sold by a cartoon bird."

"Then you're not the target audience."

Otto chuckled and winked at her, only slightly, but it was definitely a wink.

A half hour later, Otto pushed back from the table and excused himself.

"Per my earlier advice, I have to meet my client at the Sheraton for a pint."

He walked to where his umbrella was propped on a mat by the door. Next to it were two oversized black portfolios. "Paulina, do you have the goods for this weekend?"

Paulina cocked her head. "In the kitchen."

Otto walked through the hall to the kitchen and came back with two stacked boxes of vodka, leaning them against his chest.

"Another client?" Agnes asked.

Otto winked at her. "Turns out that I'll be thirty years old on Friday. Party all weekend. Starts Thursday night. You'll still be in town?"

"I don't know. I'm not really going to be here that long."

"Well if you are, you know where to come." He pointed with his foot to the portfolios and umbrella. "Could you be a good American and help me carry that stuff down to my car?"

Agnes jumped up from the table, too fast she knew. She picked up the portfolios and followed Otto down the wet staircase, now wet from a sudden summer storm, not from soapy water. Otto walked out of the archway toward a black Audi parked at the curb, putting the boxes down in the trunk and tapping it closed with the back of his fist. He came up on the curb to take the portfolios from Agnes.

"If you ever need help with your research, just let me know. A guy does a lot of research in law school."

"Thanks, I'll remember that."

Otto leaned over, putting one hand on Agnes's shoulder, kissing her three times on the cheeks, much more slowly than he had before. She watched him bend into the front seat of the Audi, his long legs filling up the room under the steering wheel. He waved and she smiled back. Her shoulder was still warm where he had put his hand when he kissed her good-bye, still warm as she watched him pull away and join the traffic headed into the center of Warsaw.

When she came up the stairs, Paulina was waiting for her at the door of the apartment.

"So?"

They traded a look and as Agnes tried to stifle a smile, a smirk escaped.

"Yes," Agnes admitted. "He's nice. He kind of reminds me of my father. How he might have been when he was younger."

"That I don't know about. But I do know that you couldn't take your eyes off him."

Agnes clumsily brushed off the comment and they said goodnight. At the end of the hall, Agnes fell exhausted into bed, while Paulina stayed up in the living room watching American movies dubbed into Polish. Agnes wasn't sure how she could hear them over the noise from the neighbor's TV. The night before and early that morning, the neighbor's volume had been unusually high. Eva didn't complain so Agnes didn't either. During the dinner with Otto, Eva had explained that an elderly man who was nearly deaf lived next door. "People just do the best they can," she had said serenely.

In the spare room, Agnes knelt by her suitcase and felt around in a hidden inside pocket for her engagement ring. After she saw her father in Berlin, she had slipped the ring off and put it in a secret pocket in the lining of her carry-on. Her finger touched a thin, circular object and she pulled it out. The sight of it made her wince. *What was she doing in Poland?* Feeling another man's hands on her shoulders that night, another man's lips on her cheeks, made her miss Krys fiercely. She went back into the living room to call him, the ring closed tightly inside her palm.

Paulina's eyes were fixed on the TV screen. Agnes touched her shoulder.

"Sorry. Could I call Krys from here, just for a minute?"

"Oh." Paulina stood. "Yeah, of course."

Paulina shut off the TV and Agnes came to sit on the edge of the couch. She dialed her apartment in Chicago. It was the middle of the day on Monday, she realized, as the phone kept ringing. Her own voice came on over the answering machine: *You've reached Krys and Agnes. We hate that hang-up noise on the answering machine. It bums us out. So please, really, leave us a message. Thanks a lot!*

Agnes held tight to the receiver and heard the beep, but there was too much to say for just a message. All she could do was hang up.

***

Much later, while Paulina snored on the trundle bed, Agnes slipped the *The Ultimate Design of Nazi Eugenics* book out from under her pillow and started reading. She looked through the table of contents and the index. A section on racial testing caught her eye and she flipped to it:

As such, the child could be evaluated from numerous standpoints for his racial desirability: physical appearance, comportment, mood, and cognitive skills. The cephalic index (measure of head shape) was employed as a determining metric. It was believed that the child who exhibited a dolichocephalic, or long-headed, result was naturally superior to one who measured as brachiocephalic, or short-headed.

She flipped back to the index and saw a chapter called "Poland, Nordic Origins."

The peoples on the continent of Europe can be classified into three groupings: Nordic, Alpine, and Mediterranean. The Nordic peoples predominated in countries of Northern Europe, including Germany, Poland, the Baltic States, parts of Russia and Scandinavia ... characteristics of Nordics are blond or red hair, blue eyes, fair skin and tall statures ... Nordic and Teuton were terms often used interchangeably, later with the term Aryan ... the Teutons were a Germanic tribe, active along the Jutland Peninsula, today present-day Denmark ... before the Middle Ages, the Teutonic Nordics commanded the waterways, expanding south along the Continent's great rivers: the Elbe, the Rhine, the Danube, and in Poland, the Vistula ..."

Agnes felt herself fighting sleep. She closed the book and dropped her head on the pillow, pulling the cord of the lamp. Sounds of Eva came from the living room. The blue glow of the TV lit the floorboards under the door, blue like a sky, blue like a river. As Agnes slipped into sleep, a new dream started. It was a dream about a great river and near it, the golden glow of wheat, like acres of shimmering blond earth.

NINE

On the Last Day of August

Agnes didn't know why the dreams of the farmer came so vividly and so often while she slept in Warsaw. Were the visions in these dreams really what happened when Poland fell to the Germans, or was it only how she imagined it? Eva's rarity of a building, a survivor of German occupation, encased her like a portal to the past. Agnes fell asleep with her hand pressed on the wall next to the bed, a wall that had stood before the war and after it, long after it, up until that moment Agnes Mueller lay there.

Perhaps her dreams were also prompted by the echo of the farmer's footsteps on the streets by the Polna Market, just outside Eva's kitchen window. Or maybe the rot of his stolen potatoes was the small, sour note in the scent of the courtyard's standing water. No matter what it was, the farmer was all around. Agnes could feel his presence when she slept. That's when she started to know his whole story. Each dream left traces in her subconscious. Just enough.

The farmer's name was Maximillian. Max. She first saw him in his field during the summer of 1939. It was one of the best seasons for farming that he had seen in all his twenty-eight years. The days seemed to last longer than they should have, a round yellow sun suspended over them like it was trapped in their upper latitudes.

Regular rain gathered into pools in every ditch, forming rivers in every furrow, enough to make the stamens of every flower droop, soggy with pollen. Near his property, the Vistula River thundered swiftly from the Carpathian Mountains to the Baltic Sea, a rumbling gray-green like the color of armies.

Everything grew wild that summer. His wheat grew above his shoulders for the first time since he took over his father's land and it made him feel good, like he was finally doing something right. *Papa would be proud of this,* Max thought, *if he could see all I've done here.* But seeing from the beyond was something Max didn't believe in—nor ghosts, nor heaven, nor the effect of prayer—so he didn't sit long with the fantasy of it.

There was so much work that summer that Max dreaded the autumn, which would bring the biggest harvest he had ever collected. But he looked forward to the winter almost greedily. On the last day of August, he boasted to his wife that that winter would be a good winter for eating, maybe the best ever.

But the following day, the first of September, Germany invaded Poland from the west. So for the farmer it meant that by October, he had different expectations for winter: he hoped only that they would all survive. By October, he was hiding his family indoors, out of view of the trolling Stukas. By October, bombs had scooped craters into his fields like giant spoons descended from heaven. By October, half his wheat lay horizontal, crushed flat by Panzers, most of it no good to harvest anymore. Aside from the wheat, he had a few acres left of potatoes and rapeseed, that was all. By October, he had decided he had no choice but to go to Warsaw, twenty miles north of their farm. He couldn't pick up a gun, he had never learned how to shoot one, but he had to do something to ensure their survival.

His main market was in Warsaw. *Or used to be,* he thought grimly. He longed to still find the carts on Polna Street, piled with beets, the beet juice running down the tin legs of produce carts and turning the gutters pink. If he could find that market, or any market, he could hold the farm and family together until the end of the fighting. Perhaps he could find out what resistance was afoot, the plans for a counteroffensive, some expectation of the end. He just wanted to find something, to do anything. Sitting still felt like suicide, like leaving his family in the path of annihilation. Although he promised to be careful, his wife did not understand.

"You're being a fool," she hissed.

"If I don't make a move, what's left will rot."

"Let it."

"Nothing on my farm is going to rot."

"We'll eat it. We can store the rest."

"There's not much left after the bombing, but there's still too much to store. I don't even have silos here."

The truth was, he didn't know if it was safer to stay on their farm, or head for the city. Wouldn't the city be safer? Maybe being in the Polish capital, with the ministers and military, was better for them at this point. The farmer didn't know what to expect in the city after the invasion, but he had to find out what was happening there. It may have been only curiosity that drove him out of the house toward Warsaw, and if so his wife was right, he was a fool.

The night before leaving, he wrapped two slices of stale bread in a kitchen cloth, wedged next to four slices of cured sausage. He filled a canteen with water, taking a swig, drying his face with the back of his sleeve, turning again to her. She had a sharp tongue, something he loved. He even wondered if he did things mainly for the chance to suffer her reprimand.

"I'll leave before dawn. You'll stay here with the girls. You won't show yourself outside the house until I'm back." His eyes found hers, insistent. "Is that clear?"

He hardened his face until he could feel small lines cut across his forehead, a stern look that begged as much as ordered. Almost twenty years working outside in the fields, either his father's or his own, had given him the countenance of a much older person. She turned her back to him gruffly, searching through the front window, and he only felt gratitude for such stubbornness. She would need it now.

***

As soon as he pulled the heavy farmhouse door closed behind him the next morning, frigid dew collected on his cheeks. Their two Irish Setters were asleep next to the porch, under the yews. He lifted his face into the dark blue air and inhaled deeply: sulfur, dead livestock, and ditches choked with displaced sand and mud. In a normal year, by that time, he would be working almost around the clock to bring in his crops. He shook the thought from his mind. It wasn't possible anymore to waste time thinking about a normal year. At the end of their fence his two workhorses kicked nervously in the shed. They were ready to work but had been without significant activity for some time, and less food than usual.

Max passed through the fence gate and began walking north along the curved road lined on each side by high birch trees, their leaves an apologetic yellow. Twenty miles, all on foot. He refused to let himself think about it. Quickening his stride, he tightened the leather harness of the satchel now strapped to his back. It sagged under the weight of as many potatoes as he could carry. He had decided the oxcart would have to stay, as would his horse. He brought with him only as much as he was prepared to lose. He would only pocket a modest sum of złoty this time, with the small lot he was bringing, but that would have to be enough. He could hopefully buy some things that his wife and the girls needed, if there was anything left to buy. And there was something about just having the weight of a few coins in his hand that he thought would make him feel better. Again, foolish.

He followed the first curve in the road as it skirted around a low hill, low enough for a man of average height to see across the top. He lamented Poland's flat terrain, almost every acre around their farm. What was a blessing to a farmer was equally so to an invading army. The landscape in Central Poland did anything but protect them—devoid of hills, valleys or forests.

He remembered the planes. They sounded like the buzz of a million bees. His wife had been in the yard behind the house where his two young daughters were playing. The planes came toward them, almost in slow motion, the buzzing getting louder until the buzz became a roar that opened over them like a screaming mouth. He had spotted black crosses, outlined in white, on the underside of the wings. Germans. He remembered watching with fascination as the first bomb fell. The dogs seemed to be watching, too, so confused they couldn't even bark. The planes' target seemed only steps away from them. A whistling came, the shriek of female voices—the girls!—then the ground rocked ferociously.

Max's throat closed from terror. He ran and collected his young daughters by the hair and necks and his wife ran behind him. His eldest fought him, blinded by panic. The little one was petrified. He pulled them both into the cellar with their legs flying behind them. Oh, how they cried with fear! He recalled the sound in his ears; his daughters' wailing was far more wretched than the roar of bombers.

Now walking through the same fields, the carcass of a once-thriving land, he spewed air through his nose as if one sharp exhale of breath could expel all the sounds from his memory.

Halfway into his journey, Max passed the farm belonging to a newlywed couple they knew. He barely recognized it. Their property comprised forty acres that had been in their family since the Teutonic Knights, bordered by a stream that trickled from the western curve of the Vistula, a line of cypress trees on two sides, and the market road on the southern edge. A young woman stooped in the yard, nobody who looked familiar to him at first. Behind her, a stone chimney stood with nothing else around it— only charred, smoking piles of rubble and the faint outlines of living spaces. A baby boy wailed by the cavity of a bombed tree trunk. The woman seemed dazed, and Max stepped off the road and called out to her. As she came closer, he realized who she was, their neighbor Ania. She was looking for her husband in the rubble, out of her mind. She seemed to not even know who he was.

"It's Max," he said gently.

She comprehended his words after a moment and her face crumpled. It looked as if a heartbreaking memory were coming to rest behind her eyes, one she refused to acknowledge as reality.

"Wait," she said, "I'll get my husband for you."

Max looked past her and could see that their property had sustained a direct hit by a bomb. Her husband was gone, perhaps incinerated, perhaps underneath a flank of his house, or flung in pieces to some patch of earth too far to see. But he was definitely gone. How had she and the baby lived through it? They must have been away from the farm.

He touched her shoulder. "Ania, go down to our place," he pointed.

Reluctantly, she gathered the baby and Max walked her out of her gate, turning her in the direction he had come. He kissed Ania three times on the cheeks and then nudged her to move. She started down the road with her child on her hip. Max took a long look at what was left of their farm, its mounds of gray ash, the wobbly stone chimney, the blackened fields behind the site of the house. *All the destruction,* he thought. *All the rot and the death.* He felt himself recoil somewhere inside, an instinct to flee itching him like the first sign of a terrible disease. He put his back to Ania, to her farm and to his own, and moved one foot after the next toward the unknown condition of Warsaw.

***

For the rest of his life, Max would never talk about what he saw in Warsaw that day. Fires raged in parts of the city, and the streets were filled with German soldiers, tanks and trucks. He went to every familiar street he knew, where markets usually operated— Chmielna, Ujazdowskie, Marszałkowska, Polna. But every market was either destroyed or under guard. Flanks of German soldiers stood in front of the one on Polna that still contained a scant bit of produce from before the invasion. Max watched them from the shadows of a building across the street, holding their rifles at an angle in front of their chests, guarding caved-in melons and half-black tomatoes that had been sitting for more than a month, uselessly policed.

What a ridiculous waste, he thought. The itch returned to him, that instinct to flee, and he chastised himself silently. He leaned against the cool concrete, and his eye caught sight of a sparrow swooping down and landing on a shallow tray of red and green apples. He had to do something, but what? He had no weapon, only the potatoes on his back, which now seemed more valuable than he first realized. But there seemed to be no place he could sell a scrap of food to anyone. Again, a chastisement: *Get out of here,* he told himself. *Get back to your family.*

He emerged from the shadow of the building and turned down a side street that would lead him through others and eventually onto Ujazdowskie, the main boulevard heading south. Taking a main road would be dangerous, possibly full of German soldiers and tanks, but almost all other roads in that zone of the city headed only east and west. He had no choice but to follow Ujazdowskie. Once he emerged onto it, the boulevard was eerily empty. As he neared the edge of the Łazienki Park, he spotted two German soldiers on the other side of the street, leaning on a section of the wrought iron fence that ringed the park. They were having a good laugh and passing the stub of a cigarette back and forth.

A man at the last corner had told him that Germany's Chancellor, Adolf Hitler, had reached the city, and that Polish authorities had already surrendered the country to him. Surrendered! Where was Warsaw's mayor? Where were the Polish generals? He watched the two soldiers by the park and wanted so much to pick a fight, to kick those two krauts in their oversized square white teeth, but somehow he resisted the urge. He stayed on the sidewalk opposite them and walked even faster. He had to get back to his family. If he could get past these two, then around the palace at Wilanów, he would be invisible again and before long, home.

As he passed, one of them called out. "Halt!"

Max slowed his gait and heard the sound of boots running across the gravel in the road. They were quickly behind him on the sidewalk. He turned to face them.

"What division are you?" one of them asked in German.

He realized his blond hair, fair eyes and squared features possibly made him look more German than Polish. They thought he was a deserter. For a moment, he wondered if he could pull it off. His mother's sister was a musician and had taught him German when he was a child. It would be unusual for a Polish farmer to speak German.

Max eyed them. One of them was tall and his coat was unbuttoned. The other was stocky with two rifles hoisted over his right shoulder. The tall one seemed to be the one in charge, so Max addressed him first.

"I have to be somewhere. Sick child," he stuttered in German.

The tall soldier stepped forward and Max immediately realized his German wasn't as good as he thought. *"Aus Polen?"*

Max felt the dust and dirt that covered him begin to betray who he really was: a Polish man who worked the land. His satchel was still on his back, but was now almost empty. Whenever he had passed a hungry woman or child, who seemed to be in every alley and doorway, he handed them a raw potato. He hadn't sold a single one to anybody and had even lost the desire to.

"Yes," he uttered, almost soundlessly. *What am I doing?* he thought.

"He's a farmer," the stocky one said, pointing. "Look at him. *Ein Bauer!*" The soldier slapped his thigh, cackling.

"What's in the sack, farmer?" the tall one asked.

"Nothing," he lied.

The stocky one lunged and yanked the satchel off his back. Four potatoes rolled onto the sidewalk.

"Where is your farm?" asked the tall one.

He saw the stocky one pull up one of his rifles and start to point it.

"South," Max answered, his breath clipped.

The stocky one shoved him in the shoulder with the barrel of his rifle. "Let's go."

They asked him more questions as they shut him into the back of a large transport truck: What kind of crops? What was ready for harvesting? Were they still intact after the German "movement," as they called it? It seemed like they had a strange interest in agriculture for two soldiers, but then Max realized they wanted to take his crops. *Control the food, subdue the people,* he thought. But these two probably had something else in mind. If a black market for food hadn't materialized already, it was about to. And with what Max had left—having seen the rotted produce in the market, he now realized his good fortune—and the land he could still plant, these two would make a killing.

Max crouched in the back of the truck as it sputtered forward. He watched the flat plain of the Vistula River basin roll by through an opening cut into the canvas. The opening was covered with three layers of netting, making everything outside—every green glade, every yellow cluster of beech trees—look hacked into pieces. When they got near his farm, he thought about not indicating to the soldiers where to stop and just let them drive on. But they couldn't drive forever, and he knew that once they realized he was evading them, they would certainly kill him. He couldn't imagine his wife on her own, trying to survive on that farm, never knowing what had happened to him. She could do it, but he didn't want her to. It had been a good growing season, he reminded himself. He would be able to give them more than what they wanted. When his blue and white farmhouse came into view, he swallowed hard and then he tapped twice on a metal panel separating him from the cab.

The truck slowed and turned into the dirt path leading off the main road. The dogs ran up beside it, barking and growling as if they were possessed by rabies. He saw his daughters rush out of the front door of the house, then stop short. It must have immediately been obvious to his wife, standing behind them, that there was trouble. She started retreating back to the door, pulling the girls inside. The soldiers spotted them and leapt out of the truck. His wife seemed too stunned to move. Max wanted to be let out of the truck. He banged hard on the side of it with the heel of his boot.

After they let him out, he spent the whole night pulling up his crops while one soldier held a gun on him and the other held a gun over his wife and daughters. Occasionally, his body would remind him of his hunger with a spurt of nausea or a rubbery feeling in his arms. After a while, he seemed to lose his senses, only moving his limbs in an automatic way, purely driven by fear and adrenaline. Every forty-five minutes, he returned from the field driving an oxcart loaded with potatoes.

At close to sunrise, he returned for the last time from the back edge of the field. Every last potato, what hadn't been destroyed by the Luftwaffe's bombs, was gone by the end of the night. His wife was sitting straight as a sentry between the girls. His daughters had both fallen asleep in the grass, which he could see by the moonlight was now coated with dew. He thought about how cold they must be, about the nightmares clogging their sleep, and that it was all his fault.

The taller soldier, the one standing over his family, lowered his rifle. He took a step over his youngest daughter's body, curved and quiet like a possum. He came close to the farmer, his red mouth revealing a barricade of teeth.

"Pest." He spat at the farmer's boots and his saliva slid off them and into the dirt. "We'll be back for the rest of the wheat. Make sure it's ready." He scraped the dirt with the barrel of his rifle. "And plant again. We won't leave here empty-handed. If you've got nothing to give us, we'll find other things here that can be of value."

The soldier turned his head and looked back at his youngest daughter, who remained sound asleep. Max anchored his feet to the earth because he knew that if he lashed out at them now, it would be the last thing he would do.

He watched the soldiers get into the front of the truck. A

moment later its engines groaned into gear. The truck climbed onto the road, heavy with the food he had worked all summer to grow. Dust rose in a cloud as the truck picked up speed, returning to Warsaw. He watched it go, standing apart from his wife for a long time. Once the truck was gone, all he could hear were the tiny squawks of crickets around them, like a feeble alarm.

"We have to leave here," his wife whispered into the night air, as if they could still hear her. "Before they are back."

Max walked past her and gathered both girls, draping a daughter over each shoulder and carrying them inside. He crossed the main room to a smaller one in back where the girls shared a bed. Their chests rose and fell as he laid them down, his hand coming over their peaceful, weary heads as his own jaw clenched with anguish.

His wife was standing in the middle of the main room when he emerged from the bedroom, still waiting for him to say something. At the fireplace, he took tobacco leaves out of a tinderbox and rolled a few of them tightly. He struck a match and lit the tobacco, wondering where he would buy matches when these ran out. Using one felt indulgent, foolish. His lips pinched the roll and he closed his eyes. For a moment, the cigarette felt good in his mouth—spicy, hot, and punishing. The smoke came into the back of his throat, caught like a hot cloud in his lungs, and escaped out of his nostrils with a sting.

"Food is going to become a problem," he finally said, breaking their silence.

"Not for us."

"Yes, for us. For all Poland. German soldiers are guarding all the markets in the city. I'm sure there will be a black market for food soon, and rations that won't keep a rat alive."

"Why do they bomb all the farmland of Poland if they care about the food?"

"They don't care about the food!" he shouted, then lowered his voice. "They want to starve us. Someone in the city told me about new calorie quotas—a quota for Germans, a much smaller one for

Poles, and almost nothing for Jews."

Husband and wife looked at each other. He bit into the cigarette and took a long drag, too long to even breathe out through it. He wondered if he were trying to choke himself. He braced both hands on the edge of the mantel and hung his head between his elbows.

"Anyplace else we go, we have less chance. We're safer here than Warsaw," he jerked his head toward the front door, "even with those two coming back."

"So we stay? We just give whatever they want if they come back?"

"Yes." He pinched the cigarette in between his fingers. "And I'll skim off as much as I think I can without them noticing. It's the best hope we have to survive."

"I'm nobody's slave!" she cried.

He turned from the fireplace and faced her. Even pale and tired, she was full of fight. His own fears, his own shameful desire to flee, squeezed around him like coils of rope.

"Mamo," a voice called from the bedroom. It was his eldest, restless as always. "Mamo!"

"I'm coming," his wife said.

He watched her turn and go into the bedroom, cradling their daughter at the end of the bed. From deep inside his pocket, he pulled out a small potato he had hidden and planned to give his wife after the soldiers left. He set it on the table and left the house.

Outside in the moonlight, a dirt path led him past his horse shed to where the wheat field began. His father had taught him how to farm wheat, how to find the flag leaf when it appeared and protect it from insects. His father had taught him how much of each harvest to save as seed for the next year. By now, he knew that each crop took one hundred days, perhaps a little more, to mature. He didn't know anything about war, or armies. He only knew about farming. He worried that he didn't have the smarts to survive.

He recalled that one year, when he was a boy, he had killed five acres of his father's wheat by overwatering. The days had been hot and he had been worried the stalks would wilt. But they hadn't been in any danger of drought, and he had made a grave error. When his father discovered the mistake, he sent him to the barn to re-shoe every horse. A gray mare kicked him in the forehead and he thought he might die from the pain. His mother stayed with him the two days that his father let him rest in the house.

Later, Max realized that his father had just been worried about the food. Max could have apologized for the lost wheat that season, but never did. He fumed about the kick from the gray mare and blamed his father—the anger, in some ways, lasted the rest of his father's life. Now the knot in his chest caused him to think about how much he wished he had apologized, how right his father had been about knowing how to survive.

There was one corner remaining of Max's wheat field that was still untouched, not by a bomb, not by a scythe. He had been able to convince the soldiers that the wheat needed more time to grow, that they would be able to get more from that patch if they gave him a little more time with it. This part of his field looked as if it had no idea what had happened in the world, as if it were still the last day of August. The stalks stood in a tall, stiff, honey-colored line. He took one step into them until he was partially hidden. He took another step, then another. Somewhere in the middle, once sure he couldn't be seen from the house, he dropped to his knees. He reached his arms out as far as he could into the darkness, around as many of the papery stalks as he could manage, and hugged the tall wheat to his chest. He hugged the wheat like it was his last friend.

TEN

In Which Agnes Starts Down an Amber Road

The next morning, Tuesday, Agnes stood in the doorway of the kitchen. Even though awake and standing, she was still trying to pull herself from the dream about the farmer, from a sleep so deep it felt partially drugged. Eva was brewing coffee in a metal carafe on the stovetop and the aroma alone started to stimulate her senses.

"Your street is called Polna, right?" Agnes asked.

Eva busied herself at the counter peeling an orange and didn't turn around. "It is."

"Is there a market near here?"

"Down the street. Tuesdays and Saturdays. Did Paulina tell you?"

Agnes shook her head. "I just have this recollection of being in that market."

Agnes sat at the raised Formica counter on one side of the kitchen, and Eva poured them both coffees. "You couldn't have been. You only got here on Sunday. There hasn't been a market day since you arrived," she said. Agnes rubbed her eyes and forehead and took a sip of coffee. "But speaking of the market, do you want to come there with me today? I have to do my shopping.

I'll show it to you."

Agnes looked toward the kitchen window and heard trucks braking and their rear gates clanging open, canvas awnings snapping, and tables sliding over patches of dirt as the Polna Market prepared to open.

"Sure," she said.

Eva came to sit on the adjacent stool and started buttering her toast. The smell of bacon wafted in from some other apartment through the courtyard. Outside the window, where the noise of market preparations continued, the air was already moist with heat. Before the dream, Agnes remembered she had been reading.

"Do you know about a place called Talisz?" Agnes asked.

The name brought a smile to Eva's face. "How do you know Talisz?"

"It was mentioned in the book the woman at the embassy gave me."

"Sure I know it," Eva took a bite of toast. "I tried to get a job in the convent there. It's very competitive unfortunately."

"There was a picture of the convent in this book."

"There was? What did the book say about it?"

Agnes didn't want to ruin the affection Eva had for the convent or for Talisz, but what she had read wasn't flattering. "It said that there had been children there, during the war."

"Sure, it was a school. That makes sense."

"It sounds like it was a special kind of school," Agnes continued. Eva looked at her quizzically. "The book said they were teaching children to speak German, to know German customs. Things like that."

Eva raised one eyebrow, her expression resigned. "That part of Poland was annexed to Germany completely during the war. It doesn't surprise me."

"The thing is," Agnes said, "the book claimed that the kids in the convent school were Polish kids. Not German kids. They wanted the Polish kids to speak German."

To Agnes's surprise, Eva wasn't shocked by that either. Agnes didn't want to tell her all the rest she had read: about how they beat children who spoke Polish and refused to learn German, how the children were kept as prisoners, how they were mistreated, how some of them died trying to escape the convent. Eva *still* might not have been shocked, but at some point, she would have to be.

Eva stood up and brought her plate to the sink. "That's not much different than what the Soviets did when they controlled Poland for the last fifty years. Learning to speak Russian was compulsory. Polish wasn't banned, but Russian was … let's say Russian was a must." Eva faced her. "Poland has lived almost every hell more than once in its history, I promise you." She snatched a sponge from the edge of the sink and started raking it across the Formica counter where they had been eating. "Do you think Talisz has something to do with your father?"

"They said children went there before being sent to Germany to be adopted. If he were born here, and adopted in Berlin, he could have been in Talisz in between."

Eva sprinkled the toast crumbs into the garbage can and laid the sponge back down at the sink. "I can take you there this weekend, if you want. I can try to make an appointment for us to talk to someone."

"Don't you have to work on the weekends?"

Eva smiled. "My boss is going with his family to the South of France for his vacation. I'm free as of Friday night, for a month."

***

After breakfast, Agnes followed Eva up the street to the Polna Market. It wasn't even ten o'clock in the morning, but the short distance they walked immediately broke a sweat at the back of Agnes's neck. Eva marched at a fast pace without a care about the heat, while Agnes slowed with every step, negotiating the poorly paved sidewalk.

"Who's the man who cleans the stairs in your building?" she asked.

"That's Piotr. The superintendent."

"He seemed very excited that I was American."

"Yes." Eva laughed. "He's only seen Americans in movies."

They arrived at the Polna Market where a maze of tables and stalls went back deeply into its grass lot, some of them covered with a green or gray tarp. Slimy cabbage leaves and onionskins covered the ground. Each farmer seemed to have his own table, piled with whatever produce he was ready to sell. One woman with a white handkerchief tied over her hair was arranging beets into a pyramid, though each time she added one, a side of the pyramid would collapse like a landslide. Eventually she lost her patience and piled them haphazardly so that the result was simply a heap of purple spheres. Some of them were overripe, tinting the table a bright pink.

"I need bread," Eva said, pointing to a far table. "I'm going to the back. There's a flea market past the food," she pointed in another direction. "Trinkets and things. You might find something to take home." Agnes turned to walk toward the flea market. "I'll come find you once I finish."

Agnes was relieved to move away from the crush of food vendors. The aisle between the produce tables was narrow and everyone was haggling for something: a pound of berries, a bunch of carrots, watermelon, radishes, cabbage, green beans, and giant ears of corn. A table full of pies wrapped in plastic at the end of the aisle caught Agnes's eye. She looked at the labels on each and couldn't understand what kind of pie they were, the oozing orange or purple or blue coming out of the crust her only hint at the flavor. Next to the pies, she spotted small cookies in cellophane bags tied with red and white ribbons. The label on each bag read: *Pierniczki.* Magda and Mr. Kubelski's gingerbread. The sweat on her neck chilled as the tree branches waved overhead. A pang of melancholy struck her.

Agnes left the pie stand and walked into the more open space of the flea market. The area didn't have tables, just piles of junk arranged around a person sitting in a rocking chair or on a stool. Some people had even driven their cars into the lot and parked,

169

opening the rear door to display sale items, or spreading embroidered linens or blankets over the roof and hood of the car.

Every imaginable type of object filled the market: old phonographs with inlaid wood cabinets and ornamental handles to wind-up the turntable, gas lamps with globes as white and round as onions, dusty paintings of ships and lighthouses, spools of brightly colored yarn, silk flowers, ceramic vases, engraved silverware, inky typewriters, Singer sewing machines, ceiling fans, old radios, and Tupperware. Then there was the glut of Soviet memorabilia, everything bearing a hammer and sickle: military ribbons, helmets, uniforms, flasks, knives, bayonets, rifles, cufflinks, bootstraps, belts, and burr-scathed wool blankets. Agnes even spotted a set of Soviet salt-and-pepper shakers. She passed a table lined neatly with dozens of square plastic packages which contained plain white t-shirts. Each package bore an image of an American flag, underneath which was written *American T-Shirt* and *100% cotton.*

Agnes came to an area with one long table, which was just a piece of plywood propped up on two saw-horses. Bolts of putting-green felt lay across the table, and jewelry had been placed carefully across. A gray-haired man stood a short distance from the table, wearing a tan windbreaker and holding an Easter bag in one hand (the bunny and pastel eggs were unmistakable). In his other hand he held up a small cardboard gift box that was propped open. Gold and silver necklaces dangled off the sides of the box. He looked forlornly at each person who came near, as he presented his small box of necklaces for sale. Most people ignored him and walked past.

Another man, not as gray-haired, stepped from behind the plywood jewelry table and barked at the man with the necklaces. His voice made Agnes jump. He was swatting the air in front of the necklace man as if he wanted him to go away. Agnes slipped to the end of the plywood table and tried to ignore them, touching a small pile of gold bangle bracelets, trying them on, thinking over if she should get one. A teenage boy in a lawn chair sat behind the table. After a minute he got up and came closer to her.

"Those would look good for you," he said in nearly perfect English.

Agnes was startled, partly by his excellent English and partly by the seeming flirtation. He was just a kid, at least ten years younger. She let the bangles drop onto the felt. "Sure, maybe. I'm just looking."

Agnes glanced away from the table and noticed that the necklace man seemed to have disappeared. She slid along the plywood table and looked at other pieces of jewelry. An arrangement of what looked like miniature amber pendants caught her eye. They were too big to be bracelets, but too small to be necklaces.

"What are these?" she asked the teenager.

"Those are amulets. For the infant," he said. "They protect the infant from the danger."

"Like from being sick or something?"

Agnes picked one up.

"From the danger," he said, his voice cracking. His eyes narrowed, as if to be gravely serious, but Agnes found the fuzz of his jaw so comical she had to work hard to stifle a laugh. "From any kind of danger."

"I see." She raised her eyebrows to play along. "Is that a Polish tradition?"

His look of danger popped like a cartoon bubble. "More Lithuanian custom to give this necklace for the infant, but in Poland maybe, too. Sure." He moved to pick something up from the table, a giant amber stone lying with others of different sizes.

"The amulet is always made with the amber," he said, holding out the giant stone. "Put it in your hand." Agnes took it. "You see? The amber has a power." Agnes closed her fingers around its smooth and heavy form, but it didn't feel like it had any power. "The amber has magic. Does it feel hot?"

"Not really," she said, a little bothered by the way he had said the word hot.

"If you wear it on your skin, it will become hot," he explained.

"That is magic working."

Agnes handed the amber stone back, and he brushed his fingers against hers for a longer time than needed. "Okay, thanks," she said, giving him a half smile and backing up to join the stream of browsers circling the lot. She walked back to where she had entered the flea market and headed for the sidewalk where she could wait for Eva and be clear of the throng of people. After a few minutes, Eva came up next to her.

"Find anything?"

Agnes smirked. "Hormones."

They crossed the street and slipped into the shade of the archway of Eva's building, upstairs through the cave-like blue of the marble stairs and their merciful chill.

***

After lunch, Agnes called her father from the living room phone. It was just past six o'clock in the morning in Chicago. Her parents would be getting up, or might even still be in bed. It had been three days since the terrible confrontation with her father in Berlin.

Once the phone rang more than four times, she suspected they weren't home. Her mother would never let the phone ring that long. Then the answering machine clicked on. *Another answering machine*, Agnes lamented. Suddenly the machine clicked off and she heard her father's subtly German-accented English.

"Mom said you went to Poland?" he said.

"I'm okay. I'm at Eva's." Agnes wound the cord of the phone in her fingers, then around her wrists. "I'm so sorry about what happened at Gertrude's." Her father didn't immediately answer, and Agnes was too nervous to leave even a second of silence. "Are you still there?"

"I am. I wish you had just come home after."

"Papa   did you hear what I said at Gertrude's?" He didn't answer. She wondered if this were the right time to press him, but realized the time for hesitation had long since passed. "I said that Liesl was not your mother. Klaus was not your father. Do you

172

remember I said that?"

He sighed. "Is this what you're doing in Germany and Poland? Chasing up fairy tale mysteries?"

"It's not a fairy tale mystery. I know from Klaus's brother and Liesl's sister. I talked to them. The Schneiders weren't able to have children."

More silence. She didn't know if he would yell at her, or just hang up. "I don't know what you want me to do with this information," he said curtly. "This is too much. Are you saying I don't have parents?"

Agnes sat forward on the edge of the couch. "Everybody has parents, Papa."

"Yes, everybody does. Speaking of my parents, Gertrude is very upset. Have you apologized?"

He was changing the subject and Agnes decided to let him. "I sent Gertrude a letter in yesterday's mail, yes. I apologized."

"You should come home," he said flatly. "Your mother is upset, too. We've all been through enough. I know I started this, but I will end it."

"You can't tell me to come home, Papa. I'm not a kid."

"You're putting your mother through a hell, do you understand? And Krys. He brought a box of your things here over the weekend, and he's bringing more today."

Agnes became defensive. "That works out for you since you didn't want me to marry him anyway."

He huffed. "I don't want you to be unhappy, but this might be better in the end. He won't even fight for you!"

She knew she had struck a chord. "You were expecting a fight with him?"

"For you? Of course I was." The TV switched on in the neighboring apartment and music swelled like it does in a feature film. "If you care about your mother, you'll come back here," he insisted.

"Is Mom there? Can I talk to her?"

He paused. "She's not here."

Agnes looked again at her watch. "It's six in the morning there. Where is she?"

Her father's voice turned faintly hoarse. "She left."

***

Her father explained that her mother had gone to stay with a college friend he didn't know. She hadn't left a number, just a note that read: *I need a few days to be out of contact.* Agnes felt sure the note contained a lot of other things that her father didn't want to tell her, and she tortured herself by imagining versions of the note all afternoon.

During that time, Eva got to work in the living room, calling the *Urząd Stanu Cywilnego* of Poland's major cities. Agnes was grateful that Eva had asked her to help with chores around the apartment while she made calls. She was hoping it would help to stay busy, but it didn't really. Her hands moved, but her head was in its own world, fretting over her mother, worrying about Eva's calls. Notes from her mother formed themselves in her imagination while she worked and she couldn't get them out of her head after a while. As she was cutting vegetables for Eva in the kitchen, she imagined this note:

Bernd—I don't know if I can forgive you for walking out on us. How could you desert Agnes on the day of her wedding? Never mind how furious all the guests were (something you left me to deal with). But what about Agnes? You should have seen her. What you did was cruel. You're not the person I thought you were.

While she was sweeping the parquet floor in the living room, she imagined a more hurtful one:

Bernd—The chip on your shoulder is poison, you know that? It's been there since the day I met you, and I never saw it. Now I see it. It's too hard to live with someone who walks around with ghosts every day, fearing them, feeling guilt for them. I'm too tired of coping with your distance from us. No matter how hard I try, I can't understand you. I'm sorry. I'm just too tired of trying.

***

In the late afternoon, close to dinner, Agnes took a bag of garbage down the marble steps to the bins on the sidewalk. Piotr was there, cleaning them with a worn sponge and bucket of water. Agnes waved and said hi in English.

Piotr smiled and began a strenuous effort to return her greeting. Finally, the little syllable fell with a strange, elongated twang from his lips: "Hiii."

He saw her full bag of garbage and pointed to the sidewalk in front of the bins. She dropped the bag and he held up a finger, saying something that Agnes didn't understand. He scooped his hand in the air—a *follow me* signal—so she did. Off the cobblestone driveway under the archway, a little metal door with windows led into a small office she hadn't noticed before. Piotr disappeared inside, then came back out holding a baggie with a lollipop inside. He took the lollipop out and held it up to her proudly. It was a Tootsie Pop.

"Amerykanska!" he beamed.

Agnes smiled back and did her best to look duly impressed by the sight of an American-made Tootsie Pop. He watched her walk back up the stairs, holding the Tootsie Pop up high as long as Agnes could still see him, like some imitation of the Statue of Liberty. It felt good to see Piotr in passing. He didn't ask much from the world or the people in it. She was grateful that, for a few minutes, he had made her forget her mother's notes.

***

During dinner, while Paulina and Eva were talking excitedly about Paulina finally selling a storyboard to Badgley's, Agnes imagined more letters. Her own fears about life had started to seep into them.

Dear Bernd—I've had enough. I could forgive a lot of the other things, but not this. Now our daughter has run off and seems bent on throwing her life away. Krys is a good boy. He would have been good for Agnes. But you just had to plant doubts in their heads on such an important day when they must have already been nervous enough. You just had to do that. She took it all to heart, and now they think they have no future together. You should be ashamed of yourself.

Paulina cackled sharply, something about her client, and it shook Agnes from her daydream. Paulina stopped laughing. "What's going on with you?" she asked. "You haven't said a word all night."

A concerned look formed on Eva's face.

"My mom left home," Agnes said.

"Why?" Eva asked.

Agnes dropped her hands in her lap. "I don't know. My father didn't say a lot. She's with a college friend."

"Can you call her?"

"She didn't leave a number. I feel like it's my fault. It's because of Krys's and my wedding falling apart. And now I'm gone. I'm sure she blames herself."

"Why don't you talk to Krys?"

Agnes knew Eva was right. Who else could she talk to now? She inched her chair back and picked up the phone, looping the cord into the hall and shutting the living room door. She crouched on the parquet floor in the entryway, knees up, leaning against the wall. The ringing of the phone seemed to go on for a long time. Then she heard Krys's voice on the machine, not her own. He had changed it. His voice was dry and self-deprecating.

"Hi, you've reached Krys. If you're hearing this it's because I'm working or out drinking. But feel free to leave a message, and I'll try to call you back when the fun lets up."

Agnes couldn't hang up again without leaving a message. The beep came, and she rushed to think of the right words. "Krys," she started, still thinking about what to say. "It's Agnes. I guess you know from my parents that I'm in Warsaw. I won't be here long, maybe until next week. I'm coming home and I want to see you. Please let's talk before you make any decisions about us. Please." She stopped, realizing how desperate she sounded. But the situation was desperate. She wanted him to know that she knew it. "I think about you every day. I wish you were here with me." She left Eva's phone number, hurrying through it before the machine could cut her off. Then she said good-bye and hung up. That's when she realized she had rushed herself so much that she never said, "I love you."

ELEVEN

Ground Zeroes

Eva had gotten them an appointment to meet with the Mother Superior at the Sisters of the Holy Sacrament Convent in Talisz on Friday in the late morning. It was the only day they met with people from what they called *the outside*, so Eva had decided she would have to call in sick so she could take Agnes.

By Thursday, Eva had called the *Urząd Stanu Cywilnego* of eleven of Poland's major cities, from Krakow to Gdańsk, asking about the birth registrations of children born in December of 1941. Warsaw had a very long list of births; they planned to get Warsaw's list, but they tried other smaller cities, too. The farther west the city, the closer to Germany—cities like Leszno, Wrocław, and Poznań— the more depleted the records. Or if they had them, the records had been Germanized such that many of the Polish names might have been re-recorded as German ones. "It could be a stroke of luck that the names are in German," Eva told Agnes while she was on hold with one office. Eva asked for boys named Bernd. Poznań had eleven boys on their list, Eva whispered to her, born in that city in that month. *Only eleven!* Agnes thought it was a manageable number. Eva talked to the office in Poznań for a few minutes longer, then hung up.

"They won't photocopy any record less than one hundred years old. I have no idea why. They didn't give a reason. Poles take great pride in their bureaucracy. The more tangled, the better. But they can send us a transcript once we send them a written request, with a fee."

"What will the transcript say? Will it name the parents?"

"Birth registrations will have a lot of information—the name and ages of the parents and grandparents, place and time of birth, occupation of the father." Eva paused. "But they said it would be four to six weeks before they can send a reply. And they didn't even sound sure about that."

Agnes lamented the bureaucracy and imagined this was only the start of it. She recalled Nepo, tangling up the entry for citizens at the embassy. "Would we be able to get it if we go in person?"

"It's about two hours' drive past Talisz. We can go there tomorrow when we're done at the convent."

***

At close to dinnertime, Paulina came in from work and found Agnes in the spare room. She held out a package. "This arrived at the agency today, via TNT overnight express. It's for you, from Germany."

"Gertrude?" Agnes looked at the package and couldn't read the markings for the return address as it was so covered with foreign stamps and tape. She sat on the edge of the bed and Paulina came to sit beside her. The package was rectangular, the size of a small shoebox. Inside there was a letter in German, a book by Rilke, and a small jewelry box. The first few lines of the letter revealed Gertrude to be an entirely different person on paper, the Gertrude that Agnes had hoped for.

Dear Agnes,

I received your letter today. I'm so terribly upset about your last visit. I don't want you to feel sorry for anything. You of all people have nothing to feel sorry for.

Your father's circumstances are confusing, I know. I've spent much of my life confused about some of the same things. I'll try to tell you what I can of the story, what might help you. Part of that story involves my dear Albert. I haven't told you about him, and I should.

Albert was a lawyer for the German government at a time when our country was struggling for its survival, after World War I. But when Hitler took the Chancellorship, Albert could sense that the plan for Germany was not one he agreed with anymore. But a person in Germany then, let alone a member of the party, couldn't dare disagree.

It's complicated to explain how, but Albert tried to slow Hitler down. There was no more dangerous thing to do then, in case someone suspected his motives. I wondered every morning, when he left, if I would ever see him again. It was a sad time for both of us, watching Germany turn into a place we feared. Albert and I wanted very much for Germany to win the war but for Hitler to lose it. That was an impossible hope, and we knew it, but we held on to it.

The truth is, at first, adopting an orphan child during the war was a chance for us to protect ourselves. I feel shameful, but it was only how it all started, not how we felt after we brought your father home. We fell in love with him. We loved him like our own flesh and blood. From the first day onward, we tried to do everything for him that we could.

As for where your father came from, at the time we only knew what the orphanage told us. I swear that to you. They gave us papers for him, a birth certificate, and that was enough. We fell in love with our boy, no matter where he came from. No matter who he was before. At the time, it didn't seem to matter. He was alone. He needed us.

Your father doesn't know about the circumstances of his adoption. None of us knew about Liesl's fate. You surprised us both in Berlin with that news. There was so much I didn't know, so many unanswered questions, so I've left it alone all these years.

Whatever happened at the beginning, Bernd was our light and life in a dark time. We didn't deserve him, but I hope we did right by him and raised him well. I have thanked God for him every day.

I hope you will keep the enclosed. The locket is something I have worn every day since your father left for America. I want you to have it. The book contains some special verses by Rilke and has been by my bedside since I was thirteen years old. Now I hope it will stay by yours.

You asked me about Poland. I think it's good that you are there. Petra might have been right, whatever she told you. Please be safe.

Gertrude

Agnes exhaled, folded the letter and put it back in the box. She took the Rilke book out and then the jewelry box, opening it gently. Inside was an oval locket encrusted with amber stones. Little pearl and platinum links formed a delicate chain. She opened the face and saw a black and white picture of her father as a baby inside. He was smiling, his light eyes beaming from on top of a pair of smooth, round cheeks. His puffy gums were studded with the few small white nubs of baby teeth. His thin, light hair stood up like the fronds of a dandelion, as if caught by some electric charge, ready to fly into the wind. She carefully flipped the locket so the picture fell out, and she read what was written in German on the back, her father's name and age in months: *Bernd, 10 Monate.*

Paulina had been reading over her shoulder and Agnes translated some of it out loud.

"It was selfish, wasn't it?" Paulina remarked. "Adopting a baby for that reason?"

"I suppose it's easy for us to think that now." Agnes laid the book of Rilke's verses down on the bedside table. "Still, I don't trust Gertrude." She looked back to the letter and pointed to the end. "She says this weird thing here that I don't think she meant to say."

"What is it?"

"She says 'we loved him *no matter who he was before.*' Why would she say *who*?"

"It's like she knows he was someone else."

Agnes placed the letter on top of the book. "Yes. It's like she knows."

Agnes and Paulina looked at each other as the mother in the courtyard started hollering.

***

After his first interview, Bernd was visited two more times by investigators from the United Nations, as well as a child psychologist. Gertrude submitted to the parade of visitors anxiously, but didn't try to stop them. Although afraid they would confirm her son had been taken from his family by force, she had resigned herself to the importance of knowing the truth.

In March 1947, Albert and Gertrude were called to a field station of the World Office of Refugees in Berlin. A brief letter from the UN had explained only that their case fell under special circumstances and had been referred on to this other organization.

The WOR's station office was on the third floor of a large concrete building in the American sector. The northwest corner of it was covered with a tarp where a bomb had left a hole that was still unrepaired.

At the time, when so much of Berlin was still under reconstruction, most large buildings served multiple purposes. In this building, there was a small veterinary clinic on the ground floor, a printing office on the second floor, and an outpost for the WOR on the third.

At the third floor elevator, a neatly dressed young woman greeted them. She led them down a narrow corridor, past several offices with closed frosted glass doors and into an office at the end of the hallway. The woman told them to wait there to meet the chief investigator on their case, a British intelligence officer named Nigel Sheffield, who would be returning from another meeting any moment. They took their seats in Sheffield's office and Gertrude hugged her elbows. A window in the office was wide open, letting in the biting late winter air.

Gertrude examined the surface of Sheffield's scuffed metal desk. It was piled with dozens of yellow folders. Each one overstuffed with paper, clips securing various notes and photographs. She thought of dandelion seeds, how they blow in the wind with barely a puff of breath. How they are lost into the air forever. Here was this man, trying to put families back together, trying to put the blown fuzz back on a dandelion. Sheffield probably hadn't imagined doing this kind of intelligence work.

After a few minutes, he entered briskly, walked past them and sat behind his desk. He was a short man with graying hair. Wire-rimmed glasses perched on the end of his nose, and his suit seemed one size too large. Tired and overworked, he had a civil servant's face, the resigned face of a person doing a job nobody else wants to do for a laughably small paycheck. The strain on his face seemed to indicate that he knew he was cleaning up an impossible mess.

"Thank you for coming in," he said, barely looking at them. They nodded as Sheffield pulled out a folder Gertrude presumed held information about her son. "We have reviewed the boy's case." He was looking through some yellow papers inside the folder, all full with a large amount of typed text. "We looked at his responses in the interview and had a psychologist review the case." Sheffield laid the folder open on his desk and looked across at them. "He doesn't appear to remember anything about a birth family in Poland."

Gertrude sat forward and put her hand on the front of Sheffield's desk. "But we told you. All this time you've just been assuming he could belong to this family you've been talking about, with this doll, with these sisters! Who are they? You see he doesn't know them at all. He can't be theirs. He has a valid birth certificate, a German one. I just don't see what the mystery is."

Nigel Sheffield tipped his face forward and looked at her over the top of his glasses. "Frau Mueller, most children who were taken from their families so young don't remember anything about where they came from. That's normal."

"But I still don't see how you can know for sure our boy is theirs. Why do you keep interviewing him?" Gertrude pressed.

"Well, there are a couple of reasons we're pretty sure it's him. The main one is that a photo from the birth mother is nearly identical to the one you gave us." He laid two pictures side by side at the front edge of his desk for Gertrude and Albert to see. It was true, they were nearly the same picture—his blond hair flying uncontrollably, his round cheeks, a few baby teeth appearing along his pink gums. "His physical description and the dates of his birth and adoption approximately match the dates his mother gave us of his birth and kidnapping. Whoever typed up his false papers at the orphanage didn't get his birth date exactly right, but it's close. Your son's actual birthdate is a month later, on January 27, 1942. Also, his birth mother told us her son had webbed toes on his left foot. So does your son, Frau Mueller. When our medic examined him, he found the second and third toes are stuck together, just like she said."

Albert held Gertrude's hand. The breeze from the window felt like needles on her face, but she didn't move to touch it, to warm it up. "We're the only family he knows," Albert said, his voice the barest rasp of a whisper.

"We know that." Sheffield cleared his throat. "That's what we told his family. To be honest, this is an unusual case. He's already five, school age now. He was a baby when he was brought to Germany. In the past two years we've sent children like him back with disastrous results. The children rebel and, well, they develop all manner of problems. Some have run away. Last year, two young girls in Eastern Poland even committed suicide together after they were sent back from Frankfurt. So we are rethinking our procedures in cases like this, in cases where the child was taken from his mother before his first birthday."

"So what procedures need to be followed here, sir?" asked Albert.

"We are suggesting a ninety-day probation on this case."

"What does that mean?" Albert asked.

"We have recommended to his birth family that he remain in Germany with you, permanently, and that he not be told about them at all. But the decision is ultimately theirs. We've played a recording for them of the interview with the boy. They talked to the same psychologist and investigators you've talked to. We made our recommendation, but if they disagree, they have ninety days to file a repatriation order to bring their son home. If they do, we have to honor it," he said. He looked directly at Gertrude. "We will all have to honor it. Do you understand?"

Albert squeezed Gertrude's hand and she nodded with him. A gust blew in and the papers fluttered.

***

Almost four months later, a letter from the World Office of Refugees came in the mail. Albert opened it after Bernd had gone to bed. Gertrude stood beside him as he read aloud, in a low voice.

"This is to notify the interested parties ..." Albert started.

Gertrude gripped his arm and squeezed her eyes shut. "My God, Albert. They're going to send him back?"

Albert put his hand over his wife's clenched fingers, scanning the letter to the end.

"No," he said, looking down at her. "It says the family has agreed to leave him with us. The agreement between us and them is sealed. It must stay confidential, even from our son."

Then Albert and Gertrude Mueller fell into each other's arms. In Gertrude's heart, she thanked God. But in Gertrude's heart, she felt herself attempting to quell an already consuming fear, like a flame catching. It was the fear that love and secrecy are incompatible. Sooner or later, one will always consume the other. Which would it be for her and her son?

***

Agnes sat on the edge of the bed holding the amber locket Gertrude had sent. She opened it and looked again at the baby picture. Without a word, she went to the living room phone and dialed the international affairs office of the US Embassy. She looked at her watch. It was after six in the evening; she would have to leave a message. To her surprise, Bobbie answered directly.

"Price," a voice answered. All business.

Agnes told Bobbie she had received a baby picture from her father's adoptive mother. "Could it help you identify him?"

"It probably won't, but you can leave a copy of it for me."

"Sure, I can come by first thing in the morning."

"I'm going to a breakfast tomorrow for President Wałęsa. Seal the picture in an envelope and leave it with Nepo downstairs. The more confidential it looks, the better."

Bobbie was ready to hang up. Agnes spoke fast. "Did you have any luck with your friends at the UN, about the Displaced Persons list?"

"Sort of. It's in the works. I'll call you as soon as I have it."

They hung up. Before Agnes took her hand away, the phone rang again. She was sure it was just an accidental callback from Bobbie, but she picked it up anyway and said "Hello?" tentatively into the receiver.

"Agnes, it's Mom."

Agnes felt the amber locket in her hand. The stones might have been warm, or she might have been sweating, but something burned. "Where are you? Are you all right?"

"Your father told you?"

"Uh-huh." Agnes pressed the amber into her palm. "Why did you leave?"

There was a pause. "What did he tell you exactly?"

"He just said you left, and you were with a friend. That you left him a note."

"I wrote a note, yes," she said. "But that was *after* he asked me to go and left me at home alone to pack."

Agnes released the amber and laid her hand on her clenched stomach. "Why would he ask you to go?"

"He said he needs time alone. I think ..." her mother stopped.

"I think he's cracking a little."

Cracking? Agnes thought. "Because of what happened with my wedding?"

"Your wedding brought everything to a head. But he was cracking before that. Work was getting to him. His life. Something happens to people in their fifties, Agnes." Agnes didn't want to ever be in her fifties if it meant cracking like this. "We see more of our life behind us than ahead. If you get to your fifties with a lot of unresolved issues, it feels like there's no time to resolve them. And your father has more unresolved issues than the average person."

"And you leaving home will resolve them?"

She paused and Agnes could tell she didn't want to answer. "Have you talked to Krys since you got to Poland?"

"I left a message two days ago. He hasn't called me back." Agnes remembered how self-deprecating his answering message had been. "Do you think he could be cracking, too?"

"Not him." Her mother chuckled. "He's too young and stubborn to crack." There was a silence, an important one. "Agnes, I don't want to see you lose him. Not over your father's issues. They're his issues, not yours. Krys is a good guy."

"I've been trying to reach him."

"You should just come home, honey."

"I'm not staying here that much longer. I'll be home next week I think."

"Then talk to him as soon as you can."

***

After dinner Thursday night, Agnes helped Paulina clear the table. Paulina urged her to come along to Night One of Otto's weekend-long birthday party, just for a little while. Agnes lolled on a kitchen stool.

"I'm sorry. I really just want to go to bed. Eva's taking me to Talisz first thing in the morning."

"I'll make sure you're awake in time."

Eva smiled. Paulina didn't look like she would give up.

"Okay. Let me try to reach Krys first, and then I'll come. But just for an hour or so."

From the living room phone, Agnes dialed Krys's office number. It was midday in Chicago. The noise of evening television blared through the wall. When Krys finally answered, she heard a voice that was even more self-deprecating than the one on the answering machine.

"Did you get my message?" Agnes asked.

"I did."

They were just two words, but they were frigid, weighty, and full of edges, like a shelf of ice.

"You couldn't call me?"

"There's a design competition, out of Seattle. I'm the lead architect."

"That's great," she waited. "I'm happy for you."

"It's good to be busy with work," he paused for effect, "right now."

Agnes didn't know what to say. The conversation left no doors open for her to enter. Finally she resorted to near small talk. "I'm in Warsaw. With Paulina."

"You said that on your message."

"I'm not going to be here that long. It's just that I was over here already," she felt like he had to understand, "and I had to follow a lead before going back."

"You're not Nancy Drew, Agnes."

She didn't want to take his bait. She didn't want to get angry. "This has to do with what happened on our wedding day. It isn't a game for me," she finally said, as calmly as she could. She longed for him to be in Warsaw with her, looking with her, being a part of what was going on with her father. But he was further away from her current struggle than the strangers selling fruit and trinkets across the street. Their sudden emotional distance filled her with anxiety.

"Getting married wasn't a game for me either," he said. "I deserved to know the truth about your family, whatever it was, before we got married."

She struggled to compose herself outwardly, while inside she was begging him to get on the next plane. "I know you feel like I've hidden something from you, but the truth is it was a long-buried part of my father's life. Not even his life, my grandfather's life." Agnes suddenly felt absurd calling Klaus Schneider her grandfather, and it almost made her laugh that a person who now seemed to be a complete stranger had derailed her future with Krys. "He actually has nothing to do with us."

"And your father? Why can't he accept me?"

"But he does."

"Of course he doesn't."

"He will. Especially once I talk to him about what I've learned over here."

"I loved you," Krys announced flatly. "That didn't matter to him?" Agnes noticed the past tense of *love* and it bit her in the heart like an angry dog. "I stood by you for more than ten years. That's more than a third of your lifetime."

Agnes hesitated. "And now?"

"Why would I stand by a person who keeps things from me?" There was a wide-open silence on the line that left only the buzzing noise of the transatlantic wire between them. *How proud he was!* "I frankly don't know why you're calling me."

"Because I love you, too. Nothing has changed."

"Yes, it has."

Agnes sensed them unraveling, right there, on the phone. She wondered if this would be the last call they ever had and it panicked her. "I am sorry, Krys. Is there anything more I can say?"

"I was waiting for *I do*," his voice turned even more bitter, "but that's right. That was last weekend."

Agnes heard the line go dead while still holding the phone to her ear, still thinking about how to repair the damage between them. Krys had hung up on her without another word, before she could even say good-bye. Her mouth was poised open to say it, and it stayed that way after he hung up as if she were a fish waiting for a hook. The call only made her feel absurd. Krys was a determined person, but she had never known him to hold such a grudge. He didn't even apologize for leaving the wedding like he did. *Something did crack in him,* she thought. *I cracked it.*

She felt a hand on her shoulder and looked up to see Eva looking down at her with a worried look. "I overheard a little. Sorry. That was Krys?" Agnes nodded. "Are you okay?"

"I messed up," she stammered. "He's too mad."

Eva sat down next to her. "He'll let go of his anger when he's ready."

"He didn't sound like he would."

"People together so long don't just stop being in each other's lives. You'll talk to him when you get home."

Eva had never been married, and as far as Agnes knew, had never had a significant relationship with a man. She seemed more devoted to her faith, and to some persistent memory of her lost brother Rafał, than to any other thing. Agnes saw her as an island, able to live on her own, unaffected by the histrionics of other people because she didn't need other people. *How could she know about being in another person's life for so long?* But Agnes was immediately sorry for conjuring such an uncharitable thought.

"I should get dressed." She stood and managed a smile for Eva. "Thanks for the advice."

She went to the spare room and left Eva sitting alone on the couch.

***

Paulina and Agnes took a taxi to a nightclub on the back edge of Warsaw's *Stare Miasto*, the Old Town. This historic section of Warsaw was a warren of narrow cobblestone streets leading into an old town square that would have been the site of the main market many centuries earlier. One tourist pub with an Italian menu had cropped up on the north side of the square, with a roped area of tables under red umbrellas spread out in front of it. Renaissance and Gothic townhouses clustered together on each edge of the square and along the tiny lanes leading toward the square, with slatted shutters held back by iron pins. Shingled signs hung out in front of a few of the townhouses near the nightclub, advertising some service or product that could be bought inside—crafts, amber jewelry, ice cream, and the powdery *pączki* donuts Mr. Kubelski used to sneak out of Magda's kitchen for her. The only way to move around inside the *Stare Miasto* was on foot, or a very small car. When their taxi got close to the club, Agnes could see a long line of people waiting to go inside. It was close to ten o'clock.

Agnes followed Paulina out of the taxi and across the street. Paulina stopped in front of a stainless steel door with the English words *Ground Zero* etched on it in a Courier stencil. She exchanged a word with the two men standing at the door and then motioned to Agnes that they could go in, ahead of everybody else in line. The door clanged behind them and they descended a long, narrow staircase until they were deep underground, inside a space that looked like any other nightclub. It was cool and dark, except for the flash of white strobes and spinning spotlights. A bar ran along the right side, lit with blue neon tubes.

Agnes stood at the bottom of the stairs, on the edge of the dance floor. The music thumped and vibrated through her ears. Almost immediately, she saw Otto at the bar in a cluster of several men and a woman. He was wearing a pair of Levi's with tan cowboy boots. What was it about Germans—and she was thinking especially of her father—that made them have such an affinity for all things American? Otto saw them and came over, a smile lighting his face.

"Thanks for getting her out," Otto said to Paulina.

Agnes put her hand up. "I don't think it's going to be for long."

"Then let's make it good while you're here."

Otto took hold of her raised hand and lowered it, not letting go, leading her into the club like he would a girlfriend, as if it were a natural thing to do. He gave her hand a slight but purposeful squeeze. He seemed to know everyone, introducing her to friends from the agency and even a table of college buddies from Munich.

They sat down at a table full of Germans he knew from law school.

"You at the agency with Otto?" one friend asked.

"I'm just visiting," Agnes replied. "You?"

"I'm in Frankfurt."

"Are you a lawyer?"

"Nah," he said. He slurped his mixed drink through a straw. "I run money."

"What does that mean?"

"I manage people's investments. But big investments. Like trusts and funds."

Agnes nodded, trying not to reveal her disinterest in the intricacies of running money. Otto had gotten up to say hello to someone who had just come downstairs into the club. A woman dressed in what looked like a French maid's uniform walked by their table and offered them Pall Mall cigarettes. The men at the table ogled her. Agnes ignored them and watched Otto talking on the edge of the dance floor. He gestured a lot when he talked and opened his fingers in a way that made his hands look larger than they were. Another French maid leaned into Agnes's field of vision and offered her a glass of a light brown liquid.

"What is that?"

"It's *Żubrówka*," the investment guy interjected. "Here."

Agnes took the glass. "What's Żubrówka?"

"It's bison vodka," he said. Agnes held the glass under her nose and smelled the liquid, not able to think past the word bison. She couldn't imagine how horrible it must taste. The investment guy nudged her in the elbow. "It won't kill you. It's just a flavored vodka. Flavored with an herb. They say it's an herb from where the bison roam in Poland."

"Does it taste like bison?"

"Just try it," he said.

Agnes took a sip and found it surprisingly sweet and easy to drink. While the investment guy told her about the many investments he ran, she drank two glass of Żubrówka without realizing. Then a voice sounded behind her.

"Schatzie?"

She turned at the word, her heart skipping a beat. Otto stood with is hand out, asking her to dance. Drinking with friends had bolstered Otto's confidence, not that he had much of an issue to begin with. Agnes didn't hesitate to follow him to the dance floor. He started them dancing, keeping a bit of distance between them, but before long he had slid his hand around her waist. Strobe lights spun over them in green, red, and blue. Music from a DJ booth vibrated through the room. Otto spun her away at fast moments, bringing her close and tucking her against his shoulder during slow ones. He hadn't shaved before going out, and his stubble brushed the top of her cheek. His cologne smelled expensive, like the inside of a luxurious car, like a memory she had of Munich. As one song ended, he placed his hand flat on her back, between her shoulder blades and pressed her body against his torso. Then she felt him kiss her hair. She didn't remember how many dances they had, or how many drinks, but they were close to each other all night. Every gesture he made that night confused her and thrilled her at the same time.

She stayed at Ground Zero much later than she planned, and had lost all sight of Paulina after the first hour. At some point, Otto led her to the bar and they found two stools at a quieter corner near the end. He drank another Heineken, and she drank a glass of white wine. She had lost count of how much they had both had to drink. The alcohol flushed her face with a tingling heat and made her extremities feel numb. She leaned toward Otto, feeling bold.

"Do you have a girlfriend?" she asked.

He leaned closer. "Have you seen me with one?"

She held her face just in front of his chin, her heartbeat loud in her ears. Otto brought his hands over her hair on each side of her head, and she didn't move to push them away. He leaned down to kiss her and she let him. The muscular touch of his lips made her feel warm and dizzy, the way the alcohol had made her feel, only more so. When images of Krys blinked through her mind like a lightbulb about to burn out, she only kissed Otto more passionately. She dropped off the stool to stand between his legs and pressed herself to him, his arms encircling her tighter. When he stopped kissing her, he laid his cheek against hers. "Nice to meet your lips," he whispered.

As the music stopped, she pulled away and looked up toward the ceiling. A concrete dome curved above the strobes and spotlights. It looked like the underside of a giant lid from a giant cast iron pot.

"What is this place?"

"It's a bomb shelter. The Soviets put it here." His arms still wrapped around her, he approached like he was about to kiss her, but stopped just short. Instead he grinned, playful, and said, "It was protection from you guys." He pecked her nose with a kiss. "The Americans."

***

Otto brought her back to Polna Street in a taxi. As they rode along Marszałkowska, red and yellow trams clanged down the middle of the avenue. Warsaw was not a beautiful city, but at least its ugliness was hidden at night. There was no real skyline, no lights to admire. Only the Palace of Culture and Science stood in the center of the city, floodlit along the ramparts of each of its four towers like a Soviet fortress. A primitive air still reigned, the Communist leftovers. Eva told her there were plans to build a subway in Warsaw, but construction hadn't started and nobody knew when it would. Half the billboards along Marszałkowska were splashed over with white paint, especially billboards for ladies' lingerie, the handiwork of elderly Catholic women with time on their hands and moral indignation they didn't know what to do with.

On Polna Street, Agnes started to say good-bye to Otto as the taxi pulled up to the curb. He paid the taxi and got out, though he could have just continued home. Agnes's head spun with things she felt she had to say. During the ride home from the club, she had started to feel guilty about Krys. On the sidewalk in front of Eva's building, when Otto leaned in to kiss her good-night, she put her hand up on the middle of his chest to stop him.

"I don't think you should kiss me again until you know something about me."

He took a step back. "Okay."

She rocked to the side, the effects of the alcohol, then struggled to regain her stance. "I was supposed to get married last weekend." He listened, his face not changing. "My wedding was … let's say it was disrupted. My fiancé left, he was angry about something. I guess you could say we are fighting over it now."

Otto tucked his hands in his jeans pockets. "Is it a serious fight?"

"At the moment, yes, I think it is."

Otto looked at his shoes, then glanced up at her. "You'll forgive me if … I hope it stays that way, at least for a little while." He looked sheepish. "I know it's not very kind of me to say."

No, it wasn't kind, she thought, *but I'm so glad he said it.* She kissed him, but on the cheeks three times like the first time they kissed, the way Poles kiss not the way Germans kiss. She stepped away from him with a smile and a shy wave that felt ridiculously girlish. He smiled back and winked. Then he started walking back toward Maszalkowska.

As Agnes passed through the archway of Eva's building she was startled to hear music coming from Piotr's little office. She peered into his doorway as she walked past. The tune was something from Chopin, something she remembered playing in a piano recital. Piotr was tapping it out on an old Casio keyboard he had laid across his desk, the kind of thing they sold at the Polna Market for twenty złoty. When he saw her, he stopped playing.

"*Dobrze?*" Piotr asked, which Agnes knew meant *Good?*

Agnes felt ashamed of herself for being so drunk, a nice Amerykanska girl, so she didn't dare try to say anything or mime anything back. She just smiled and nodded good-night. A moment later, she heard Chopin again.

She crept up the stairs and into Eva's door, pulling it closed. In the spare room, the trundle was still tucked neatly under the bed, no sign of Paulina having come home. Agnes lay across the bed, not bothering to even take off her shoes. She picked up the book from Rilke and flipped to a random page, trying to decipher the meaning of one of his poems with her basic, school-taught German, in her fog of drunkenness.

Tucked into the back of the book, she found an old snapshot of Rilke's grave in Switzerland and a scrap of paper on which Gertrude had written the writer's epitaph, with part of it underlined:

> Rose, oh pure contradiction, _delight_
> _of being no one's_ sleep under so
> many lids.

Delight of being no one's, Agnes thought. _Delight of being no one's._ She wanted to know what it would be like to be Otto's, just for a little while. She imagined it could be good to be Otto's. She fell asleep with the book in her arms and she dreamed, on that particular night, about love and the siege around it.

***

First, she saw the same wheat farmer, Maximillian, the same wife and daughters, the same two men from the SS. Max was forced at gunpoint to give every crop to the soldiers. After five months, his wife could barely stand their predicament. She came to him in the toolshed one steel-gray afternoon in the early spring of 1940, the Irish Setters circling her ankles and barking in a blur of copper-colored fur.

"It's time to leave," she said. It was winter and the soldiers came less often then, only for radishes, potatoes, and squash. "One day they will just kill us. What would stop them? Can't you see how they hate us?"

Max remembered when he went to Warsaw the previous fall,

stupidly looking for an open market. His mind caught sight of a memory, a woman begging a German soldier for food. He had shot her in the mouth.

"Where do you want to go then?" he questioned.

"Just away. Away from Poland." There were tears in her eyes. Max knew it was more from shame than from fear.

Max couldn't look at her. He picked up a spade to clean it, with the intention of bartering it for seeds if he could find someone who needed a spade more than a seed. He would have to start the spring planting in another three weeks. His wife was right, like she always was. Why was he waiting for the soldiers to keep coming back? Why didn't they leave? The soldiers' winter visits were so far apart they would never be able to find Max and his family if they left the farm.

But Max knew somebody would. The world beyond their fence seemed a hundred times more treacherous than their own farm. Every day felt like a calculation. A farmer in Kazimierz Dolny, the nearest village, had told him the British were preparing to liberate Poland. Maybe they would even bring the Americans with them. But the Americans weren't part of the war. Still, somebody had to come. He held onto this thought like he was gripping a high wire with both fists. How can the world let a whole country starve to death? He had confidence enough to stay put. It felt safer.

"We're not leaving Poland."

Just then, the handle of the spade twisted loose and the tool split in half. It was useless. He pitched it against the wall of the shed where it landed with a bang.

"Don't suggest it again," he said.

***

By the spring of 1941, a strange quiet had settled over the countryside around their farm. Less people seemed to be on the road. The same farmer in Kazimierz Dolny said the Germans had built work camps around the country, hundreds of them. All the cities had ghettoes for the Jews. Even if it were true, Max tried to talk himself out of worrying. He was able-bodied and they would want him farming for them, not rotting in a camp. He just had to outlast the war, and they would be fine. But it had been close to two years since Hitler had invaded and occupied Poland and no other country had come to their aid. *When would the rest of the world come to its senses?*

Max lay in bed one night at the end of April that same year, next to his wife. The Irish Setters were quieter than usual. Even peaceful. The weather had turned warmer that week. He could only gather enough seeds to plant half his field that year, but he had seen buds of wheat start to break through what had been planted in the autumn. It gave him confidence, if only fleeting. But their life was still treacherous, and as he predicted it had become difficult to keep them all fed. His family was no more than four bags of bones. The girls' skin had turned yellow. His wife's clothes hung on her like her shoulders were made of wire hangers, the fabric not touching any other part of her body. Although they had been skimming food from what they gave the soldiers, it was barely enough to live on.

That April night, his wife stirred next to him. Her breath moved in and out of her. He rolled nearer and kissed the coil of her ear. After a moment, she turned her face to his. Worry filled her eyes as she came out of her sleep, so he pressed his mouth quickly over hers so he wouldn't have to see it. If she spoke, with her frail voice, it would remind him how hungry she was, what world they were really living in. As he kissed her, he reached for her breasts and felt his fingers circling only a loose pocket of skin that used to be full and round. He wanted to bring her back to the way she was before the war, so he kissed her harder. He kissed her harder than he thought was right, and she let him.

***

He hadn't thought that night about the possibility of conceiving a child. With his wife so emaciated, such a thing seemed impossible. But that was exactly what they had done. When she became pregnant, a strange multiplication seemed to happen within her body. She would eat one potato but would appear in the fullness of her belly to have eaten three. Her hair shined again. The loose pockets of skin that he had held on the night of conception became round and full once more. A pink light tinted the flesh on her face. It was almost as if he had brought her back, like he had wanted. He even convinced himself he had more power over the fate of their lives than he really did.

He knew that bringing another child into the world, one they would barely be able to feed, was pure folly. But when the birth came on a cold morning at the end of January 1942, and he saw that it was a boy, he was overcome with the feeling of a good omen. He had a son. And the Americans had entered the war the month before he was born, after the Japanese had bombed their naval base in Hawaii. The Americans would come to their aid, if nobody else would. The end had to come and they would have made it through.

Two weeks before his son was born, Max had sent the soldiers away with six sacks of radishes. It would be months before they came back for the spring lot. For the first few months of their son's life, he and his wife stayed busy planting and growing as much as they could with their dwindling resources, so their baby boy grew under the watchful care of his sisters. Max found him one afternoon, three months old, in a makeshift pen under the girls' bed. A doll made of hay and tied with blue and green ribbons perched next to him.

Max kneeled and put his hand under the bed, sliding his son out.

"I see they've finally made you their pet," he teased.

His boy grinned, a skill the baby had just begun to master. His mouth was full of bright pink gums. He seemed afraid of nothing, not even being trapped under a bed. Max brought the boy's chin to his own nose and nuzzled it, feeling how soft and perfect he was. His eldest daughter would admonish him later for forgetting the boy's doll under the bed, an oversight that caused his son much agony later on.

In the spring and summer, as expected, the soldiers began returning more frequently. One August day, when Max's son was almost seven months old, the farmer heard their truck approaching from the north. By the time he looked up from what he was doing, the two soldiers were already standing over the boy, who was in front of the house playing with the hay doll his sisters had made for him. Max was furious with his wife whenever she let any of the children play outside, but the years of war had worn her down, and new motherhood had added to her fatigue, and she was more careless lately.

One of the soldiers leaned down to pick up the boy's doll, and move it several feet away. The boy eyed it, then rolled forward onto his hands and crawled toward the doll. He clutched it in a swift movement of his fist and broke into a laugh. The sight of the soldiers so close to his son petrified the farmer. He came upon them as fast as he could without appearing to challenge them.

"Clever boy for pest parents like you," the tall soldier said, grinning like a monkey.

His boy was now pulling himself up on his father's pant leg. Max scooped him up and locked eyes with the soldier. "Come. I have berries in back. And tomatoes," he said with a stony expression. He wanted to smash the soldier in his smiling face, just like that day by Łazienki Park when he had learned that Poland had surrendered. His boy's white blond hair waved in the breeze like the whitish yellow of baby chick feathers, tickling Max's jaw. He walked ahead with his son, careful to keep the soldiers at a distance behind him.

TWELVE

Baby Toes

Early the next morning, Agnes opened her eyes to find Eva standing over her wearing a pained expression. The trundle bed was still empty.

"Is Paulina okay?" Agnes asked.

"She stayed with a friend in the *Stare Miasto*."

Eva held up the crucifix from her living room. "My Jesus fell."

Agnes pulled herself up on her elbows. "What happened?"

"Something must have shaken the wall, I don't know. It fell during the night."

"Did it break?"

Eva inspected it. "No, but I'm useless at hanging things. The nail and hook fell somewhere and I can't find them."

"I find it hard to believe you're useless at anything."

"I'm extremely resourceful about everything in the entire world except for hanging things on a wall. I just didn't get those skills."

"Do you have tools?"

"Why would I have tools if I'm useless at hanging things?"

"Would Piotr have tools?"

"Probably."

While Eva made breakfast, Agnes threw on a pair of shorts and a T-shirt, grabbed the Polish-English dictionary from the kitchen, and went to the bottom of the stairs to look for Piotr. A blue glaze of fluorescent light emanated from his little office. She found him there, sitting on a stool, holding a pencil over a folded back page of the newspaper *Gazeta Wyborcza*.

Agnes looked up the few words she would need as she came down the stairs. When she reached him, she tried to say the words for hammer—*młotek* and the more difficult nail—*gwóźdź*. No matter how many ways she tried to say those two words, Piotr remained puzzled. It was clear that Agnes and the Polish z were not good enough friends yet. With her hands she mimed hammering an imaginary nail with an imaginary hammer. He still looked confused. It might have been clearer if she had brought the Jesus with her.

When she was about to give up, he suddenly seemed to get it. He turned his back to her, scanning a section of cubbies behind his desk. After a moment, he saw what he was looking for, spun back around, and placed a hammer down. Almost there, Agnes thought. She spooled her thumb and finger up tight and tried to make it look like she was rolling an imaginary nail between them. She picked up his broken pencil and, in the margin of his newspaper, she drew an ordinary nail. But as she had always been good at drawing, he got it immediately. He smiled and produced a nail from the drawer of his desk. They both chuckled.

Agnes returned upstairs, and after a little hammering, she replaced the Jesus onto the wall. Jesus looked none the worse for wear.

"What time do we have to leave for Talisz?" she called to Eva in the kitchen.

"Ten minutes, give or take."

Agnes dropped the hammer on the couch and sprinted to the bedroom.

"Sorry, I should have woke you earlier like I promised," Eva called. Agnes whipped open Paulina's closet and pulled out a long white cotton skirt and one of Paulina's lavender tank tops. "But it sounded like you came in pretty late last night."

Had it been late? A recollection of Otto walking away under the streetlights flashed through her mind, and the memory of his kiss in the club. Agnes lifted Gertrude's amber locket from the bedside table and looped it around her neck. They would get a copy of her father's baby picture and leave it at the embassy on the way out of town. At the last minute, she thought to grab an oversized black cardigan, to cover her tank top when she went inside the convent.

***

Eva led Agnes around the corner from the apartment building to where her car, a red Polish Fiat, was parked. The tiny car was shaped like a box with two doors and a hatchback cut at a steep slope at the rear. The square headlights sat far apart, like the eyes of a toad. The car was so tiny it seemed impossible that anyone could fit inside. It reminded Agnes of a little clown car. She couldn't imagine someone like Otto, who had to bend to even fit into an Audi, ever being able to drive one. Even Eva had to scrunch up to sit in the driver's seat. But she seemed pleased with it anyway.

"It's about as powerful as a go-cart," she explained. "But it's cute, isn't it? Its nickname is *Maluch.*" Agnes looked at her quizzically. "In Polish that sort of means *small one*, a name you give to a little child." She started the car and it coughed and sputtered as it turned over. "A friend of mine said that the wait list to get one of these cars during Communism was thousands of people long."

They veered away from Polna Street and into traffic on Marszałkowska Avenue. After the stop at the embassy, they headed west out of the city, the early morning sun rising straight through the back window. The buildings thinned and farms started to appear. "How far is it to Talisz?" Agnes asked.

"Three hours, maybe a little more."

They had started along a divided highway. Agnes glanced at the speedometer, which showed they were traveling slightly over fifty miles an hour. Eva's shoe rested flat against the gas pedal, which was flat against the floor. The car shimmied left and right as it sped down the road.

"I like these drives," Eva said, not seeming to mind how the car struggled with the speed or how it vibrated with road noise. Agnes looked out the window, the bright green grass more like how she thought of Ireland than Poland. In the distance, clusters of tall trees formed mini forests broken up by plots of farmland. "We're coming into the Wielkopolska." Eva gazed ahead of them. "That means *great Poland*. Where the state of Poland was founded a thousand years ago."

Eva steered them around a farmer who was leading an empty horse-drawn cart along the right edge of the road. The cart was made of a weathered, gray wood, the sides high and opened outward, like hands raised to the sky in prayer. Heavy iron chains clanged at the back, holding the gate closed. His horse was light brown with patches of white on his head and lower legs. As they passed, Agnes looked more closely at the farmer and was reminded of something, or someone. He noticed Agnes looking and he gave her a quick glance, but he made no expression of greeting. His mouth stayed closed tight, his lips pulled straight like a seam across his weathered face.

About two hours into the drive they turned onto a different highway that was smaller with less traffic. There were fewer farms and more churches, cemeteries, and village lanes that curved away from the road. Down the lanes, Agnes imagined there would be little town squares with small markets and village churches in which everyone knew everyone else.

While Agnes was lost in thought about village lanes, an eighteen-wheeler passed them at high speed, a flatbed with its contents tied down under a tarp. Agnes felt a pop under her feet. The car swerved to the left, jumping into the lane that the truck had just left. Eva turned the wheel hard and put them back in the right lane, slowing. Now the Maluch was bucking and sluggish.

"Agh! It's a flat," Eva said.

She muscled the wheel to get the car onto the shoulder. They rolled down it at a fast pace, dust kicking up around them. Another farmer had stopped on the shoulder about a hundred feet ahead, his cart piled high with potatoes. Eva pumped the brakes but the car barreled forward at too high a speed for the shoulder.

"Can't you stop?" Agnes asked.

Eva pumped her foot harder. "It's not responding."

Agnes spun her head and looked behind them on the road.

"Put us back up on the highway, in the right lane. There's nobody coming."

Eva tried it but the edge of the asphalt was too high for the Maluch. The hobbled car couldn't climb out of the dirt. She pumped the brakes and beeped at the farmer, who whipped his head around, startled. He jumped away from the cart at the last minute, into the tall grass. Agnes felt a skid and the car slid forward. It stopped just behind the cart, tapping the back of it.

Eva crossed herself. "Mother Mary!" she gasped. "Are you all right?"

"Uh-huh."

Eva leapt from the driver's seat and walked around the back of the car to the farmer, who was already at the front right wheel well of the Maluch, pointing with a dirt-covered hand. Agnes got out of the car. The farmer was saying something to Eva with a commanding tone, like he was giving instructions. Eva took her phone out of her purse and started speaking Polish. The farmer checked the back of his cart and returned to point again at the blown tire. The horse upfront was jumpy, his bridle and reins knocking against the wood of the cart. The farmer knelt at the front wheel and slapped both hands authoritatively on the deflated rubber. Eva hung up.

"Paulina said Otto is nearby today, visiting a friend in Łódz. She's calling him to come get us."

Eva said something to the farmer, and he immediately raised his hands clear of the wheel. He stood and lifted his cap, saying good-bye. Eva smiled so Agnes did the same. The farmer left them and climbed into his cart, taking a seat on the wooden bench at the front. He whipped the horse twice, but the animal only swatted itself with its tail. After two more swats, it sidled forward lazily.

"I'm sorry about this," Eva said.

"Don't be. I've heard *little ones* can be temperamental."

They both laughed.

"The farmer offered to drive us to Talisz in his cart."

"Where would we even sit? On the potatoes?"

"Not only that. It would have taken us the rest of the day to get there."

Agnes gestured to the tire. "Do you have a spare?"

"Not anymore. I bought the car secondhand. The spare was probably used when Gorbachev was talking about perestroika and glasnost!"

Eva pulled an old plaid blanket out of the tiny trunk and spread it over the ground. Eva made another call, this one to a tow truck. They sat in the tall grass, under the shade of a beech tree, waiting for Otto's arrival. Agnes watched the cars passing by on the highway, and she studied the makes and models. Fiats were plentiful, also Renault, and Peugeot. Ford Escorts passed once in a while, and the German cars were notable for being larger and more luxurious than most others, not to mention also driving the fastest as they headed toward the German border.

Agnes's gaze fell for a moment on the grass in front of them and she saw a few potatoes that had fallen from the farmer's cart as he was leaving. She leaned forward, rolled two of them toward her and held one in each hand. As hot as the day was, the potatoes were cool like the inside of a cellar. They were covered with a film of clay and chalk that made them especially soft. Agnes ran her thumb across the ridges made by the eyes, squeezing the potato with her whole hand. It yielded, only a little bit, to the pressure of her fingers. She squeezed it over and over and watched the road. Next to her, Eva had started to nod off.

Close to forty minutes later, while Eva was still dozing, Agnes spotted a black Audi coming up the road in the right lane. It slowed and jumped down onto the shoulder, kicking up dust, braking a medium distance from where the Maluch had slid to a stop. Agnes stood and smoothed her skirt as Otto got out of the car and came over. "I shouldn't have let you girls come out here in that death trap," he said, jerking his hand at the Maluch. "That car isn't really meant to be driven out of the city."

Eva stirred. "It drives out of the city all the time."

"Well come on. I'll drive you both the rest of the way to Talisz."

"What about Eva's car?" Agnes asked.

"Nobody is going to bother that little thing," he said, moving to help Eva stand up.

Eva waved him off. "It's okay, I'll stay," she said. "I already called for a tow. I'll hopefully not be far behind you."

"I don't want you out here by yourself," Agnes said.

"I'll be all right. And your friend is Polish, yes?" Eva asked, straining to see into the passenger seat of Otto's car where a dark-haired man was sitting, talking on a cell phone. "He can do the talking for you?"

"It can be dangerous to let him, but I guess he can," Otto said. "You're sure?"

Eva waved them on. "I promise I'll be right behind you. You'll be okay."

"But you'll be here by yourself?" Agnes worried.

"I promise I won't cause any trouble."

"That's not what I meant!"

"Don't worry about me." Eva reclined on the blanket. "It's a good day for sitting in the grass and going nowhere."

* * *

The two climbed into the Audi and Otto introduced Agnes to his friend from Łodz, Damian Orlowski. Otto merged into traffic and soon they were moving at twice the speed as the Maluch with barely a noise in the car.

"What do you do in Łodz?" she asked.

Damian ran his hand through his hair, a brown mane cut with

layers, very thick. "I'm in the film school," he said. His face was unshaven, and he scrutinized Agnes like he was trying to decide how to light her for a scene.

"What kind of films do you want to make?"

"Ones that people will go see," he said, a wry grin escaping. He was the kind of person who was fond of his own wit.

Agnes tried not to indulge him. She looked past Damian at fences and small cottages, the patches of green, brown, and yellow fields. "I didn't know there was a film school out here."

"You've heard of Roman Polanski?"

"Sure."

"He went to the same film school in Łodz."

As with his wit, Agnes could tell that Damian was impressed with his choice of film school. She turned around to watch the road to avoid the risk of seeming too interested. Otto exited the highway and drove down a ramp, stopping at a traffic light at the bottom. He turned south onto a two-lane road. Damian was in the mood to keep talking.

"What are you going to Talisz for?"

Agnes stumbled through the beginning of an explanation. She would have preferred if Eva had been there to do the talking, but now that she wasn't, she had to bring Damian up to speed. But where to start? When Agnes didn't immediately answer, Otto jumped in to help, and she remembered that the previous night she must have told him why she was in Warsaw, when alcohol had made it easier to talk. Otto gave the barest of details and Agnes wondered if it was because that's all she had shared with him, or if he knew much more and he was protecting her.

After he heard the story, Damian leaned against the backseat. "You're gutsy to come out here," he said. "I think a lot of people would just leave that whole thing alone."

Agnes felt suddenly unsettled. She met Damian's eyes, brown with small rings of light green around the pupils. She hoped she wasn't making a huge mistake in coming out to Talisz, now having no choice but him as her interpreter.

A half hour later, Otto slowed the car and the road turned into a street with stoplights every few blocks. They turned right and passed over a bridge, the old city rising to the left, a cluster of orange roofs reminiscent of a miniature Munich. "We're here," Otto said. "Do you know where the convent is?"

Agnes pulled a map Eva had given her out of her purse and directed him straight ahead. They went over a second bridge and after three more turns, Otto pulled the car over to the curb and parked in front of an iron gate, behind which was a plain, whitewashed building and a cobblestone courtyard. "I think this is it."

"Eva already made an appointment with the Mother Superior. We just give them her name," Agnes explained.

Agnes and Otto followed Damian up the sidewalk to an intercom at the front gate. Damian tapped the button once, which elicited a static beep. A woman on the inside answered. Damian said something in Polish with a commanding tone and the gate buzzed open.

They crossed a cobblestone courtyard. At the main door, they went inside and Damian spoke to a woman sitting at a desk, a young nun in a white shirt and gray calf-length skirt with a white wimple covering her hair. The nun picked up the phone and made a call. Agnes turned in the foyer, looking around. Incense perfumed the hallways, which were faded and reverent in the dim light. Small waist-high alcoves adorned the walls with statuettes: the Virgin Mary, the Saints, the Apostles. Agnes struggled to identify any of them besides Mary.

The young nun hung up the phone and motioned for them to follow. In a moment they were standing in a vestibule outside the office of the Mother Superior. There were two desks in the vestibule. A nun sat behind each one, typing, eyeing them cautiously.

"You should wait out here," Damian whispered to Agnes.

"Why?"

He inspected her and lowered his voice further, until it was almost inaudible. "Because your face looks nervous."

Agnes was immediately self-conscious of her facial appearance. "But it's my appointment."

"Let me warm her up for you."

Warm her up? Agnes thought. Reluctantly, she sat and Otto stayed with her. Damian walked into the office and, as he entered, Agnes could see inside: the space was long like a boxcar, the walls painted a hospital white. A large wooden cross hung on the wall at the far end, behind an oak desk. Damian disappeared through the door and shut it gently. Agnes and Otto sat back while the eyes of the typing nuns flicked up occasionally to watch them.

"He's very dramatic, your friend. How do you know him?" Agnes asked.

"We went to the same summer camp in England when we were teenagers. Just kept in touch. He talked me into coming over to Poland for a while when I was fed up with law school."

"So he's a good friend?"

"One of my best."

The door opened and Damian looked at both of them. "Agnes? Come on in."

Agnes stood up and left Otto sitting outside to wait so the Mother Superior wouldn't feel overwhelmed by the volume of visitors. As she reached the door, Damian eyed her critically. "Wait." He put his hand on her shoulder. "Can you look less … scared?"

Agnes threw up her hands. "I don't know what I'm doing that makes me look nervous or scared."

"Your eyes are too far open. Close them for a few seconds, then open them again. But, you know, more relaxed."

Agnes did as instructed. "How's that?"

Damian was disappointed. "Now you look lost. But it's better than scared."

Agnes followed him in, exasperated. Damian shut the door and sat with Agnes in front of the Mother Superior's desk. The Mother Superior and Damian began talking, and Agnes did what she could to follow each person's body language. At one point, Damian sat forward. Agnes thought she heard him use the word for children, and later the words for World War II. The features on the Mother Superior's face drew together, as if she had caught a whiff of sour milk. Damian kept talking, using his hands more, trying to convince her of something. His voice softened. He held out his hand in front of Agnes, as if she were an exhibit in a trial. The Mother Superior looked a long time at Agnes, her eyes becoming gentler. She got out of her chair and walked around the side of the desk to stand in front of Agnes.

"I told her about your father," Damian said in a low voice. "I told her your father was here during the war."

"But we don't know if he *was*," Agnes hissed from one side of her mouth. "That's why we came."

The Mother Superior held out her hand, laid it on top of Agnes's head, and started to say a prayer. Agnes recognized some of it from when she had heard Eva say prayers in Polish at home. Agnes shot a look at Damian, who was stone-faced, solemnly focused on the prayer, or pretending to be. After she was done praying, the Mother Superior walked to face the window and started to talk, her back to them, while Damian translated.

"She said she was a child in the town of Talisz during the war, when orphans were brought to the convent ... there were so many orphans that conditions became desperate ... she remembers when the nuns went through the streets of the town begging for food ... they said they only had enough food to feed the children one meal a day." Agnes watched the Mother Superior, her back straight, her hands together. "They heard that a baby died one spring of starvation and suddenly the nuns weren't begging in the streets anymore ... the rumor was that the convent had been taken over by the Nazis and the children expelled, but nobody knew where any of them went."

The Mother Superior turned around to face them and Damian continued to translate what she said, with brief pauses that made every sentence feel more dramatic.

"She says that years later, when she became head of the convent ... she learned that the Sisters had worked with the Germans to send the youngest children to Germany ... to save them. The older ones were sent to work camps in Poland and Germany ... Before the Germans took control of the convent, the Sisters hid all the records of the children's families because some of the children were Jewish."

"Do they know where the records were hidden?" Agnes asked.

Damian and the Mother Superior exchanged words and then she slid the bottom right-hand drawer of her desk open. "She says that they couldn't locate the records, but that they started to keep a list of parents ... who came asking for their children after the war." The Mother Superior wedged a thin wooden panel loose from the drawer, a false bottom, and put it on top of the desk. From the drawer, she pulled out a black and white photograph of a baby's foot, a close-up that showed the spaces between the child's toes. Adult fingers were in the frame of the picture, holding the toes apart. She spoke and shortly after Damian continued. "She said the Sisters marked each child who was taken away ... between the toes of the left foot, where the mark would likely not be found." Agnes could see the marks between the toes in the picture: T+ between the big toe and second toe, then numbers between each of the next toes, then two initials between the fourth toe and the pinky. "She says the first marking meant the baby had been at the convent in Talisz, then the baby's birth month, then birth year, then the two initials of the mother."

"So if my father has these markings in between his toes, he came from Talisz?"

"She says Talisz wasn't the only place to do this ... it became a kind of underground system to track young children who were forcibly separated from their parents. Even the female German guards and nurses in many of the concentration camps did this. She says it seemed to be happening to millions of children."

Agnes marveled at the image of the baby's toes and the markings.

"Will she let me have a copy of the list of parents?"

Damian inquired and then shook his head. "No. She says it's confidential."

Agnes spoke directly to the Mother Superior rather than Damian, raising her voice and using a tone that she knew probably lacked respect. "But I'm trying to find my father's family. Doesn't she understand I have almost no information to go on?"

Damian put his hand on Agnes's arm to calm her as the Mother Superior said a few words. "She knows," Damian said. "She said your father should look for these markings and if he has them, come back." Agnes put her head in her hands. "If his markings have the T+, she says she'll give you the list. But you have to bring him with you."

Agnes's head sunk further. "*With me?*"

The Mother Superior said nothing more. They stood up and Damian thanked her. The Mother Superior rose and brought her hands flatly together. She recited another short prayer to Agnes in Polish that Damian didn't attempt to translate.

Outside in the waiting room, Otto looked up as they came out of the office. Agnes passed him and walked quickly into the corridor, to get out of the earshot of the typing nuns at the desks outside the Mother Superior's office.

"What if he has these markings, Damian?"

"Then it would be a big breakthrough, wouldn't it?" Damian said.

"What markings?" Otto asked.

They exited through the courtyard while Damian explained to Otto what the Mother Superior had told them. Otto opened the car door for Agnes and they all got in. "She made it all sound rather innocent," Agnes said.

"What do you mean?" Otto asked.

"The book I'm reading says the nuns here were actively helping Germanize the kids, teaching them German, forging birth certificates. It wasn't so innocent."

Damian's voice turned philosophical. "Maybe they really were just trying to save them. Maybe that was the *way* to save them. Isn't that what Sophie tried to do for her son, you know, because he was blond and blue-eyed? In that movie *Sophie's Choice*?"

"It was actually a book before it was a movie," Agnes retorted. "And yes, she did."

Agnes fished in her purse for the cell phone Paulina had gotten for her. "I should call my mom. Can I call the States on this? I never tried."

Otto examined it. "Not this one, but you can use mine." He pulled a phone out of his jeans pocket and handed it over.

"Won't it be expensive to call the States on this?" she asked.

"Nope. It's on a global system. You can call anywhere."

Agnes looked at both of them, then back at the phone, and waited. "Can I … call now?"

"Oh, sorry," Otto said. "We'll take a walk."

They got out of the car and started walking up the street, around a curve, until Agnes couldn't see them anymore. The car was hot, the black leather like a heating pad under her thighs. She cracked the window, looked up at the convent, and realized one of the nuns might hear her so she put the window up again despite the suffocating heat. It would be morning in Chicago. When she reached her mother, she didn't even take time for small talk. She explained the markings and where they would be on her father's body. She didn't hear her mother take out a cigarette, which Agnes interpreted as a sign of shock.

"They *marked* babies?"

"She says there could have been millions of kids. I saw a picture of it, Mom."

"Honestly … I've never looked in between my husband's toes before. Ever."

"Has he ever said anything about it? Hinted at it?" Agnes closed her eyes and tried to imagine all the scenarios. "Has he ever resisted wearing sandals or flip-flops?"

"He almost never wears that kind of stuff, you know how he is. He would go to the pool in a dress shirt and tie if we didn't stop him."

"Can you look at his toes?"

"I can't imagine how I would do that right now. I don't even live at home for the moment."

"You have to figure out a way."

"You really think this is some kind of lead?"

"It's the best lead so far. This place was a major ... processing center, I guess you could call it. He could have been here. And if not here, they said the same kind of markings were used in other places. So if he was born in Poland, and then transferred to Germany, it's very likely there is some mark on him somewhere."

"The only way I could really get a good look at his feet is if we made up."

Agnes warmed. "Good, then make up. That would make me feel better either way."

After Agnes hung up with her mother, she called Eva's cell phone.

"A mechanic came with a spare," Eva said. "They fixed it on the road. I'm headed to Poznań to get the list of birth registrations there."

"Can I meet you there?"

"It would take Otto pretty far out of his way, and I would be backtracking to get you. Why don't I meet you back in Warsaw?"

"Are you sure? It's a lot of driving. Shouldn't I be there when you talk to them?"

"I would do all the talking anyway. Just go home with Otto. I'll meet you there, hopefully with some information."

Agnes hung up and put her head back on the seat and closed her eyes. Her father had to have these markings, it seemed a certainty to her. In the warmth of the car, her mind felt slow and tired. The lack of sleep from the late night before was starting to catch up with her. She probably dozed, because when she heard the doors open, it made her jump and her eyes flew open. Otto slid into the seat next to her and Damian climbed in the back. She told Otto they should just head back to Warsaw, that Eva's car was fixed and she would meet them there.

"You called your mom?" Damian asked.

"Yeah."

"Why not your dad? They're his toes."

Damian's exigency was starting to lose its charm. She ignored him and spoke to Otto. "My father has webbed toes on his left foot. His second and third toes are stuck together."

"Then they would have just marked him in between the toes of the other foot, don't you think?"

Agnes remembered once water skiing with her father on a lake in Minnesota. They sat next to each other on a dock waiting for the speedboat to make a loop around the lake and pick them up. She remembered laughing with her father about his so-called duck feet. He wiggled the toes on the left foot, then on the right, which wasn't webbed. She tried to remember what the toes on the right foot looked like, if she remembered seeing anything in between them. But it was impossible; the memories didn't contain such detail, only feelings. The feelings had been good, the sound of his laughter and hers blending together like ripples on the water's surface.

All three of them remained quiet during the drive back to Warsaw, where Otto was bringing Damian for the weekend. She was relieved that Otto didn't quiz her the same way Damian had. Though he seemed to keep one concerned eye on her during every mile they drove back to the capital city.

THIRTEEN

The Clue of the Amber Locket

Eva appeared at home late Friday night, exhausted. She had waited close to two hours outside the office of the manager of the *Urząd Stanu Cywilnego* in Poznań. He hadn't wanted to cooperate, finding her request for a list of births from more than fifty years ago—and during the war—to be highly irregular. *That information is private for the persons who were born then,* he insisted. *If it's private, why is it recorded in a public office?* she shot back. This gamesmanship continued until the manager took a long coffee break near closing time, and his secretary took pity on Eva's request. Eva left with a list of every child born in or near the city of Poznań in the last half of 1941, printed from records that had just the month before been made electronic.

Back at home, Eva explained the list to Paulina and Agnes.

"She cautioned me that it's somewhat incomplete."

The three of them sat together on the living room couch. Eva laid the twenty-five-page transcript on the coffee table and they all regarded it as if it were a set of Biblical scrolls. "These are the records they were able to recover from Berlin after the war, combined with records that were left in Poznań."

Agnes scanned the typewritten transcript. It was a strange mess of Polish and German names: Werner, Fritz, and Wolfgang interspersed between Andrzej, Jarosław, and Krzysztof. To Agnes's American eye, the list almost looked pleasantly multicultural.

"Where are the ones named Bernd? This looks alphabetical by last name," Paulina asked.

"It is. Unfortunately we just have to pick through it," Eva replied. "The secretary who gave it to me couldn't figure out how to sort the list any other way." Eva picked up the first page. "She told me that not all of these births were necessarily forged or Germanized Polish births. Poznań was part of the German Empire for almost fifty years, until the end of World War I. Some German families have been in Poznań for generations."

Agnes was already reading the second page. "I found one— Bernd Anstel, born August 5, 1941," she said. She marked it and scanned to the bottom of the page, picking up the next one. "Here, Bernd Arnold, born October 20." She put another mark.

"This is only one city," Paulina said. "Poland has hundreds of cities. How do we look through all their lists?"

Agnes stopped reading. "Did any of the other cities you called have Bernds on their birth registration lists?"

"They wouldn't tell me on the phone. Each one has the same procedure—send a written request and payment, and they'll send a list in a few weeks or months, unless we go in person like I did in Poznań. Then we'll see what's on the list and if it even helps us. We got lucky in Poznań. It was this same secretary who gave me the list that I had first talked to on the phone. She was sympathetic. Most of them won't be, it's not really a Polish thing … we're not quick to sympathize."

The kitchen clock ticked six minutes past midnight when they finished looking through the twenty-five typed pages. They had found eighty-six boys named Bernd who were born in the Poznań region in the last half of 1941, with the names of the parents and grandparents of each child.

"Do we go house by house?" Paulina asked.

Agnes was on the floor with her knees pulled up. "And if we do find them, how do we get them to prove my father is their son?"

"When will the woman from the embassy have a list of Displaced Persons?" Eva asked.

"She didn't know. She just said it was in the works."

"Then when you have that list, we can see if any of these names match. Until then, we go city by city. We call all of them."

Agnes's head grew heavy. She gathered the twenty-five pages of birth registrations, marked with the eighty-six boys named Bernd. "I'm going to bed." She held the list up. "Thank you for this, Eva."

It occurred to her that they were only looking for boys named Bernd, and she remembered Bobbie Price's advice to look for other names, Polish names, especially ones with a B or a D in them. But what names?

As she walked into the spare room, she heard a cell phone ring and Paulina start to talk to whoever was calling. A moment later, Paulina called to her: "It's Otto and Damian. They want to know if we're coming out. Tonight is Otto's actual birthday."

For a moment, Agnes thought about it, but sitting on her bed soon led to lying down, and in a few moments she stopped thinking about anything. Like the night before, she was still in her clothes and didn't have the energy to change. "You can go," she murmured. "I just can't, not tonight."

Her eyelids fell closed, dead weights, like the ballast off the side of a boat. She was so tired that for once she didn't dream of anything.

***

When Agnes woke on Saturday morning, the sun in the courtyard was already high. She was supposed to be back at work in Chicago on Monday, as Mrs. Sobota, returned from her honeymoon. She hadn't bought a return ticket to Chicago for the next day and didn't think she would, so she would have to come up with a story for her boss and call him on Monday morning.

She rose and went to the bathroom, looking at herself in the mirror. After her eyes adjusted, she took note of the mascara she had forgotten to remove from the day before. It had left large black smudges under her eyes. Her skin looked pasty and irritated from sleeping with makeup on and her hair was stuck in a loose ponytail, forming a knot of blond hair on one side of her head. She looked down at her neck and noticed there was nothing hanging there. Her hands flew to her neck. She went back to the bed and searched through the sheets and under the pillow. There was no sign of it. She checked on the floor, under the bed, in between the pages of the Poznań list. The locket was nowhere.

"Eva!" she called. "My locket's gone!"

Agnes ran from the bedroom and searched on the floor near the couch, between the couch cushions, on the coffee and end tables. Eva appeared, looking concerned.

"You mean the one from your grandmother?"

"It's gone." Agnes slumped on the couch, trying to think when she last felt it on her neck. "Oh, Eva. How could I have lost that thing?"

"Let's check the stairwell and the sidewalk outside. Maybe it fell as you were coming in?"

They both exited the apartment and went into the stairwell. They crept down, step by step, scanning every surface as they descended. They reached the bottom and still hadn't found it. Agnes was too tired, and the loss of the locket and the Goliath task ahead of searching birth registrations in a country of forty million people was starting to overwhelm her. She fell to a sitting position on the bottom step, her feet in the cobblestone driveway, and dropped her head into her hands. She heard Eva start to speak Polish. Piotr was there.

Her breaths came in and out, labored, as she tried to let go of her anxiety, to let go of her need to have the locket back. It was just a locket. She would be all right without it. It wasn't everything. But at the same time, it felt like everything. It felt like the only concrete thing she had. And it was gone.

A hand came down, gently, on the top of her head. It wasn't Eva's. It was thin and large and there was strength in the tips of the fingers. "*Spokojne,*" Piotr whispered over her. "*Spokojne.*"

Agnes had seen Big Bird say this to a crying baby during a show the week before. Big Bird rocked the baby in a cradle, saying this word, and then four older children sang a lullaby to it. After a moment, the baby obediently stopped crying. Agnes didn't know what the word meant, but it started to have the same effect on her that it had on the baby. She felt better.

Outside, she heard a car pulling up on the curb. Otto and Paulina walked through the archway a minute later.

"Oh good, you're here," Otto said.

Agnes pulled the tie of her disheveled ponytail out in a quick yank and straightened her hair. She remembered the black marks of mascara. There wasn't much she could do and admitted to herself that for the moment, she was beyond caring about appearances. Even in front of Otto. He stepped toward her and pulled something out of his pocket.

"I think you left this in my car yesterday. I guess it dropped."

Agnes leaped at him. "My locket! You found it!"

"It was on the floor, on the passenger side. I figured it had to be yours as I haven't had a locket-wearing passenger in my car for quite some time." He winked. "By the way, that Adam is a cute baby," he said.

Agnes stared. "Who is Adam?"

"On the back of the locket," Otto pointed. "The name is engraved—Adam."

Agnes flipped it over and looked at the scratched silver back. Along one side were the letters A-D-A-M. She could hardly believe her eyes. There was his name, all this time, hung around her neck. She sprang to her feet, turned on her heels, and started taking the stairs two at a time. Eva and Paulina ran up behind her.

"Where are you all going?" Otto called from the driveway.

Agnes thrust open the apartment door, her heart racing. "How could I not have looked at the back of the damn locket?"

All three of them tumbled into the spare bedroom and dove at the Poznań list on the bedside table, scanning it for boys named Adam. There were already twenty on the first page Agnes looked at.

"Is this a popular name?" she asked.

"Adam Bernard Mickiewicz," Eva announced with an important air.

Agnes shot a look at the page Eva was holding. "Adam Bernard? That name's on the list?"

"Oh, no. He is Poland's national poet. He's considered one of the greatest writers in all of Polish literature. So what that means is yes, the name Adam is popular."

Agnes sat on the bed and stopped reading down the list. Otto had come upstairs and was standing in the doorway of the spare room. "Can I help with anything?"

Agnes's eyes met Otto's. "You found his name," she said, disbelieving.

A revised picture of her father formed in her imagination, with the name Adam next to it. It had the hard consonant D, like Bobbie said. She got up from the bed and walked into the living room. "I have to call Gertrude."

Otto followed her and Paulina and Eva both filled the living room doorway, holding sections of the Poznań list. Agnes dialed Gertrude's apartment in Berlin and waited. A woman answered, but it wasn't Gertrude.

"Is Gertrude there?" Agnes asked in German.

"This is Freya. I am Gertrude's nurse."

A nurse? "Is she okay?"

"Could I know who is calling?"

"This is Gertrude's granddaughter, Agnes."

"Then I'm sorry to tell you … she is now quite unwell."

Agnes clutched her chest. "Oh, God. How …"

The question was *How long?* but Agnes couldn't ask it. Freya spoke as if she anticipated the question anyway.

"They said it was only a matter of days."

"My father is in Chicago, her son. Did you notify him?"

"Not at the moment, no."

A matter of days and they didn't notify her son? "I'm going to call him now. He'll be there. I'm coming, too."

"We'll look for you both, dear," Freya said.

***

Agnes landed at Berlin Tegel less than four hours later, on Saturday afternoon. Otto had driven her straight to Okęcie Airport so she could get the first plane to Berlin.

"I'm sorry about skipping your birthday yesterday," she told him as they said good-bye at the curb.

"Are you kidding? This isn't the time," he held her shoulders. "We'll talk about birthdays another day."

"We will?"

"Maybe yours?"

"Mine's in October."

"Then we have time to plan a good celebration." He kissed her three times on the cheek, but slowly, as if thinking about kissing her on the mouth, but did not. "Will you be okay?" he asked tenderly.

Agnes nodded. "I'll call you guys," she said. "After I see Gertrude."

Agnes stepped back from him and into the small terminal of Okęcie. They waved to each other until the sliding doors closed and made it impossible for Agnes to see anything but herself.

***

When Agnes arrived at Gertrude's apartment in Charlottenburg. Nurse Freya answered the door. Narrow eyes pierced her face and a brittle ball of gray hair stood like a sentry at the nape of her neck. Agnes followed her into the bedroom where Gertrude was lying straight and flat in her bed, appearing to be asleep.

The room smelled like antiseptic, but somewhere Agnes could still detect Gertrude's own smell—chamomile and baby shampoo.

Agnes crouched on a small stool and leaned into the white skirt and cloud-like duvet that hung down the side of the bed. On the bedside table, a small bunch of white edelweiss was tucked into a silver vase. Next to it stood a framed picture of a young couple, teenagers, who she guessed were a young Gertrude with Albert. They stood on the edge of a dock, a luxurious ocean liner looming behind them. Albert had his hand loosely around her waist and was looking at her, smiling. Gertrude's head was slightly back and her mouth was open wider than a normal smile, as if the photographer had caught her in the middle of a laugh. Maybe something Albert said. They both looked so young and happy. The picture was smaller than the frame, and Agnes could make out something written in ink on the white border: *Vaterland, Hoboken 1915.*

She turned from the picture and peered at Gertrude's sleeping figure. Her face had no makeup and her white hair was undone, combed back off of her pale forehead and falling in thin strands around her on the pillow. Her eyelids were still and stretched over the round protrusions of her eyeballs. Agnes sat on the stool for a long while and studied her, trying to imagine how long a life she had lived since being a teenage girl in 1915 until now, nearly eighty years later.

Gertrude's lids drifted open for a moment, and her body flinched under the duvet. Agnes had been holding the locket in the palm of her hand and held it close to Gertrude's face so she could see.

"I received it," Agnes said. "I'm wearing it."

Gertrude didn't make any movement, but somewhere under the skin of her forehead and eyes Agnes felt like she saw some glint of comprehension, some peace.

"Can Gertrude hear me?" Agnes asked Freya.

"It's unlikely."

Agnes wanted Freya to go away. "Could you leave me with her for a few minutes?"

Freya retreated into the hallway, stepping a few paces toward the living room, but she was still within earshot. Agnes moved to the door and shut it gently. She came back to crouch on the stool by Gertrude's bed. Her cheeks, mouth, chin, and neck were as motionless and white as Carrera marble. The only sign of life was the small flutter of her eyelids and a monitor next to the bed that beeped out her heart rate. Agnes alternated between extreme pity and a blinding anger. If Gertrude died, the identity of her father's parents might also die. Agnes thought about all the Adams on the Poznań list. There were hundreds. And that was only one city, and she wasn't sure she was even looking for the right name. How would she ever know who her father was if Gertrude died now, if she knew and could tell them? Why wouldn't she tell them?

Agnes held up the locket again, turning it to show the backside. "His name was Adam?" she asked. Gertrude made no sound or movement. Agnes asked it again. Again no sound or movement. "I'm trying to find some record of his birth. I looked in Poznań. I'm looking in every city, in Warsaw, Krakow. Am I looking in the right place? Am I looking for the right thing?"

Gertrude didn't stir. Agnes opened the locket to reveal the baby picture of her father—his cheerfully gummy smile, the flyaway blond hair. Gertrude's eyelids were half open. Agnes held the picture over Gertrude's reclined face, where she imagined Gertrude could see it if able to see. Agnes held it until her arm started to hurt. Gertrude didn't make any noise or move any part of her body. The heart monitor beeped at the same rate it had been beeping since Agnes walked in.

Agnes shifted on the stool and looked around the room. Her eyes fell on the closet, the bureau, another antique desk by the window, and a small bookcase. Did she dare rummage through Gertrude's things looking for clues? Agnes closed her eyes and gave it a thought, but just as quickly realized the indignity of nosing through a woman's personal things while she lay dying. No matter what Agnes needed to know, she wasn't going to find it that day, not that way.

Freya knocked at the door. "Are you fine here?"

"Yes, thank you. I'm going to sit for a while. I'm staying in

Berlin tonight, and my father will be here tomorrow."

"Do you want me to make up one of the other beds for you?" Freya offered.

Agnes thanked her and Freya slipped away again.

***

On Sunday morning, Agnes was relieved to open the door to the apartment and see both her parents standing there together. They had reconciled and it gave Agnes more relief than she expected.

She and her parents took turns sitting next to Gertrude's bed. Her father read to his Mamo late into the night on Sunday and again on Monday, from another book by Rilke. During one of his reading sessions, Agnes took her mother into the kitchen and showed her the amber locket.

"Gertrude sent this to me," she said. She showed her mother the baby picture inside. "There is a name on the back of the locket." She turned it over. "Adam."

Her mother took the locket in her palm and looked closer at the name. "Why would it say Adam?"

Agnes explained the naming technique the Nazis employed for stolen children. "This could be Papa's name, couldn't it? If he had another name, a Polish name. Why else would Gertrude have a locket with a boy's name 'Adam' on the back of it?"

Her mother handed her back the locket, after looking again at the picture. "There are any number of reasons it says Adam. It could be a secondhand locket. Did you think of that?"

No, Agnes hadn't. She looked down at it and closed her fingers around the face.

"I looked at his feet, Agnes," her mother said.

"And?"

Her mother hitched open the kitchen window, sitting on the sill. She pulled a pack of cigarettes out of her purse and eyed the door, as if expecting an admonition from Nurse Freya at any moment. "There's nothing there."

***

Agnes returned to Warsaw on Tuesday morning. Her parents planned to stay with Gertrude as long as they could. During the three days Agnes was there, Gertrude's condition hadn't improved or worsened. Her life seemed suspended at the very edge of its end, with them only able to watch and do nothing.

Her parents tried to talk Agnes into remaining and coming home with them to Chicago. It was tempting, she told Otto, when they talked on the phone Monday night.

"All the leads I thought I had, now they feel like phantoms," Agnes told him.

"I think you're doing the right thing," he replied. "Fine if your leads are phantoms. They could lead to real ones, ones that aren't phantoms. Couldn't they?"

"My father could just be German, with missing papers."

"He could. But you seem to have a strong feeling now that he's not." Agnes was silent and Otto continued. "I told you, if you want help, you just ask. Tell me what I can do."

"I don't know what to tell you to do, honestly. But thanks."

"Are you going back to Chicago?"

"I'll come back to Warsaw tomorrow. But I think it's just to say good-bye. Then yes, I think I need to go back to Chicago. I've about used up all the vacation time I took for my honeymoon and had to ask for more for this week. It's time I went home."

"Then I'll pick you up at Okęcie tomorrow?"

She told him when her flight arrived and they hung up. After they hung up, she kept her hand on the top of the phone for a moment, thinking of the next day, realizing with some amount of guilt that she was dying to see him again.

***

As he promised, Otto was waiting for her in his black Audi at the curb outside of the Okęcie terminal. She emerged through a throng of mafia taxi drivers and spotted him getting out of his car. They kissed on the cheek three times and again she wished it were more of a kiss. He had kept a respectful distance since she told him about being engaged, and she had to admire his respect for her. But the trouble was, the admiration only made her want to kiss him more.

They drove toward the center of the city, Otto taking the traffic circles in smooth shifts of the gears, passing the clusters of umbrellas at roadside food stands, the whitewashed lingerie billboards, the flower carts and the gray rectangles of apartment blocks. When they pulled up on Polna Street, Agnes looked across at the Polna Market, which was in its full Tuesday afternoon swing. She remembered what her mother had suggested, about the locket possibly being secondhand.

"There's someone at the market I want to talk to," she said.

She got out and slammed the door, crossing the street. Otto followed. Agnes walked up the sidewalk to the far end, the section with the flea market, and entered between two Maluchs parked in the grass lot, their rear doors open and displaying handmade linens and loads of gleaming silverware. *Someone's grandmother must have died,* Agnes thought, then was shocked at herself for thinking it.

She walked by the man selling Soviet relics arranged on a plastic tarp—he had an abundance of black fur hats that hot day. A man and woman selling antique phonographs called out to her as she passed. She then spotted the necklace man with the Easter bag. She motioned to Otto, who was doing his best to keep up. The same amorous teenage boy was there, in his lawn chair, sitting behind the green felt jewelry table. His father was leaning against a Peugeot minivan holding a cigar, his arms crossed and resting on the top of a beer gut. Agnes waved to the boy.

"I wanted to ask you and your father about something," she said.

The boy popped out of his chair and came to her. She pulled the amber locket off her neck and showed it to him. "It's full of ambers. I was wondering if your father might know anything about this necklace, if it came from Poland? There's a boy's name on the back," she turned the locket over, "a Polish name."

The boy raised his eyebrows. "May I?"

Agnes let the locket drop into his palm. He turned and showed it to his father and they exchanged a few words. The father didn't look at all interested in examining the necklace. He looked more bothered by having his time alone with a cigar interrupted. The boy returned to Agnes.

"He says it's just plain locket, possibly of Polish amber. He can't tell. But he says name on the back isn't Adam, it's Adamska. Look," he ran his finger along the bottom edge of the locket, "the *ska* has just been worn away."

Agnes craned over it and sure enough, the last three letters of Adamska had all but disappeared. The angle of part of the *k* was still visible and she knew he was right.

"Is that a person's name?" she asked.

"It was a store." He held up the locket and laid it in her palm. "This locket was certainly bought at Jubiler Adamska. It was very important jeweler in Warsaw, some years ago. He says they closed when the Martial Law came."

"When was that?"

"1981."

"Where was the store when it was open?"

The boy turned and asked his father, then faced Agnes. "He says it was on Nowy Świat—New World Street, before you get to the area of Royal Castle."

Agnes glanced at Otto, who she could tell from the look of calculation in his face was already planning the fastest way to drive there.

"Thanks for your help," she said to both of them.

The father grunted and popped the cigar back in his mouth.

***

They crossed town in mid-afternoon traffic that seemed unusually thick for a Tuesday in July.

"Am I keeping you from work?" Agnes asked.

"I told them I had to scout a location out of town today. A fib, but it was for a good cause don't you think?"

He winked at her. She had begun to adore his wink.

"Do you speak any Polish?" she asked.

"I can order a beer or pizza delivery. That's about it."

"I should ask Paulina to meet us." Agnes phoned her while Otto looked for a place to park near the Charles de Gaulle roundabout, where the elegant stretch of road called Nowy Świat—New World—began. Paulina told them she would meet them in front of a Latin tapas bar called El Corazón.

As they waited outside El Corazón, Agnes looked down Nowy Świat. It was a long, gently curved street with a cobblestone sidewalk and a narrow lane down the middle, only wide enough for small cars to slip by each other. Gas lanterns perched at the top of tall black lampposts. Pots of fully bloomed red geraniums hung from the equidistant lampposts, lining the street with dots of red like beads on a necklace. Awnings and umbrellas shaded the sidewalk in front of cafes and bakeries.

Once, when she was twelve years old, Agnes had gone with her parents to New York City. Agnes remembered Fifth Avenue most of all, how important it looked, how the sidewalk gleamed, how every shop had deep, dreamlike windows displaying minks and jewelry, elegant women's clothing, scarves, and handbags. Things the average person could never afford. New carpet aromas, air conditioning, and the scent of expensive perfume wafted out of every doorway. Nowy Świat reminded her of Fifth Avenue. But, winding toward the medieval Old Town, the burgher's rows of townhouses, and eventually leading to another lovely street and the onion-domed tower of the Royal Castle, Nowy Świat had a fairy-tale aura Fifth Avenue could never have. It just wasn't old enough. It hadn't to endure the same history. Otto noticed her admiring the neighborhood.

"It's really something what they were able to reconstruct here after the war," he remarked.

Agnes gaped. "This is a reconstruction?"

"Almost every brick. This part of town was the first to go. It was Poland's heritage. After D day, when it was clear the German army was going to lose the war, they bombed all of Warsaw and came through this part with flame hoses to destroy each building door by door." Otto kicked his feet at a crack in the sidewalk. "There almost wasn't a brick standing at the end of 1944. They said it looked like Ezekiel's field, from the Bible."

Agnes heard the remorse in Otto's voice. "You know a lot about this."

"It's just a shame. There was no point to it really. The city started out having over a million people living in it. By the end, there were only 100,000 or so." Otto looked down the street. "Warsaw was meant to be wiped out forever."

"That's sad to imagine." She waited for him to say more but he didn't. "What made you want to come live here?"

He put his hand on her shoulder, like her father had in Berlin, and gave a little squeeze. "I guess I have a soft spot for survivors."

Next to them at the curb, the back door of a Mercedes taxi swung open and Paulina exited. They started walking north up Nowy Świat.

"How will we know where the jewelry shop was? Did the guy at the market give you an address?" Paulina asked.

Agnes shook her head. "He just said it was along this street. Maybe one of these shopkeepers knew them."

Paulina went into a women's clothing store where three mannequins with expensive handbags dangling from their wrists posed in the window. She came out a minute later.

"This shop opened last year. They haven't heard of the Jubiler Adamska. They told me there is a jewelry shop on the same side of the street, down a bit more. We should ask in there."

They walked past more shops.

"Maybe that one," Otto pointed to a small shop with a blue awning. Across the front edge of the awning, in white letters, was written Jubiler Kasia Moda. They hurried to it.

Agnes opened the door and led Paulina and Otto inside. A

brunette with black-framed reading glasses stood behind a display case at the rear of the store. The shop was dim, the walls covered in royal blue velvet, the same blue as the awning. When they entered, it felt like stepping inside a jewelry box.

The woman greeted them in Polish and Paulina started talking. Agnes pulled the locket off her neck and handed it to Paulina, who showed it to the jeweler. While they talked, Agnes scanned the cases in the shop and saw one case with the same small amulets she had seen at the Polna Market. She pointed to them and when there was a pause in the exchange between the jeweler and Paulina, she said "Very beautiful," in English. The jeweler nodded blankly and Agnes figured she hadn't understood. After a minute more, Paulina gathered the three of them in a corner by the shop window.

"So we have some good luck. Kasia is the owner of the shop." Paulina tipped her head to the jeweler. "She said she took over this shop about ten years ago after it had been empty for a few years during Martial Law. She said that before her, this was the shop of the Jubiler Adamska. She confirmed that this locket was bought from Adamska. She doesn't have sales records, but she told me that the owner …" Paulina paused and looked at the case of miniature amulets Agnes had been admiring before. "Well, Agnes, when you pointed to the amulets in that glass case, she happened to mention to me that when the Adamska shop first opened in the 1960s, they only made one kind of jewelry."

"The baby amulets?"

"That's right."

Agnes remembered what the kid at the flea market had told her, about how the amulets had been gifted to babies for protection *from any kind of danger.* She looked again at the glass case. In her mind, the bright, blue color of the shop began to magically turn shades darker, like a deep sea.

Paulina explained more. "She said the woman who owned the shop, Daria Adamska, had lost her brother during World War II when he was still a baby. Everyone in Warsaw knew it because she kept a picture of him inside the shop in a gold frame."

"How did she lose him?" Agnes asked, even though she somehow knew the answer to the question already. Paulina's eyes met hers and the pause between them was cavernous. Paulina seemed to be waiting for something, for the moment to be right. Agnes knew that everything was about to change.

"Daria Adamska's brother had been kidnapped by German soldiers."

Agnes couldn't speak or even think. She only heard Otto speak for her, the next question she would have asked if she had been able to. "Does she know where Daria Adamska is now? Does she have an address or anything?"

"No. She believes the owner and her family left Poland after the shop closed, maybe to London, but she doesn't know. She says Daria Adamska was in trouble with the secret police back then. That's one of the reasons her shop closed."

Agnes felt like she couldn't breathe, like the darkness of the shop had gone from deep blue to a thick, edgeless black. She reached for the door and stepped out onto the sidewalk. Otto came behind her.

"Could it be my father who was Daria Adamska's brother? Is it a coincidence that Gertrude has a locket from this shop, from this woman who lost her brother that way and we happen to not know who my father's parents are?" Agnes asked. "Is this just a coincidence?"

Otto waited, then laid his hand on her back. "It would be some coincidence," he said.

Paulina appeared on her other side and handed the locket back to Agnes. Agnes held it in her open palm and gazed hypnotically at the face, studded with ambers. When Gertrude had sent it, it seemed like a last-ditch attempt at bringing them closer, nothing more, just a memento. A gift from a grandmother to a granddaughter.

"She wanted me to find these Adamska people. That's why she sent this to me?"

"It seems …" Paulina whispered.

Agnes started walking south on Nowy Świat, retracing her steps back past the gate in front of the university. Students clogged the sidewalk and she weaved through them in a daze.

"Now I know the family name," she mumbled, more to herself than anyone else.

She walked faster and pulled the cell phone out of her purse. She punched the first memory button and heard an operator answer. "How can I direct your call?"

"Bobbie Price."

"I'm afraid Ms. Price is traveling in Moscow today. She'll be in the office tomorrow. Would you like to leave a message?"

Agnes left her this message: "The family name is Adamska. That's the name I'm looking for. I'm sure."

***

Otto drove them back to Eva's apartment on Polna Street and they shared what had happened on Nowy Świat with Eva. The news shocked her like it had all of them, but Eva reacted with her characteristic pluck. She pulled out a fat book with the title *Ksiazka Telefoniczna,* and the four of them sat around it at the living room table flipping through the Warsaw phone book. Listings for Adamska were easy to find, right up front, running for five pages. All the Adamskas in Warsaw. Hundreds.

"How do we do this?" Paulina asked. "Just start calling?"

"I'll call ten, then you, then me again, until it's too late to call," Eva said.

Agnes felt useless. "I'm sorry I can't speak Polish."

"Me, too," Otto added.

"Don't worry. You two can handle dinner," Eva suggested.

The calling commenced with Eva and Paulina continuously explaining the same story to each number they called. Otto ordered two pies from Telepizza and he sat with Agnes on the couch, both of them watching Paulina and Eva with phones held to their ears, Eva's the home phone and Paulina the Nokia. Agnes

234

couldn't understand what they were saying, but more than a few times she heard their tones turn apologetic and knew that what they were saying was some version of, "I'm sorry for bothering you."

Otto disappeared into the kitchen and returned to the couch with the list of birth registrations from Poznań. "We should see if there are any people named Adamska on here too, right?" he suggested.

The Poznań list, how could she have forgotten? And they had the one from Warsaw. They would look at both of them. Agnes sat forward and they each started scanning the list. Agnes found only four children named Adamska and Otto found eighteen, but strangely they all seemed like female names. On the Warsaw list there were many more, but again, all girls. After several hours, she gathered Otto's pages and her own, marked with Bernds and Adams and Adamskas, and folded them in her lap. It was close to ten o'clock at night. Eva put the phone down.

"We shouldn't call people this late," Eva said. Paulina stopped in the middle of dialing the next number. "We've called this page and a bit of the next one," she said. She held the phone book up to Agnes. They had gotten through dozens of numbers. "We'll call more tomorrow. Don't be discouraged by this."

"I'm not," Agnes said. "I hope I'm not sending you on another wild goose chase."

Eva stood up and started collecting their plates and silverware. "I don't mind chasing a wild goose now and then. It's better than some other things a person could chase."

***

When it was nearly midnight, Agnes walked Otto downstairs to his car. Piotr's office was dark, a rarity. She hoped she would see him around the next morning. When they got out to the sidewalk, Otto turned and leaned against his parked car, folding his arms in front of his chest, looking pensively at her.

"You're patient to put up with all this," Agnes said. She felt glum, even though it seemed like the jeweler's information had been a breakthrough, the search still seemed an impossible one. "I have a hard time giving up on something once I get started. But I can see the wisdom in letting up."

"No letting up now, Fräulein," Otto encouraged, affecting a thick German accent, even though his English was nearly perfect. "And no reason to apologize." He paused and looked at her more intently. "Any progress with the fiancé these days?"

"I haven't had the strength to call him again. Our conversation last week was terrible."

"Perhaps he'll feel some sympathy for what's going on now with your granny? Does he know?"

"Actually, he doesn't. Do you think I should call him?"

Otto stood and took keys out of his pocket. "If you were my fiancée, I would be waiting by the phone for you to call."

Otto leaned to her, his hands along the sides of her shoulders like he had done the first night. He kissed her right cheek, then her left, then her right again. Each touch of his lips was tender and slow, his fingers gripping her arms more tightly with each kiss. Agnes didn't want him to let her go. "I have a few meetings tomorrow, but I'll try to break away as much as I can. You tell me what I can do."

"Thank you. I'll phone you after I talk to Bobbie Price."

He let go of her and went around the front of the car, his long strides confident, his shoulders square and strong. "I'll wait by the phone for you to call," he said.

He started the engine and again Agnes stood by the street and watched the car drive off until it was gone.

***

Agnes couldn't call Krys that night, despite Otto's advice. She knew Krys's pragmatism would take over and drain her of the small amount of determination she felt she had left. If she told him that Paulina and Eva had spent the evening cold calling every person named Adamska in the phone book, he would point out the futility of what she was doing. She half believed in that futility, and if she heard another person voice the same concern, it would be enough to derail her. She needed people around her who didn't believe that what she was doing was futile.

Paulina was asleep on the trundle already when Agnes came into the spare bedroom. She pulled the lace curtains across the window and crept into the upper bed. She laid her head on the pillow. The sheets and pillow were cold, like they always were, the spare room facing north and shaded all day. She looked through the lace at the glow of moonlight in the courtyard. In those days, high summer, the sun in Warsaw's northern latitude set at ten o'clock but was up again just after four o'clock in the morning. Once it was high enough to reflect against the white stone of the building, Agnes didn't sleep much longer. The early mornings left her tired all day.

Agnes let her eyes close on the vision of the moonlit lace. She knew the night would be full of dreams, and not good ones. She thought about Daria Adamska, her trouble with the secret police. What kind of person was she to stir them up? Did the day she lost her brother turn her into a person with nothing to lose? Then, thinking of Daria, the next dream came.

***

The two soldiers were arriving in a jeep this time instead of a truck, to the same farm Agnes had seen in earlier dreams. They parked in the garden and entered the horse shed, finding the farmer, Maximillian, sifting dung out of pad of hay that was so rotten he didn't know how much longer he could use it to line the horse's stall.

"What do you have for us?" one of the soldiers growled.

"I have leeks, more potatoes, some cabbage."

Max stayed calm, but something didn't seem right. The taller one, the one who did most of the talking on every visit, seemed drunk. He shook his head to get his hair out of his eyes. Max studied him and then realized: these two had been found out, or were about to be. His theory had probably been right. The men were selling his goods on the black market and pocketing the money, going around the calorie quotas for their own gain. If they had been found out, it would certainly mean a court martial. Max knew that the soldiers' misfortune was the worst thing that could have happened to him and his family. He had been dreading it. Both soldiers swayed to one side, overcome with drink. Neither was clean shaven.

"No," said the tall soldier. "Forget that." He motioned to the draft horse in the next stall. "We want you to cut up this horse and pack up the meat," he said, tossing a cigarette into the hay between them. It smoldered slightly and distracted Max for a moment from the horror of butchering his own horse. He worried about the barn catching fire, but realized the hay was so wet from rot it probably couldn't burn.

"Schnell!" the soldier barked.

His horse. What could Max say to save it? "But then I can't plow—"

"You won't need to plow anymore, farmer. Just do it!" the tall one ordered.

"But I don't know butchering—"

The other soldier, the stocky one, lunged and butted Max on the top of the head with the handle of his pistol. Max's ears started to ring. He dropped to his knees, put his hand up, and felt blood ooze through his fingers. But he wasn't thinking about his head or the blood. He wondered what he was going to be doing if he didn't need to plow anymore and it terrified him.

"We'll show you how to butcher, you useless Polack!" The stocky one hurled with laughter, kicking Max in the gut.

Wincing with pain, Max scrambled to a stand, fearing another kick. His eldest daughter—they called her Daria—charged through the open barn door and kicked the stocky soldier in the back of the knees until they doubled and he fell to the ground in surprise. The tall one moved to slap her, and she dodged his hand, bobbing up again and biting him hard on the thumb. He yelped and grabbed her by the hair. Daria spat and kicked him. Both soldiers grabbed her, one by each arm and she writhed between them, her legs spinning. She cursed at them in Polish and they cursed back in German. The years of starvation and subservience to these two men had driven his daughter mad. Max yelled for her to stop but none of them heard. His Daria was like her mother, fiercely stubborn, and also like Max's father, swift to recriminate. A cowardly bone she did not have, not a one, but she had plenty of foolish ones. Max feared that her blind rage would get her killed.

"Stop!" he shouted as loud as he could manage. The rafters shook. All three of them spun around. Max grabbed a short sickle from a peg on the wall. "Stop! I'll kill the horse for you. I'll kill it now!"

The tall soldier shoved his daughter hard, and she tumbled backward, tripping and falling against the barn door. His wife was at the door then, screaming, the littlest daughter holding the back of her mother's skirt and crying.

"Get them out!" Max ordered.

His wife snatched Daria by her dress sleeve and yanked her out, all of them disappearing. Max moved quickly into the stall to stand by his horse, desperate to keep the soldiers focused on the imminent slaughter of the horse, not on the retreat of his family. The horse was a hefty cinnamon-colored beast that had done more than its fair share of work during the past few years. As Max turned the wooden handle of the sickle in his palm, he tasted the salt of his blood in his mouth and spit into the hay. He looked again at the soldiers with their rifles drawn. He knew there was no question: it was the horse's life or his own.

He caught the horse's gaze; one bluish-black eye locked on him and following his every move. *The horse knows what I'm going to do,* he thought remorsefully. The animal snorted several times and moved its weight over the hay, swaying its tail in high, nervous swings over its rump. When Max touched its back to calm it, the animal's coat twitched with nervous spasms.

He planted his feet and held the matted tendrils of the horse's dirty mane with his left hand. Terror filled him. He felt the urge to say a silent prayer, and was suddenly angered by his own feebleness. A vision of his father's gray mare kicking him in the forehead flashed in his memory, and it was what he needed to finally commit the act.

He brought the sickle across the front of the horse, and in one quick thrust, sliced the horse's neck. Its head started to thrash and Max had trouble keeping a grip on the mane. He sliced the neck again. The horse deserved a merciful death and that meant Max had to kill it decisively.

The animal bucked and immediately collapsed in the middle of his jump. Blood gushed across the hay. Max fell with the animal, his fingers still knotted through its main, feeling almost transported by his own brutality. He pulled a short blade out of his pants' leg pocket and stabbed the horse three times between the eyes, straight into its brain. The horse jerked violently from the spasm to its nervous system. Then it was as still as if it had never lived.

Night approached, and Max cut and wrapped the horsemeat in paper that his wife had brought him. When she ran out of paper, she stripped the beds of their sheets, tearing them into sections. Their son was strapped to her chest tightly and the girls were nowhere to be seen. She must have hidden them.

Long after nightfall, the soldiers became bored of waiting. They had loaded most of the horsemeat into their jeep along with a paltry quantity of leeks. The soldier who struck him climbed in behind the steering wheel while the tall one turned from the jeep and approached his wife and son. Max watched him, then scanned the grass for the sickle blade, but couldn't see it in the darkness.

"Give him to me," the soldier said.

His wife recoiled away from him. She couldn't have understood the German but it was clear from his arms, outstretched in the direction of their child, what he meant.

"Give the boy to me, I said." He hissed through clamped teeth.

When his wife didn't react, the soldier grabbed at the boy. She tried to hold the soldier back with a stiff arm. Retreating toward the house, she stumbled backwards, dragging the soldier with her as he cursed and spat in her face. The soldier shoved her and she tripped and fell backwards, knocking her head on the stone stoop of the house. While she was flat on the ground, dazed, he ripped the boy from her chest with one hand and drew his gun with the other, aiming at her face.

"Mamo! Mamo!" The girls burst onto the stoop and threw themselves over their mother. Max had been frozen by the barn door, dumbstruck. But the sight of his wife and daughters in front of a loaded gun and his only son in the hands of an enemy soldier shocked him into motion.

Max lunged. He finally spotted one of his scythes on the ground and grabbed it as he ran. He gripped both handles and swung it into the air, training it on the soldier's trigger arm. In the corner of his eye, he saw the other soldier leap from the jeep, bearing down on him. Max turned to strike him first, but was too late. The soldier kicked him in the middle of his back and Max buckled, gasping, slumping to the ground.

The soldier carrying his son was at the jeep by now, putting the boy into the back, still pointing his gun. Max's mind raced. *Where was the scythe now!?* He scrambled to get to his feet, his eye sticky with dried blood and his heart throbbing wildly in his throat. The kick to his back had knocked the wind completely out of him. He struggled to get his legs to move, but his feet felt glued to the dirt.

At that moment, he sensed a shadow over him and he shrunk under it, loathing himself as he did it. *Fight, man! Get up!* he chastised himself. The shadow grew until he saw nothing, and then a fire shot up his left arm. A hideous, roaring pain slammed through his body and he felt his consciousness blink. He fought the darkness and crawled toward the jeep. *Where was the scythe?* He could see his baby son wedged next to bundles of sopping red horsemeat. A snap of a memory took the farmer back to the moment he found the baby under his sisters' bed with the hay doll when he was three months old, fearless. This time his son was wailing, his anguished cries like an apocalyptic thunder.

Max stumbled forward on his knees, hurled himself to his feet, as the jeep's engine roared. The jeep started moving, and he knew he wouldn't be able to run fast enough to catch it; he didn't even have a horse to ride in pursuit. Desperation choked him. He stumbled again, watching the jeep speed away. He screamed after it, running now. *"Nie możne! Nie możne!"* Again and again he screamed until he had no voice left and the jeep had completely disappeared. *You can't! You can't!*

Max saw the jeep go and his mouth hung open in a scream that wouldn't stop. His knees buckled and he fell onto the dirt road, wanting someone or something to kill him. He rolled sideways, stunned, sobbing. Dust swirled after the jeep's departure and he inhaled it as he cried, coughing through his tears. His left hand throbbed, the pain blinding, and he knew he was near losing consciousness.

In the last moments, before his eyes shut on the world like a curtain, he glanced down at his hand, where he felt the pain. But where the pain was, at the end of his left arm, all he saw was a stump. His hand was gone.

FOURTEEN

Warsaw is the Heart

Agnes woke on Wednesday morning bathed in sweat, her hair wet as if a bucket of water had been poured over her.

Paulina touched her cheek. "Are you sick?"

Agnes sat up and felt her forehead. It was cold and wet, her cheeks pasty. The muscles of her arms and legs ached as if she had been fighting something in her sleep. "I don't think so."

"You were screaming during the night, 'Get out of the barn!'"

Agnes looked at her, only half remembering. "What barn?"

"I don't know. I don't remember where I was."

Paulina stood up and slid the trundle under the bed.

"Do you want to try to eat?"

An aroma of sausage frying wafted in from the kitchen. "I should."

She felt around her neck, which was bare. There was a sensation from her dream of something being lost, and she immediately feared again for the locket. "Where is the locket?"

Paulina pointed. "Relax. You put it on the bedside table. It's right there."

Agnes picked it up and clutched it to her chest. She laid her head back down, flipping the pillow to the drier side. "I'm going to lay here a minute."

"Okay. I'll bring you some food."

Paulina went out to the kitchen and Agnes lay still, feeling the desperation of losing something more important than life itself, but having no idea what it was.

***

At five minutes after nine o'clock, the phone in Eva's apartment rang. Agnes and Eva were in the kitchen and Paulina had just left for work, planning to come back at lunch to help them make more calls. Eva went to the living room to answer the phone.

"It's the woman from the embassy," she called.

Agnes went to her and took the phone.

"Bobbie? Did you get my message?"

"You should come in," Bobbie said. "I got the DP list on Monday, but I had to go to Moscow and couldn't call you. But I got something else with it. Classified. I can't talk about it on the phone."

***

Nepo was unusually vigilant that day and insisted that Agnes couldn't enter the building because she wasn't listed in any of his appointment books for a meeting with Bobbie Price. He refused to even call upstairs. Agnes tried every tactic she could think of, but he rebuffed each one, enjoying his paper-hat authority.

"Why don't you do everyone here a favor and get your own job next summer," she said.

"What did you say?"

"A circus monkey would do a better job." She was frantic to talk to Bobbie, and Nepo was going to suffer for it.

"You are being …" he was searching for a word that seemed beyond his vocabulary. Finally he said, "You are being belligerent. Don't make me have a guard escort you out."

"You need a guard for that?"

Nepo left his podium and walked to the side of the lobby

where two Marines were standing in full regalia. Agnes only let a few seconds pass before she decided to take matters into her own hands. She slipped out of the lobby and walked to the right-hand hallway, past the elevator, and found the stairs. She climbed to the third floor and was at the door of Bobbie's office just as the phone rang. Agnes entered without knocking, slightly winded.

"That's probably going to be about me," she said.

Bobbie picked it up. "I'm in a high-level meeting," she snapped. "I'm not taking calls now." She slammed the phone down and flicked her hand. "Agnes, please shut the door."

Once they were behind closed doors, Agnes sat down in front of Bobbie's mahogany desk. The oaks at the edge of Łazienki Park were waving brusquely, the bottoms of the leaves turning up. A storm was coming.

"One of the people I know at the UN is my ex-husband," Bobbie started. "You're lucky my marriage ended badly."

"What do you mean?"

"Well," Bobbie sighed and tilted her head. "My husband cheated on me, so I left him. But his fling only lasted for a year and then he was on his own again. Richard can't be on his own, he doesn't know how. He's been begging me to come back for years." Bobbie rolled her eyes. "There's a bigger chance I would get married to Nepo."

"Did he want to help with this then?"

"Help? Oh, yes. He's still trying to win me back, and I'm happy to let him try. But I didn't know how far he would go."

Bobbie pulled a large red envelope out from a drawer in her desk. It was laminated, with a triple closure along the top like a Ziploc freezer bag, only even sturdier. It had lots of official-looking markings near the closure. "It was stupid of him to send me this, but he did. He could lose his job, or worse."

"What is it?"

"Richard knows someone at an organization called the World Office of Refugees. It's not a very well known group. My whole career it's seemed like nobody knows anyone there, but Richard does. What they do is politically expedient, but it isn't very popular. The information in this envelope was sealed by the WOR Secretary General in 1949. It was filed as classified for seventy-five years, until the year 2024."

"Bobbie, listen," Agnes stood and raised her palms. "I don't want anybody to risk their career for me."

"It's mainly Richard who's risking his career. And Agnes," Bobbie's eyes softened. "I really want to help you. I thought I would just make a few calls, but once I did, I realized you were on to something that you wouldn't be able to understand without my help. I didn't want to send you away with a few DP transcripts and leave you to figure them out on your own."

"Are you sure you won't get into trouble though?"

"Just sit down," Bobbie said. "When I get in trouble, I usually know how to get myself out of it." She opened the file. "And as long as we have this, we should use it."

"What's in the file?"

"A list of Permanent Expatriation Settlements made between 1946 and 1949."

"What are those?"

"Richard told me it was when the WOR took over handling the repatriation of Displaced Persons decided, for whatever reason, to *not* make a person return to his home country. There weren't many settlements, because when the WOR let a person stay permanently in refugee status it was considered politically unpopular. The Allies did everything they could to get people to go home. Poles especially were a burden on the West because there were so many of them. There is some evidence the Allies even used coercion to force people to go back to Poland."

"But wouldn't they want to go home once they could?"

"For Poles, it was frying pan or fire. Stay in the West and be treated as a second-class citizen, an interloper, or return home to a decimated country that had fallen under the control of the Soviets. There really was no going home. Richard said that settlements of children were usually because the child didn't remember their family. Many of them had been taught to hate Poland. They violently resisted the notion of returning. The worst part is that these settlements were with the permission of the birth parents."

"You mean the birth family would have given their child away?"

"The child wouldn't have remembered them. You can't really give away a child who doesn't even know you exist. Not quite. At least, it must have seemed best for the child."

Agnes swallowed and looked at the red envelope. "Was the name Adamska there?"

"Not Adamska."

Agnes was relieved.

"But then I realized my mistake." Bobbie shuffled through the papers in the envelope and pulled one out. "I looked up Adam*ski*. Adam*ski* is the same family name as Adam*ska*. The jeweler you told me about in your message was a woman, right?"

Agnes nodded.

"Then her name would have ended with an *a*. But any male in the family would have had the name ending with *i*." She held out a page to Agnes and pointed to the name Adamski that was almost at the bottom. It was right there, in front of her.

"But how do we know if that's my father's family?"

"The settlements are also indexed by what they called the *assumed name*—in this case the German one. So I looked up Bernd Heinrich Mueller."

She pulled out another sheet of paper and handed it to Agnes. It had a name highlighted.

"Bernd H. Mueller is on the list of settlements, right here,"

Bobbie held the page out and Agnes took it in her trembling fingers. She saw his name, the whole name, the name she knew, the father she knew. Her heart caught in her throat. Under that name was another one: Bogdan Adamski. Under that were the names of what were termed *assumed parents*, Gertrude and Albert Mueller, and *natal parents*, Janina Adamska and Max Adamski.

Blood pulsed in Agnes's neck. She looked at the date of the

Settlement: July 3, 1947. She counted back. Her father would have been only five and a half years old. She tossed the paper onto Bobbie's desk and stood, circling the floor.

"How could these Adamski people not have wanted him back?" she said, throwing a hand out, her voice cracking. "They let him spend his whole life thinking he was an orphan!"

Bobbie laid her hand on the paper Agnes had discarded. "I know it's hard to accept this, but it had to be the best thing for him. There had to be no other choice. It had to be hell for the Muellers also."

"The Muellers would have known about this?"

"It was a settlement, so that means everyone knew. But like I said, it was fully based on the permission of the birth parents. So at that point, he couldn't go back, and his relationship to the Adamski family was never to be revealed per the settlement. Remember that the Muellers were bound by this settlement to never reveal their son's true identity for his own good, and the good of the birth family. It must have been brutally hard on the Muellers to keep this kind of secret for so long."

All Gertrude's secrecy, it all made sense to Agnes now. She had been bound by this agreement not to tell Agnes—or anyone— anything about her son's birth family. But now she was dying. The poor woman.

"But wouldn't Gertrude and Albert have known before about this Lebensborn plot? That all these orphans were really stolen kids from occupied countries? Wouldn't they have known that?"

"That plan was a very secret one, Agnes. Even to most Germans, even to people high up in the government. Hitler must have known that German civilians would have a hard time tolerating the outright theft of children. Supporting the war is one thing, but participating in state-orchestrated kidnapping of tens of thousands of children is another. Don't blame the Muellers. I feel almost sure they couldn't have known what they were part of, not at first."

She thought of Gertrude, near death in Berlin. "How do I find the Adamskis? Is there an address?" she asked, looking at the Settlement agreement.

Bobbie's finger met the spot where Agnes was looking. Next to their name was only the name of a town—Kazimierz Dolny—but no road, house number, or post box.

"It says Max Adamski's occupation was farming. So they must have been on a farm and this Kazimierz Dolny was the nearest village to them," Bobbie said. "If they still live there, people in this town must know them. Any farmer working the same farm for more than fifty years will be known by everyone, if he's still alive."

Agnes wrote down the information from the classified Settlement agreement on a scrap of blank notepaper and watched as Bobbie resealed the document in its red envelope. She clutched the scrap of paper. She knew everything now, almost everything. She just needed to find them. As she thought about that search, a new one with more information, her thoughts shifted to Eva. She wanted to have information for Eva, too.

"Did you ever come across the name Rafał Rozbrat?" Agnes asked.

Bobbie shook her head. "I'm sorry. It's likely that he didn't survive the war. Many boys in the Polish Underground didn't." She put the file back in her desk and locked the drawer with a key.

"You did more than anyone has ever done for me," Agnes told her. "Thank you."

Bobbie stood up and rounded the desk. She faced Agnes and took her hands. "You remind me of my little sister, Susan." Bobbie paused. "I miss my sister."

Agnes noticed the mournful look on Bobbie's face when she mentioned Susan and got the feeling that something had happened to her. She could tell that even if Bobbie had wanted to see Susan, she was never going to again. Agnes kissed Bobbie Price three times on the cheeks. Then Bobbie called a Marine guard to escort Agnes past Nepo and outside into the gathering storm.

***

Once outside, Agnes crossed the street and entered Łazienki Park. She wasn't ready to call anyone. It felt important to sort out her anger and her regret as well as the cauldron of emotions that ranged from fear to sadness. And she had to think how to find a farmer with only the name of a village as her reference.

She thought achingly about Gertrude. All this time, Gertrude had known everything. All this time she had been forced to keep the settlement classified, even within their own family. It was a terrible burden, one Agnes finally understood. All the years Gertrude had refused to come to the States to see them, to keep in touch, to have a relationship with her father, it wasn't because she didn't love them. She was trying to keep the secret. Agnes felt the locket that lay in the middle of her chest and closed her fingers around it as she walked. The amber felt hot, but then so was the day. The air was growing dense, the clouds blackening, the tree branches whipping the air over her head.

When Agnes got to a clearing at the bottom of a gravel trail deep inside the park, she looked down a long, narrow lake and discovered a small palace built over the water. A columned arcade crossed from one bank of the lake to the other, in front of the palace. Agnes walked to it. Marble benches lined the walkway under the arcade. She sat on one and took the cell phone out of her purse, this one Otto's. When he had picked her up at Okęcie, he insisted on swapping phones so she could reach her parents in Berlin, or even Krys in Chicago if she wanted to. But she hadn't wanted to.

She propped her feet in between the marble posts of the arcade railing. The water under her feet was completely still, the way water gets before a storm, as if the water knows and is even afraid. The surface was a dark green, deeply shaded by the tall oaks and pines on either bank and the darkening sky. She dialed Gertrude's apartment in Berlin and felt her breath tighten when she heard her father's voice.

"Schatzie?"

"Oh, Papa," her voice came out breathy, a whisper. Knowing

what she now knew about him, his voice hit her like a punch. She bent her head and covered her eyes with her hand.

"It's good you called."

His voice was raw. He had been crying. She had never heard him cry. Not once.

She took her hand away and looked out across the water. "Are you okay?"

"Mamo is gone."

***

Agnes walked for many hours after talking to her father, even though the cell phone in her purse rang four times—two calls from Paulina and one each from Otto and Eva. The sky finally gave up and the rain came in a ferocious summer downpour. She took cover in the underground passageway of a roundabout on Ujazdowskie Street. The rain came in sheets, as if God were pouring buckets over them. Agnes leaned against the tiled wall and watched people—Polish people is how she saw them now, like her—rush down the stairs to stand underground and escape the deluge.

When it finally stopped, Agnes left the passageway and returned to the street, the tires of passing cars and buses hissing on the wet road. She walked down Wyzwolenia Street toward the Politechnika and Eva's building on Polna. There was nothing more she could do to make amends with Gertrude. Gertrude had died believing that the secret would be buried with her. It must have tortured her to die with it. She didn't know Agnes had discovered the name of her father's family. And it was only a fateful luck that connected Agnes to Bobbie Price, and then to the ex Mr Bobbie Price, and then to the list of Settlements. All fateful luck, and Gertrude must have assumed Agnes would never find out, even on her luckiest day. Agnes wished she could have told her, she wished she could have told her grandmother that it would be okay now. That it would all be okay. But then, Agnes wasn't sure of that, not yet.

Piotr was at the door to his little office when Agnes walked through the archway of Eva's building. He put his hand to his heart when he saw her. That's when she realized her face must be stained with tears, her eyes red, her posture downcast. She couldn't blame the rain.

"*Dobrze?*" he asked.

Agnes remembered this was the word for *okay*. She shook her head. "No *dobrze*."

Piotr took her gently by the elbow and led her into his office, sitting her down on a wooden box. He sat across on the metal stool. They looked at each other for a moment, and Agnes saw how Piotr had been worn down by circumstances far beyond his control, how resigned he was—happy, yes, but resigned to be happy and ask for nothing. He had lived out his life in a country that had been nearly annihilated by one neighbor and then controlled for half a century by another. Oppression had defined him. What would Piotr's life have been like without the Soviet Union controlling Poland all these years? If Piotr could have pursued any life he wanted, what would he have done?

He smiled, as if he knew Agnes were worried for him, and his face filled with kindness. From the wall behind his desk he pulled down an old postcard of a tomb inside a church and handed it to Agnes. He pointed to the tomb and raised his eyebrows, questioning.

Agnes wished she could communicate with him, but even between people who speak the same language, death is impossible to understand. Death can't be explained by words.

"Yes, somebody in my family died today."

With his finger, he pointed to the middle of the tomb where a name was inscribed—*Fryderykowi Chopinowi*.

"Chopin?" Agnes asked.

He nodded and held up his index finger: there was more. On the backside of the postcard, he drew the reclining figure of a man—head, body, arms, legs. Then inside the chest, on the left side, he drew a lopsided circle and colored it in. He tapped his finger on the circle.

"The heart?" Agnes asked. Piotr flipped over the postcard and pointed to the tomb. "Chopin's heart is in this tomb? Only the heart?" she said. Piotr nodded.

Agnes looked at the picture of the tomb. It was made out of marble with scrolls and harps decorating it and a bust of Chopin at the top. She flipped the card back over and ran her finger over the reclining man.

"And the body? Where did they bury the body?"

Piotr drew something next to the reclining man. It was the Eiffel Tower.

"His body is in Paris and his heart is in Warsaw?" Agnes said.

Piotr touched her on the shoulder and she looked into his eyes, really seeing them. They were as green as spring grass, as clear as if he were still a boy and he were still living in the world like it was when he were a boy, a Poland before any war, occupation or Soviet sphere.

"*Warszawa*," he said out loud, pointing to his own heart, "*to serce*."

Warsaw is the heart.

Agnes felt her face tighten from the dried tears. Piotr couldn't have known how much that very idea meant to her just then. But then again, maybe he did.

"Tak," she replied. *Yes.*

***

Otto drove them south to Kazimierz Dolny that afternoon, leaving his client's office midway through a meeting. Agnes sat in the front with him and Eva and Paulina sat in the back. The rain had cleared, bringing cooler temperatures and a rinsed sky, clear blue without a single cloud.

The road leading out of Warsaw to the south cut straight through two lines of birch trees, with their flaking white bark looking like ribbons on church pews at a wedding. Fields as flat as carpets rolled away on either side of the road. Some fields were green where the stubby shrubs of root vegetables were growing. Other fields were padded with dried, golden hay where wheat had recently been cut down. Occasionally a dog would bark at the road and run a few steps next to the car before he ran out of breath and veered into the brush.

"I'm sorry about your granny," Otto said. "How is your dad?"

"He's shaken." They passed a paddock of horses, and Agnes watched them droop their heads over the grass, lolling there, as if bored by chewing. "I think he regrets living so much of his life away from her."

"Is he going to come to Poland?"

"I asked him to come, when things with Gertrude were settled. I asked both my parents to come."

"Do they know why?"

Agnes shook her head. "There was too much news today. I couldn't add this to it. And we may not yet find the family out here. I want to find them first if I can."

A little more than an hour into the drive, the land ahead rose toward a small hill over the Vistula River, with the ruins of a tower and a castle at the top. They passed a white sign that read: Kazimierz Dolny. The road narrowed and small cottages and houses clustered on each side, each one ringed with a picket fence. Colorful stems of cosmos waved where the grass met the asphalt. They soon arrived in a cobblestone square with Baroque and Renaissance houses circling it and a water well in the center, enclosed by a wooden turret. A Gothic church towered over the square at the north end. Otto rounded through it and parked the car in front of a building with the letters PTTK over its large wooden doors.

"The PTTK is the tourist office," Paulina said as she got out of the car. They all stood together on the sidewalk. "We might as well start here."

They followed Paulina into the dank lobby. A woman with frosted blond hair was sitting behind a Plexiglas window, like a bank teller. Paulina started talking to her. Agnes circled the edges of the lobby, looking at brochures. She pulled out one that had a map of the entire region, known as the Lublin Upland, showing small roads and a few highways. The major cities were Lublin, Zamość, and Kazimierz Dolny. Ukraine bordered the region on its eastern edge.

Agnes took another brochure with a picture of a bearded man on the cover, dressed in gold robes covered with red eagles. Casimir the Great, it said. *Kazimierz Wielki*, in Polish, King of Poland from 1333 to 1370. Agnes turned it over and saw a picture of the castle ruins at the top of the hill that they had passed coming into the town, a castle Casimir the Great had built. She counted back and realized the ruins were more than six hundred years old. Paulina stepped away from the window.

"She said there is a town hall in the other square, the small one, which might have farm registrations for the region. If not, we might need to go to the bigger town halls in Lublin or Puławy."

They left the PTTK and walked out of the square, past two arcaded merchants' homes whose façades were ornamented with bas-relief figures of what looked like artisans and traders and decorated with painted frescoes. Eva led them now, reaching the far end and the front door of the town hall.

"I've had some practice with these town halls," Eva said. "Let me do the talking. They can't give us any more trouble than the chap in Poznań."

They followed Eva inside what seemed more like a house than an official building. Two worn couches faced each other under the front windows. A young woman in a white blouse and flowered skirt stood up from her desk when she saw them come in. Eva greeted her and started talking in Polish. As with the Mother Superior, Agnes tried her best to tease out the meaning of what was being said by watching the body language of each person. It was encouraging that the young woman never stopped smiling, and nodded her head as Eva spoke. Agnes clutched the brochures she had with the map and Casimir the Great's bushy-bearded picture, his intense gaze. She looked again at Casimir's face and was reminded of Pope John Paul II.

The young woman crooked a finger and the group followed her up a set of carved, wooden stairs. At the top, they entered a small library where the young woman pulled a long book full of maps off the shelf and laid it open on a high table in the center of the room. She spoke to Eva and turned the book over to her.

"She said this book contains all the farm plots in the area, with acreage and crop yield and ..." Eva flipped one page, then two, pointing at the top of the last page where there was a typed name, "the name of the family owning the land." Eva started flipping the pages faster. "So we just need to find a farm owned by Max Adamski," she said.

The young woman pulled down two more books identical to the first and laid them down in one of the deep window ledges along the side of the room. Agnes took one and Paulina took the other. As they flipped, they saw her lay another book into Otto's outstretched arms. Soon, all four of them were turning pages with maps of farms, looking for the name Adamski at the top.

"They don't have any kind of database or index?" Otto asked.

Eva snickered. "Are you kidding? To be honest with you, this is more than I thought we would find."

Agnes scanned the pages, turning one after the next, as Eva murmured the names of the crops: *Wheat farm. Rapeseed. Potato. Rye. Barley. Another wheat farm. Three more potato farms. Hops. Sugar beets. Another rye farm.*

For a long while, there were only the sounds of Eva's absent-minded crop recitations and dusty pages turning. Agnes noticed the young woman from downstairs standing at the sill of the next window, carefully turning pages in another book.

They were in the wooden-paneled confines of the small library long enough for Agnes to notice that the sun had moved. Her cheek became hot standing next to the window, the glare of sun on it, but now afternoon shadows were creeping in. She turned the last page and looked at the others, who were each at the end of their books.

"Did any of you find them?"

All four of them—the young woman included—dejectedly shook their heads.

"Are these all the farm records they have here?" Agnes asked Eva.

"Tak," the young woman said, apparently understanding the question.

She returned her book to the shelf and came closer to Agnes, hesitating, twisting her fingers together and seeming like she was searching for how to say something Agnes would understand.

"I am sorry," she said in very careful English. "I hope you find family."

Agnes said thanks, in a careful Polish, *"Dzienki."*

Eva led them out of the library and back down the stairs. When they got out to the cobblestones of the small square, Otto spoke first. "What now?"

"It's getting late," Agnes said. "We should go back to Warsaw and maybe we can look in those other cities' town halls tomorrow."

She started walking toward the square and their parked car, feeling weary, her shoulders slumping. Otto touched her elbow to slow her down.

"Let's get you something to eat first, at least," he said.

Agnes agreed. As they walked toward the square, Otto opened his hand near hers. Agnes hesitated, then she slipped her fingers inside his palm. She felt an immediate relief. Otto couldn't change anything that was happening or find her father's family faster, but she was relieved just the same. Just to feel his hand around hers.

They passed the Renaissance merchant houses and the tourist office. Otto headed them toward the Gothic church and the cluster of white umbrellas near the base of it. A sign over the umbrellas said *Restauracja Krolewska*. The King's Restaurant.

The three women followed Otto through the canopy of umbrellas and into the cool darkness of the stone-walled restaurant. A young girl with brown hair in a high ponytail motioned to an empty table and they sat down. Five men in their fifties and sixties, her father's age and a bit older, clustered at the adjacent table. They seemed to be well into their third or fourth round of beers. A soccer game was being broadcast on a small TV in the corner of the room, and the men were intermittently cheering or booing depending on what had happened on the screen.

"What's your team?" Eva asked Otto.

"Bayern Munich," he grinned. "Of course."

"Of course," Eva smiled back.

They each ordered a beer, an EB, as that seemed to be the house drink. Eva patted Agnes on the back of her hand. "Don't worry about today. There are other cities in the area. I'm sure they are just registered somewhere else, not Kazimierz Dolny."

"But that was the name of their town in the settlement record," Agnes said.

"A lot has changed in this country since World War II. Don't let that bother you."

"What if the family all left to England, like the jeweler said?"

"Then maybe there will be some record of the dissolution of the farm, or transfer of ownership. It will still lead us somewhere. Whole families don't just vanish." But just as soon as Eva uttered the words, Agnes realized they could. If a whole person could just vanish, so could a whole family.

The men at the table next to them reared back in their seats and hollered at the TV. There was a close-up of a referee holding up a red card and ejecting a player wearing yellow and white from a team called Motor Lublin. The men's booing and cursing became intense, and one of them slammed his fist hard on top of the varnished wood table, startling Agnes. Otto noticed her jump.

"Do you want me to say something?" he asked.

Agnes waved a hand at them. "For God's sake, it's just soccer."

"I'm going to pretend you didn't say that."

Otto drank his beer, taking a long gulp. Agnes watched the game resume and looked at each of the men. One of them stomped his feet on the floor after a near miss at the goal and his boots caught her eye: they were caked with mud. She looked at the boots of the other men. All of them were wearing boots covered with mud. It was not the mud of walking the streets during a rainstorm; it was the mud of trudging through a sopped field. Agnes leaned over to Eva.

"Look," she pointed at their boots. "They're farmers." Eva's face brightened and Agnes knew she understood. "Ask them about the Adamski farm."

Eva tapped one of them on the shoulder, and he looked annoyed at having his attention taken away from the game. Agnes saw the referee pull up another card, this one yellow. This card elicited less cursing from the table, so Agnes assumed it was for a player on the other team. The man kept talking to Eva, turning more to face her when one team called a time out. His eyebrows rose, and he pulled on the short sleeve of one of his friends.

Eva started talking to the friend, who was a little older, his hair fully gray and his round belly trussed into his pants with a wide leather belt. He nodded and said "Tak, tak" several times. Agnes sat forward. He raised his hands and pointed in the direction of the river that was beyond the square, circling his hands, moving them up and down, together then apart. He was giving Eva directions. She listened hard to what the man was saying and then heard him say, in the middle of many other things, *"pinch knee beeski."* Pinch knee beeski? she thought. A memory of Big Bird triggered in Agnes's head: the number of the day is *pinch* and the color of the day is *knee beeski.*

Eva finished and turned around to their table. Agnes blurted out, "Five blue what?"

"Well look at her," Eva raised one eyebrow. "Yes, he said their house has five blue-shuttered windows. When he was a baby, he and his mother, Ania, lived with them off and on during the war after her husband died and their farm was destroyed."

"How far is it to their farm?" Paulina asked.

"By car, he said about twenty minutes from here. To the north, back in the direction of Warsaw."

Otto stood up. "He told you the way?"

"He did."

"Let's go then."

All four of them were out the door before the next player of Motor Lublin had a chance to make another goal, or suffer another penalty.

***

The light was failing as they drove and the edges of the country road became more difficult to see, even with the car's headlights. Agnes strained to look at each collection of buildings every time they passed a farm, looking for a house with five blue-shuttered windows. Once they had been driving close to twenty minutes, following the directions the man had given Eva in the restaurant, Agnes strained even harder to make out the houses. Anything blue was only going to look black in the dim light.

"There!" Paulina yelled from the backseat, pointing out the window to the right side of the road. "Stop!"

Otto pressed the brakes hard and the car lurched. He stopped at a dirt driveway that led off the road toward a house with five windows, framed by blue shutters. Just like the man said. "Is this it?"

"This is the road," she said. "There are the five blue-shuttered windows. This has to be them."

Otto pulled into the dirt driveway, passing through an unpainted picket fence. Beyond the house, enormous rolls of hay lay in the wheat field every twenty feet or so, darkened so much at sunset that they looked like slumbering elephants. Mechanized farm equipment, mainly plows and threshers, were parked in a line behind a large wood-slatted horse shed on the left side of the driveway. Two aluminum silos rose behind the barn. Past that, at the end of the driveway, were smaller sheds that looked like they housed more equipment and feed for animals. It was a large operation.

To the right of the driveway, behind a row of rose bushes and yews, was a one-story manor house made of whitewashed concrete with five windows across on the first floor, each window framed by a pair of blue shutters. A blue door could be seen under a small, triangular porch roof. Agnes looked through the windshield at the house. Two of the windows, to the right of the door, had lights on. Agnes turned to face Eva in the backseat. She felt like she couldn't move, she couldn't find the courage to get out and knock on the door.

"They gave him away. They *settled* him," Agnes said.

"You can't think it was all that black and white, can you?" Eva replied.

"Would they even want me to come here?"

"Listen," Otto put his hand on her shoulder. "You're here now," he tipped his head toward the house. "Go on."

"Do I just go up and knock on the door?"

Eva slid out of the backseat. "That's about all you have left to do, sweetie. I'll go with you."

Eva took Agnes by the arm, and they walked closer to the house. Off the driveway, the ground was like a bog, soaked and soft. Mud squelched under their feet and covered their shoes after only a few steps. They stepped up onto the porch. Agnes raised her hand and knocked. Voices sounded from inside, then the blue door opened. A woman with cropped, light brown hair and modern, frameless glasses was standing in front of them. She said something to Eva in Polish. It looked like she had been crying for a long time. Agnes noticed Eva's face whiten with shock.

"What is it?" Agnes asked.

"She asked if we were here to pay respects."

Agnes looked up at the porch light beside the door and noticed it was sheathed with a piece of black silk. "Respects? You can't mean ..."

"Yes. Their mother, Janina, died. Just this morning."

FIFTEEN

I am Agnes

As I looked at the shrouded porch light, I realized at that exact moment that my identity had been robbed right along with my father's. It was the first time this had occurred to me. I prepared to open my mouth and introduce myself with *I am Agnes Mueller*, as I had for almost thirty years. But I wasn't that person. What I should have been saying was *I am Agnes Adamska*.

I couldn't bring myself to speak that sentence, which was true, or speak the other one, which was false. Eva must have sensed my struggle so she did my talking for me. She explained to the woman standing in front of us who I was and why I was there. The woman's name was Sophie, and she was Janina and Max Adamski's younger daughter, my father's sister, my aunt. She stepped onto the porch and put her arms around me, embracing me like I had just left that morning and now returned and my coming and going had been a regular occurrence for years. It should have felt like the strangest embrace of my life but it was the best.

Sophie led us inside. Her father and her elder sister, Daria, had walked out together into the wheat field after hours of sitting next to Janina's reposing body. The only other person in the house with Sophie then was her son, who was named for my father. He was sheepish as he shook my hand.

"I never thought there was other Bogdan," he said in halting, schoolboy English.

Sophie spoke English better than her son, from the time she spent in medical school in England. She didn't look much like my father and neither did Bogdan. Her hair was fine and light brown, not the slightly curly nap of sandy blond that my father had. Even though her eyes were also blue, they were set closer together than my father's eyes. Sophie also had a sharper nose and more pointed chin. I realized I was hunting for resemblances—in every person I met, every picture I passed on the walls. I was trying to convince myself that all of this was real, and I was somehow a part of it.

Sophie eventually took me to the room where they had laid her mother's body. I had never seen a person's dead body. I had come close a few times, but I had never truly seen one. That was all I was thinking as I followed her to the back of the house where the bedrooms were.

We arrived at the doorway of a small bedroom. A lamp on the dresser across from the bed emitted a sickly yellow glow. A mirror over the dresser had been covered in black silk like the lamp on the front porch. Janina's body was laid in the middle of the bed on top of a board. A sheet covered almost her entire body, up to the bridge of her nose. Only her eyes and forehead showed. Three hourglasses stood on a small table next to the bed, turned upside down, the sand gathered in a conical hill at the bottom of each one. Sophie took a seat on a wooden bench next to the bed, and I timidly sat down next to her.

"She would have liked to meet you," Sophie said.

"Me, too," I whispered. I pressed my hands together between my knees. A curtain of white lace floated on my left, by a window which was thrown wide open. I glanced through it. The sun had set completely. I could see the wheat field, lit only by the bedroom light. Sophie held her palms together in her lap, each finger aligned with its mate on the other hand. Her nails were unpolished, each one clean and trim. She told us she worked as a pediatric oncologist, and as I looked at her hands they indeed seemed like a physician's hands: tender and productive. I felt better sitting next to her. She seemed like the kind of person who knew how to navigate a crisis, or handle a difficult conversation, as she must encounter them on almost a daily basis. So I asked the question that had been on my mind since I saw Bobbie that morning.

"Why did your parents agree to leave my father in Germany once the UN found him?"

Sophie looked wary and a touch surprised. "You know about the settlement then?"

"Yes, someone helped me."

Sophie shifted on the bench. "It was a difficult decision, to leave him there. Believe me. We heard his interviews with the child psychologists. Toward the end of every one of them he wanted to know when Mamo was coming for him. He adored her." Sophie gestured toward Janina's body. "That is what we all called our mother, including him. When we lost him that day, it was the only word he knew how to speak."

The room was still and dim. I looked at the gentle slope of Janina's forehead, the gathers of wrinkles around her eyes. The word *Mamo* only made me think of Gertrude.

Sophie continued, "The World Office of Refugees made their recommendation, and our parents decided to leave him there. My mother had to beg my father to do it. The decision nearly broke our family. My father and Daria have always resented it."

"But you haven't?" I asked.

"I suppose I was sympathetic to my mother. You have to remember, we had lived through a war. To find my brother still alive, that was a miracle. He hadn't died, he wasn't put in a camp. These were our greatest fears. I didn't want any more harm to come to him, and I began to believe that separating him from his new Mamo would have hurt him deeply. My father and Daria didn't see it that way."

I heard a door open at the front of the house and looked in the direction of the sound.

Sophie stood up and held her hand up to me to stay there. "That will be my father with Daria," she said. "Let me talk to them first."

Before I could say anything, Sophie had left the room and pulled the door closed behind her. It occurred to me that I was sitting alone in a room with a dead person. There should have been a more familial way for me to feel about Janina Adamska right then, the woman who gave birth to my father, perhaps even in that very room, but I couldn't manage it. My basest feelings seemed to have taken over and I felt only fear and dread.

I stared at her closed eyes and forehead and her thin hair, which was a mix of blond and gray. Sunspots dotted the skin around her right temple and the middle of her forehead. Deep indentations marked the bridge of her nose where glasses must have once rested. Her hair was combed straight off her face and forehead. It looked soft, like the pelt of a newborn animal. I leaned to her and looked closer. I raised my hand and touched my fingers to her hair, which was soft like I thought. It was the softest hair I had ever felt, in fact. I slid my fingers off her hair and laid two of them on the middle of her forehead, barely touching it, but touching it enough. Her skin was hard, drained of life, like the molded plastic of a doll's head. My hand sprang back.

All at once, the alarming sound of a male voice groaning in agony, almost from a physical pain, erupted at the front of the house. Then a female voice burst into angry shouts and feet stomped through the hall. Another female voice cried out and then all the voices calmed. My dread mounted. *Would they hate me for coming too late, or coming at all?*

I heard steps approaching the room, the heavy stamp of boots. The wooden door of the room creaked open and Max Adamski stood before me, the others hovering behind. He filled the doorway with his broad shoulders and long legs. His face was sinewy and weathered, but his eyes were sharp and blue. There were tufts of white hair on either side of his head, but nothing on top.

At the end of his left arm there was a steel hook where his hand should have been. He saw me jump at the sight and he bent his arm at the elbow, concealing the hook behind his back. The day I met him, Max Adamski was eighty-three years old. But, like a tree, he seemed like a thing that only became harder to cut down with each passing year.

He entered the room and I stood up. We both regarded each other as if each of us were something from the other's imagination that had inexplicably materialized. He craned over me and I gawked upwards. He put his good hand, his only hand, on my cheek and held it there. The touch of his fingers calmed me. His hand was coated with a smooth film of clay like I had felt on the potato after Eva's car broke down. The pungent smell of the earth was in every part of his hand, just like my father's hands always smelled like lead from drafting pencils. Max Adamski spoke something softly in Polish, enunciating each syllable, his z's sounding like a mother hushing her baby.

Eva translated: "He says that you coming is a sign of God's mercy. That in taking Janina, he has returned Bogdan. And brought you."

Another woman's voice spoke from behind Sophie.

"Gdzie jest Bogdan?"

Daria Adamska stood by the open door, arms crossed in front of her chest. She had dark blond hair that was cut in short layers near her face. Her hair had a slight curl in it like my father's, like mine. The contortions of her face were like my father's when he was angry, or like mine when I was stressed: the twist of the mouth, the steep slant of the eyebrows. I couldn't believe my eyes. We both looked just like her.

"She's asking where Bogdan is," Eva explained. "Did he come with you?"

I stood away from Max just as a gust of humid air blew in from the window, so thick it felt like it could push me back toward them all.

"He's in Berlin. His mother," I stopped and looked over at

Janina. "I mean his ... Gertrude passed away," I said. "Also today."

Eva translated and Sophie came around her father and hugged me again. I sank a little bit into her. Her hand caressed the back of my head. I noticed her looking down at her mother on the bed. Sophie spoke in her softly accented English.

"Surely God is making a peace between Janina and Gertrude, right now in heaven."

I rested in Sophie's arms and considered my two grandmothers—that's what they would always be to me—meeting each other finally in some place beyond the physical world. I hoped they could be at peace. I hoped Gertrude Mueller knew I had found her son's family and that Janina Adamska knew she had been found.

***

Otto and Paulina had been sitting in the car for what must have been hours. When I came out of Janina's room, I didn't know what time it was because all the clocks in the house had been covered with black silk. It was dark. In that way mourning has of seizing time, it felt like we were deep into the night, even if we weren't. As we prepared to leave, Sophie walked with us to Otto's car.

"My mother will lie with us at home for three days, then she will be buried at the end of the third day. That will be on Friday. Please can you bring Bogdan here before then?"

"I'll try to bring him by tomorrow."

"During my whole life, I have never heard my father speak of God until today, what he said about God's mercy when he met you."

"He doesn't believe in God?"

"He was angry at God. I hope he has forgiven him now."

Sophie took my hand and said good-bye and we kissed three times on the cheeks. Before we parted, she threw her arms around me and held me to her and I felt a heaviness in my chest that made me feel like I could cry for days. I felt a fury toward people and armies who were long since dead, who had forced me away from this family for almost thirty years of my own life and more than half a century of my father's. I held all the feelings in. I couldn't let the tears start right there and then because they would never stop.

Inside the car, we were all quiet. I knew Otto and Paulina must have been bursting to know about my meeting with my family, but they didn't ask me anything. It was as if we all knew there were no words, or at least, there were no words right then. Maybe there were certain things that would never have words.

***

When the silence in the car had become too stifling, I was the first one to speak, but I still felt like I was speaking from a far-off dream.

"The mother died," I murmured. "How could the mother have died, just today? If I had come one day earlier ..." My voice trailed off.

"The fact that you came at all is what's important now," Eva said.

"But I felt something wasn't right for so long, even when I was twelve years old and learned about Klaus and Liesl. I could have come fifteen years ago."

"To Poland?" Eva said. "No. Even I wasn't coming to Poland fifteen years ago."

"What could you have done as a twelve-year-old kid?" Paulina asked from the rear seat.

I gazed out the window, into the borderless black of the flat, Polish countryside. She was right, how could I have come until now?

Otto, silent all this time with both hands on the wheel, finally spoke. "In your German studies, did you ever learn of something called Heimat?"

"I don't think so."

"When I was at the boys' camp in England, where I met Damian, I was always very homesick. I missed home but could never say what thing I missed about it, or what my parents could send over to make me feel better. I just missed being there. One day my mother told me about this idea of Heimat." The road straightened and Otto accelerated. "I guess it's quite a German concept. It has no real translation in any other language. It's about the relationship a human being has to a space or a community, but also to familiar traditions and the people that have surrounded him since childhood. It's an attachment to home, but not so much to the physical place," Otto paused, "or even to the country. It's a love and attachment to just the *idea* of home."

I started listening more closely to Otto. I could guess where he was going with his discourse on Heimat. Papa's childhood traditions, relationships, community have all been German. He has lived more than fifty years as a German; being Polish would have no meaning for him. But there was nothing I could do about what attachments my father had to Germany, or the ones he wouldn't have for Poland. His life had been full of mirrors, a madhouse full of them, and I was trying to pull him out. I hoped it was the right thing to do.

"I had time to think about the concept of Heimat while I was away in those summers. I developed my own understanding of it. To me, Heimat is a space inside each person, a feeling of home in the soul. Heimat is meant to be an attachment to something external, but I came to feel the best part of the Heimat is an attachment one feels to some part of himself, deep within himself."

We drove steadily on over the unlit road, the headlights of the Audi carving a path in front of us.

"The reason I mention this is, well, you don't know what the *home* is inside your father, Agnes. Perhaps that home has always come from this place," Otto gestured to the road behind them, "from that farm."

Otto shifted gears to move around a slower car. I looked into the car as we passed. It was a small Peugeot with a young couple in the front seat. The woman was laughing at something the man had just said.

"I don't know what *home* he feels inside. To be honest, it's always seemed like there wasn't one. My father tends to push people away, to isolate himself."

"Perhaps he seems isolated to you because he has been distanced from what he felt inside, from a Polish home, a Polish Heimat."

Otto's words struck me. The notion of my father missing a Heimat felt like it could explain so much. Otto decelerated slightly and slid the car back into the right lane. I glanced back at the couple, at the man smiling. I considered what a different person my father might have been if he had known who he was from the very beginning.

***

When we returned to Warsaw, to Eva's apartment, I knew I had to make the phone call I had been dreading. I had to call my father to tell him that I found his family and that they wanted to meet him. The timing seemed macabre. How could I tell him this while he was mourning the loss of his Mamo? It felt like an intrusion, but I didn't see how I couldn't. I had promised the Adamskis I would bring him to the farm before his birth mother, Janina, was laid to rest. I couldn't go back on that now. Eva and Paulina left me alone in the living room and I tapped out the number for Gertrude's apartment in Berlin. Thankfully, Mom answered.

"How is Papa?"

"He's heartbroken. I don't know another way to put it. It seems like something has kept them apart for so long and they will never be able to reconcile now."

Oh, God, I prayed silently to myself. *Please let this be the right thing to do.*

"We need you here for her service this weekend. You're coming back to Berlin?"

"I ... yes, I will be there. But first I need you both to come to Warsaw. I need you to bring Papa to Warsaw tomorrow, the first flight you can."

"What's going on?"

I bit my lip and fumbled with my fingers. I kept opening my mouth and closing it before any words came out. Finally all I could say was, "I found them."

Mom gasped. "Oh, Agnes."

"I found them near Warsaw, on a farm."

"Are you absolutely sure about this?"

"I am sure. I met them." I waited. "But it's important he comes here tomorrow, Mom."

"Tomorrow? We just can't. We're in the middle of preparing Gertrude's funeral service."

"He has to. His mother," I paused again, that term mother confusing me, "the one here, she also died. She will be buried on Friday. He has to come before then."

I heard my mother sniffling. As with my father, her outward emotion was so rare that when it did happen, it unsettled me profoundly. "How can I ... tell him this now?"

"I'm sorry," I said. "But she's going to be buried. He has to know. He has to see her, at least just once."

***

Otto offered to drive me to the airport when my parents arrived, but I declined. It wasn't the moment I wanted Otto to meet my parents. When he met them, I wanted it to be right. I asked Eva to take me and, after stopping at the airport, drive us in the Maluch on to Kazimierz Dolny. They had known Eva for a long time so it would make things easier. We arrived at the airport and Eva parked across from the terminal. She wanted to stay in the car and wait.

"You should have a minute alone with them," she said. "I'll be right here."

I left the parking lot and crossed a roundabout. At the curb, I wedged through a thick line of Mafia taxi men, ignoring their pushy entreaties of "Taxowka? Taxowka?" I entered the terminal and stood, weak-kneed, at the exit of the baggage claim. I watched people streaming out of a pair of swinging doors. I checked the Arrivals board. The flight from Berlin had landed fifteen minutes earlier, and soon I started to see people come out carrying nice leather backpacks and wearing good, sturdy shoes. Germans, I thought, and laughed inwardly at the stereotype. A group of college-age men, tall and square-jawed came out in a cluster, nearly every one of them dressed in Levis. Stereotypes were stereotypes for a reason, I thought.

When the cluster of college boys cleared, I saw my father. Mom was holding his elbow and walking a step behind him. His face was drawn and colorless. I put my hand in the air to get their attention. When he reached me, there was nothing either of us could say. I just threw my arms around his neck and held on as long as he would let me.

"Papa." I squeezed him. "I'm so sorry."

He brought my arms down off his neck. He regarded me with wonder through eyes that were so burdened by grief that they had lost their color.

"How did you do this? How did you ever find them?"

"I had help," I said. "You had to have parents, Papa."

He kissed me in the middle of the forehead and cupped his hand on the crown of my head. We walked out of the terminal with his arm around my shoulders, his grip tight, as if I were an anchor that he couldn't let himself drift free of.

We found the Maluch parked outside. I sat in the back with my mother on the tiny rear bench, and my father sat upfront with Eva, his legs almost folded into his chest. Eva pointed the car out the airport exit and soon we were back on the highway, headed south. I watched my father look across the landscape: the carts of hay, the horse-drawn plows, rows of birch trees lining fields of vibrant yellow rapeseed that was the color of hot butter. This wasn't his first time in Poland, but for him it must have felt like it. I wondered if anything scratched the tiniest surface of his memories.

When we had been driving what felt like a long time, Eva turned to him and said the only thing she would say during the whole drive. "Your daughter is the most tenacious person I have ever met."

My father looked thoughtfully out the window a moment longer, as if absorbing the idea of my tenacity, then he said, "It doesn't hurt to grow up with tenacious neighbors, I expect."

I saw the crease of a smile on the side of Eva's face. We drove on, the summer sun blazing through the windows on my and Eva's side of the car. Shortly, we were driving on a section of the road close to the Vistula River, and I recognized the landscape. Eva made a turn and another until she reached the opening of the fence that ringed the Adamski's property. She turned into the driveway, pulled in past the horse shed, and turned off the sputtering engine of the Maluch. My father was drinking in the view, studying every wooden slat of the barn and rail of the fence.

"Do you recognize anything?" I asked.

He looked out the front and side windows, his head swiveling. "Nothing at all."

Eva urged him on. "Let's get out."

My father didn't immediately open his door. He rolled his window down and a starchy sweet smell of hay wafted into the small car. He scanned the landscape—the horse shed, the farm equipment, the silos, the white house with blue shutters. I remembered what Otto said about Heimat. I wondered if Heimat could show on a person's face.

He finally pushed open the door and we both got out, standing on the dirt driveway. Just then I saw Sophie come out the front door and stop at the edge of the porch. She was dressed all in black. I approached her but she didn't look in my direction. Her gaze was held fast on the figure of her brother walking toward her across the lawn.

"Bogdan?" she whispered.

Sophie stepped down and they reached each other, but didn't touch. My father was awestruck, as if he were seeing a ghost.

Daria came out the front door and my father looked up. Seeing Daria, his face broke, and I saw a recognition I had thought would have been impossible. Daria ran to him and embraced him with such a force he almost fell over. He hugged her back just as hard.

In a tree above our heads, I heard the twitter of a rosefinch. Its trill rattled quickly and then it released several long, fading caws like the triumphant sounds of miniature trumpets. Sophie and Daria wrapped their arms around their brother. He bent his head between theirs and I could tell from the tremble of his body that he was crying.

The sound of the front door opening drew my eyes away. Max Adamski stood at the threshold of the house, witnessing the embrace of his three children, the first time they had been together in front of him for more than fifty years. He stepped onto the porch and raised his hooked left arm to the sky. The hook glinted and shook as Max pumped it into the air, like he was trying to catch a fish in heaven, or wound an angel, or maybe a little of both. My father left his sisters and went to him. I was struck again by Max's tree-like presence; my father only came up to his nose. Max reached for him, a fierce hold that enveloped my father. He rocked his grown son in his arms and wept openly.

"Wybacz mi, wybacz mi … wybacz mi," he moaned.

"What is he saying?" I asked Eva.

Eva choked back tears. "He's saying *forgive me.*"

***

We buried my father's mother, Janina, on Friday in the cemetery of a small wooden church two miles away. During the evening of that day, there was a *stypa* gathering at the farm. Dozens of their friends came, everyone bringing food, filling the house with it. Daria and Sophie cooked and I did my best to help them. The presence of my father was a shock to everyone, and I was amazed by how many of the people there knew the story of his disappearance. An elderly woman came up to my father and thrust her hands at his face. Sophie introduced her as their neighbor, Ania, who had stayed with them briefly at the start of the war when her farm had been bombed. Near her, I recognized her son, the man we had met in the King's Restaurant, who had directed us to the Adamski's farm.

Ania fell against my father, overcome, embracing him around the chest with her frail arms. She was giddy with joy. *"To dziecko!"* Ania cried. *"To dziecko!"* Papa seemed to almost be holding her up. *"To dziecko należy Janina!"*

Sophie ran a hand across Ania's back, calming her. "Tak," Sophie whispered. "Tak."

Eva gestured to my father. "She says *this child belongs to Janina.*"

***

On Saturday, we said good-bye to the family in the yard in front of the house, not wanting to. We all felt like there was too much time lost for us to leave any day spent apart again.

"When will we see you again?" Sophie asked.

I thought of the family on this farm, my family. I thought of Otto, Eva, and Paulina. I even thought of Piotr. I had a hard time thinking back to my life in Chicago. "I'm not leaving Poland," I said. "Not for a while."

"Come see us again with your friend, Otto. Bring your parents."

"I promise I will."

Eva started talking to Sophie. They were almost the same age, and I imagined they could be friends. As they talked, a round brick building behind the main house caught my eye. I walked up to its short wooden door and tried it. The door was stuck so tight into the frame, it didn't move when I pulled the handle. I yanked harder and it didn't yield an inch. It seemed like it had to have been years since it was opened. Possibly decades. With my last pull, it burst open and I stepped inside.

I saw in an instant that the room had been set up to be a daytime nursery, like a kind of playroom. A rocking chair sat to the left of the door. A low table was positioned in the middle of the room, encircled by three stools. On the table there were children's picture books, all in Polish, with old bindings and faded hand drawings. My eyes stopped on a handmade doll made out of hay, the parts of the body tied with blue and green ribbons. Years of handling had left it tattered and stained, but it nevertheless looked as if it had been lovingly made for someone.

I heard my name being called and turned to see Sophie appearing at the door.

"What is this room?" I asked.

"It was the old kitchen. After we improved the property we put all of Bogdan's things here."

I picked up the handmade doll. "Do you mind if I keep this?"

Sophie nodded. I looked down at the doll. Holding it, I was reminded of the dreams of the farmer I had in Eva's spare bedroom, about some familiar feeling inside, something coming to rest. I wondered if this was what Otto meant by Heimat.

"Are you good?" Sophie asked.

I was so much more than good. I didn't feel curious, for once in my life. I didn't have any unanswered questions, any unfinished business. I was, at that precise moment, only thinking of being there, not of what came before and not of what would come after. Inside me, there was only a sensation of connection to the deepest part of myself, to the spirits that formed me. I finally knew who they were, and felt their presence, and was at peace with all of them.

Sophie shut off the light and I left the room. I closed the door to my father's childhood tight behind us. Overhead, out of sight, another rosefinch twittered. Three dogs barked to be heard above its song.

***

Historical Note

This is a work of fiction. However, it is a fact that during World War II, the Nazi regime conspired to kidnap Aryan-looking children away from their families as part of a program known as the Lebensborn. These children were taken to Germany, taught to speak German, and forced to forget where they came from. In the process of being Germanized, they were given false birth certificates and new German names. Many German families were persuaded to adopt them and told that they were German orphans. Between 1940 and 1945, historians estimate that as many as 200,000 children were successfully taken from Poland under this plan. The majority of these children, now in their seventies and eighties, have never discovered their true identity. Most never suspected that the identity they have might not be their own. The Brown Sisters were real, not an invention of mine or the Brothers' Grimm. The historian Richard C. Lukas is a good source for further reading.

It is also true that Chopin's heart was buried in Warsaw and his body in Paris. Most historians attribute this to his fear of being buried alive, and removing his heart before burial seemed like a secure enough method to prevent the mistake. Chopin was Polish. He was born in a small village outside of Warsaw called Żelazowa Wola and spent most of his life abroad. After his death, his sister smuggled his heart into Warsaw inside of an urn where it was interred in the Holy Cross Church near the Warsaw University. The church was destroyed by the Nazi forces during World War II but was rebuilt. The heart inside it, reportedly removed for safekeeping, was returned to the church after the war and reposes now under an inscription from Matthew VI:21: "For where your treasure is, there will your heart be also."

Book Club Discussion Guide

1. How did you experience the book? What were the first emotions you felt when reading it and how did those emotions evolve, if they did? Which part of the novel was the most intense and why?

2. What themes does this novel explore? How did they relate to things you've experienced in your own life?

3. How did the plot evolve? Where did characters behave in ways that you didn't expect?

4. How do the main characters change by the end of the book? Have they learned something about themselves or the world? Who has changed the most and how? Who has remained the same throughout, until the end of the story or the end of their life? Is that a good thing?

5. Consider the situation Gertrude and Albert faced during World War II. Do you think the actions they took, in particular related to adoption, were defensible? What would you have done?

6. Discuss how Eva Rozbrat feels about Poland—think of her experience leaving Warsaw during World War II, her feelings during the Cold War, and her views about the country once it is a free democracy. How has Poland changed? Have Eva's feelings about Poland changed during that time? Why or why not?

7. What reasons does Bernd Mueller have for distancing himself from his mother, wife and daughter? Why do some people choose to isolate themselves from others? What things does Bernd do to make his situation worse? What does he do to make it better?

8. Discuss the attraction between Otto Bauer and Agnes—why do you think Otto is drawn to her? Why is she drawn to him?

9. What passages strike you as insightful, even profound? Perhaps a bit of dialogue that's funny or poignant or that encapsulates a character, or a comment that states the book's thematic concerns?

10. Discuss Poland and Germany: where have characters *in this story* of each nationality been victimized and how? Were you surprised? Who are the 'good guys' and 'bad guys' in this story?

11. Were you familiar with the history this novel is based on? What did you learn that you didn't know before reading? What is your feeling about this history? Why do you think it has been so little documented?

About the Author

MELISSA TOMLINSON ROMO is an American writer with a wandering soul. She spent the last two years of the 20th century living in Warsaw, an experience which inspired her to write *Blue-Eyed Son*. She lives in London with her husband and two sons. Contact Melissa at www.melissatomlinsonromo.com.